Thirst For Revenge Trilogy

Book Two
Lawrence the Son

By

John L. Kinsler

A-Argus Books
USA

Thirst for Revenge Trilogy: Book 2,
Lawrence the Son © 2013 All rights reserved by
John L. Kinsler

A-Argus Better Book Publishers, LLC

For information:
A-Argus Better Book Publishers, LLC
9001 Ridge Hill Street
Kernersville, North Carolina 27285
www.a-argusbooks.com

ISBN: 978-0-6158778-2-2
ISBN: 06158778-2-6

Book Cover designed by Dubya

Printed in the United States of America

Dedication

This book is dedicated to the true Llewellyn... my loved and departed father.

......JLK, November, 2013

"The beast alone was reacting... The beginning and end of all his thoughts was hatred; that hatred which, if not checked in its growth by some providential event, becomes a hatred of society, then hatred of creation, revealing itself by a vague, incessant desire to injure some living being, no matter who. Jean Valjean "is a very dangerous man."

... Les Miserables 1863, Victor Hugo

BOOK TWO: LAWRENCE THE SON

CHAPTER EIGHT

Killing The Dog

"You killed Frick, didn't you, Petey?"

Peter Lawrence never felt any compunction about forcing him to tell the truth. Confessing conceived by man's gods and written on church scrolls, neither of which were viable to Peter Lawrence. He believed that what was not written was what made man, not the creation of human gods but human survival. Lawrence loved his Uncle George. Uncle George was a small man, five-feet two inches at most, who claimed to be a Texan, Mexican, Filipino, Japanese or Native American from whatever tribe worked best at the time. No one, not the ignorant of the most ignorant would believe him to be Chinese so he gave up telling people he was also part Chinese. Uncle George was an alcoholic but a slow drinker. He used his booze consumption as an all day tour de force that ended when he passed out late at night. He was never too drunk to miss a free drink when he roamed the neighborhood with an empty glass in hand. The kids in the neighborhood made fun of him but loved him, including his nephew Peter Lawrence. Their behavior was playful fun which Uncle George encouraged thus making him a legend in his own mind. His face always had a bearded stubble and on his lip always dangled a cigarette, usually a Camel. He dressed Early American hobo which gave his wife, Aunt Louise, the sister of Lawrence's mother Evelyn Southern, a good enough reason to avoid being seen in public with her booze hound husband. Yet Lawrence never heard Aunt Louise chastise Uncle George about his dress or drinking or smoking. The two boys from this union shunned their father as a stigma with which they had to suffer. Basically they were their mother's protégée that brought additional problems to the family besides their alcoholic father.

Lawrence smiled, "Killed? Frick? Frick's dead?"

Uncle George got that shit-eating grin on his face that said "gotcha" and pulled small pieces of loose cigarette tobacco from his lips. He managed this with his right hand still holding about a half-inch of cigarette butt. Both hands had an overlay coat of yellowish-brown nicotine. Today in his other hand was tonight's dinner, a live chicken.

"Ain't found his body yet, Petey."

Uncle George carried the doomed hen to the blood-stained stomp. The chicken fluttered a bit but was unaware of what was about to befall her. Lawrence tried never to miss one of Uncle George's chicken beheadings. It was a strange and maybe maudlin passion but not for brutal passions. Lawrence had read about a doctor who studied death in France during the great guillotine beheadings of the French Revolution. The doctor was trying to see if life existed immediately following an execution. To accomplish this goal, the doctor got permission from the French authorities to be a witness during the beheadings. The doctor went further than just watching the heads fall. In his experiments he visited the doomed victims prior to their execution. He became very close to them and even exchanged messages for them between friends outside of prison. It was not for compassion that he acted as liaison for these soon to be beheaded people. His experiment involved getting so close to the prisoners that when he addressed them, they would recognize his voice and respond.

His experiment worked only once, but that was enough for him. He waited at the basket below the head pillory. As soon as the blade fell and the head dropped into the woven container, the guard lifted the basket from the guillotine, placed it on a table, and lifted out the head for the doctor. The guard was glad to do this since he was paid an extra bonus for this grisly task. When the head was sitting on the bench, the doctor called out the name of the executed. Each drop of the blade, there was nothing. The eyes were blank and dull. He was ready to quit the experiments. One last time he called a name to a bleeding head. The eyes turned to him and stared in recognition. The doctor fled in fear! Getting what he wished for, turned into getting what he did not want; his wish scarred his life forever.

Lawrence got no such horror from the chickens. Uncle George would hold down the poultry's neck on the chopping block while Lawrence grasped the body between his hands. Unlike many butchers, Uncle George did not let the chicken run around with his head cut off unless there were children from the neighborhood watching. While he did not like to let the chicken run loose since it would bang into anything in its way and bruise the meat. Uncle George knew the kids loved to watch and scream at the beheaded chicken.

There were no neighborhood kids there today and Lawrence's job was to quickly drop the body into a plastic basket and put a lid on it until the headless bird stopped fluttering. Lawrence knew to avoid that sudden gush of blood, which many times before had splattered all over his clothes. His mother would know that he was again killing chickens with Uncle George and reprimand him for being a monster. Lawrence was usually good at containing the body while staying clean. He needed to be, since he was doing his own experiments. While Uncle George was honing his hatchet, Lawrence would chase the live chicken around the fenced-in yard calling, "here chickee-chickee." Every once in a while he could get the doomed bird to recognize his call and turn his head.

Thunk, went the hatchet and quickly Lawrence had the blood spouting carcass inside the plastic basket, the lid closed preventing a headless escape. By the time Lawrence turned back to the chopping block, Uncle George had set up the bodiless head on the stump.

"Here, chickee-chickee," and sure enough its eyes turned toward the sound of Lawrence's voice. It worked every time that he trained a doomed poultry.

"I always wondered why that guillotine doctor fled when his experiment worked? If he was that scared, why did he even try? You know, if you're going to do something like that, you better make sure you can survive getting the result you want."

Uncle George knew Lawrence killed Masabi Frick. He definitely knew it by what his nephew just said.

***

Peter Lawrence grew up caught in the world of desegregation in the late 1970's. Sacrificing its young children to the tyranny of a country fearing race riots, Lawrence and thousands of other nine to eleven year olds were forced by a superior court judge buckling under to the vicious harassment of the NAACP, black leadership, and wealthy white radicals whose children attended private schools, to bus white fourth, fifth, and sixth graders into the city slums and black fourth, fifth, and sixth graders into the suburban public schools. Lawrence, who only lived a half a mile from his grade school, had to ride a bus over twenty miles into the city every day. No matter what logic was applied, it was punishment meant for the dead adults who created local school systems well before Lawrence or any other child was conceived. The sins of their forefathers were visited upon the infantile souls of the babies born to working class whites who had no say in the matter. No one, neither white nor black, understood what was to be proved.

The black child gained no more than what that child would have learned in the inner city. White children were rewarded with a view of the ghetto, a cesspool created by dead bigots. The creation of the black ghetto had nothing to do with white children of the middle and lower classes, nor with the white children of the upper classes who saw no slums, only the insides of private or chartered schools. These private institutions complied with desegregation by recruiting black children of their choosing into the halls of their elite education.

Lawrence's mother had been put into a conundrum. With financial help from Peter's grandfather, George Lawrence, Peter could have attended a local private school. Lawrence's mother was a teacher at the local high school and for her to divert the court-mandated desegregation order would have been an insult to her profession. Yet, it barely entered into her decision. Peter's Canadian mother saw no reason to segregate Peter's education. Excepting the daunting daily ride, she was very positive about her son's education.

Peter learned to live with it. Prior to desegregation he had very little contact with blacks and grew up fearing black American, this fear caused by the prejudices harbored and espoused by many of the white parents in the community. A few of his friends were Catholic and circumnavigated around desegregation by going to parochial schools. Even the bus ride did not bother Peter since he was an early riser and loved to read. Ironically his three years attending a black school gave him very little insight into colored people. Blacks and whites to Peter were simply ships passing in the dark of the morning ride. Lawrence already knew the city and knew its slums. He and his grandfather had ridden through them many times as they traveled to fishing spots along the main river through town. While not a place they would like to live, the northern slums bore no comparison to the slums in the south.

Beyond Lawrence's contemplation at his young age, there worked the schemes of the white power elite. Millions and millions of white dollars had bitterly fought desegregation, but millions and millions of black dollars had fought for it. The powers to be realized after years of financial combat, that they could not keep wasting their fortunes and so conceded over time. The United States District Court had combined every school district within the whole county into one. What the court thought was a simple blending in the creation of a grey school district became a tremendously huge disaster to control. Without proper management, the county education system became a debacle. The rich gave cursory support but smiled as they watched millions of young lives barely survive getting an education in a public school.

The power elite entered and in one fell swoop closed down the two main city school systems, reconsolidating the entire county into four individual districts each with its own little sacrificial black piece of the pie from the old system. There were no longer city schools, the only places to be educated now where within the new county schools. No white students rode buses out of their district and all black students achieved racial balance by being bused into previously white schools. The fight had been a brutal battle, integration forces against a financially superior defense fending off of segregationists. Not only did the reorganization of the schools close down the inner city schools, but social change virtually eliminated slum schools in the cities. The state mandated all districts send their students to the school nearest them. Ironically both sides won.

Peter Lawrence would make it through elementary school and would not care what went on during his secondary years. Eventually he would go to the nearest high school and accept the twenty percent of black's quota as just other students. His acceptance never worked out that because he met Masabi Frick and his gang.

Never in the three years did any white kid riding a bus into the ghetto ever think about not riding home on the school bus. This was not the case for high school black kids now being bused into the suburbs. Why should they ride home to slum houses and broken glass covering their playgrounds? As their yellow school buses rode back and forth daily, they saw the white neighborhoods with the parks, playgrounds, and basketball courts with nylon nets hanging from the hoops, not steel chains. The black students thought that somebody actually cleaned up these areas since they saw little trash littered over the playgrounds and courts. Why ride home each day when they could walk home through the white suburbs and use these fine facilities?

Masabi Frick was a tall, cocoa-skinned boy who ran a gang of African American high school kids called The BAN aka Bad Ass Niggers. His eyes were coal black with blood shot veins running through the sclera. He sweated through all the seasons, reeking of a dank bacterial smell that even if he tried, could not be washed away. His annual and sequential failings in school put him in the junior class at age nineteen. Both his parents were fiery and would take any teacher, principal, superintendent, or school board member to the mat over their son's continued heinous behavior in school. The Frick family usually won. The played the race card. It was the same tactic that had proven so successful for Masabi Frick against the police and the court systems when he was arrested for crimes ranging from shop lifting to sexual assault. He was virtually left to do whatever he pleased.

What pleased Masabi the most was drugs. He had been a user since he was seven. He had seen his ten year old brother die of an overdose. The Masabi clan regularly shot up together including both parents. Masabi Frick reaped a gold mine when the desegregation order was amended to send him to white schools. Back in the city, few blacks had the kind of money to satisfy his need. White kids, on the other hand were loaded with money. Now that the white kids shared the real, they were eager to do whatever drug, usually weed, was available and at whatever price it cost.

Masabi was also untouchable in school. For any teacher to report Masabi Frick for any violation immediately brought out the race card to trump the violation. The teacher was automatically a racist. Masabi's mother would be in the school faster than the sound waves echoing her voice, "that teacher don't like my boy 'cause he black. That white woman pickin' on him cause he colored. Masabi a good boy you leaves him alone and does you job!"

Even with the power of his mother, Masabi Frick still spent the majority of his time attending in school suspension. There was no way his mother could get around Masabi doing non- racist behavior like cutting class, being late, to class, fighting in the halls, or failing to dress for physical education class. The teachers learned quickly that you did not want Masabi on your class roster. Even the most devoted, student directed, and highly motivated teacher would wind up being used, made a fool of, and losing the respect of the rest of the class. He was best left, as the adage called for, as a sleeping dog that you do not disturb. If you tried to reach him, he would laugh in your face, his vile stench with spit putting you down. A teacher, any teacher, could not face the subsurface of violence Masabi brought to confrontation. Masabi was best left to sleep or be suspended for any misbehavior a teacher could find.

Lawrence had little or no contact with Masabi and his gang of thugs in school. It was outside of school that Lawrence had his first confrontation with gang violence, specifically with their attitude of shear inhumanity. It happened on the neighbor playground as the end of the school year neared.

The mid-Atlantic states are not known for their excessive heat nor cold since neither is a condition that prevails for long. The heat that drops in near the beginning of summer rides a wave of spring humidity that can make life intolerable but not unbearable. It redeems itself in its brevity as does the sporadic winter storms that can turn the area into a Middle States rendition of upstate New York. Lawrence and his friends were sweltering through a game of "groundies and airies" on the playground baseball field. Youth league baseball had gotten started but it did not reach full swing until the second week of June when school ended. They got a jump on weekend practice by the four of them going to the diamond after school once or twice a week.

They could not stay long since Zinni had to deliver the evening newspaper around 3:30 PM. Their game required at least four players. The batter decided what position you held. You got to be the batter by skill or lack of it. If you were the pitcher and could throw three strikes past the batter, you got to bat and he pitched. If you were playing short stop, the only infielder, you had to catch a short fly ball or grounder to step into the batter's box with the batter taking your position. Similarly the outfielder could come to bat but only on catching a fly ball. There was one more rule for the batter. He had to tell the other players which side of the field to play. If the batter hit a ball to the right of second base without stating he was hitting to right field, he was automatically out and everybody moved in one position while the batter headed to the outfield.

Groundies and airies was a tedious game but economical. It allowed a very few players to practice at four different positions in a baseball game. On a hot day like today, the game was one nobody wanted to play unless you were the batter. The worst place in the heat was outfield; you could not even run in and grab a quick drink of water from the thermos Tony Guest brought with him each time. Zinni was sitting in the outfield waiting to take short stop from Bobby Finney should Tony Guest ever get Peter Lawrence to ground out, air out, or strike out. Zinni knew his odds of getting to bat before he had to serve his paper route were totally against him. He rarely could get under a fly ball to left field. While he sat and pulled up grass, he did not realize that Masabi Frick's gang of seven was walking up behind him. He also had forgotten about Rags, his rusty red Irish setter. A leash tied the dog was to the fence behind the players' bench on the first base side and behind the steel mesh back stop.

Masabi came up behind Zinni and kicked Zinni's baseball mitt about ten yards in front of Zinni.

"Hey, watch ..."

Zinni stopped. Zinni was a short chunky kid who would eventually outgrow those physical shortcomings, but not today. He was no match for Masabi or any other of the black kids walking past him, one of which back-handed Zinni's head and knocked off his baseball cap.

"Fuckin' white shit ain't goin' do nothing!" said the last black kid passing Zinni.

Bobby Finney heard the noise and recognized its source since every other word had 'fuck' in it. Bobby was short but sinewy. He also was no match for any of these thugs either since all but one of them were juniors and Bobby was only fourteen. Bobby moved out of their way as they sauntered onto the infield, breaking up the game being played. Masabi saw the pitcher and avoided the pitcher's mound.

Tony Guest was not extremely muscular but he was taller than Masabi by two inches. His face was sharp-angled, pock-marked from acne left untreated, and physically threatening when he got mad. Tony knew how to fight, had been forced to fight after two years in Ferris Reform School. His long arms could stand off blows while finding their way through an opponent's defenses causing damage to a foe's upper body and head. Guest was not only a hard kid to take down but one that would not stay down. Masabi knew Guest; they shared classes together since both were seniors, although it was Masabi's third try at graduating. It made no difference anyhow since he would turn nineteen this summer. Whether walking at graduation or walking through a criminal line-up, the school would be rid of Masabi Frick this year.

Masabi and Tony nearly squared off at the beginning of the year during gym class. In one of his rare days showing up for physical education, Masabi was forced by the gym coach to play soccer. It did not last long. Masabi tried to trip Tony on a drive to the outside and Guest passed the ball between Masabi's feet with a follow through that caught Frick in the testicles. The entire class, including the black kids, laughed at Masabi rolling around on the ground. Guest stood over him, daring him to attack. Before Masabi could recover, the physical education teacher grabbed him and sent him inside to get dressed. Masabi chose to just leave school and go off campus to meet up with his suppliers.

Today Masabi and his gang circumvented pitcher's mound, they walked to the batter's box. Lawrence steeled himself thinking Masabi might go after Tony. There were seven thugs coming his way. He knew what Uncle George would say, "avoid it. In any fight, everybody gets hurt. More against you, more you get hurt."

Peter Lawrence let his left hand slide into his front pocket, the thumb and forefinger gently pulling up the folded steel blade of the jack knife. One slide backwards locking the blade and he could bring it fast out of his pocket, and gripped for a fight. Before Tony could get into it, Lawrence knew Masabi and his gang would hurt Tony. Lawrence knew he would kill one of them if they went after Tony. Was it worth it? It would have to be their choice but he would help Masabi's thugs decide. He used his wrist to roll the steel baseball bat back and forth, extending it in front of him. They stopped ten feet away from him. Lawrence knew a baseball bat was a useless fighting weapon. Attacked by a gang, he could only hope to knock down the first one and go for his knife to maybe get another. Obviously, neither Masabi nor any of his thugs wanted to be the first one Lawrence knocked down.

"Dumb mother-fucking piece of white shit," said Masabi, staring at Guest. He walked over the third base line and out through the batters bench enclosure.

Lawrence just watched them saunter out of play like they owned the baseball field. The arrogance was enough to make Tony head toward them.

"Don't, Tony. They're nothing. Come on, pitch the ball."

Lawrence took a couple practice swings as Tony returned to the mound. Turning to throw a pitch to Lawrence, Tony's head jumped up and to his left. Lawrence dropped his bat and tried to find from where the horrible sound came. It was a high pitched whine followed by loud choking groans. They heard Zinni screaming before they turned to see him come running in from left field.

"Rusty! Rusty! What are you doing?"

Behind the players' bench, Lawrence could see Masabi looking down at his feet. He was repeatedly kicking at something. He was kicking Zinni's dog. The other thugs got into it and added to the kicking even though the dog had been kicked to death.

Zinni made it to the players' bench, and propelling himself with one leg, leaped over the fence knocking Masabi down. Masabi rolled away from the fat Zinni and his thugs took over.

Tony grabbed Lawrence by the neck of his shirt to stop him. It was a horror Lawrence would never have imagined happening to a human being. He had seen wolves attack a wounded stag once on a hunting trip with his grandfather. This attack was nearly the same. One black kid came up behind Zinni and punched him in the side of his head. Zinni turned, only to have another black kid kick him in the kidneys. Zinni went down on one knee and a thug slammed him in the back of the neck. When Zinni's head came around, the thug ran away and Zinni was kicked on the side of his head by another black kid. They ringed him, moving in at every vulnerable position that Zinni exposed. None would stand up and fight him face-to-face. They were animals, animals like wolves taking down a prey. They picked at him, one at a time and each inflicted pain, and then backed off giving another thug a chance.

Lawrence turned to Bobby Finney but a bit too late. Bobby was gone but Lawrence still knew his message would be delivered. He could see Bobby at the Stephens house. When he turned back, he saw Guest walking over to the driveway that winded through the park. He did not quite understand first until he saw Tony pick up stones from the road, brick sized pieces of basalt with sharp edges. Lawrence was lost, not sure what to do. Throw stones with Tony? Pull out the jack knife and kill somebody? Swing the bat?

Tony caught one thug in the side of his head with a rock. The kid screamed and pulled his hand from the head wound seeing it covered with blood. The other thugs saw the blood running down the boy's face and looked to Masabi. Tony quickly caught another black kid in the chest while distracted. While not wounding the thug, it did knock the breath out, making it difficult to inhale or catch his breath. He fell. Now there were five against two. The thugs were backing and Masabi was at a loss of what to do. Zinni was covered in blood but was able to pull himself up by holding on to the fence. His legs initially gave out on him from the severe kicking to his thigh muscles and shins but he got up again and went to his dog.

"Jesus Christ! Why did you do that? Why did you kill my dog?"

"Cause he a white man's dog, mother-fucker. Black man's dog'd kill anybody come near him," said Masabi as he walked over and shoved Zinni out of the way. Masabi kicked the dog again, his foot ripping through the dog's belly, causing intestines and blood to erupt out from the body.

Guest had had enough. He let loose a rock at Masabi's head that Masabi blocked with his hand. Blood flowed from his knuckles. Lawrence put his jack knife into his pocket when he heard the siren. The police car came hurtling over the playground toward the baseball field before Tony and Lawrence had the chance to attack or run. Lawrence thought it was over. It wasn't.

The first policeman out of the passenger side of the patrol car was a black man, a big black man with very dark skin and the broad shoulders of a weight lifter. The slow driver was white, not as big. He was physically fit and walked toward them as the black cop rushed between Tony and Masabi, screaming at both of them.

"What the hell's goin' on here? Who's that boy there with that ... Is that some kind of animal, somebody's pet?"

"Yeah, mine ... er, officer," said Zinni.

"What happened to him?"

"These niggers ..."

"You hold it right there son. You ain't goin' be calling anybody names. You understand me, boy?"

"Officer, these thugs .."

"What'd I just tell you? You come here," said the black cop to Masabi. "What happened to your hand?"

"That white meat there, " Masabi said pointing to Tony, "threw rocks at me. Threw'em so's I'd stop kickin' that fuckin' dog."

"Why you kicking this dog, son?"

"Fucker attacked me. That's why. Got loose from his leash and came after me."

The black cop turner to Zinni. "He says your dog attacked him? That true?"

Zinni was ready to blow and Lawrence saw it. Lawrence also saw that the white cop was avoiding the situation. Lawrence spoke.

"Officer, that dog belongs to him," Lawrence pointed to Zinni. "It was tied securely to the fence. Rusty, that's ... was the dog's name, was the tamest animal I've ever known. Loved kids and kids loved Rusty. These boys here just kicked him to death. Rusty never attacked Frick."

"You Frick?"

"Yeah, Masabi Frick. Fuckin' dog bust loose and attacked me, that's what."

The white cop picked up the leash, "How come he's still attached to the leash?"

The black cop had big eyes, dark brown. They were bloodshot like one eyes in a heavy drinker. "Answer the man, Mr. Frick."

He could not.

"What's your name, son?" The white cop asked Zinni.

"Zinni."

"Okay, Mr. Zinni, did your dog have shots? You know like rabies shots?"

Zinni and Lawrence both caught the cop's direction. "I don't know, sir?"

"Masabi, right?"

"Yeh."

"We're going to have to take you right now down to the hospital. His dog might not have had up to date shots. You're going to have to get rabies injections or you'll die. You understand?"

"No, what the fuck's rabies?"

The black cop knew what was going to happen. He knew Masabi did not get bit but he also knew that killing the dog would mean Masabi and his friends would have to be charged.

"Listen to me, son. I'm getting' a little tired of hearing the "f" word. You understand?"

No, Masabi did not understand, "Who the fu ..." he did not have time to finish as the black cop grabbed him by the neck and took him off the baseball field toward some picnic benches where they could not be heard.

"Son," spoke the white policeman, "I'm really sorry about your dog. I'll be honest with you. We can charge that boy but he's just gonna to get off. Even if the dog didn't actually bite him, he and his pals are going to make it seem like the dog went after them. You can't win."

Zinni was in tears. The policeman handed each of them a business card.

"We've got some problems in this area with gangs, and especially with drugs. You boys can help. You see something not right, get a hold of us. Hopefully we can get to you before something like this happens again."

Lawrence and his friends knew that would not have happened today nor any other day. The policeman also knew.

"Hey, you," said the black cop to Tony, "he says you hit him with rocks? That true?"

"Yes, sir."

"Who you think you are," said the cop grabbing Guest by the shoulder and yanking him away from Lawrence. "That's assault and battery. Mr. Frick here's goin' press charges against you. Let's go. Get in the police car, now!"

Lawrence, Zinni, and Bobby watched their friend get handcuffed and his head shoved into the police car, and pushed down as he slide into the back seat. This would be Tony Guest's second criminal offense. He would not go to a reform school again he was now eighteen.

CHAPTER NINE

The Dog Killer

"Sure did, Uncle George."

"But you're not going to tell me how you killed Masabi? I mean I know the why. You've told me about Zinni's dog and Tony getting busted ..." Uncle George paused a second.

"Did you ever hear about Tony after he went to prison?"

"He was gone, gone for good."

"Not as good for gone as Masabi is. So?"

"It's gotta be a tradeoff Uncle George."

"How's that, Petey?"

"What's the real story about my dad?"

"Your mother told you everything," Uncle George said, turning to grab a cold Piels beer.

"Bull shit! I know she's lying. It's not hard to figure that out. All my life my nobody talked about him."

"Sure we did. We've told you about being captured ..."

"Come on, Uncle George. He's the stuff heroes are made of but nobody discusses. That doesn't work. It never has. You've left too many loopholes. Plus you're the only one who knows, besides my mother."

"That's not true."

"What do you mean?"

"I mean your mother doesn't know."

This set Lawrence back. His mother had repeatedly told the story of Lawrence's father being a war hero. He was sent to a prisoner of war camp and died there. Nobody could verify what happened. The United States government only listed Llewellyn Lawrence as MIA and never actually honored him as a war hero.

"How could you not tell her? This doesn't make sense. It's not like you, Uncle George. You've always been a straight shooter. Hell, you're a hero to me. You're the man who suffered through my father's imprisonment with him. You returned home and helped raise his son, a son who never knew. How could you not tell my mother what actually happened?"

"Whoa, Petey. You've got to turn it around. Your mother asked me to never tell her what happened. It was her decision, not mine. And I agree with it."

"You agree to not tell me, his son, what happened?"

"Again, Petey, I agreed to not tell you because your mother asked me to never tell anybody. But that was when you were growing up. Well, you're grown up. Before I tell you, there are two conditions."

"They are?"

"First you've got to talk to your mother about it."

"So she can stop you?"

"No, talk to her. Even if she tells you she doesn't want me to talk about your father, it'll be your decision."

"Okay, I'll talk with her. I don't see it changing my mind but I know it's because you don't want her to lose respect for you."

"No, not just me but you also."

"Second condition?"

"How did you kill Frick?"

***

Uncle George already knew the basic story of what happened at the baseball field and the killing of Zinni's dog so Lawrence started up with the aftermath.

"What do you remember about after they took Tony away?"

Uncle George had taken the dead chickens into the kitchen and returned with two cold Piels. "By then the whole neighborhood was out telling a hundred different stories. Mr. Zinni had taken his kid to the hospital and Mrs. Zinni was on the phone challenging the cop's story of what happened."

Lawrence remembered well Mr. Zinni and his wife. They had been raised in Philadelphia's Little Italy and made a stark and sudden move out of the city to the suburbs when Mrs. Zinni got pregnant. Both saw the black cloud edging ever nearer to their homestead of Little Italy. Businesses were failing since the new city dwellers were basically poor southern blacks moving into the abandon areas of the city. Tenements went up, growing like weeds around the Zinni's community. Die-hard Italians tried to hang on but few outside consumers would venture through the ghetto to help keep the economy of the Italian grocer, baker, or haberdasher flowing. Not only were businesses not making enough money to pay mortgages but the stores were being robbed, looted, and burned. The city police could do nothing to stop the incipient crime, even if they truly wanted.

Castigated and almost disowned by their families, the Zinni's headed to the suburbs, only a few blocks from where Lawrence lived. Mr. Zinni thought he had saved his family, and like a plague, new vandals and criminals were rearing up and threatening to crush his family once again. The Zinnis may have left their heritage back in the city, but they would never leave their spirit.

"Old man Zinni begged off work the next day and he and his wife headed to the high school. His son's injuries were bruises from the punches and kicks. In a couple days, he was good. I think what they did to him was the scariest thing I've ever seen."

"How's that? You've been in fights before. Why did this bother you so much?"

"It was the animal nature of it. Except animals do what they need to do to survive, not for pleasure. At first it seemed to be an attack, like wolves downing a deer herd, you know, attacking the weak. When I got back home and after I explained what happened to Mama, I sat in my bedroom trying to put a finger on why it seemed so familiar. Then it hit me. My biology teacher showed a video tape about chimpanzees hunting. They behaved the same way as Frick's thugs behaved that day. They came at Zinni like bared teeth chimps came at a small monkey on the tape. It wasn't a matter of food. They just didn't kill it. They ripped it apart while it was still alive. It was as if the chimps took pleasure in the horror of the killing. That's how Frick and his thugs treated Zinni. They had smiles on their faces and were laughing as each one snuck in to take a shot at him."

Lawrence felt a chill go up his neck. It got more frightening each time he brought back the images of the attack. "I think they were one second from ripping him apart and eating him. Cannibals couldn't have been worse. Their sheer pleasure and ..."

Lawrence could not pull up a mind image of what he saw. It kept eluding him.

"Humor?" said Uncle George.

"Yeah, that's sort of what it was like to them. They were actually laughing, joking with each other as first one than the other reached in to hurt Zinni. How'd you know that?"

"Your father and I saw it in the camp."

Lawrence paused a second. It was the first time that Uncle George mentioned the Prisoner Of War camp which meant Uncle George was going to talk.

"Anyhow, Old Man Zinni and his wife were put off by the principal and had to deal with the assistant principal. It was like the stupidest thing they could do. The assistant principal's a black man. I don't know exactly what happened in the assistant principal's office, but Old Man Zinni was arrested and charged with assault and battery and the assistant principal was taken out of school on a stretcher unconscious and rushed to the hospital. Zinni told me that before his father even got to the police station, his mom had made enough phone calls to the right people that all the charges were dropped. She's the secretary of the PTA and works for one of the political parties."

"Zinni told me that the assistant principal started calling Old Man Zinni's kid a liar and their dog a vicious animal that Frick had to stop from tearing off his leg. Said the rest of us were racist liars trying to get ourselves out of trouble by blaming a poor black kid for something he didn't do. According to Zinni, his father told him, "my kid ain't no racist, but I am, you fucking nigger." The assistant principal jumped out of his chair and … Well this is where the story takes on different versions. The Zinni's version put them one up on the assistant principal when Mrs. Zinni called school board members. According to the Zinnis, when the assistant principal rose out of his chair, he came after Old Man Zinni for calling him a nigger. According to the assistant principal, he only got up to show the Zinnis to the door. Mr. Zinni decked the assistant principal. Two witnesses, Mr. Zinni and Mrs. Zinni, against one. Mrs. Zinni contacted all of her political contacts attacking the token black school administrator, a man who already had a reputation for disciplining white kids severely and letting black kids off free."

"How tough is this principal, Petey?"

"He's a little guy, maybe five-four or five. Kind of scrawny but claims he was a great football player in college until his shin splits got to him. Would've made the pros."

Uncle George laughed. "My guess is the Zinnis were lying. Mr. Zinni's built like a brick shit house and survived in Little Italy with his fists. He's a fair match even for your Uncle Ralph."

"Sounds like a fair fight to me after that black cop nailed us for starting trouble."

"How did this go over with the Zinni's march on the school?"

"Old man Zinni went straight from jail to the school. He and his wife walked into the school principal's office without even asking. They demanded that the school press charges against Frick for killing Rusty and attacking Zinni. The principal tried to whitewash it, claiming she's not responsible for what happens outside of school. The problem was that the school is responsible. Mrs. Zinni had done her homework. She dug out a school board rule that is used to nail kids carrying cigarettes and drugs to school. School board regulations say that a student is subject to school rules and regulations the minute they leave their house until the time they step off the school bus. Frick and his thugs were the school's responsibility and should have been on the school bus, not prowling the playground."

"So what did the principal do?"

Told her she'd check on it and tried to get the Zinnis to leave. They said no. Told her they're staying right here until she checks out the school board rule. Woman got on the phone, right away. The Zinnis wouldn't budge, kept staring at her while she talked with five or six different people in administration. Finally she hung up the phone and told Mrs. Zinni that the school board decided to not press charges against Mr. Zinni if they would drop the complaint. Mr. Zinni told her to go fuck herself.

"Jesus, that sure sounds like him. He's a scary man. Scares me."

Lawrence registered this. His Uncle George was a very dangerous man. Like most dangerous men, he avoided letting you know that he was anything but quiet and withdrawn until you gave him reason to defend himself.

"Before the principal could stand up and order them out, Mrs. Zinni slapped Mr. Zinni across the face and told him to never use that kind of language around her again. Then Mrs. Zinni took it to the principal. Laid it out plain to her. She was the administrator responsible for this school. She was the ultimate authority to prevent what had happened today. By law she had failed to prevent the Zinni's child and pet dog from being harmed. She was culpable."

"Mrs. Zinni used the word culpable?"

Lawrence smiled at Uncle George "Well, I guess she said that. Zinni was on a real tear when he told me about it. Maybe I'm embellishing a little."

"A little?"

"Yeah, Uncle George, just a little! Anyhow the Zinnis stayed put. As to be expected the principal got back on the phone. She tried turning around so as to not face the Zinnis but instead yanked the phone right off the desk, according to Zinni. The Zinnis laughed at her. When she finished talking with central administration she asked the Zinnis if they would accept her word that Frick would be punished."

"My guess, Petey, is that both said no?"

"Yep. I was kind of surprised that the Old Man didn't drop another "f" on her. The principal did not even hesitate. Told the

Zinnis that Frick was expelled as of this moment and his case would go before the school board for final expulsion. Before the Zinnis could nail her, the principal told them that the school would pay for all of the medical bills and for a new dog."

"Why does it take so much effort to get school people to just do their job? Your Mama says the same thing about them."

"I think it's a power situation, Uncle George. Figure it. They start out as a teacher with this powerful and almost absolute control of a classroom full of kids. That's probably not enough. So they become principals and can control not just the kids but the teachers. They think their power goes beyond the rights of others."

"Through all of this, Frick got out of it with an expulsion."

"And he could care less. All of these people in conflict and the son of a bitch that deserved to get punished ended up getting what he wanted. Frick didn't want to be in school. He hated school."

"If he disappeared, then ... wait, you didn't ... Frick disappeared over a year later? How did you catch up with him?"

"Bobby, Bobby Finney. There was one loose end in the whole tragedy with Zinni and his dog. I could never figure out how the police got there so fast."

"That's right! You guys had just heard the dying dog yell and the thugs kicking at him when Bobby went to a neighbor's house. Why were the cops there in less than a couple of minutes. How?"

"I tried to tell Bobby to go call the police but he wasn't there. He had already left once the gang walked past him in the outfield."

"Why would he call the cops before anything actually happened?"

"Bobby was buying grass from Frick. Frick told him to get lost, and quick. Bobby took off and we didn't notice it."

"Bobby came back and told you that?"

"No. It wasn't until almost two years later that I found out about Bobby. It was my first year of college and when I came home for Christmas vacation, Zinni told me Bobby was in the hospital. He'd ODed on horse, heroin ..."

"Yeah, I know what horse is, Petey. You never knew he was a user?"

"Frick got him into it in the typical one step at a time scenario. Little pot, let's up the thrill a bit with some coke, and wham he's shootin' H. It wasn't what happened that day at the baseball diamond that made me kill Frick. It was seeing Bobby die."

"You saw him die? That had to be hard."

Lawrence did not respond. He never wanted to revisit Bobby's death but wanted to tell his uncle how he killed Masabi Frick.

"Before he died, Bobby told me enough to find Frick."

***

Bobby Finney had never been a big kid. He was sinewy and slightly above average in height. When Lawrence visited him at the hospital during Christmas break from college, Lawrence got choked up and had to restrain himself from crying. Bobby looked like a chicken that had been plucked and boiled in water. Flesh draped from his bones, his ribs tracing lines, even through the hospital gown. His face looked more like a skull painted off-white. Lawrence finally put a handle where he had seen a person like Bobby – in concentration camp photos. There was no doubt Bobby was going to die. No amount of nourishment could stop the residual narcotics from neutralizing his normal bodily functions.

"Hey, Pete. Look pretty bad, don't I."

"Jesus, Bobby, how could you do this to yourself?"

"I don't care, Pete. It took me right out of the anger. Got past that bitch and her boyfriends."

Lawrence knew about Bobby's life. Bobby's father had been a brutal man who beat his son for any offense. He was ashamed of his son and constantly compared Bobby's lack of manliness to Lawrence's athletic and outdoors life style. It never made a difference in Lawrence and Bobby's friendship. Bobby Finney knew that Peter Lawrence was the son Bobby's father wished he had. Having that man for a father was worse being fatherless, like Peter Lawrence was. Lawrence and Bobby both knew that Bobby enjoyed the outdoor life whenever he was around Lawrence's family, especially his two uncles.

Bobby's father had a massive heart attack a year ago. He did not even live long enough to tell his son he loved him, which he would not have done even if he had had the opportunity. Before his father's death, Bobby had started doing drugs, usually marijuana or OxyContin, which he stole from his mother. His father's death was not to be a reprieve for the tortured son, because within two weeks his mother started searching for a man. It was as if she intentionally looked for a clone of Bobby's father, only to bring home mutants even more hateful than her deceased husband. While his parents had no sex life in their last years together, his widowed mother sought out and found the most violent lovers possible. Bobby had no choice but to leave the house whenever she had one of her Greco Roman Romeo' over. He could hear her screaming obscenities from her bedroom, the garage or the bathroom or from wherever else they were screwing.

Masabi Frick and the narcotics he could offer became Bobby's source for freedom. For a while Bobby was able to finance his drug menu by stealing from his mother. She would usually pass out after her latest man left and having taken too many pills or too many shots. Bobby would ransack her purse or the desk drawer where she kept large amounts of cash. She had not been stupid with her finances when her husband's high blood pressure continued rose and he still continued to smoke three packs of cigarettes each day. He had little regard for money, not caring as long as there was food on the table and plenty of smokes. Therefore he knew nothing about the Finney's cash flow, including the million dollar life insurance policy his wife struggled each month to pay for. But it paid off when he died. She could grow old and still have her boyfriends. Bobby could get his drug money by ripping off her finances, as long as it was just Bobby and his mother.

When she decided to remarry, that all changed. Her new husband took over all the finances; Bobby was left without any cash to buy his drugs. Caught stealing, his step father threatened him with jail. That was when Bobby became a seller for Masabi Frick. Bobby had access to the white neighborhoods. He became so good at selling drugs that he bypassed the kids and got their parents as clients instead. Frick paid him in drugs, that was all Bobby needed to kill himself.

"Where's Frick now, Bobby?"

"Why, Pete? Whole thing's my fault, not his."

"Bobby, where's Frick? How do you contact him? How do you get the drugs and pay up your collections?"

"Pete, I'm gonna die. I know that. I'm kind of looking forward to it. Just let it go. What're you gonna do, beat him up? I got myself into this. It could've been any dealer. Just happened Frick got started at our school when deseg went down. Best thing happened to him, he said, was killing that dog. Got him expelled and a chance to roam the neighborhood. He didn't have to limit himself to the high school. Said the first place he ever did was the middle school."

"Bobby, where's Frick?"

"Come on, Pete. I don't want to lay here dying thinking he'll kill you like he did that dog. He's got a whole network going for him. Why do it?"

"I liked Zinni's dog."

***

"So did he tell you anything, Petey?"

"Yeah. Frick worked out of Price's Run tenements downtown."

"That's a pretty tough area. You go down there looking for Frick?"

"Yeah, but I'm not dumb. Price's Run was like a castle for Frick. Single floor tenements lined up row by row with big, unkempt lawns between each building, blocks and blocks of low income to dirt poor colored people. Every house had bars on the windows and most a dog chained out front, some with a dog chained in the back also. The city spent a fortune maintaining the whole project. Basketball courts nearly every other block and playgrounds with profanity spray painted on every square inch. Every day a crew goes down there to clean up all the glass and trash and black paint over the ghetto gang graffiti."

"Did you find Frick?"

"Right were Bobby told me, the epicenter of the war and whore zone."

***

To Lawrence it appeared hopeless. There was no way he could get to Frick with the hundreds of black people living only feet from him. At least a third of them looked to Frick as a source of income if not as their source for drugs. The other blacks would never allow a white person within ten feet of a brother. To even think of walking through Price's Run in the dark was to participate in an act of suicide. Lawrence spent a week reconnoitering the entire area. Only one white person. That was the man who ran the Boys Club on the edge of Price's Run. Deciding it was useless; he quit patrolling the area and went back to his college work.

One day toward the end of summer vacation, Lawrence was looking through the classified ads for a part-time after school job and saw a listing for a games room manager at the Vandover Street Boys Club. Had he not known there was a white man who ran the Boys Club, Lawrence would have never believed he had any chance for the position. He applied and was given the job. He was the only one who even applied. The manager told him that since it was part-time and paid minimum wage, no local would take it; trying was a waste of time. Getting somebody like Lawrence, a white college student who did not even live in the city, to take a job in the projects where most of the members were African-Americans, was impossible. Lawrence was surprised and glad to hear the man's honesty.

"Mr. Lawrence, it's not that I'm prejudiced or anything."

"Lawrence, people just call me Lawrence."

"Yeah, well that's good. Of course here, you're going to get called all kind of names. How are you around black people?"

Lawrence had an idea he would be asked about race, considering where the Boys' Club was located. "I've had very little contact with colored people …"

"Whoa, you better hold it right there, Lawrence. You don't call anybody colored. In fact you best avoid any racial comments. We're very careful about that. You might think this is an all black boys' recreation center, but it's not. Vandover avenue splits between Price's Run housing and St. John's Church diocese. We get pretty much half and half. Usually the Catholic kids come in during afternoons and weekends. The black kids are here mostly after dinner around 6:00 or 6:30. We close at 9:00 pm. Also forget using the word boys as in Boys club. While they haven't gotten around to officially changing the name, we're both sexes. Don't get a lot of girls but some of the more athletic ones use the gym on their nights."

"You've got special nights just for girls?"

"If we didn't, they would not get a lot of court time. That's important here since right now we're the only place for these kids to go."

"Is there an age limit?"

"Yes, and that's important for you to check. Part of your job is to register new members. Got to be eighteen or younger to be a member."

Lawrence pondered the age limit. If he was going to get at Frick, it would not be here. Frick had to be 21 or 22 by now. "Listen, Mr. …"

"Larry, just call me Larry. Kind of coincidental you being called Lawrence and I go by the name Larry. I've been here for nearly seven years Lawrence. It's a good institution. The kids that come here know that this is their place, not mine, theirs. They also know me, and the people that work for me have a duty to see that this place stays usable to them. You can see the game room. Pool tables, ping-pong and even shuffle board tables, are all there but their usage of it is my responsibility. I'll bounce them out if they horse around, leave trash lying on the tables, leave the cover off the pool tables when they're finished. Watch tonight when we close. Nobody leaves until the tables are covered, equipment's back in storage, locker rooms without trash."

"And these kids do that?"

"They do or they're out. I get a few punks that'll mess around but I out them fast. Police are just three blocks up on Market Street. Police want the club to stay open and stay clean. It keeps the kids around here from trouble. They stop by without even being called. Twice a month we have a boxing tournament. Cops love to come down here on their own time and referee the bouts."

Lawrence smiled and asked "was Spenser Tracy your father?"

"This is the Boys' club, Lawrence, not Boys' Town. I'm not that old," said Larry with a big smile on his face. "You want the job?"

Lawrence took to this man instantly. Throughout his life, young as he was, he had learned one important concept from his mother, aunts, and uncles. You can benefit from any person. No matter how much you think you know, there's somebody else who can teach you something. Would this job put him into direct contact with Frick? No, but it would give him proximity since the kids with which he would work probably would know Frick. It was just a question of taking it slow and finding his way through the people who came here. Also he could use the extra money he would make now that he was commuting to college.

"That simple? Just like that you'll hire me? You didn't even check my credentials?"

"You write well. Great resume. Mom's a teacher which usually means a smart kid. Plus I got a letter from a man named Ralph that said give you the job or he'll come down there and break the place up."

"My Uncle Ralph told you that?"

"Not in so many words."

Lawrence had no idea how his Uncle Ralph knew he was applying for a job at the Boys' Club.

***

"I told him," said Uncle George. "I figured that if anybody in this family knew somebody that knew somebody, it'd be Ralph. Of course he called the Boys Club."

Uncle George and Uncle Ralph had a strange and strained relationship between the two of them. George had been a prisoner of war with Lawrence's father and returned to the United States to tell Llewellyn Lawrence's Vietnam War widow a story Peter Lawrence had yet to hear. To Peter's knowledge, nobody, not even Peter's grandfather, heard that story, only Peter's mother. She had made Uncle George pledge to never repeat what happened in the Vietnam POW camp where George met Peter's father, Llewellyn Lawrence. Evelyn Southern had married Llewellyn Lawrence before he shipped to Vietnam. Their son, Peter, was born while Llewellyn was a POW.

When Uncle George met Peter's mother and her family, he took a real interest in Evelyn's sister Louise. Louise, along with Evelyn's third sister, Alsace, moved to the United States from Canada when Llewellyn Lawrence was sent to Vietnam. The sisters were very close and would stand by each other to maintain their family, even if that meant moving to the States while Evelyn was pregnant. The Southern family had tried to convince Llewellyn Lawrence to flee the draft by immigrating to Canada, but he would not.

Not long after Peter Lawrence's birth, Alsace Southern met and married the man who became Lawrence's Uncle Ralph. Uncle Ralph was a Master Sergeant in the Air Force, responsible for fighter plane maintenance and technician training. He was never sent any farther than the East Coast of the United States, so he always had a closeness to the Lawrence family. After the fall of Vietnam, Ralph took a job as a mechanical manager for an airline. Uncle Ralph was also an amateur boxer with a very big ego that matched his very big body. The family grew together so a fatherless Lawrence was never without a father figure. Ralph had two daughters which helped lead him to take on Peter as the son he wished he had. As to be expected, he trained Lawrence in boxing, with one condition being set by Evelyn Southern; Peter would not fight outside of the local gym. Both Ralph and Peter agreed to the same condition. He enjoyed the camaraderie of the local bouts but feared he would easily go over the edge if he ever began fighting outsiders. He could square off against the other boys at the gym without anger. One time in the middle of fighting another, his anger got the best of him and both he and his antagonist got hurt. As long as he could laugh and relax at the boxing arena, it was fun and challenging. He could accept losses and hug opponents as long as it was a game. When it became a toe-to-toe fight to hurt, he lost consciousness of the sport. It became survival, survival by destruction of the opponent. That fear rested angrily inside of his psyche like a sleeping monster. It's snarling and violent head raised up just once for Peter Lawrence and it scared him more than the boy he fought. Would he kill, or even worse, would his violent anger educe the same rage within his enemy? Would he take down his foe so violently, that he could not get up, beaten and destroyed? He feared it and avoided it. As much as his Uncle Ralph nudged him into the ring, Lawrence's fears and his mother's wish would not let him move on to tournaments or the golden gloves.

Lawrence began work at the Vandover Street Boys' Club a week after college started back up. Lawrence was entering his third year and had opted to be a commuter instead of staying on campus. While the near hour drive to the university was a grind, it served to stimulate his mind before getting to class. When he was living on campus, many days he barely got out of bed in time for class. Now Evelyn Southern was on top of his lazy life, waking him up and having breakfast ready for him. Best of all Lawrence was not stuck living on campus and he loved the freedom. In two months he would be twenty-one and while he had a few drinks once in a while, now he would be legal. The extra money from working the Boys' Club would cover the cost of his books. Yet the rewards merely an excuse, for Lawrence's actual purpose remained finding Masabi Frick.

Larry showed him his job at the Boys' Club in ten minutes. Lawrence would basically sit on a stool at the entrance and check names coming through the door. The system was very simple, just like the job To be a member of the club, you had to have your parents come in and fill out an application. The parents got to know the club and had to sign an oath on the application that they were responsible for the boy or girl's behavior at the club. After the history-making progress of Title IX and Women's Liberation, the boys' clubs across the nation stood out as a beacon for equal rights. Despite their origin as a boys' club, the organization had easily and eagerly took on both sexes of young people in the early years, years before the radical Sixties.

A new member had to pledge in front of a parent to take responsibility for his actions and behavior. The parent backed up this pledge in writing and in front of his child. Lawrence had a Polaroid camera behind the long entrance counter and used it to take a photo of all applicants. He would run a security check on each applicant by calling the home address to verify actual residence and contacting the city police force. The city police were very amenable to assisting the Vandover Boys' Club since it bordered Prices' Run Projects, one of the worst crime spots in the city. Anyway they could help the Boys' Club would result in less street crime; kids were in the club and not on the streets. The club did not tolerate misbehavior. A patrol car periodically drove by the club a few times each day. Its presence signaled to the neighborhood that police would be on top of any problem at the Vandover Street location.

Lawrence pulled a member's card as he or she entered. The card went on to a pocket board with pockets hung on the wall behind the front desk. This allowed the desk monitor to know who was in the building at all times. In order for a member to use one of the gaming tables, he would ask the desk person for pool balls or ping pong equipment etc. and his card would be pulled and placed on another board which showed all of the club's equipment that could be checked out. This prevented lost materials since Lawrence or any other monitor could pull the kid's card and know what the kid checked out.

Lawrence had full access to the membership list. This is what he was hoping to use to find Masabi Frick. The problem was that Lawrence had not allowed that Frick was now too old to be a member of the Boys' Club; the maximum age being eighteen. The club still provided Lawrence with access to the community at large. The first chance he had, Lawrence went through the membership cards, seeking anybody named Frick. He had hoped to find a brother or sister. He did not. Lawrence was undaunted. Garrulous by nature, and friendly in a humorous way, he talked with every boy or girl that came into the club. Lawrence was also smart. Any hint that he was searching for Masabi Frick could backfire in his face. Frick was a drug dealer which meant he worked for criminals, criminals that were much larger in the crime syndicate then a junior in college seeking revenge for the death of a pet dog and a close friend. If Lawrence insinuated himself flagrantly in search of Frick or talked with the wrong boy, Lawrence would be noticed. If it got back to Frick, Lawrence would have his prey turned into his predator. This indeed was on what Lawrence thrived. Grandpere George and Peter had stalked many prey, ever since Peter was old enough to fire a 30.06. They had spent entire days stalking animals with nothing more than the creature's spoor to follow. They had come up empty-handed some days and they had snared their prey on other days. They also had been circled by the prey and were stalked by dangerous animals.

Lawrence knew he could stumble into a rattlesnake's nest by investigating Masabi Frick. Frick was not a deer. Masabi Frick was a syndicate drug dealer and a convicted felon who could kill Lawrence as easy as he had stomped to death Zinni's dog. Lawrence knew this but still felt the same rush he felt when he had to hike into the wilderness north of the city for a week stalking a rogue wolf. It was why he kept his 30.06 rifle locked in the trunk of his car with his hunting license in the glove compartment and a .22 automatic pistol duct taped in its holster under the left rear suspension of the car.

Even though Larry's expectations for Lawrence were high, he was not foolish enough to bypass the initiation period. Not too many young adults find it easy to get along with and tolerate supervising preteens and teenagers. Lawrence's work hours were Monday to Wednesday from 2:30 to 5:30 and Saturday mornings. While the hours worked well for Lawrence's studies and social life, it added another barrier to his tracking down Frick. Lawrence mostly saw the St. John's kids during these hours, which meant he saw white kids. Few of them would know Masabi Frick. Only a very few black kids came to the Boys' Club before 5:30. Those that did were usually the students that did well in school and were not being bused great distances. What it did allow Lawrence was a chance to do something he had never experienced before, teach. Since it was the start of a new school year, it also brought a new batch of members to the Boys' Club.

Most of new kids needed to learn about the various activities the Boys' Club provided. While Lawrence knew how to play ping pong, he had not played much billiards or table shuffleboard. Larry showed Lawrence how to teach these activities by teaching them to Lawrence like he was one of the kids. This was not much of a stretch since Lawrence was still a minor.

The kids that Lawrence met were well behaved but for occasional confrontations of "he cheated … No, I didn't. Liar," which one always expects with young kids. Lawrence quickly learned to use his sense of humor when talking with kids. He liked making the sourest kid smile with some stupid joke, of which Lawrence had hundreds. He saw very few older kids because of his hours. He would play shuffle board with the kids and get them talking about their neighborhoods, families, and friends. They became very at ease in discussing their lives with him, especially when he told them stories about hunting and fishing with his Grandpere George. They picked up on his use of French, which he told them was his mother's family language, to the point of calling their grandparents by their French titles and getting laughs at home. This helped.

During his shift Lawrence made no distinction. They were kids, between the ages of eight to twelve, and they behaved like kids who knew the Boys' Club was theirs. With that ownership came a responsibility to use it properly. The Boys' Club served more than a place for kids to play after school. It taught them responsibility for their actions, how to get along with other kids, and it provided them with a excellent venue for learning how to play with others and enjoy one's self.

Lawrence had been working about six weeks when Larry told him about the after school tutor program the Boys' Club was getting together. Larry had contacted the university about getting some education majors to help out at the Boys' Club by tutoring kids who were having difficulties in school. The Boys' Club would pay the tutors and give incentives to attendees. The tutors would use the Boys' Club library on Tuesdays and Thursdays from 4:00 to 5:00 PM; Lawrence needed to keep track on a log sheet of those members that showed up and actually worked with the tutors.

Lawrence could not believe who showed up to tutor the first Tuesday. It was a girl in his American Authors class at the university who was directly behind him and with whom he was embarrassed to speak . One morning during lecture he had kicked of his loafers and put his feet under his seat. In a few minutes he felt somebody's toes rubbing up and down on the sole of his sock-covered foot. It had caught him off balance. Lawrence was not a prude and had been involved with girls throughout his teens, but he had never met an aggressive female. After class she went by him and smiled. She was alone but too embarrassed to acknowledge her, he just let her go. He did note that she was a blond, almost platinum, maybe five foot three or four, and would have seemed heavy except that it was her large breasts that really created that image. Lawrence had been waiting her out for a few classes, to see if she would repeat her soul-searching. She did not and he had been trying to get his spine up to approach her. Now she was here.

"Hey, strange isn't it? You're in my Am Lit course. Sit in front of me. You ever going to ask me out?"

"Lawrence, just call me Lawrence." He shook her hand gently.

"Marilyn, Marilyn Otto. You tutor here?"

"Nope, I watch the game room. What're you going to teach?"

"Probably English. I not only get paid to tutor but get credit for it. It's one of those lazy education courses where some professor's supposed to come out and see you working with kids but he never shows up. You just get a little check mark on your card by the boss here, show it to the professor and take an "A" for three credits."

Larry came down the hall from the gym and introduced himself, "Miss Otto, right? What year are you?"

"Junior. Two to go."

"You've met Peter? Except he likes people to call him Lawrence."

"Yeah, we've got a class together. Where do I set up with the kids?"

Larry took her down the hallway to the library as Lawrence watched.

This was her first day and she was here early to get introduced to the Boys' Club. At 5:30 when Lawrence went home, she was still in the library with Larry, so he walked down the hall to tell Larry he was leaving.

"Joey's here, right?"

"Yup, I already told what kids are here and what they checked out. How she doing?" Lawrence gestured with his right thumb toward Marilyn Otto.

"She'll get by. I think she's got the attitude it takes with kids from this area" said Larry as he turned from Lawrence standing in the doorway to Marilyn Otto working her way through a stack of books.

"You've got quite a selection here. I don't know about these kids or any kid in this age bracket reading Charles Dickens?"

Lawrence had been in the library a few times and spoke, "Don't worry about these versions. Look at <u>Moby Dick</u> over there. I don't think Melville's book is under two hundred pages like this one."

"Yeah, I did notice most of these books are a bit condensed. You think that'll be a problem with the kid's lessons?"

"I doubt it. I don't think any of these classics, abridged or otherwise, are used in the schools."

"Thanks. Are you here every day? You could be a great help to me."

"Wrong hours. I get here at 2:30 and leave every day about now unless I gotta sub for Joey."

Larry broke in, "But you'll see him on Saturday mornings. Both of you are here from 9:00 to noon. Maybe in a few months I'll give you more time. Joey's getting itchy to find full time work somewhere else but he's got no skills. Who knows, maybe a pizza parlor will need a man."

Lawrence and Marilyn Otto sat two classes a week in American Writers with Dr. Dougherty. Lawrence had liked Dougherty and his class, but now he even liked it even more. He increased his participation, knowing he was showing off for Marilyn's benefit but he also knowing Dougherty appreciated it. It was like pulling eye teeth to get anybody to participate during class. Most of the students wanted him to just lecture, get the fifty minutes over with minimum involvement so they could go to their next class with minimum involvement. Lawrence and Marilyn had no next class on Thursdays.

"You will probably not be surprised that I hold Twain in very high esteem among American authors," said Dougherty, now that they had left James Fennimore Cooper mercifully resting in his grave. Dougherty had been harsh with Cooper's place in great American writers but eased off a bit when Lawrence mentioned that James had written Pathfinder in longhand and it had gone to press without one editorial or grammatical change. Dougherty was going to call Lawrence's bluff since he thought Lawrence had the wrong Cooper book, but was stunned at the amazement in the faces of the other students. Even if he had the wrong book, to see his students recognize the tremendous significance of Cooper's writings was great. At least Lawrence had not asked what role Randolph Scott had in Last of the Mohicans like one of the other students.

"Why do you think I praise Mark Twain as one of the greats in American literature?" asked Dr. Dougherty during one of his classes.

Amazingly for the first time since the class started, Marilyn Otto raised her hand and was called on, "because he was one of the few southern writers to recognize the shame of how black people were treated."

Dougherty was mildly excited, "I assume you are not forgetting Stowe."

"Stowe defined slavery and white aggression toward other races. She will go down in history as one of the great humanitarians but I'm not sure that many people tackle <u>Uncle Tom's Cabin</u> much anymore. Probably it would be rare to meet anybody that has read it unabridged," Marilyn addressed the comment of Dr. Dougherty.

Lawrence liked to ruffle a professor's feathers but always did so with a smile across his face and a pseudo shock on his face when challenged, "She's a lot easier to read then Mastah Samuel tis."

Doughty needed only to swivel his head a few degrees as Lawrence sat right next to Marilyn Otto, "A lot easier to read, Mr. Lawrence?"

"Hey, just Lawrence works for me," said with a broad grin.

Dougherty could not resist Lawrence's sarcasm. "Maybe I can find you an old copy of the Classic Comic book for our reading of <u>Huckleberry Finn</u>, Lawrence?"

"Already got it, Dr. D," replied Lawrence gaining a mild laughter from the class. "No, I'm not kidding. You shouldn't really get your back up about Classic Comics. Really and seriously, I read a lot now and I doubt I would've had I not had someplace to go to like Classic Comics to learn about the <u>Count of Monte Cristo</u> or <u>The Three Musketeers</u>."

"I don't have a problem with little children acquiring their reading habits from comic books. At some point though, you've got to grow up. What is your problem with Mark Twain?"

"I think it's mostly me. I have spent more effort in reading through Twain's southern dialects than when I read <u>Les Miserable</u> and I read it in French."

"Come on, Lawrence! You read <u>Les Miserable</u> in French?"

"Ah, Moi Mere, est francais. She is French Canadian."

"I think that Twain is trying to make the reader take a roll in the story as a southerner," added Marilyn.

"He's doing it at the expense of the reader though," added another student. "He makes it hard to follow. That's not necessarily wrong, though. If you have to work at reading Huck Finn, you'll get more out of it."

"That's a fair concept," responded Lawrence. The conversation went on for a few more minutes, then Dougherty went into a lecture. Lawrence had been very surprised at Marilyn's analysis of <u>Huckleberry Finn</u>. He had taken her for a slogger, an education major plodding through an area that was best left for

English majors. They left class together, knowing they would see each other tonight.

After his afternoon at the Boys' Club, Larry had asked him to stay on to cover for Joey. Lawrence had nowhere to go except home so he called Evelyn Southern and told her to not hold dinner for him. After a quick run to Burger King, Lawrence sat at his desk position and had his dinner. Marilyn walked in with another education major who tutored math just as Lawrence was finishing.

"Hey, you could have waited and took me to dinner."

"I can still do that. I'm going to be here until closing," said Lawrence. "Want to do something after that?"

"It's the end of the week. I've got no classes tomorrow, so it sounds good to me."

"Same here, we can both stay in bed and sleep all day tomorrow," replied Lawrence who turning red when he realized how suggestive his comment sounded even though it had passed quickly from his mind to his mouth.

Marilyn went off into the library as two of her students checked in with Lawrence. The Boys' Club closed at 8:30 during school nights. Lawrence began sorting through his options with Marilyn Otto. There was no doubt she was attractive, especially sexually attractive with her well developed breasts. He had no idea if she was seeing someone else, which he was. That was an advantage for Marilyn since the girl he was dating was a Catholic and limited their sex to coitus interruptus. She was also putting a lot of pressure on Lawrence to get engaged. She worked full time as a secretary for a downtown investment firm and she preferred to not see each other during week nights. Her intellectual discussions were limited to whether when they got married, she could shed the pounds that she gained having babies and still keep her premarital shape. Lawrence hoped that if they did consummate their romance by getting married and having babies, she might actually develop breasts and nipples he could find without tweezers.

"Yo, Lawrence? How about some paddles and a ping pong ball?"

Lawrence turned from his personal thoughts and took the boy's membership card from the file, put it into the ping pong board slot, and gave the boy two paddles and a ball. He reached under the table and took out his copy of Robert B. Parker's Spenser novel, "Catskill Eagle." If he ever taught college English classes, he knew he would include Parker.

Marilyn came down the hall at about 8:00 ready to leave.

"I've got to stay here until 8:30 when we chase them out."

"I know Lawrence ... Do I have to call you Lawrence for the rest of my life? How about Petey?" She had a slight but obvious smile that curled toward her right cheek than the left.

"It's bad enough mon mere calls me that and my uncles ..."

"Your who?"

"My mother. It's just a habit, a long habit that I keep using. Remember I told Dougherty that my mother was French?"

"Oh, yeah. It's sort of a family thing. Kind of cute, Peter. Peter okay?"

"I can live with it," responded Lawrence although he really did not want her to get that close. "When you have kids, you'll probably tease them with some kind of cutesy name ..."

Lawrence noticed a very slight drop at the edge of her smile.

"I'm going to go home and take a shower. Guys don't seem to realize how you don't stay fresh going to school and working all day. I think you'll appreciate me smelling bathed as opposed to all sweaty."

"How far from here do you live?"

"Washington Street, just six or seven blocks up Vandover and two blocks north on Washington."

"What's the address? I'll pick you up when I'm finished."

"No, I'll be back. Just wait," she said without thought. Quickly she was out the door before Lawrence could ask her why.

He did not have to wait long in front of the Boys' Club for Marilyn Otto. Marilyn locked her car and met him before he could suggest her car might be more comfortable. He led her around the other side of the building where he had parked and opened the door for her.

As she got in she asked, "Kind of a fresh smell in here, Peter?"

"Is it that bad? My grandpere and I do a lot of outdoor activities, fishing, hiking, and hunting. I try to keep the wagon cleaned up but I've sort of gotten use to the smells of the equipment and the catches we've made."

"No, it's not a bad smell. It's like ... I guess sort of earthy? Does that mean anything?"

Lawrence did not know how to respond. His present girlfriend refused to go anywhere in Lawrence's car. She shuddered at the thought of actually sitting in a vehicle that had dead animals in it. Lawrence just laughed at her, since she did not have any problem eating the fresh fish Lawrence would bring home and have Evelyn fix for dinner when she visited the Lawrence's. She even fell for venison once she put it out of her head that she might be eating Bambi. She was not snobby about it and Lawrence and Evelyn laughed with her.

"Is it a fishy smell?"

"Yeah, that's it. My father used to bring home carp and catfish from the river downtown. When he … What do you call it?"

"Cleaned them?"

"Yeah, that's it. When he cleaned them, that's what I smell. Kind of a good smell when you take the strong aroma as a sign you're going to eat fresh fish."

Lawrence was feeling very good about Marilyn Otto. She was not an outdoors person, yet. But she appreciated and could probably enjoy weekends in the mountains and fishing. Hunting would probably be too much for her though. It was rare to find any female that got into hunting. But maybe she might just be one of those predatory females.

"Did you have a chance to grab something to eat?"

"No, I figure I could do that at the drive-in."

"The drive-in? Is that where we're going?"

"Is that okay with you? I mean if you want to go somewhere else …"

Lawrence had no problem doing the drive-in, "What's playing?"

"I have no idea."

There was only one drive-in left in the area. It catered mostly to families, not only with the movies it showed but it also had a playground for those arriving early with a little train that circled the drive-in area. Kids got free rides while their parents stocked up on the goodies at the snack bar. But that was ten years ago and now the train was a rusty pile of nothing left behind the screen and the playground was overgrown with weeds. Another piece of Americana was becoming extinct. People could pop in a video tape, sit the kiddies in front of the television, and nuke up their own popcorn and drink cheap soda from cheap plastic bottles.

Lawrence was going to ask if Marilyn still wanted to do the drive-in when they saw the marquee "Now s owing G ost usters and Grem ins." Either the letters "h" "b" and "l" had fallen off the marquee or the schools were really destroying the English language. A teenage girl sat at the entrance window. She looked like a toll booth cashier on the Jersey Turnpike.

"That'll be six dollars. You're kind a late, Mister. Movie started a half hour ago when it got dark. You still got to pay the full price."

He paid and took the FM car speaker from her.

"Two classics, Marilyn. Remember, you picked them."

"Come on, Peter," she said as she moved next to him. "You don't like Gremlins?"

"It's not bad. The scene with Snow White and the gremlins tearing up the town's funny. The only good thing about Ghostbusters is Sigourney Weaver. She I can handle."

Marilyn wasted no time. She undid his belt, popped the waist button, pulled down his zipper, and had him in her mouth. Lawrence's vision of Sigourney Weaver was gone, replaced by the pleasure of Marilyn Otto's hands and mouth.

CHAPTER TEN

They Killed The Ice Cream Man

Every man should have that experience of getting and giving great sexual pleasure. There is no physical pleasure better. It is what we were made to achieve and therefore made to enjoy more than any other pleasure. It cannot be exceeded nor even closely equaled, for if it were, than we would not be here. It is the loss of consciousness during the unfathomable pleasure of ejaculation. Be it obscene to many, a duty to more, an embarrassment to others, each in his own can comprehend no greater physical pleasure and only deny himself that ecstasy through stupidity.

Lawrence was not there yet. Marilyn Otto had no hesitation about having sex with Lawrence. She was not very good at it, but just good enough. Lawrence was bad and she did not care. If Marilyn felt pleasure, it was only at a very minimal orgasmic level. She would take Lawrence whenever and however he wanted it. Lawrence had orgasms more times in the next five weeks than he had ever had in his entire life, including adolescent masturbation. He would never again in his life equal the sheer number of sexual releases. Lawrence and Marilyn would fuck in the university library elevator, the girls' room at the Boys' Club, while watching a movie at a local cinema, or parked on any number of different streets throughout the city, sometimes in broad daylight. She would once, twice and at the most of their copulations three times feel a slight itching and tiny release when his organ rubbed that spot, but she did not care.

Not once did she say no to getting Lawrence off, even during her periods when she would have oral sex with him.

Lawrence started their affair using condoms but Marilyn stopped him. She made it very clear that she took the pill and there was no need. Lawrence was uneasy about this and the fact that they never had an opportunity to have sex at her home. This she avoided due to her mother. Marilyn's father was dead. A former steel worker, he had worked his life away for the company literally, by being killed in a plant accident. A loose bar of steel being moved by chains and pulleys had ripped off half of his head. This now dead German steel worker had left a very young widow who was pure Italian and extremely beautiful. Marilyn favored her father but facially intellectually, sexually, and in her body build she was very much like her mother. Lawrence only knew this by picking up bits and pieces of the family history from Marilyn when they were between sex acts and the one time he visited her house unannounced. Marilyn's mother was probably sixteen or seventeen years older than Marilyn but Lawrence only saw that she was gorgeous.

Marilyn tried to blame her mother as the reason Lawrence rarely visited the Otto house. Her mother had boyfriends, many boyfriends. Her mother had maintained a place in the Italian community even during the years her German husband was alive. The family home was in the German sector of the city but on the edge of little Italy. Her mother's beaus, being Italian, were extremely jealous and Marilyn feared that bringing Lawrence around to her house might cause some friction. That one time he actually did sit down in the same room with Lisa Otto, Marilyn had erupted, but quickly cooled once they were away.

Lawrence knew Marilyn was lying. Lawrence knew when most people were lying. Neither he nor any of his relatives could explain why this was. His mother conceded that Peter's father had the same intuition when with people not telling the truth.

Marilyn was a "B" student. She was in the School of Education working towards being an English teacher. She was very good at retaining what she read but not so good at applying the knowledge. Marilyn could comprehend and analyze well but had problems evaluating and synthesizing. Her rational for criticisms of writers during Dr. Dougherty's American Writers class showed very little cohesion; the other members of the class would tear her presentations to pieces. Not so Lawrence, and not just because he was having sex with her. Lawrence derived no pleasure from proving others wrong unless they either intentionally failed to properly evaluate the challenges Dr. Dougherty set before them or they just had not done their work and were trying to fake their analysis. Marilyn did neither of these and thus Lawrence would rise to her defense when attacked by others, even Dr. Dougherty.

There was time when Marilyn presented a critique that even Lawrence could not handle. The assignment was to demonstrate how a contemporary American writer has addressed a major social problem, either successfully or unsuccessfully.

Lawrence took John Irving's <u>Cider House Rules</u> as his example of a contemporary writer tackling social problems. Dr.

Dougherty was ready for Lawrence to get ripped to pieces on this. Cider House Rules deals with abortion. The student with the very first hand up after Lawrence's précis went for Lawrence's throat.

"Abortion is not a social problem," this from the first hand up which had barely beat out the other four hands, one of which, surprisingly, was Marilyn's.

"It was before Roe v. Wade," said Lawrence.

Dougherty could not help himself. "But Lawrence, Irving's book just came out this year."

"That's right, but while the book is the story of abortion, it's really about the people portrayed in the book and how life should adjust not to what others see but to what others suffer. Irving could rewrite it ten years from now and attack a problem we solve in the future by showing us how it's people with problems, not people with self-righteousness that we must consider.

"John Irving wrote about a time when to even use the word abortion was a very socially stigmatizing faux pas. To even consider abortion the "holier than thou" egoists would tear you apart and see you in jail. Does the social misfit only need to be having an abortion? Who knows? Irving puts identifiable characters in challenging situations. That's what literature is about."

Dr. Dougherty called on Marilyn. "But Irving is glorifying a procedure that is wrong. How can you feel sorry for somebody that kills a child?"

Lawrence knew Marilyn was in deep trouble. She was past the entire concept of the problem. There was no query in the class problem about social issues. The question dealt with a an American writer and how he dealt with a social issue. She had taken up the issue and lost the writer. He saw the other students turning their eyes from each other. Dr. Dougherty was a good man, a very knowledgeable English professor, but he also was a good teacher. Where Lawrence could find no words to get her past this incredible embarrassment, Dougherty found them.

"Have you read Irving's novel, Miss Otto?"

"No, sir. But ..."

Dougherty held up his hand and smiled an avuncular smile, "Neither have I, Miss Otto. I only know what the reviewers have written and what Mr. Lawrence has told us. Your comment has given your friend, Mr. Lawrence here, and 'A+' on this assignment."

Lawrence looked at Dougherty but got no eye contact. Dougherty was deep into Marilyn's eyes. He saw something that Lawrence could not see until later.

"Irving, apparently from what Lawrence has told us, made people step past their ignorance and feel empathy for people with severe problems, people who got caught pregnant with no one to help. Whether abortion is right or wrong, Irving did not crusade for abortion. Legally that problem has gone. For a writer to show people as they are with all their problems and make the reader care is not short of a Charles Dickens. Wouldn't you say so, Miss Otto?"

Lawrence looked at her. She had no idea what to say but managed to say the right thing, "Yes, you're right."

Dougherty asked her to do her précis to the class. Marilyn's problems were not over.

Lawrence just shook his head and smiled while looking down as Marilyn began, "As you know I'm an education major. I will probably teach junior high school English although I will also be licensed in elementary school education. With that in mind I have chosen as my writer Dr. Theodor Seuss and his book The Butter Battle Book."

***

"Marilyn, what you did was very brave but you didn't think what Dougherty's class is about. The class is American Writers, as in the great novelists of the United States. Dr. Seuss' The Butter Battle Book is a children's book for God's sake!"

"That's where you're wrong!" It was the first time she had ever yelled at Lawrence. It took him back. "Kids, hell all of us, including you have, got to start looking at what you call 'them'!"

Lawrence had no idea what she was talking about, "I know the Seuss story, Marilyn. It's a classic, probably will be remembered long after John Irving or even Charles Dickens. How do I fit into this?"

"Not you personally, but every white person that …"

"Wait a minute. The Butter Battle Book is not about racism. It's about countries building weapons, the nuclear arms race."

"And about differences. I see it that way."

"Who told you that?"

Lawrence got no answer. "Come on, Marilyn. Who told you it was about race?"

She still did not reply.

Lawrence pushed her. "You've made some insinuations about me and race before."

"How many friends of yours are African-Americans?"

Lawrence could not believe what he was hearing. "The same number as the number of my friends that are Icelanders!"

"You fucker, you know what I'm talking about!"

Lawrence put both his hands on her shoulders and gently shook her.

"Marilyn, what's with this change?"

"I'm just starting to see you as ..."

She stopped. She put her head on his shoulder and she cried. Lawrence nestled her head firmly in his shoulder.

"You got to tell me, Marilyn. We're just getting started here. We're good with each other but something's gotten into you and is eating your guts out. I don't like seeing this pain."

She reached behind him and pulled out his handkerchief as she had hundreds of times after having sex with him. "Clean one, Lawrence?"

He knew there was a confrontation at hand when she dropped the Peter. He shook his head in the positive.

"Let's go back to my house. My car's on campus and so is yours. I'll meet you there. Okay?

It was a forty-five minute drive, during which Lawrence had no idea what would happen. Somehow a screw had come loose in her brain and she was going off a very deep end. They had been seeing each other for only nine or ten weeks and Lawrence was feeling very at ease with Marilyn. While there was still a distance between them, he felt it could be overcome. In a few more weeks Thanksgiving would arrive to be followed by Christmas. It would be time for both of them to open up and get to meet each other's families.

Then it hit him. She must be pregnant. That's what this is all about. He knew she had been lying about the pill, but with total lack of intelligence had let her fabrication absolve him of responsibility. His mind ran through her actions in class and he saw how her outburst about The Cider House Rules and abortion lead directly to her sudden lunacy and the attack on him in class.

Marilyn was getting out of her car when Lawrence pulled his station wagon up behind her. He got out and she came over to him and hugged him. Holding his hand she walked him up the steep steps to her porch. Lawrence took the message and turned the door knob letting her enter first.

"Mother, you've met Peter, Peter Lawrence before." Mrs. Otto was sitting on a couch watching her soap operas on the television. She got up, turned off the television and spoke, "Yes, I have. You have taken me by surprise, dear. Do you want me to go to my bedroom so you can have some privacy?"

"No, mother, it's time. It's been bothering me."

"I think you're right, dear. I told you that weeks ago. Should I bring Rubicon down?"

"Yes, please."

Lawrence was in an unusual predicament. He had nothing to say. If she was pregnant, then what or who was Rubicon? Why all the mystery?

"Why don't you sit down, Peter?"

"Marilyn, you aren't taking any birth control pills, are you?"

She hesitated but spoke, "No, I'm not."

Lawrence's ability to detect a lie was still at one hundred percent.

"Isn't that kind of risky? Is it just something you put off?"

"No, I've been doing it on purpose."

"Jesus, you want to get pregnant?"

"Yes. It would not be my first."

"Is that why you had a fit with The Cider House Rules précis I did?"

"Not because I'm pregnant, which I'm not. Because I'm prolife."

"Mama, who's he?"

"Mr. Lawrence, here is Ruby. This is my son, Rubicon Otto. Come here, Ruby."

The boy looked to be about three, maybe four years old. He had his mother's chubby cheeks, slightly tilted smile, and pudgy legs and arms. He had his father's tight curly hair, black eyes, and brown skin.

"I'm sure you recognize that Ruby—that's what we have shortened Rubicon to—was fathered by a black man. No, not really black, more Jamaican cacao."

"He's why you wouldn't let me … why we avoided your home?"

"Peter, Peter I'm not going to fight with you. I'm still a kid. Fuck I was a kid when his father and I were screwing like you and I do now!"

"Marilyn, you're child, please," said Mrs. Otto.

"Come here, Ruby," said Marilyn. She held her son first with both hands, looking into his eyes, then rubbing his scrub brush hair with her right palm.

"Mama, stop that! I don't like you to do that."

She said nothing, just hugged him. She looked Lawrence in the face.

"He loves <u>The Butter Battle Book</u> which is why I used it today. After the hundreds of times I read it to him, I finally saw that Seuss meant more than just nuclear warheads."

"No, Marilyn, you're stretching it to fit your son," said Lawrence. He could hear and see her stifle a slight gasp in her throat. She knew it was over.

"Peter, I've seen you, seen you with those kids at the Boys' Club. You don't even notice if a kid's white or black or brown .."

"Yup, I don't see purple either. What's your point?"

"Us. It's wrong of me to hide what I am. Hell, I'm twenty-one, a full grown adult and I've got to hide my kid to get a lover."

"You mean husband, don't you, Marilyn? It's not screwing … I'm sorry, Ruby. Marilyn, I can tell when you're lying. I've caught you before and I caught you now. I just sense people when they're being untruthful. It's their tone or physical bearing or whatever. What are you after?"

"Mama, take Ruby back upstairs, please."

Lawrence waved his fingers at the boy and watched him and his grandmother ascend the stairs and disappear.

"Somehow I knew you could see it when I lied. It is not that Ruby needs a father. He's got one. His father's in a prison in Arizona doing three life terms for premeditated murder. He tried to kill me when he found out I was pregnant."

"I see why abortion upsets you. To have a man try to beat you enough to cause a miscarriage and fail, has got to tell you losing the child would be wrong. Go on."

"I can't make it alone. My mother's all I have. That's not a family."

"You're scared, aren't you?"

"Yes, I fear being alone. Until my father died, I lived in a family. I saw my mother being taken care of by my father. Even now that he's dead, he's taking care of her."

"Marilyn, if you did not have Ruby it might have happened with me. I don't know. What I do know is I can't accept him."

Lawrence got up. He was dizzy. A whole new world had been thrown at him and Lawrence knew what to do. Back away. He did not love Marilyn. He knew he liked the tremendous amount of sex they had, but also knew it could be better. It never would be with Marilyn.

"You can't accept him because he's black?"

Lawrence had to ponder this. What he felt was exactly what she said. If Ruby had been a white Jimmy, Lawrence might have tried. Not with a colored kid. Did this make him a bigot, a racist? If he told her his thoughts, that is exactly what she and every protester and antiracist in the country would say. They would be wrong. Lawrence had no desire to discriminate against African's or African-Americans. He also had no desire to have them as part of his life. Was he a bigot? Lawrence did not like being around blacks that wanted you to make sure you knew they were black. His relationships with the kids at the Boys' Club never involved a black kid forcing himself off as black. Still there was a deeper problem inside of Lawrence. He could read off a litany of black people that he respected but he had no desire to be close to any of them; His hackles immediately rose whenever he was. Something internal raised his metabolism in an almost tribal personification whenever he was exposed to blacks. He had felt it not in school when black kids worked on projects with him, but when colored kids strutted down the halls their pants hanging down to their knees, forcing white kids out of their way. He had not felt it when shopping when black people were in line waiting for the cashier in front of him, but when colored people looked around the store for security then stuck merchandize into their pockets. He had not felt it when he watched the Olympic relay runners win gold for the USA and they were all black men, but felt it when he watched professional football on television and gorilla-like colored men danced and mocked their opponents in front of the camera.

Lawrence did not like Africans. He could exist with Italians, the French, Israelis, Samoans, or just about any other nationality possible, but he did not want to be around Africans in his personal life. He sensed antagonism, aggression, and violence much in the same way he could tell when a person was lying. This he sensed around blacks.

"Marilyn, I don't have to like or dislike black people. It is my life. I choose who's in my life. You are paying for a bad choice you made years ago. I can't help you with that problem. If you try to handle Ruby's part in your life with other men like you did with me, he's going to lose. Even if they say they'll accept him, the odds are they won't. Don't hide your kid, Marilyn."

Lawrence was shaky. Here he was, just barely twenty-one, and facing a problem very few adults could handle. He did what was right for him, which in turn would have to be what would be right in any relationship he had in the future. Was he selfish? No. His life would have shaped the life of not just Marilyn's but Rubicon's and any other children they might have.

At the door he turned toward her. It would have been easy to say he still loved her but he would be lying. It had been pure sexual excitement and that was all. He opened the door and left. When he got home, he called Dr. Dougherty and told him that a major personal problem in Marilyn's life was the reason why she destroyed her précis on an American writer's influence on society. Dougherty, being a good man, said to tell her that if she tried again, he would drop the "D" he gave her. Lawrence said he would tell her. He wrote a note to Marilyn telling her that Dougherty agreed to give her a new grade if she did a new précis. He recommended that Tom Wolfe's <u>Bonfire of the Vanities</u> might be right up her alley, considering the racial conflicts in it and how white people perceive black people. Lawrence would see her on Saturday at the Boys Club Halloween Party and give her the note.

* * *

"After you broke off like that, she still showed up at the Boys' Club?" asked Uncle George.

"Marilyn is a funny person, Uncle George," said Lawrence. "She lets things sort of roll off of her."

"You learned that much from her in that short time?"

"Here's the strange part. Halloween fell on a Saturday and I worked Saturday mornings in the game room. The club has a special day for the younger kids, sort of a Halloween party. Larry lets some of the older members bring in their younger brothers or sisters. He also lets the neighborhood kids who aren't members come to the party, has a sign up out front. He feels that if more children in the neighborhood knew what the Boys' Club offered, they might sign up."

"I couldn't believe it but Marilyn showed up just after lunch with Ruby. Had him dressed in a clown suit. You're not going to believe this but she brought me a birthday present. She had wanted to give it to me but it seemed the time was never right."

"After what you went through, she still gave it to you? It had to hurt her to do that."

"No, in fact she told me I deserved it more now than on my birthday. She said that I was the only honest boyfriend she had ever had. How I treated her … meaning what I said about my feelings toward Rubicon …"

"Before you go any farther, where did she come up with a name like Rubicon?"

"Remember I told you her mom was Italian? I mean true Italian, right from the old country."

"Crossing the Rubicon, nickname Ruby."

"Yep, it kind of fit, what with her having a child by a black man. Trouble was that she kept Rubicon out of her life, except at home. Even though I had no intention of making her see that she shouldn't hide her child like she did, Marilyn realized she had to make Ruby part of her life."

"Which is why she brought Ruby to the Halloween Party?"

"Want to know what she gave me as gift?"

Uncle George had a big smile across his face. He knew Lawrence better than he knew his own kids and knew there would be something funny about Marilyn's gift for Lawrence.

"The video tape of "Ghostbusters". It had a little birthday card attached that said now I would have time to actually watch it."

***

Larry held a big day for the neighborhood with the Boys' Club Halloween party. The club was filled to over-flowing. Larry had also called the Jack and Jill local distributor and they had sent out an ice cream truck later in the afternoon. Annoyingly playing "Jack and Jill went up the hill" for over an hour, the truck driver left the Boys' Club just before dusk. The driver had other merchandise to sell as part of his summer revenue. Getting a rare chance to rake in more dollars, the driver began searching the streets of Price's Run for sales opportunities.

Lawrence did not leave the Boys' Club at the end of his shift. He could see that Larry could use some help. There was no doubt that his recruiting gamble was drawing larger numbers than anticipated. Larry was very glad that Lawrence stayed.

On Saturday afternoons, Larry held a boxing club for members sixteen and under. He very much needed Lawrence to help out in the game room while he trained the young boxers. Marilyn stayed for a while, but Ruby was too young to last the whole afternoon.

Giving Lawrence a polite and proper kiss on the cheek she said, "Thanks, Peter. You didn't tell me anything I didn't already know. You just got me to do it."

As the Halloween kids gradually filtered out to go home, eat, and get dressed back up for tricking and treating, Lawrence meandered to the gym to watch Larry's boxing club. Lawrence had been in a similar boxing club when he was a kid. It was part of the Air Force base recreation activities program which his Uncle Ralph helped run. Uncle Ralph was a good boxer, not an outstanding boxer, but good. He was a large man whose physical stature gave him that initial advantage in the ring. Before his opponent would realize that Ralph was not great on technique, Ralph usually had so bullied the man physically that he was already beaten.

Larry had about a dozen or so kids in the boxing club. They varied enough in age and physique that Lawrence saw the pairing up did not force an extreme advantage to any particular pair of boxers. He also noticed that Larry had been very inventive in setting up his instruction. The Boys' Club gym was not very big. Larry had a large vinyl covered mat going from one end to the other of the gym. There was a three row set of typical gymnasium pull out seats or stands. Larry had used duct tape to quadrant off four boxing areas. In each of the four corners, two kids were sparring. Larry stood in the center and rotated through each twosome. There were about five or six other kids sitting on the pull out bench seats listening intently to Larry's instructions. Lawrence was getting to know Larry quite well. He did not need to be a Boys' Club director when he obviously could be a school teacher par excellence. Lawrence could see a few weaknesses in Larry's training but knew there was no need to interfere. Larry had made a few more circles of the gym, getting to each mini boxing ring before he blew his whistle. All the kids went to the storage room. Larry had equipment there and jumping ropes. It was rope jumping time. Lawrence had not even noticed this room before.

"Lawrence, you still here? Thanks a lot for helping out this afternoon. I can't get you any more than I'm paying right now, but I'll let you shave off a few …"

"Larry, just forget it. You did a good thing for the kids around here and I had a good time. I saw the boxing club posters out front but didn't really think about them. You've got a good program going here."

"Helps a few of these guys deal with bullies. Board of Governors were a hard sell but I finally got them to let me run the boxing this year. You ever box?"

"The first rule of survival is do not let anyone know how good or bad you are" was Uncle George's advice. Opposite was that of Uncle Ralph's, "if you can make them think you'll wipe the floor with them, do it." Larry was neither an enemy nor foe here, but Lawrence learned to keep his self-awareness to himself.

"A bit when I was a kid. My Uncle Ralph would take me down to the Air Force base gymnasium and let me go at the bags. Once in a while somebody else's kid would show up and we'd duke it off for a couple rounds."

"Lawrence I know tiddly squat about boxing. Everything I teach down here, I find in books. Say, it's getting dark outside, isn't it?"

Lawrence looked up at the gym windows near the top of the ceiling and saw that it was night. He always had a problem living with the end of daylight savings time. Larry told the kids to start putting away equipment. It was time to go home. Lawrence helped Larry and the boxers clean up the gymnasium. They escorted the kids to the front door just as they heard sirens raging in the heart of the tenements not many blocks from the Boys' Club.

"Thank God those are all police sirens," said Larry. "I always get scared when I hear the fire trucks."

A bunch of teenagers came down the street away from where the police were headed, hooting and doing high fives. Larry went down the steps of the Boys' Club and stopped them. None of the boys were recognizable to Lawrence and all but one was in their late teens. All were black.

"What's going on, gentlemen?" Larry stood in front of them.

"Killed the fucking ice cream man! See that building 'bout four block down there," said one of the young men pointing to the north east.

Larry's eyes were wide, "Which ice cream man?"

"Jack 'n Jill man. Tried to sell some bad weed," said another and all of them began laughing, banging knuckles, and prancing through a dance ritual.

"Weed! That's just what the kids here need," said Larry. "You know, Lawrence," said Larry, "you can't beat these bastards. Not in my wildest imagination could I have thought of using an ice cream man to sell drugs. Damn it, though what a smart way to get it into a community. Son of a bitch."

"Why did they kill him?" Lawrence could not grasp why they would kill off their source.

***

"So why did they kill him, Petey?"

"When I came to work, there were two police cars out front. Very few kids showed up when we opened the club. In this neighborhood police cars are scatter alarms. Inside Larry was sitting at a ping pong table with three uniform police officers opposite him. There was an obvious plain clothes officer walking around the game room as if he was doing a search."

"Lawrence, come here a minute. These are the police investigating the ice cream truck driver murder ..."

"Sir, could you avoid using the word murder for now. That's what we're here for. We're not too sure what happened yet. What's your name, son?"

Lawrence gave the police officer his name, address, phone number, and was asked if he had been in any trouble with the police before.

"Am I in trouble, now?" asked Lawrence.

"Why do you ask that?"

Instead of telling the policeman that his use of correct language made his question assume that presently Lawrence was now in trouble with the police, Lawrence instead said, "Guess anybody that gets questioned by cops feels the same way."

The plain clothes man put his hand on Lawrence's shoulder and spoke. "Cop is not a good word here, kid. We're investigating a potential homicide and don't need some teenage hoodlum ..."

"Twenty-one."

"What?"

"I'm twenty-one and you're not a cop, okay?"

Larry stepped in, "Lawrence is a good ..." He was going to say kid but stopped short. "Man ... he's a good man. He's only been here for a couple months, but he does his job and gets along with these kids."

"He's also a smart ass!"

"Okay, enough. Mr. Lawrence, Peter, you were here Saturday night when the ice cream truck driver had an accident, right?"

"Lawrence, just call me Lawrence. Yeah, I was helping with the Halloween party."

"That's what we need from you. What the people who caused the problem didn't know was that Jack 'n Jill have been installing video cameras in all of their trucks. They've had so many cases of robbery and vandalism that they can replay the video tape whenever a driver has a problem. They also can replay the video without the driver knowing. This guy did not know the tape was running, recording. That was the bad news for the driver. We can see from the tape that those little plastic bags were not orange pop sickles. He'd be in jail today ..."

Lawrence added his own ending, "If the mob hadn't killed him?"

"We don't exactly know that."

Lawrence looked at the scattered black and white photos printed off of the video tape and currently on the ping pong table.

"How can you look at these photos and not think he was murdered?"

The plain clothes man spoke, "Look, Sherlock Homes ..."

"That's Holmes with an "L". Nearly every picture shows somebody visibly attacking the man. How can you say it isn't murder?"

"Because we don't want anybody clamming up on us," said the policeman sitting next to Larry."Just keep what you see here to yourself for a while, okay Lawrence?"

Larry spoke, "Lawrence, I've gone through them. I didn't ..."

"No, keep what you saw to yourself. Let Mr. Lawrence go through them before you look at them again. That way there's no collusion. Could jeopardize our case."

Lawrence slowly scanned through the photographs one-by-one. There would be no one here to recognize. Almost every person in the pictures was older than the Boys' Club members, most probably in their late teens or early twenties. He found no one until he came to the next to the last one.

"Why are you hesitating? Got an ID on someone?"

Lawrence held up his hand and the police officer quieted. He looked very closely at the photograph, even picking up the magnifying lens the police had left on the table. He had to be careful in how he examined the photograph. One of the two people Lawrence recognized could easily be identified by Larry. The other could not, and Lawrence had to make sure not to dwell on the face of Masabi Frick or the police would spoil his hunt.

CHAPTER ELEVEN

The Fight

Uncle George spoke, "Frick? Frick got caught on the video tape? You could actually recognize him?"

"Remember Tony hit him with a rock? It caught him over the right eye lid and left a scar. Frick never got stitches. I learned that when the cops questioned us about Zinni's dog and Frick's gang. They said Frick refused to go to a doctor. The pictures from the video tape recorder in the ice cream truck were very poor, but Frick's dark skin made the cut show white, plus his Neanderthal-shaped head and hollow black eyes I'd never forget."

"Who was the other man you IDed?"

"Not a man. A kid that I only saw once in a while at the club. I didn't know his name so all I could do was point him out to the policeman. They asked me if I was sure and I was. They gave Larry the picture and asked him if that was the same person he recognized. It was. I didn't know his name but Larry knew him and IDed him. He was a white kid that lived in the projects with his mother. His name was Danny Scott."

Uncle George popped open two more Pabst , handed the second beer to Lawrence and spoke, "So you didn't tell the police about Frick. I'd guess that was to keep them off your spoor trail?"

"I knew the video tape was nothing. All you saw were very vague images and nobody actually beating on the truck driver could be positively identified. Frick would avoid any charges. But that didn't matter. That son of a bitch had this big smile on his face and was high fiving the Scott kid. That trapped him as far as I was concerned."

"How about your boss? He knew the white kid but didn't know Frick?"

"Yes, remember Frick was too old to join the Boys' Club. Larry and the cops asked me if I had any idea who the guy with Scott was. I told them I didn't. I also told them that I knew nothing about Scott, which was the truth. Larry knew him. Scott was one of the kids in the boxing club. He missed last Saturday's class. The day the ice cream man was killed. Larry told them the kid was a bully; he had much trouble with him. Scott would always try to pair off with kids he knew he could beat up. He especially liked big kids, the fat ones that were still mommy's boys."

***

Lawrence knew he had a strong lead to finding Masabi Frick, Danny Scott. After the police left, Larry and he had a long talk about Danny Scott and the boxing club. Larry wanted to kick Scott out of the Boys' Club, but Lawrence was able to cool him down enough to see the harm that would do. Basically was it better to keep a wolf on a leash or let him roam free? Scott had no idea that Larry and Lawrence had identified him. The police would keep their information to themselves since the video pictures showed nothing criminal about Scott's being at the homicide. The police had asked both of them, after they had reviewed the photographs a number of times, if they knew the man who was slapping palms with Danny Scott. They harped on it, told them to look very closely and to take note of the scar. Larry could give them nothing and Lawrence would not. Frick was his kill.

"I see your logic, Lawrence," said Larry. "Hell, maybe we can bring this kid around, straighten him up."

"The kid's a wigger, Larry. He's a little kid, a short kid. From what you told the police, his mom's on welfare and has ..." Lawrence did not want to offend Larry, "boyfriends that help her pay for the low income project housing plus her booze."

"I didn't exactly say that. But you are right about him being ... I got to be careful with what I say, Lawrence. I hope you don't use words like wigger or worse around the club. You'd get us both in trouble. No, I'm sorry, Pete, I know you're smarter than that. You like the kids down here, black, white, yellow ..."

"And I really love the purple kids, Larry. Listen it's the kid that matters, Larry. Keep at Scott and you might keep him from hurting somebody else. I don't think you can ever change him, not with the environment he goes home to each day. He's learned that violence works and the kids and grownups he hangs around with let him survive because he boosts their egos."

Larry was quiet for a while, looking away from Lawrence and across the game room, "Lawrence, you said you've done a little boxing, right?"

"Yeah, my uncle taught me how to take care of myself."

"I've got a new guy coming on that can do the game room on Saturday afternoons. How's about helping me with the boxing club?"

That got Lawrence one step closer to Frick.

Lawrence's assistance with the boxing club was a major gain for the kids involved. Trying to keep a dozen or more ten to fourteen year olds busy during the lessons had been nearly impossible. With Lawrence helping, Larry was able to have two sparring bouts going at a time and thus made him better able to referee the bouts. Lawrence took the other kids into the huge storage closet where Larry had installed an old canvas weight bag and an almost bare speed bag that had to be inflated every ten minutes. Lawrence kept the kids at the bags, shadow boxing, or skipping rope. He avoided showing them techniques. The very first Saturday after the killing of the Jack 'n Jill man, Danny Scott showed up. Larry knew he would since it was rare for Scott to miss a chance to punch out some weakling and send him to the mat. Lawrence knew it was too soon to move on Masabi Frick. It would be too suspicious since he was sure the police were still interrogating potential witnesses.

Larry had pegged Scott perfectly. He was a short red-headed kid with a crew cut and a temper that cut loose on any provocation. No matter what Lawrence told him about bag work, Scott would not listen. On the heavy bag he would flail away like he had an opponent ready to fall. Lawrence pulled the five kids in the workout room together and explained how to work the bag, how to make sure their hands were taped. You never work the heavy bag until you have warmed up properly and shadowboxed for a good five to ten minutes. At their age, the heavy bag work is meant for one or two minutes. You do not stand flat footed and swing away at it. Jabs, slow jabs, picking up in intensity, starting with body movement on the balls of your feet around the bag, were the moves necessary. Lawrence showed them the slow movement around the bag and the left jabs circling the bag and following with a 1-2-3. Once comfortable with circling on the balls of your feet and landing the 1-2-3's, then you pound with jabs flat-footed.

Scott totally ignored the advice. He went right at the bag, smashing his gloves into it and throwing upper cuts which were useless on the heavy bag. At least the other boys ignored Scott and followed Lawrence's instructions. Lawrence had to physically pull Scott from the heavy bag so others could use it. Scott called Lawrence names and then refused to skip rope. He was covered with sweat and had no idea how to slowly cool down. Scott would burn out quickly in the ring against any kid with a basic knowledge of the sport.

The speed bag was fun to teach because it is very hard to grasp the rhythm. It is like riding a bicycle for the first time, but a tremendous pleasure once the technique is mastered. Scott lasted one shot on the speed bag and the laughter from the other kids made him quit. Lawrence trained the others slowly, very slowly with a warm up speed of counting the rebounds before striking, 1-2-3 and hit. As they mastered the punch, rebound 1-2-3, punch again softly, they began to feel the rhythm which kept them from missing the bag. When they lowered their miss level to two or three misses, they started picking up the pace slowly. For some reason that Lawrence could not imagine, Danny Scott came back to the speed bag and started slowly. His red hair and red face began to match in intensity but he got a feel for the rhythm and could do a moderate pace on the bag.

"How those guys in the movies get the bag flying?"

"They didn't behave like little babies when they first started."

"Who you calling a fucking baby, white ass?"

Lawrence smiled, not wide or even a sneer, just the smile of a hunter when the prey turns into the sight at the end of the rifle. It was not a time to bag the hunted. The distance was too chancy. It was a time to draw him into the zone.

"You've got me there. Whitest ass you'll ever see. Those guys in the movies learned how to speed bag or some stunt man did it for them. You go into a ring flailing away like you started on the bag, and some baby who's learned his rhythm on the speed bag will 1-2-3 you onto the mat."

The boy's eyes were blood shot and while his face was still red from the bag work, his body was as white as filleted sole.

"Scott, you use any of that language again and you're out of here, maybe forever. If you can't handle the workout, than leave."

Scott went back to the speed bag while Lawrence lifted up an old medicine ball and began tossing it around in a circle of the other kids. He held up after a few rounds and showed them how to use it as a punching bag with another person. Larry called to Lawrence to bring his group out into the gym for their turn in the sparring rotations. The first group was too fatigued to go with Lawrence into the storage closet, now a punch bag room, so Lawrence sat down with them to watch the sparring groups. Larry checked each kid's head gear and gloves before assigning them a partner. They were to only spar with no intentions or attempts at landing solid blows. This worked for the first three groups. The fourth group had Danny Scott against a very skinny and very black opponent. Scott went right after the boy with a left jab and right crosses to the boy's head. Lawrence saw that Jemarius had paid attention to Larry's training. None of Scott's crosses landed anywhere but on Jemarius' arms. The boy had trained well with Larry and kept moving in a circle around Scott, his feet balanced on the ball of each foot. Scott kept at Jemarius with little harm but Jemarius had no offense. Larry broke up a hold that Jemarius got around Scott's shoulders and separated the boys. He warned Scott about throwing vicious blows, reminding him that this was only sparring with minimum contact. No sooner had Larry backed off then Scott went after Jemarius with another vicious onslaught of right and left crosses. Before Larry could get between them, Lawrence, who had been timing the one minute rounds called, "round! Stop and sit down."

"Larry, Larry come here a minute."

Larry was getting furious with Danny Scott. "This kid does it every time we spar. I bench him and he stews over on the bench, just waiting to get back to throwing hay makers and scaring the daylights out of the other kid. What do you think I should do?"

"Let the other kid loose."

"Are you kidding me? Scott will tear him to pieces!"

"That won't happen. The other kid's paid attention to what you've taught him. Scott will never land a solid blow. But what he will do is wear himself out, big time."

"Hey, you're right. The way Danny's flinging blows all over the place, he's going to burn out fast. Jemarius moves very quick and easily keeps out of range."

"Tell Jemarius to wait on Scott until the third round. Also, he's got his hands up too high. Scott's short and isn't going to reach his head. Right now all Scott's got to do is body punch the kid. That'll wear Jemarius down. Get him to lower his hands below his chin," Lawrence said showing Larry where he should put them. "This will keep the body punches off him. It'll also get Scott's blows deflected upwards."

"Why should he want that?"

"Last round, when Scott's punches go off Jemarius' arms, they'll go up, not to the side."

"Which means he'll be open to a counter punch."

"No punches until the third round."

"Okay, we'll see.

Larry walked around to all the boxers and spoke with each in turn, giving them advice about how their were doing and what they should strive to correct. He spent a little more time with Jemarius and a little less time with Danny Scott.

"Okay, back onto the mat. Second round. Timer ready?"

Lawrence held up his watch and signaled, "Go."

It was easy to see Lawrence's evaluation about Scott's propensity to keep throwing wild punches and how it would fatigue him. By the time Lawrence called the end of round two, Scott had sweat flowing down his face, covering his chest and back. Jemarius looked tired but not worn. Lawrence walked over to him.

"How you feeling Jemarius?"

"Little tired. Larry said not to throw any punches, just block him out."

"You see Scott over there?"

"Yeah?"

"Who's more tired?"

"I think he's about to fall down dead, Mr. Lawrence."

"Lawrence, Jemarius, just Lawrence. You know what a 1-2-3 is?"

"Yeah, jab at the body, straight in with a right, then the left hook."

"Let him take two or three of his round houses at your head. When you're ready, block his first left upward. I mean lift it above your head. It'll put him off balance. He's tired and his right arm is hanging. Follow with a jab right at his mouth and turn your glove as it lands. Do it automatically, like on the speed bag. His left will arm will be up and you throw in a straight right hand at the other side of his face. What do you think next?"

Jemarius was smiling, "I think a short and fast left hook; I'll put him on the floor. Mr. Larry might not like that, though."

"Yes he will Jemarius. He'll probably yell at you, then give you a kiss."

"Don't want no kiss, Lawrence."

"One last thing. When you punch, don't stay on the balls of your feet. Power comes from your feet, up the legs, and your hips put the power of your whole body into the punch."

"But Mr. Larry said we should dance around on our toes, keep on the toes."

"Right, when working the other guy. Wrong when you need to put him down. Good luck, man."

Scott was sluggish, flat-footed when being flat-footed was your enemy in the ring. His wild, flailing punches caught

Jemarius' arms but Jemarius could feel the lack of power Scott had in the first round. He danced until Scott came in with a left hook, planted his foot firmly on the mat, and, too fast to appreciate, put Danny Scott to the mat.

"Jesus Christ," yelled Larry as he screamed at Jemarius to move back off the mat and went to Danny Scott who was now laying on his back with sweat running off his chest. Through his head gear, Larry could see that Scott was not out cold, and he thanked heaven for that. Scott's eyes took a long time to focus together. Scott tried to get up but only fell on his stomach.

"Lawrence, call for an ambulance."

Scott sat up and spoke, "No, man. I'm okay. Give me a second."

He shook his head and Lawrence had a wet towel ready when Larry got the head gear off of Scott.

Lawrence wiped Scott's face with the wet towel, "You're alright. Just take in some breaths. I think you overworked yourself, Danny. You had him but you tired out your arms and let them down, which let you be put down. Just luck, Danny."

Scott stood without wobbling. His eyes were back focusing together.

"Yeah, guess I gotta work on them rope jumps and the bag speed."

Larry took hold of Scott's elbow and spoke, "Come on. Let me get you into the locker room. Lawrence will work with you on jump rope and speed bags next Saturday."

"Gotta be ready for the fights, man."

***

"Danny got me to Frick," said Lawrence to Uncle George.

"It sounded like Scott didn't want anything to do with you," said Uncle George.

"That's right, except Scott was too groggy to be sent home on his own. When Larry came back from the locker room, he asked me if I'd walk the kid home. He lives in the projects, about three blocks from the club. Larry wanted to make sure he got home without passing out or something worse"

"Sounds like he should have sent him to the hospital."

"Nah, he was just a little shaky. With Scott, that was almost normal. Larry wanted to cover himself and the club by making sure an employee told his parents what had happened and ensure them that the Boy's Club would take care of it if there was any problem."

"Why didn't Larry just take him?"

"We were the only two Boys' Club staff there and the club still had a few hours to stay open. It shouldn't have taken me but twenty or thirty minutes to walk him home and get back. Larry would hold down the fort."

***

Lawrence tried to help Danny down the first step of the Boys' Club building but Scott shook him off.

"I'm alright. Leave off of me."

"Okay, but you heard Larry. I got to stay with you or call an ambulance."

"Yeah, I heard. Don't want no ambulance pickin' me up. My mom would beat the stuffing out of me. Can't afford no doctor bills."

Lawrence knew to keep his mouth shut. While his mother had signed off on a boxing class permission slip, those protection papers rarely held up in court. Larry had tried calling Scott's mother but the line had been disconnected.

It was getting late and the sun was low behind the two of them as they walked the streets in the tenements passing hidden alleyways, casting long shadows. Lawrence had ridden through Prices' Run Projects many times, trying cross Masabi Frick's path. All he ever saw were run down two story brick units usually painted with gang hieroglyphics across every available place. The city had no way of cleaning off the graffiti so they painted over the trash words in black. This meant the next barrage of gang signs were painted white or some color that was associated with a particular gang. Of course this forced the city to paint over the graffiti again and again, on and on.

Scott tried to shoo off Lawrence when they reached his home. Lawrence had strict orders to talk to someone, anyone, that he could verify as a witness that Lawrence had escorted Danny home and offered to take him to the hospital. Before Scott could dash into the tenement, Lawrence tried the bell, heard no sound, and knocked on the door which Danny was trying to close. The steel door hung inside of a screen door that was missing the screen. Lawrence knocked then banged a few times on the steel door which was still ajar.

Danny disappeared and Lawrence waited as he knew he must. Knocking every ten seconds or so, he finally got a response.

"What the hell are you banging on my door for?"

The voice had such a shrill timbre that the hair on Lawrence's neck rose. The door opened a trace and Lawrence had to stand back a step or two. It was not the appearance of the face that stirred his retreat, although it easily could have sent him running, but the rank odors that aired from inside the house through the small gap between the door edge and the threshold.

"I said what're you banging on my door for?"

"We tried to call you but ..."

"We? Only one of you fuckers out there," said the female face. "Phone bill ain't paid. You after some money, might as well forget it. Get in line, I say."

"No, I work at the Boys' Club and I brought Danny home."

"That bastard's in trouble again? I'll fix him good," came out of the crackling and salivating mouth. "Danny, get on down here. Now!"

"No, Ma'am, he's not in any trouble. He took a slight punch to his head and it seemed to shake him up a bit."

"Come on, Ma. Leave me out a dis."

Lawrence could see Danny behind his mother. The mother turned to Lawrence.

"He ain't in trouble, right? You ain't after any money, right?"

"That's about it."

"Come on in," she said opening the door.

Lawrence had to swallow to keep the bile from rising in his throat. He had hunted and killed many times. He knew how to dress the carcass and save out the edible parts while disposing of the tripe. The smell in the tenement house overpowered any rotting creature he had ever smelled. It would not have bothered him had he been prepared for such an atmosphere contained in this small living room. The best he could figure, the smell was a combination of putrefied meat, cat urine, and the obvious stench of poor whiskey. The room itself was not a mess, even though it obviously had not been cleaned for months. The furniture was Goodwill bought but it served its purpose. The papered walls had a few water stains near the ceiling A couple pieces were flapping from paste no longer adhering o the wall. The floor was tiled with a travel path worn around the entrances and exits from the living room. A once tan six by eight foot rug was centered in the room worn and torn, and dirty from lack of vacuum cleaning. A large RCA color television stood like a holy Madonna in its niche against the wall, with a freshly cleaned screen and a coaxial cable running out of the wall. The pile of HBO magazines on top proved that at least one monthly bill never went unpaid. The alcohol odor in the room proved that the other important pay day expense was always met. The room reeked of booze much like the antiseptic aroma in a hospital operating room.

Cats, five followed by a sixth one, appeared gaving Lawrence no idea how many others roamed the house. Their odor justified Lawrence's guess that there was very little attention to cleaning their litter box. The cat piss smell was overwhelming and Lawrence did not know how much longer he could stand it.

"Got a few cats?"

Lawrence got his first full view of Danny Scott's mother. Had she kept herself fit, she would still be barely tolerable to look at. Medium height, extremely thin, but what stood out most was the color red. Danny's red hair obviously came from his mother. She had nits and sores visible in stripped areas of her fiery tangles. That she washed it more than once a month was doubtful. The locks were stretched and tangled. In places it was plaited, as if she had tried to make corn rows on her own without using a mirror. The red did not stop with her hair. Her face and her amply revealed chest were covered with orange-red freckles. The eyes were the eyes she gave her son, blood stained and unfocused. With each breath inhaled and exhaled, her alcoholism spoke loud and clear. She was barely more than a cadaver. Her face was booze gaunt, with wrinkled valleys carving their way from ear to jowl. Her cheek bones protruded like a corpses making her face skeletal with eye sockets sunken into orbital skull niches. Almost disgusting as the odor of her breath when she opened her mouth was her lack of teeth. Her body did nothing to hide her death like visage. Bones and joints with bony knobs holding together her upper arms and forearms showed alcohol aggravated gout. The muscles could pass for nothing more than sinews that have eaten away every ounce of meat leaving draping tubes of lateral muscles barely keep her body from disjointing. They also held the ubiquitous orange-red freckles. If she had once been pleasantly plump, her body did not show it. Danny Scott's mother was not far from being a walking rack of bones, ready to be interred.

"Have a seat Mister. By the way young man, what is your name?"

"People call me Lawrence. I'm used to it."

"Lawrence, huh? Maybe I should just call you Larry Boy."

"Whatever you want …"

"I'm Liz, Elizabeth. Either is good," she said walking into the kitchen and returning with a Flintstone's jelly glass, three quarters full with whiskey. "So how'd my boy get hurt?"

"I ain't hurt Ma."

Liz ignored her son. "He was boxing? Must a been a lucky punch. Usually Danny beats hell out of others."

Lawrence smiled slightly, then quickly retracted the smile in fear that Elizabeth Scott would think he was smiling at her. "Not this time. Kid out boxed him, put him on the floor."

Liz turned to Danny. "What kid was this son?"

"Just one of the ones down the Boys' Club, that's all," replied Danny Scott.

Lawrence notice a trace of fear in Scott's face.

"You know what I mean boy. Was he a black kid? A nigger?"

"It was just an accident ..."

Lawrence jumped backwards when he saw Scott's mother wallop him. The sound of her knuckled fist was followed by an eruption of blood from Danny's left ear. The boy grabbed his ear and fought off the tears of shame in front of Lawrence. His red strained eyes were watery as the boy yelled "Fuck you!" Danny went up the stairs two at a time. Lawrence could not handle the embarrassment he felt for the boy. He started to say something to the mother then wised up, knowing it was a waste of time talking to a drunk. When a person is as far under as she was, logic cannot win against the alcohol. One of the cats rubbed against Lawrence's leg and to give his hands something to do besides strangling this horrible woman, Lawrence picked it up. The cat was fat.

Liz Scott turned her attention to Lawrence since she no longer had her son to beat on. "We used to have more cats."

Lawrence thought she was going to ease off, maybe forget about Danny in her alcoholic maze. Lawrence spoke. "We used to have a cat or two around our house."

"As I said Larry, we used to have more but times got tough. Sometimes that fucking welfare check wasn't enough to feed us so we scrounged some up. Did you know that in China cats are a meat source? People eat them."

Lawrence slowly inched towards the door. Liz took another sip from the Flintstones glass. "I used to be quite a woman Larry, then I took up with Danny's father. Son of a bitch wino wasn't even good for fucking. Had a good job working the docks but drank all his wages up at the bar with his buddies. Hard to live when you got three people who need to eat and one of them is drinking all the income. It's why we had to move down here, here in the projects. Only place we could afford. Worse thing was that shithead, asshole starting drinking with and screwing these bubble butt jungle bunnies down here."

Lawrence was ready to walk but stopped. Despite the obnoxiousness of Elizabeth Scott's drunkenness, it offered him a chance to pry information out of her. As nauseating as it would be, Lawrence began questioning her. "Blacks give you a lot of trouble?"

"Not anymore. I got into a fight with one bitch and cut her real good," said Liz. She pulled out a razor-edged, carton opener knife from a pocket in her dress. Lawrence stood still. "After that, the rest of them backed off. They leave me alone and I leave them alone."

"That's got to be tough on your son. Nobody to be friends with? I mean I didn't see many white kids when we walked over here."

"Only one you'll see is my boy." She sipped the cheap whiskey. "Danny don't see what they are. He hangs around with them and don't mind that nasty jungle smell. Don't bother me. Puts more food on the table."

Lawrence did not quite comprehend what she was saying. Elizabeth Scott was very clearly a racist, a racist of the worse kind. She had denigrated herself physically so low, that her only way of surviving was living with people she detested. Then Lawrence stopped and rethought it through. Maybe she does not really hate blacks. Behaving as badly as she wants and consuming liquor is what led her to Price's Run. By living here, she had a stature in the projects that anywhere else would put her in an asylum. What Lawrence did not quite understand was how did Danny being friends with the neighborhood black kids put food on her table and Jack Daniels in her jelly jar glasses?

"Danny helps you out?"

"Better or I'd kick his ass out of here. Boy's got friends. His friends sell things." Liz smiled or was it a sneer. "You know what I mean, Larry."

"No, you've lost me."

Liz finished the last drop of whiskey, went back to the kitchen, and returned with a second glass that had the same yellowish, tea-color as her Flintstone glass. She offered it to Lawrence.

"You look old enough and it ain't bad. Still make you feel good. Makes life a little better," she said turning to a framed mirror on the wall the one corner cracked and missing. Primping her rusted, steel wool hair, she continued, "sometimes it makes people you look at look even better. You know?"

"I can't drink alcohol, Liz. I have diabetes. It'll kill me," said Lawrence glad, he could think quickly at times. "How's Danny help you out with money?"

She had already finished half the jelly glass. "You white boys are pretty dumb sometimes. What do you think makes money down here in nigger town? The boy sells dope, usually only weed."

"How in the world can he get drugs down here, in a black neighborhood? Why would a dealer work a white kid like Danny into his gang?"

Liz did not say anything. She was looking at her jelly glass, determining if she had one more swig. "He's safe to hit on kids in school, especially white kids. He sets the white meats up for Masabi …"

Here it was a link, a trail, fresh spoor. Danny Scott obviously had contact with Masabi Frick. Lawrence recalled in the video camera still photographs from the ice cream man's death. How did a white kid get friendly with a black man, an adult probably six or seven years older? Masabi used him for his drug deals with white kids.

Lawrence had to be careful here. He was not downwind of Frick yet, but one bad question could have Elizabeth Scott's negative attention. How stoned was she? It did not matter. Lawrence had to remain out of the picture completely before he played his cards. He took sight of the prey.

"This boy Danny deals for, does he live here in Price's Run? I never noticed any kid at the club with that name."

"Frick's not a kid. He's a grown up. He don't live here, just sells here." Liz downed the swig and put the glass on a table. There was only enough left in the bottle for perhaps three, at the most, four drinks. It was just turning dusk, barely any light flowing through the dirt smeared windows, and she would have to adjust her drinking until Danny came up with some more money. The welfare check got spent in the first week.

"You want some smack? Mary J? Danny can get you some real fast."

Lawrence read her eyes and knew she was sizing up her booze supply, "I do some weed once in a while. Got some friends that go as far as horse. Danny can get that? How's he get it from this Frick guy?"

"Can't tell you that. Probably get us killed. Answer's he can get you whatever you want, at a good price too."

"I'll have to think about it. Could get me in a lot of trouble." Lawrence had to end it now. Liz was not suspicious yet. If he pushed too much, she would grow leery and his spoor trail would disappear.

"I've got to go," said Lawrence seeing that as far as Elizabeth Scott was concerned his being gone meant little in terms of the possibility her alcohol would be gone. She did not reply. Lawrence quickly went out the steel door, trying to fully close it but failing since the hasp from the door lock was bent out of shape by somebody shoving a screwdriver into it to break in.

***

Uncle George was shaking his head. "I can't imagine how anybody can use their kid like that."

"I find it hard to see how you can get that drunk for that long without passing out," said Lawrence regretting his words as he finished speaking to Uncle George. Uncle George was considered the family drunk.

George could see Lawrence was embarrassed, "I can. Petey, I know I'm a souse, on top of being a cigarette addict. But I usually control both. I count them, count the drinks each day and I'm down to one pack of Camels a day. Used to be rolled over drunk up and smelling like a smoke stack every day. I took some responsibility to stay alive a couple years ago. Lot a people, especially in this family, think I got that way because of your Aunt Louise. She had nothing to do with it, neither keeping me drunk or getting me started on it. Don't let anyone say any other. Never took it out on her. Don't know why. Usually the drunk beats up somebody when he's on his booze, takes it out on family. Never did."

Lawrence loved his Uncle George but he also loved his Aunt Louise. His two cousins, Louise's sons, used to be his play mates when they were very young. Lawrence had a very good sense of reading people and knew Uncle George was not quite lying, but near enough to facing his habits that Lawrence had to speak against him, "Uncle George, you know that's not true. I know you never did violence against anybody close to you when you were

- 64 -

smashed, but you know damn well what it did to Aunt Louise emotionally."

Uncle George looked Lawrence square in the eye, "I ought to be pissed at you for saying that, but I'd be attacking the wrong man."

Nothing more needed to be said.

"So you had your spoor trail now. How'd you get to Frick?"

"Like I said, I couldn't go right after Danny. First, he didn't know me from scratch and second, it would only get Danny and his mother in deep shit if I was flushed out. I needed Danny to give me a lead to Frick without him knowing it. I especially had to make sure that Frick couldn't tie me in with Danny Scott. So I stalked Scott, figuring he had to meet up with Frick or one of his cronies to get the drugs. If I could catch them doing a deal, I wouldn't need Scott. I could follow the primary dealer."

"Primary dealer?"

"Yeah, Danny was dealing besides supplying himself and his mother. I set up a surveillance in my car at a street where I could see the Scott's tenement. I took an educated guess that deals were not going down in daylight. Police knew all about Prices Run Projects and the drug users, but didn't care too much about a bunch of welfare users getting stoned. You never see a patrol car anywhere near the projects except during daylight. It was easy to see their attitude about catching the slum druggies. Patrol during daylight, avoid at night unless there's gun fire or bombings."

"Bombings? You're kidding?"

"Not many, but there'd be major blow ups between the residents; one slur would turn into a punch up the side of another's head, man went down would crawl off and come back with a spent wine bottle filled with gasoline and a rag hanging out, and boom the other man's house was on fire. Police had no choice then. Fire trucks zooming there and ambulances sirens would rage through the tenements alleys, echoing that the slum was at war. Cops would take their time. One more building burnt down was one less nest of the poor, the drunk, and the drugged."

"And you staked out the place? You did this at night?"

"Good thing about having an old Ford station wagon with rust spots hidden by fast food stickers is that nobody wants to steal it. Hell, they don't even want to waste time smashing it. Like I said, I set up a watch on the Scott's home at night. I'd get to my spot, one block s just after dark. The stake out was across from a well-traveled street and I could see the front of the house easily.

Too many cars, buses, and patrol cars went up and down the street for thugs to hang around. I'd sit there with a small battery-powered tent lamp and do my studying. I rarely got bothered other than some wiseass teenager banging on the hood and running away. Actually that was a plus side, since many nights I fell asleep."

"Many nights? How long were you there?"

"I did three weeks, including Saturdays and Sundays. I'd go home usually about 12:30 or 1:00 AM most nights. The Scott surveillance was almost a waste at tracking Frick. Danny would get home from school and be out of the house in minutes. He only returned late at night."

"My guess is that considering what you told me about Liz Scott that was his safest way to live. Get away from that bitch fast. Did you ever follow him?"

"No, he would be out the door, around the facing tenement houses, and by the time I got the car started and headed to where he disappeared, there was no trail. He was gone. I must have gone on a dozen wild goose chases during those three weeks. But the overall surveillance wasn't a total waste of time. While I was trying to catch him meeting up with Frick, he did give me an even better way at Frick."

"How did he do that since you never could follow him?"

"After the first two weeks, I noticed a change in Scott's backpacks. Every day but Friday he took a black backpack with black power images in red written all over it. But not on Fridays. On Fridays he wore a backpack right out of G.I. Joe, totally camouflaged with no writing on it at all."

"You're kind of grabbing at straws here aren't you?"

"Maybe, but it didn't make sense. Even if he used two backpacks for school, why would one only be used once a week? Why would it only be used on Fridays?"

"Was it larger? Maybe he had more homework then?"

"Both the backpacks were nearly the same size. You're forgetting something that I missed when checking him out."

"What's that?"

"When did I spy on him? When did I see the backpacks?"

"When he went ... No, you only saw it when he came home. But ..."

"That's the point, Uncle George. Did he actually take it to school? The next Thursday I didn't set up to watch his house. Instead I set my alarm clock to get up earlier on Friday. I parked my car a couple blocks away from Scott's house and walked through the tenements to his house. About 6:45 AM Danny came out the front door with the red black power backpack. I thought he had just destroyed my lead on him. Maybe he caught me and changed his routine? I was just about to give up but thought it over. There's a major gap in between times here, the time he leaves the house and the time he comes back to the house."

"I ran back to my car and drove to where I knew the project kids caught their school bus. I got there just as Scott was getting onto the bus. He still had his black backpack. I dogged the school bus all the way to his school and caught him."

Uncle George did not immediately see what Lawrence caught. "Caught him? Caught him getting off the bus? So, what'd he do, go off and meet with somebody at the school?"

"No, he got off with the U.S. Army camouflage backpack!"

"Holy shit. He traded with somebody on the school bus. Probably the school bus driver."

"I thought that too. But I also watched all the other kids get off the bus. The last one off had the black backpack. Instead of going straight to school, he looked around the school campus, turning completely about, and headed up DuPont Avenue. I followed him, but not for long. There was a black Cadillac with tinted windows less than a block from the school parking lot where the busses left off students each day. I parked in an alley parallel to DuPont and walked around a couple of houses until I could see the car. From the edge of a house, I could see the kid standing next to the black Caddie, waiting."

"Come on, man! D'ese gonna catch my ass fo' sure you don't harry up!"

"The window went up, and a brown envelope came out but, not the black backpack. The kid went down the street and away from the school."

Uncle George was getting lost, "Okay, back track for me. What you think was happening?"

"You figure it out. Remember every Friday I assumed that Danny took his U.S. Army camouflage backpack to school since he took it with him from home. He didn't. He exchanged backpacks. What about Mondays? I only saw him getting home with a red backpack."

Uncle George thought he got it, "So they exchanged backpacks again on Monday. You saw him come home with a black backpack."

"The liaison kid isn't a student there. Bus drivers have no idea who the kids are. The bus is filled to overflowing. Kid meets up Friday mornings with Scott, trades backpacks, and walks off school grounds. That's easy enough, considering the couple of thousand   students all milling around the busses. Monday afternoon they exchange backpacks again, which is why I assumed Danny went off to school with the black backpack. Guess what?"

"My guess is that you tailed him on Monday morning and he went to school with the good old U.S. Army backpack."

"Bingo! And he came home with the black back pack. Guess what else?"

"Go ahead, Petey."

"The next Friday I didn't even watch him get on the bus. I went to the school, parked about five blocks from the DuPont Street rendezvous spot, and sure enough the liaison kid comes walking back to the same black Cadillac.. This time I was across the street and had a pretty good view of the car. Soon as the kid gets to the car, the driver side window motorizes down. Guess who's driving?"

"Frick, it's gotta be Frick. Shit, Petey, you nailed him!"

"Not quite yet, Uncle George."

"Why didn't you just report him and his stooges to the police?"

"Because I wanted him!

***

Lawrence had his quarry in his sights but he was too far afield to bag him. Danny Scott carried more than a few bags of pot on these trips to school and back. The set up was too sophisticated for something so simple as marijuana . Why Frick used Danny was obvious. Danny Scott was white. Lawrence would bet that Scott sold drugs throughout the high school. For Frick to put a black kid in there would have been a poor choice. With desegregation all but over, black kids now being bused to the schools presented a small minority and the communities watched and followed them closely. So did school administrators and the police. Danny Scott would be the sacrificial lamb if the operation was busted. Lawrence was guessing that as little time as Scott spent with Frick, Frick probably was also busy running similar operations in other high schools, maybe all of them. It was very obvious that Frick had money when you saw his Cadillac.

Lawrence did not want Danny Scott. He had to somehow draw Masabi Frick out in to the open. Where and when that would occur had to be controlled by Lawrence. Lawrence could just rat them and the operation out to the police. At the most Frick would get a couple years in the state penitentiary. He would probably be out in less than a year and back running his drug operations once again. Even while in prison, Frick's cronies would keep the operation running, allowing him to walk out of jail not only free but also very rich.

It was not what Lawrence wanted. Lawrence wanted Frick dead. He could read the man, he read him completely the day he killed Zinni's dog, read him even better now knowing he was supplying narcotics to people who would eventually suffer or die from their effects. Frick had no sense of compassion for any living creature. He kicked animals to death and beat helpless children into blood-stained pulps. Masabi Frick, down and simple, was a non-human being that needed to be removed permanently. Was it revenge to Lawrence? Yes, the best kind, where a truly evil act can be done to a truly evil creature and be called justice. Life and victims would be rectified and a vile human would be eliminated from society. Killing Frick could not rid his victims of the horror Frick visited on them, but Masabi Frick would suffer like them and die.

Lawrence remembered Grandpere Lawrence telling him about Peter's father Llewellyn and their hunting trips into the forests north of the town just above the coal mines. George Lawrence had given his son a Winchester 30.06 that traced back through Llewellyn's grandmother. George got the Winchester back when the U. S. Army notified him that his son Llewellyn was missing in action and presumed dead at the end of the Vietnam War. This came about when Uncle George returned to the United States and explained to Evelyn Southern about her husband's life as a prisoner of war and how he probably died. Evelyn gave the Winchester 30.06 back to George Lawrence as a keepsake. George gave it to his grandson Peter on his sixteenth birthday, along with a story.

The gun was a buffalo rifle and one of the reasons the buffalo had virtually disappeared from the plains of the United States. Because of the Winchester, buffalo herds grew small and the kills were few. Very few pelts could be had in a horseback charge on them. The bulls and cows scattered so fast and were so far removed from each other, that horseback riders got off very few shots. One of the few Indians remaining near the herds taught Lawrence's great-great grandfather the way the Sioux took down more buffaloes, despite the fact that the white man with his 30.06 was depleting the herds. The other tribes refused to hunt the white man's way as did most of the Sioux. They believed it was unholy. Before the white man came it was believed to be a very bad practice to take down a whole herd especially the calves. It would ultimately destroy all of the revered animals.

The Sioux knew that the female buffalo cows would not leave their calves if injured. They would stay with the baby until it died, hoping it could survive the hunter. To kill an injured calf was considered punishable by banishment from the tribe or even death since the tribes believed the soul of the calf and the mother would not leave the earth, but follow each other behind a tribe that committed such an unholy act. The Sioux, in the late 19th century, knew the curse but they also knew the curse of starvation caused by the white man would be worse. They stalked the small herds, never attacking until they could get a shot at a calf. The purpose of the kill was to wound the calf so that its bellowing kept the mother tending to her calf. The hunters would then raid the herd, killing off the cows and finishing the kill of the calves. The herd was not just diminished by one or two or three mothers and children, but also lost the ability to increase the size of the herd. Herds became sterile with cows that were sickly and bulls with no mates.

This story from his grandfather ran through Lawrence's mind as he contemplated Danny Scott and the Frick drug gang. Scott was small prey, could do little harm to Frick's syndicate by being eliminated. But somehow, removing Scott as a player in the drug syndicate had to cost the gang and Frick. The whole basis of Frick's syndicate revolved around kids like Danny Scott. It was an almost perfect set up. The Scotts' did the leg work and would suffer little harm if caught. The only way Frick could be caught was if Danny or one of his other gang members ratted him out. The chance of this happening was nil. Frick's gang was loyal and ruled the impoverished neighborhoods. Turning on Frick would have more dangerous consequences than the legal system could exert. It was a status symbol to underprivileged kids to be in Frick's gang, and as a bonus you got paid for it.

Lawrence had to pull Frick in by using Frick's own scheme as the trap. If you wound the calf and waited, the cow would join it. His thoughts ran over and over in his mind, intricately trying to imagine how the drug gang worked. Frick could just give Scott the drugs and collect the payoffs without the elaborate ruse of the backpacks, but he did not. Why? Lawrence again came back to the need to have a kid like Danny running the drugs, a white kid, especially a white ghetto kid. The police knew Masabi Frick very well. He had already been in jail twice on drug charges. Anybody seen associating with Frick was sure to be tagged for surveillance. If Frick used one of his cronies to supply Danny, he ran the danger of losing control and possibly one of his cronies skimming funds. Masabi trusted his black brothers even less than he trusted the white members. A black kid associating with white kids in their community would be a red flag to the police. Frick had already been shut down dealing drugs directly in the schools. It had worked for a while but not well. Suppliers were caught too often, but school officials rarely reported the crimes. Schools worshiped their purity beyond any sense of stopping the crime at its nexus. If a student was caught with drugs, he spent two weeks in a school drug program and went back to class. Even when some of them were caught three and four times, the schools looked the other way. Too much paperwork, too much time, kept the school from prosecuting.

Frick's operation ran on a minimum risk factor. No drugs in school but anything you want through thugs like Danny Scott. No exchange of money or narcotics on school property.

Lawrence guessed that the drugs went out with Danny's one backpack on the Monday school bus jaunt and the money came back with another backpack on the Friday morning bus ride. Since they used a backpack, there had to be a considerable amount of drugs on those Monday rides. Even worse than burning a seller, was losing a shipment of drugs. Get Danny on Monday and you've got your buffalo calf, thought Lawrence.

***

"How did you get him? Just grab him off the bus?" asked Uncle George.

"I couldn't chance that. I didn't want Danny Scott in trouble or hurt. I also didn't want him to be a target for Frick's gang. Scott lived right in the middle of Frick's thugs. His tenement was their tenement. If anyone suspected he was involved in the takedown, he probably would get killed. When the dust settled I wanted the confrontation to be me and Frick, no one else."

"I set it up for Monday, the drop day, when Scott got off the school bus. I was waiting at the stop so he would see me as soon as he got off the school bus. I breathed a deep sigh of relief when I saw that he had on his red backpack, which meant the switch had been made …"

***

"Danny! Danny, come here!"

Scott saw Lawrence and started to bolt but not quickly enough. "What'd the fuck you doing? Let go of my arm."

"Listen Danny, you're mother called from some neighbor's home and pleaded with me to get to you. You are not to go home."

"She wouldn't tell you that, Lawrence."

"Well she did about an hour ago. She said there's cops all over your house. They got a search warrant. She asked me to keep you at the Boys' Club and she'd get a hold of you or me when it's clear."

"What are the cops searching for?"

"I have no idea but they went straight to your bedroom and asked her for a key."

"She ain't gotta a key!"

"Danny, keep it down. She told them so and they busted in the door. Come on."

Danny kept both of his hands firmly on the backpack straps. Nothing was going to make him let go and nobody was going to touch it. Lawrence noticed three black kids watching them. That was good since Lawrence was sure it would get back to Frick. The Boys' Club was only a short walk. Once inside Lawrence pulled Danny Scott's membership card and marked him as present. Danny would still not unleash his hands from the backpack straps. His fingers were turning red from the pressure. Lawrence left him alone and went into the office. He could see Danny out of the office window. Lawrence did not have to worry that some kid would tell Danny the truth about his mother and their house. Lawrence had called the city police ten minutes before the school bus would arrive and reported a violent family quarrel raging at Danny's house. He had called from the pay phone outside which, made for a good Caller ID to the police. He told them a small boy was screaming from an upstairs bedroom that his mother had a knife and was going to kill him. The response from the policeman on the phone was perfect. "She's at it again! Thanks Mister. What's your name?" Lawrence hung up the usual result of asking the name of someone reporting violence at Elizabeth Scott's house.

Danny was hanging at the side window looking at his house. He could see squad cars in front of it. Lawrence gave him about ten minutes then went over to him.

"Danny, the police must have found something. You're mom called and told me they're on their way here."

Scott's freckled face blanched and his eyes widened.

Scott headed for the door but Lawrence grabbed him. "Look, you'll never outrun them. Whatever they got on you, it must be bad if they're going to all that trouble. Just be cool, do what they say. I'll help you through it."

"Lawrence, I got to get away from her. Got to go ..."

"Danny, you can't out run them. They'll be all over this place in a couple minutes."

"Look, Lawrence, they can't get this backpack. I'm dead if they do."

"Come on, Danny! What are you carrying, drugs?"

"Yeah, they'll nail me for sure."

The only way into the Boys' Club was through the front double doors, which was obviously the only way out too. Lawrence could see Danny Scott searching for another door or a window, but no such escape existed. Danny dared not run out the front doors since his home was too close.

"Lawrence, hide my backpack. Come on man. I'll get you some free smack, best around. You got to get rid of the backpack," said Danny as he shuffled his arms out of the straps.

"Sure, Danny," said Lawrence, now knowing for a fact that indeed Danny Scott was carrying drugs. Lawrence had wounded the calf and needed the baby to cry for his parent. "Give it here."

Lawrence took the backpack.

"Danny, calm down. Wait here."

Lawrence went out the front door to his car. He opened the rear hatch of the station wagon, flipped up the lid to the spare tire compartment, and fit the bag into the space where a spare tire, that had not been replaced belonged. Locking the car, he returned to Danny Scott. The boy had small streams of tears running down the sides of his freckled, white face. Lawrence feared the boy would faint, especially after talking to him.

"Relax Danny. There's no cops on the way. The ones at your house are there because I called them and told them your mother was beating the hell out of you. Danny, I need a meeting with Masabi Frick."

"I don't know who you're talking about asshole."

"That's okay, Danny. I'm sure he'll ask to meet me. By the way, when you walk out of here, so do I. I'm not working here today. Frick will know where to find me tomorrow, right here. I'm sure he knows where to find you."

***

"You really put your ass on the line, Petey. You were messing with drug dealers. These guys will kill you for a postage stamp."

"Except I had the backpack. They also had no idea if I was in this alone, or not."

"So you were setting yourself up with a few dollars of pot?"

"You don't know too much about what was going on here, Uncle George."

"Yeah, you're right. The whole thing still sounds like a lot of grease in the pan to char a piece of bacon."

Lawrence laughed at his uncle's adage. "Danny Scott was just one kid. Don't you see what that means?"

"Frick would lose a seller. Probably could have another kid dealing in a couple days."

"Yep, but Frick had no idea whether I'd talked to anyone else. Why do you think he created this convoluted syndicate? Why not just hit on some kid without using the backpack scenario? Think spider, Uncle George. Frick's network was like a big web. It probably ran across the whole county. You're the spider at the edge of this big web. Places all over the web run to your corner. What's gonna happen if you jump on every insect that trips the net?"

"Probably nothing. The spider will nab the prey, wrap him up in silk, and go back to wait for another prey. Seems that's all he had to do."

"But the spider isn't just the predator. Or is he?"

Uncle George had to rethink the analogy but took a stab at an answer. "Like a spider in the web. Guess he's got some birds out there that'd like to make him their dinner."

"In Frick's case the predators know him and can find him. His predators are the police. Frick's been up the river a couple times. They're well aware of his drug dealings. So he's set up his territory so that the prey the cops can get don't lead back to him. It's like a big spider having small spiders around his net to grab pieces of the captured flies, just like Danny Scott's dealing directly with the buyers. The cops would not even see the Danny Scotts. What's the only contact Frick has with Scott?"

"The boy that rides the school bus and trades backpacks with Scott. So the cops should be able to nail Frick by nabbing the in-between man. They should be able to do that. How come they don't?"

"Frick rotates the runner after every drop and pick up. I think Frick has two or three different runners riding the school bus every day."

"How come the drivers don't catch them?"

"You ever see how crowded those busses are? Years ago, before desegregation, the busses held just about the legal number of riders. Now they're crammed. Also, and this I'm just guessing, the runners are probably set up to not get caught for anything more than hitching a ride where they don't belong. Think. If there's more than one Frick thug on the bus and somebody calls that kid out, the odds are he's got nothing. Even if he is the runner for that day, he'll see it coming and just drop his cache on the way out. He'll easily see that the driver is eyeballing him and waiting for him to get off the bus. So another crony picks it up."

"You think that's how it works?"

"I think that's how it's set up. Like I told you before, I watched the kids that the bus drops off at the school. I never saw any kid stopped from getting off the bus. That means any particular runner on any day is probably not going to be stopped. The school personnel supervising the bus drop off zone at the school don't pay any attention to the kids. There's a couple thousand kids being unloaded. How're they going to catch one of Frick's thugs?"

"So did Danny tell Frick about you?"

***

Lawrence pulled up to his normal parking space on the street next to the Boys' Club at the precise time he did every day including the day after his snatch of Danny Scott's backpack. He did not even have time to turn off the engine before the black Cadillac pulled up behind him. Lawrence had not anticipated it coming this soon. There was no one on the streets. All of the children in the area were still at school watching and waiting the bell to release them to the school busses or the walk home. Pedestrians on the street were rare on any day. Lawrence had shook the web and been caught.

He quickly put the gear into drive and maneuvered the car to face directly at the black Cadillac. Squealing his near bald rear tires, he pulled his front end to within a yard of the Cadillac's front end, rolled down the driver side front window, and put his left foot firmly on the brake pedal as his right foot gassed the engine.

While Lawrence has making this turn maneuver, a huge, very black man exited the passenger side of the Cadillac and made it to Lawrence's door. The black man grabbed the door handle a split second too late as Lawrence hit the lock. The driver side window was open and the black man started for the drop button of the lock when Lawrence spoke.

"Hear that engine, Bozo? Got my foot running it and my other foot on the brake. You grab me this car's going ram your Caddy like a dump truck. Want to explain that to the police? The black man backed up. He looked at Lawrence's feet, both off the floor and onto pedals. It was easy to see Lawrence was not conning him. The black man started to yell at him.

"Listen you mother fucker ..."

Lawrence was sweating like a glass of ice on the equator, but like that glass he was cool. It was not much different than when he and his grandfather hunted black bears and one charged them. You sweat it out, hold it still, and kill it.

"Tell Frick, he wants to talk to me, I'm waiting. Pretty soon there's going to be school busses coming down the street. That's a lot of witnesses."

"You fucked white boy."

The black man went back to the car. Lawrence could see the man lean into the rear driver's side window. The black man repeatedly pointed to Lawrence, shaking his head, and eventually holding his arms up in surrender to Frick's dictates. The man walked slowly down the side of Frick's Cadillac turned to his right, and crossed directly in front of Lawrence's car. Lawrence revved the engine and the man dove onto the side walk. Neither car moved. The man rolled off the sidewalk and looked at his hands. They had scrapes and cuts along the edges of his palms. Lawrence was surprised the man did not pull out a gun. Instead he walked along the curb edge, avoiding the street, and stooped down to Lawrence's window.

Lawrence laughed and spoke "Five and half, sorry that's all I'll give you."

"What the fuck you talkin' 'bout?"

"Worse dive I've ever seen. Better try another sport. Black folks can't swim. You oughta know that. Where's Frick?" Lawrence knew Frick would never show his face. The last mistake Masabi Frick needed to make was to be IDed at the scene of a crime.

"He says to meet him ..."

"No, wrong answer. I knew he wouldn't come out of that Cadillac. Let me make myself very clear. I know how much money's in that backpack. The street value of it could buy him another Cadillac and probably a Buick. Hit me and kiss it good bye. Call the Boys' Club after six tonight. We'll talk."

The black man had had enough, he yanked open Lawrence's door. Lawrence eased his foot off the brake pedal. The station wagon lurched, quickly followed by a blast from the black Cadillac's horn. Lawrence just smiled into the black face in front of him.

"You've got pussy breath, boy! Ought to try fucking cunt instead of eating it. Damn stuff is making you stupid."

"What's the fucking phone number dis here club?"

"Try the phone book. Right now my ankle's getting stiff. You punks don't get out of here soon, there's going to be a big crash right out here in plain sight."

The black man caught his temper. He smile broadly, "You ain't bad, white shit. I gotta say as much. Lotta balls. You'll go down and I be the one take you down."

He slammed the driver side car door, walked to the Cadillac, got into the front passenger side, and the Cadillac slowly rolled past Lawrence's rusted and ugly Ford station wagon. Lawrence feared that a window would roll down and a gun muzzle would stick out.

***

"I can't believe you took those kinds of risks. Damn, Petey, those weren't the right kind of people to be challenging like you did. They'll kill you as soon as look at you," said Uncle George.

Lawrence paused a couple seconds, gathered his thoughts, and knowing Uncle George was right about the danger said, "That's the strange thing about it. I went after jerking them around. You're completely right. Frick and his thugs would kill me on the spot without any thought, squashed me like a bug. It was scary but I went after it."

"It's the hunter in you," said Uncle George. "You sound like you let your conscience tell you that you're doing a good thing by getting rid of vermin like Frick, but that isn't what gets you going. Your grandfather's like that. He kind of likes the facing of danger, makes him feel more alive."

"Sort of. When Lew and I went black bear hunting, we had to lead the bear along. He kept staying just out of reach. Many a time Grandpere wanted to take a shot at him or wanted me to give it a go. Range was close, but I held back and held him back. Worse thing would be not making a clean kill. It wouldn't even be like shooting a deer without bringing it down. Deer's not going to circle on you and attack. Deer's not going to go out of range and maybe hurt or kill somebody else in a dying rage."

"Guess you looked at Frick as that kind of kill?"

"At first, then I realized that when Lew and I hunted down the black bear, I didn't actually hate the bear. In fact I was pretty sad when we did get him. It was the hunt, not the kill that charged me. I never stalked a creature that could disappear and then turn on me, make me the hunted, that night's dinner. Originally I went with Grandpere because he said bear meat was one of the best. At least he and I both let ourselves think that. It turned into more than that. I got scared; scared the bear would turn on me without me being ready to stop him. I felt his total ability to make me the hunted, that he could rear up all of a sudden and tear me to pieces. I didn't hate him but I wanted to face him. I don't think I really needed his body as much as I needed to know I triumphed."

"Isn't that what was happening with Frick by the time you had the face-off outside of the Boys' Club?"

"Yes, it was. His thug scared me, scared the hell out of me. Yet, I caused my own fear but relished that fear. It wasn't being afraid; being scared means being unable to overcome your enemy. It was the fear, not of facing Frick, but of not being able to beat him. The bear never had a shot at us but we feared he would. The fear kept as at our maximum. Even when we cornered him and he came at us from twenty or thirty feet away, we both felt the fear and made a clean kill."

"So what was going on was a bear hunt, only with Frick as the prey?"

"As wrong as that sounds, I wanted to kill him. He never actually did anything to me. At worse, he killed a dog and beat up my friend. My wanting to kill him was murderous. Yeah, you could see it that way. We killed the black bear not for what he had done to us but because of the hunt. It had nothing to do with bear steaks for dinner. Fact is, they had a sickly taste and were tough. We threw away most of the meat. I tasted the first bite and didn't much like it. But I ate it any way."

"Sounds like an Indian ritual, Petey. You took his spirit and had to release it from the earth by consuming it and uniting it with your spirit."

Lawrence smiled at his uncle. Uncle George understood him.

"That's not why you wanted to kill Frick."

"You're right again. I would never want the spirit of a creature like Masabi Frick. He had no compassion for anybody but himself. Frick thrived on those he could either subjugate or violently tear apart. Frick's eyes told Frick's spirit. When he was kicking the intestines out of Zinni's dog, his mouth was salivating, his eyes were red from the rush of adrenaline. Then his eyes got a second helping when they attacked Zinni. I took the bear and felt guilt. I pacified my sins by eating his flesh. The bear was an elevation in my spirit that I could find him, fight him, and take him. With it I took guilt and would never take an innocent animal's life again. Frick is a vile and evil being. If anything, I avenged my guilt at killing the bear by ridding the world of Frick. The bear's spirit was inside of me. The bear's hunting, stalking, and killing, had prepared me. I would need the prey to give me fear during the battle with Frick. When I came face-to-face with that cancerous scab of a monster that festered itself on others, Frick's potential to kill me and my killing him would give me the fear but would not cause guilt when I finally took his life. This was why I so enjoyed the fear Frick and his cronies provided. Had he been easy to kill, I would have enjoyed it less."

Uncle George understood the spirit of killing that which is not human or inhuman. He also had taken lives when necessary for his survival and in Vietnam went the logic of being drilled into believing he was in the right killing Vietnamese. Evil and good were only separated by of who told the story. The living cannot be evil and the dead are or were. Uncle George also knew during all the years watching his nephew grow, Peter had developed a profound ability to judge life and especially humans. It was impossible to lie to Peter.

"Weren't you pretty much at crossroads here, where you would now become the hunted? I mean they knew you, knew what to stalk."

"That's what Frick wanted to believe until I flushed him out of his niche. As soon as he pulled away, I went into the Boys' Club and got out the business card the city police detective gave me. When he had showed the pictures of the killing of the Jack and Jill ice cream man, I told him I thought I knew another one of the people in the picture with Danny Scott. He brought the photographs back over. I went slowly through them, and pulled out the one with Frick and Danny Scott."

"He asked me how come I didn't identify him before? I told I had never seen him before but that I just got hassled by him in front of the Boys' Club. The two police detectives looked at each other with glances that signaled a lead. I explained one of his men had rousted me from my car and forced my arm up behind my back. He took me to the car where the man in the pictures was sitting. When the rear window rolled down, I recognized him from the police photograph. With my arm bent up my back, the man in the car asked me if I ratted on him. I told him I couldn't since this was the first time I had ever seen him. He told me to keep my mouth shut or I'd be stealing crèmesicles from the dead Jack and Jill man. As soon as they left, I called you. I didn't like being hassled."

"What did the cops do then, Petey?"

"They asked if I would testify against the man who assaulted. I told them I sure would. Uncle George smiled, "I'll bet the police went straight to Frick's place to confront him.""

"Better than that. I added that maybe there were other people in the area being harassed to keep quiet, especially the kids that come to the Boys' Club. I told them I was getting scared to work here now. They told me that they would have the station assign a patrol car to watch this area starting now. To prove it one policeman used our phone to call the station to set it up. He also made a point of letting me hear that he and his partner were leaving to interrogate Masabi Frick right away."

***

Lawrence waited for Masabi Frick's promised phone call. He had to wait until the next night's shift at the Boys' Club. Lawrence thought Frick would be outraged and threatening on the phone, but he was neither.

"You a pretty smart fucker, White Meat. Set those pigs right after me, didn't you?"

"Best way to get a good shot is to flush the bear out of an ambush."

"That's good. I don't know what the fuck it means but it sounds good. You making me out to be a bear coming after you, huh?"

"Been there. Killed me a black bear once. I judged you would be too stupid to go after me since I have your stash. I think I guessed wrong."

"Nah, I ain't gone after you, White Meat. Least not til I gots my goods back. Still, it was a smart move. Ebony wanted to hit you last night, but then you did scare the shit out of him when you revved that sad looking car of yours. Sic the bacon on us got you out a town before we could follow you. By the way, you knows you not listed in the phone book," said Frick with his loud, and guttural laughter.

"You want the drugs. I been through them. They aren't really that valuable unless your operation is the same nickel-dime level as that stash in the backpack. You need them that badly, what you willing to pay to get them back?"

"I knew, White Meat, that it'd be pesos! Like you said, White Meat, ain't worth enough to get busted. What's in there? Enough weed for a dozen or so smokes? Maybe a couple hundred dollars to me. That's chicken shit,"

"There's a least a kilo of marijuana. On the street that would bring in a couple grand at least. What about the powder?"said Lawrence. "You got enough 8 Balls in there to blow apart a major uptown party tonight and rake in what? About 10 thou or more?"

"I underestimated you White Meat. You a user? You gotta be, knowing what you know. So let's cut the bull shit and name a price."

"Seven thousand and you get back the backpack. Nothing missing. I call the cops and tell them I made a mistake. Better yet, I don't give them the tape I'm making of this call."

The phone went into a disconnected buzz. Had Lawrence pushed Masabi Frick too far? Hunting's worst trial is the patience to wait, bide your time. If you try to push them, you will lose them, the prey.

Lawrence let the phone ring five times before picking it up, "Boys' Club, how can I help you?"

"Okay, White Meat, you get seven thou. Let's do it. Where we meet to set this up?"

Lawrence saw his opportunity open up. "Here."

"You fucking kidding? The cops already been over my apartment cause of you talking. What you think de's gonna watch me walk in there, hand you over a bag of bread, and walk out with a bag?"

"No, because you're going to be clean walking in and clean walking out. We meet here and talk. All out in the open. Police will even let you in, let us talk."

"How's that, White Meat?"

"Next Saturday's the boxing club's tournament. I'll be there, but only as a spectator. You come in about an hour after it's started, find me, and sit next to me."

"And the cops won't be all over me?"

"Why should they? Out in public? Sitting in a gymnasium. Watching boxing matches. Think they'll arrest you for sitting next to me? Come on, Frick. They'll be ecstatic, watching us like crows over road kill, just waiting to get at me about what you had to say."

"You know, you a pretty smart white boy. Shame someday I'm have to kill you."

"You agree or not?"

"Give me the times."

CHAPTER TWELVE

Feeding A Bear

Uncle George was more than just amazed at his nephew's deadly scenario. "Petey, I know you were pretty young at that point and I understand why you just didn't turn Frick over to the authorities, but it's a miracle you aren't dead."

"Why Uncle George, if I died how could I ever tell you how I killed Masabi Frick?" Lawrence smiled. "Wasn't the first time I got near biting the big one. In fact my first shot at testing my mortality gave me the way to keep it when I finally killed Frick."

"How's that?"

George popped off a Schlitz beer can tab and handed it to Lawrence. It had been a long afternoon, the chickens were beheaded and cleaned, and now inside with Aunt Louise. Lawrence took the beer and slowly felt the cooling effect of the Schlitz running down his throat while waiting for the small spark in his brain telling him the alcohol had reached his nervous system.

"You know Grandpere Lew sort of took me under his wing. I guess he saw his son, my father, in my eyes. Only rarely did I ever take advantage of it. Never did he interfere with Mon Mere disciplining me. I was a rascal and ornery but I pretty much avoided totally pissing either of them off enough to whoop my ass. But it did happen once and Mon Mere rear ended me."

Uncle George was snickering since he knew how the rest of the family felt about his sister-in-law's molly coddling of Peter.

"Me and Bobby Finney took off for the hills one late fall weekend. Bobby's a pretty good archer and he let me borrow his dad's old bow and shafts. It didn't bother his mother since his father had been dead for a couple years. In fact she told me to just keep them. Our destination was the Adirondacks, you know like going to Mon Grand pere's cabin except as we drove toward the forest I realized this was a chance to check out a place where we had been forbidden to go, the old Scranton Mining Company hills."

"How come now?"

"It was the first time Mon Mere had agreed to let me go out more or less on my own. Seeing that I was old enough to drive, she figured I could do a camping and fishing trip without getting into trouble."

Uncle George's mouth gaped incredulously. "Did she think you were gone hunting?"

Lawrence just smiled, "Mon Mere only thought fishing. We headed east toward the old mining camp. It'd been closed I guess near about five or six years. All they had done was board up the entrances and stick up a cheap old wire fence that was easy enough to crawl under."

"Probably the real reason we wanted to do the mine was to brag about spending a night in the mine. Nobody I knew had ever tried it. We'd a been okay if we'd done it much earlier. Like I said it was late fall and getting close to some snow signaling winter."

"We had no trouble getting under the fence and yanking boards off a mine entrance. Only trouble I had was remembering what Grandpere Lew had taught me about bears, black bears. I failed to notice a couple things about black bears. The mine was just above a small stream and the entrance was fronted by an understory of blackberry bushes and oak trees that had scattered acorns all around their roots. I shouldn't have missed the acorns. It was just plain stupid."

"Shouldn't have been any acorns around the trees, not in the Fall with Winter getting ready to send the squirrels to their nests. You were pretty negligent there Petey."

"Not just that but the blackberries were ripe enough to make wine out of …"

"That's just how black bears love them. You'd think you'd a seen their spoor around?"

"Gotta have your head up your ass to not see anything. Guess what else?" said Peter.

"Couldn't be much dumber than that?"

"The mine entrance was so simple to bust because the right side lower boards had been torn away. How's that for being ignorant?"

Uncle George just shook his head, "you idiots were going to walk into a bear cave. Obviously you didn't. Cause if you had, he'd got you both. You couldn't have even used your bows in a mine shaft. Probably the son-of-bitch would just wait for you to walk into him and killed you both."

"Well, Uncle George, you're just about right, but you got to do an about-face. We met him when we were running out of the mine. I think we even invited the bear to get us, since when we were knocking down the entrance, the wind was coming down off the mountain in our faces."

"You were down wind in a bear's feeding niche and his den entrance. You shouldn't be there, Petey. Bear didn't kill you but your mom should have. Why were you running out of the den and the bear was running into his den."

"I wasn't totally stupid. My nose was working. We went down the tunnel, following the tram tracks, and I started smelling rotting meat. I wanted to chalk it off to mice or opossum, but we would have heard some noise. Bobby kept his flashlight low to see that we didn't fall through any sink holes in the shaft. We should have heard some scurrying. By the time I figured it out, my eyes told me why the smell and no rodents. The entrance shaft branched to a T. The smell at the T was a putrefied carcass, probably a deer, but could have been a small elk. Then I knew where we were. I knew we had to get out."

"Bobby started to run when I told them we were in a bear's den. The bear was probably foraging to store up fat under his fur for hibernation. I quickly grabbed Bobby to stop him. If we ran out of the cave the way we came in, there was a good chance he'd be waiting for us. Neither of us gave the bears credit of having an acute sense of smell. No sooner had I explained our troubles to Bobby then we heard a slow but heavy shuffling echoing down the shaft where we entered. Either he was stalking us or he was returning to his nest for the night. Bears aren't good nocturnally, best in the morning or early darkness."

"Bobby wanted to fit up his bow and hit him when he came down the shaft. That would just get us killed quicker. The arrows we had couldn't stop an anemic squirrel. We had one option which was to go back to the carcass and take one of the other shafts. Bobby argued that it would only put us in deeper. I know it wouldn't from stories Grandpere Lew had told me about the abandoned mine. The bear wouldn't trap himself in a deep cave like stupid teenagers. I convinced him that at the worst we'd be stuck down here until morning when the bear went out to forage. Maybe we'd find one of the shafts leading to another exit."

"So is that what you did? Sounds to me Bobby had the best idea. Aren't bears spooked pretty easy?"

"Remember, Uncle George, the carcass was putrefying very badly. I mean I couldn't tell if it was a deer, moose, or somebody's large hunting dog. The bear smelled us and was coming down the shaft. Bears avoid human scents unless they're hungry. We had to get out or die, but I couldn't tell Bobby that. He'd a shit his pants like I damn near did."

Lawrence put the empty beer can down, shook off Uncle George's offer of another Schlitz, and leaned back on the bench stretching his back muscles.

"So how did you get out of there?"

"I guessed right, because we took the right. The shaft went down maybe a quarter a mile and came out facing the moon, the ground devoid of fallen acorns and no berry bushes or streams."

"I don't understand how you got whooped by Evelyn when you could've just kept your mouth shut?"

Lawrence held up his right arm and pointed to a long white scar running at least a foot down his forearm. "Damn fence got me. We were in such a hurry to get out of the mining camp that I caught an edge of the wire going over it. Bobby saved my life probably. Got a tourniquet on it fast, stopped the bleeding, and ran about two miles down to the main road to where we had pulled off and parked my Ford station wagon in the bushes. He was back quick enough and drove fast enough, that I didn't bleed to death and a tetanus shot was given in time to keep me from lock jaw."

"So the hospital called Evelyn. She came, got you and ... "

"Smacked me up one side and down the other. Sent me to bed. But when I woke about ten hours later, she had the greatest breakfast ready for me that I had ever eaten."

"Your mother makes the best pancakes I've ever tasted. Don't tell Aunt Louise that, though."

"Grandpere Lew was ready for me. I knew he was close to smacking me, but he just couldn't. I held my head down at every word he said. He came very close to saying he was ashamed of me, but he didn't. I knew he wouldn't. In fact once he finished his tirade, he had me tell him the whole story. He almost slugged me when I told him about all the scents I ignored. Guess what happened after everybody cooled down? Bobby, me, and the bear started to take on new twists as it became a legend told at family gatherings."

"It would seem you'd be grounded for the rest of your life and never allowed back in the forest again. That's what would happen with a normal, chicken-shit family which ours isn't."

Lawrence smiled, asked for another beer, popped it, took a long swig, and spoke. "A month and a half after getting caught in that mining shaft, Grandpere Lew took me back up there."

"That wasn't hard to see happening."

"He showed me the new signs. Most of the foliage was brown and dead. We didn't see any game at all, but somebody had come up from town to put new boards and big warning signs all over the mine entrances. Guess what happened to the entrance had gone?"

"Had a hole in it?"

"Just enough. Grandpere knows his stuff. He taped over a flashlight, making a small slit in it, ready just in case the entrance was open enough for the bear. We crawled down the shaft on our hands and knees, stopping every ten feet so that he could edge the light forward. First way we knew the bear was in the cave was we could hear him. Grandpere stopped me; we waited about five minutes, both of us listening to the bear sleeping. Then he turned me around and we came home. He said that the Peter Lawrence Great Bear Hunting Story would be worthless if we didn't know for sure that there was an actual bear."

"Petey, that's a damn good tale. I'm proud to be a member of the Lawrence hunting party, but why did we get into the Great Bear Hunt when you're telling me about Masabi Frick?"

Lawrence used his plying smile to turn up the corners of Uncle George's mouth. "Bear's still there."

"What? How do you know that?"

"Don't fight an enemy on his territory. I think Davy Crockett said that in the Disney movie when he was trapped in the Alamo. Frick had me dancing to his music and in his ballroom. If you want to kill a bear, you've got to draw him out into the open. You've got to have control. After the phone call with him, I knew he'd have too much of an advantage in the city. I needed to put him in my niche, out here in the suburbs, or best of all in the forest where I was raised to hunt, fish, forage, and basically survive. I remembered the mine. You know how the bear had his kill at the T of the shafts? What saved me and Bobby?"

"Choosing the right shaft. By the way, where did the other shaft go?"

"Not out but deeper into the mine. It also had a ventilation shaft going straight up. We could have shimmied up it. So we had two escape routes.

"I killed Frick in the bear's den."

***

Lawrence imagined and worried about all sorts of attacks on him and his family. He could not help it. Seeing fear is part of the human response system. Inside of himself he knew that for Frick to kill him would not be easy. Still he had trouble sleeping, reading, and not starting at any sound or movement. What Lawrence had going for him was his mother never took the name Lawrence and so her residence was listed under E. Southern. No Lawrence's in the phone book would direct Frick to him since his Grandpere hated phones and refused to own one.

Lawrence had to keep Frick out in the open. Frick was a sadist that grew from mutilating dogs and kicking helpless kids into committing street crime. Given a chance to do violence to Lawrence, Frick might even give up the drug stash in the backpack in order to savor watching and maybe even taking part in the killing of Lawrence. He had to keep the fight out in the open. This was his reason for meeting at the Boys' Club boxing club.

Boxing club night was a culmination of the Boys' Club sponsored activity and parents of the boxers would show up to see their sons participate. The gymnasium was so small that Larry had to assign bout times and only allow a boxer to have two spectators in the gym during his bout. Lawrence guessed that Frick would be one of Danny Scott's guests, and was right. The other guest was Frick's thug. Scott's mother, Liz, would never be seen in a place so public and with so many black people. Lawrence caught Frick's eye when he and his body guard walked past the game room counter where Lawrence sat on a stool. When Frick walked over to Lawrence, Lawrence told him to save a spot for him in the gymnasium. He would be in before the fight started. He asked Frick who he was here to watch. Of course Frick told him Danny Scott. Frick and the other black man walked down the hall and sat on a bench against the wall leading into the gymnasium. There was one group of spectators ahead of Frick.

The bouts were only two minutes long, three rounds with thirty seconds between bells. When Lawrence saw Frick move to the next and last position, he walked down the hall, smiled at Frick's thug, made a pistol with his pointed index finger and thumb and did a pretend gun shot at Frick. Frick smiled and told him he better use the real thing next time. Both sneered. Lawrence went through the closed gym door, opening it just enough to slip through. He sat one row up and near the rear concrete block wall. There was no way to exit unless you climbed the twenty-five feet to the sealed glass windows and broke through them. Lawrence now had what he needed. There was no way Frick could try anything here, especially since Larry had gotten the city police to patrol the activity. Even better were the two detectives that had interrogated Larry and Lawrence about Frick. Both were in casual clothes and seated on the highest bench row near the only exit out of the gym, besides the locker room. Frick would recognize them, Lawrence was sure.

One of the kids who helped Larry manage the boxing club and was sitting at a bench across the mat from the two combatants, held up an old cow bell and shook it. Larry threw his hands in the air crossing each other back and forth while separating the boxers to indicate the bout was over. Larry did not announce a winner. The one outcome Larry did not want from sponsoring the boxing club and training the young pugilists was to make any kid a loser. In all the training or in any of the exhibitions there had been only one fight that ended in a decision and that was when Jemarius had knocked Scott to the floor and out cold.

The friends and relatives clapped for the fighters. Exuberant mothers hugged their embarrassed boxers and the group exited the gym, letting in the next spectators. All in all there was enough room for four groups of fighters, and Frick now walked in for the subsequent battle Danny Scott would have. Frick sat down next to Lawrence, and his sat on the other side of Lawrence.

"Now I have the honor of being an ore," said Lawrence to Frick.

"Start talking, White Meat. You ain't amusing me." Frick wiggled in his seat enough to jab the gun he wore on his belt into Lawrence's side. His red jacket over a black turtle neck sweater concealed the weapon. Lawrence was sure the thug had a pistol on his right side.

"I got money for you. It's right outside in my Caddie. Where's the backpack?"

"Right here," said Lawrence as he reached under his seat to grab the backpack he had left there when he got to work this morning. The bag was empty.

"You mother fucker! What's ..." Frick could not get out another word before a very heavy set, well dressed black woman sitting behind him slammed the side of his head.

"You watch yo' mouth nigger! I got boys here I tryin' to teach right and manners. Don't need any that filth!"

Frick put his hand in the face of his thug who was reaching inside of his jacket.

"Cool it! I'm so sorry ma'am. You right. I just got one a dem' trash mouths and I forget when I'm with cultured folk. I'm truly sorry. Ain't happen again."

The black woman shored herself up and made a growling sound,. "Thank you. Keep it that way."

Lawrence thought that Frick and his cohort were going to start shooting right in the gym and that he might owe his life to that woman.

"You think I'm dumb enough to bring drugs into here? Look around you, Frick. See the patrol officer over there? I'll bet you know those two guys behind us. They know you. They've been all over my case about you."

"Boy, this is gettin' tiring. Where's it?"

Now came the downwind, the scent that would force the prey to move his niche, "not here, not in my car, not even in the city. Not only don't I trust you, but even if you were playing straight with me, you've got cops breathing down your neck with every step you take."

"How do you know that? You just rapping to me. How you know."

"Because I told them you wanted to do a deal with me."

"Now let me get this straight, White Meat. You ratted out our deal to the pigs? You stupid or something? They shake me down, I'll blow you away before than can cuff me. I don't, he will!"

The thug nudged Lawrence. Lawrence looked him straight in the face. The man was not just ugly, he had made himself uglier by having one whole side of his face tattooed in three different colors.

"Wow, nice tats! It just goes to show you what a faggot can do when you give him a box of crayons."

The thug just smiled. "That'd be a new one. Last guy made fun of my mamma's picture is pushing up daisies."

"Frick, for someone that runs a ... let me reword this. For a businessman like yourself to get caught in this kind of situation makes no sense. We do it here, we're both nailed. One thing I've got going for me is that you don't dare kill me, even if you don't care about the ... product. It can't be here."

The audience was standing up and clapping for the finished boxers. Danny Scott came out of the locker room with his gloves on, shadowboxing along the far wall. Ironically, Jemarius followed him. Usually Larry rotated fighters. Larry walked over to Lawrence before starting the next fight.

"Lawrence, see you got a couple of friends here?"

It was a question that Lawrence did not answer. "What's going on with Jemarius and Danny?"

"Jemarius has been sparring with Scott, teaching him a few things. They're kind of friends now. Danny asked to have a rematch, so I thought, hey why not?"

Larry went back and started the next fight.

"Danny's a powerful boy, Lawrence. I heard you got a thing for his mamma," said Frick.

The thug started laughing. He reached in front of Lawrence and gave Frick a high five.

Lawrence could smell a set up. Somebody got to Danny Scott and did something with him. They had set up Danny to take down Jemarius. Jemarius was a good kid and Lawrence did not want see him get hurt. There was nothing he could do to stop it except know that Larry was a good referee and could control the fight.

"In the backpack are instructions. They tell you where to meet me after we leave," said Lawrence. Frick was not paying much attention. He had his eyes on Jemarius as did the thug.

"You interested here? I'm trying to ..."

"Shoo man, just a minute." Frick stood up and motioned Lawrence to move over in his spot, which Lawrence did. Frick now sat next to his associate and began whispering in his ear. Lawrence could not hear what was being said between the two. Lawrence was in disbelief, not realizing that Frick knew how to mislead protagonists. He was putting Lawrence and the drug deal into a small meaningless situation that did not interest him too much. If you belittle your foe, then he will be little.

When the fight was in its last seconds, Frick turned to Lawrence, "okay, you gonna meet me somewhere and give me my ... yeah, my product. Sure man let's do it. Do it now. Soon as this next bout gets done."

Frick went back to watching the fighters and Lawrence continued to feel insignificant. He was having serious doubts about what he was trying to do. Here he was a young man, barely old enough to buy a beer and yet up against a mobster who ran a citywide drug syndicate.

Lawrence stopped thinking about what Frick might do and brought his thoughts to what Frick could do. He saw his fears and he knew their source. It was that time before the kill. The time when you ask yourself if you have what it takes to bring down the animal. Can you stop the creature or will you fall apart inside of yourself? It hit him hard, just like the first creature he ever killed. This hunt was eating at him because it would be his first human kill. He knew he had to either walk away from it or get on top of it.

Danny Scott came out swinging like he always did. Jemarius was different, though. He kept on his toes all the way, jabbing and backing, never really using his power. Danny had no stamina but Jemarius just kept at Danny's head, at his left ear. Danny would come in, Jemarius would do a left jab, right cross, but fake the left and come back with the right jab at the ear. Jemarius backed up constantly, making Danny chase him. When they came by Lawrence's front row bench, Lawrence could see Scott's eyes. They were blood shot and dull. He was drugged.

Lawrence's mind erupted in thought, "What the hell's going on here? Is Frick trying to get his dealer to blow away Jemarius by not feeling any pain?"

By the third round Scott kept dropping his hands, but continued heading into Jemarius. Lawrence could not understand why Jemarius did not just one-two-three him and end it. Danny chased him and took a wild stab, his arms so tired he could not make contact. Jemarius threw two left jabs at Scott's right ear, faked a right cross to the left, then caught Danny thinking there would be another shot at his right ear. Jemarius threw an upper cut that came up underneath Scott's jaw with such a force that Lawrence could hear the jaw bone break. Danny was down and might never get up. Lawrence finally realized what was happening. Frick was paying Danny back for losing the drug exchange. By now everyone was standing up to see if Danny would get up. Larry sent the kid who was working the bell to the office to call an ambulance. The uniformed patrolman came over to keep people away from Scott and to give Larry room to tend to Danny. Jemarius walked over to the thug who unlaced his gloves and pulled them off. He did a 'give me five' slap with the black man, the slap that black men do when they want to praise each other and at the same time to dehumanize and ridicule their opponent. Frick slapped Jemarius on the back and hugged him.

Lawrence's hunter's edge was back. The fear of the kill was gone and his adrenaline was flowing. A smile broke out on his face as he walked over to the threesome. Jemarius refused to make eye contact. Lawrence had the backpack and when Frick turned to him, he slammed it into his chest.

"I can see that it's true you should never trust one of you in a wood pile."

The thug started at him but Lawrence turned his head and, with the palm of his right hand, gestured to the two police detectives watching them from the stands. The black man backed off.

Frick started to speak but Lawrence stopped him. "No more. Read what's in the bag."

Frick opened the flap, found an envelope, ripped it open, and looked up for Lawrence. But Lawrence was already out the door. At the door were the two police detectives who now stood waiting to take Frick for another ride downtown. On his way out, Lawrence had told the policemen about the weapons Frick and his thug were carrying.

"Shit," said Frick. He realized Lawrence had taken control. When he finally got the envelope opened, he took out the piece of typing paper, read it, and asked the policemen now standing in front of him, "where the fuck is the Scranton Mining Camp?"

***

There was zero chance of snow with temperatures ranging from 35 to 40° and slight winds running at peaks of 2 to 3 miles per hours. This was mid-Atlantic United States lodged between the Adirondacks and the Appalachians which meant there was little or no predictability. Lawrence waited on top of the hill thirty or so yards above the entrance to the Scranton Coal Mines, trying to scan the state road two miles below and south of the mine entrance. The fallen snow was a gift to him since it covered his tracks of two hours ago. He established a reconnoiter point and was using his binoculars, waiting for Frick and his thugs to show up. The wind negated a clear view. The gusts were strong enough to force him to lean against their blasts and the wind driven snow made it difficult to even see his gray Ford station wagon parked conspicuously in front of the trail leading to the mine entrance.

Frick and his cohorts waited until dusk before driving past the only path from the state road to the mines. Lawrence guessed that their two hour trip from the city had found them unprepared for an abrupt change in the atmospheric environment. Frick's gang was black and worked their terror at night, taking advantage of skin camouflage. Snow trumped that advantage and that put Lawrence one up on them.

The state road had a speed limit of forty-five but most sane drivers knocked it down to thirty five with the snow, which had now accumulated enough that soon state snow plows would hit the road for their winter season opener. Lawrence correctly guessed that the black Plymouth sedan contained the first cadre of thugs whom were doing a ride by of the site Lawrence had mapped for Frick. A black head with dreadlocks was poked out of the passenger side window. The car could not have been traveling more the fifteen miles per hour. While their approach was slow and careful, their drive by, which was trying to not draw attention, was ridiculous. Not only was it too slow but its passengers were a rarity in this predominantly white area. Just as they went around the bend north of the road and to the right of Lawrence's vantage point, Frick's Cadillac slowly cruised by using the same tire tracks that, despite the falling snow and gusty winds, had remained very visible. The gap between cars gave Lawrence consternation. His defense of the mine entrance was based on the situation of there being only one path leading to the hill from which he reconnoitered Frick's approach. Frick's car went past Lawrence's parked car, slowing down considerably. The first car had not returned and this worried Lawrence since they might attempt a two front approach to the mine entrance. It would not change his strategy but it would require him to watch both of his flanks.

Frick's car did not go as far as the bend. Lawrence watched it pull over to the shoulder and stop. Lawrence could see Frick get out of the passenger side door and stand up. He was holding a car phone to his ear, the helix cord stretching from inside of the car. After a couple of seconds Frick handed the phone into the car, bundled his arms around his body in a shiver, and turned to where the first car had gone around the bend. He was waiting and watching for his cohorts to return. It did not take long. With wiper blades slushing hills of snow off the windshield, the Plymouth came down the far side of the state road and turned immediately into a space next to Lawrence's gray Ford Station wagon. No sooner did it stop then two men jumped out of the right side of the car, pulled out pistols, and holding them with two hands, shot out all four of Lawrence's tires. When they finished, they fled to the far side of the Plymouth keeping their guns aimed at the Ford station wagon.

Lawrence smiled and thought, "damn, Pep Boys just had a sale on tires and I missed it!"

By this time Frick's Cadillac had u-turned and was parked off the shoulder on the south side of Lawrence's car. Despite the wind, Lawrence could hear dogs, quietly at first but then more discernible when the Plymouth rear doors were opened and the driver tugged on two choker leashes. Frick's men had two pit bulls, one black and one white, roaring and busting at their leashes now held by two of the hugs. They had gained a one up on Lawrence. He had never expected them to use dogs. It meant little to tracking Lawrence; once they opened his Ford, they would find detailed instructions of how to find him. Pit bulls were not tracking dogs anyway. Probably they were to be used to attack him. Lawrence had made a good choice in weapons. While he loved the 1898 lever action Winchester 30.30, this venture needed automatic fire. The Winchester would blow away the first target and maybe give him a shot at a second, but with more than two or three pursuers, he would be under fire too quickly. Grandpere's Marlin 30.06 with 4X scope was as close as he could get to automatic firing without having an illegal weapon. Lawrence could send off at least five rounds before the prey even knew what hit them or where the rounds originated. With a little bit of luck he could get off an additional two or three more rounds before they finally targeted him.

The thug, Frick's huge black man, exited the driver's side of the Cadillac and stood with the door opened, using it as a shelter from arms. He waited. A third black man emerged from the Plymouth and stood with a pistol aimed up the trail in front of Lawrence's now flat tired Ford station wagon. The pit bulls were loud and vicious, attacking each other. One of the gunmen took the leash of one and separated the fighting dogs. The thug continued to wait behind the car door but motioned to one of the men to go to Lawrence's car and open all the doors. Every thug had his weapon focused on the doors as they were flung open. Nobody fired. The huge black man spoke, Lawrence could only see through the binoculars his fat lips moving; he could not hear the commands. It was not difficult to interpret what he said since the pit bulls were lead around the car, and gradually over the terrain surrounding both cars. Lawrence again smiled, knowing pit bulls were not good at tracking and usually scented only very pungent odors that most humans could recognize and follow. After scavenging through the first bush line leading to the mine entrance, the two dogs were brought back and one of the men emerged from the station wagon holding the piece of paper Lawrence had left on the front seat.

Lawrence carefully adjusted the scope on the Marlin rifle by focusing on the front bumper of his station wagon. It was getting too dark and the distance was obviously too great to take down anybody. He traced backwards with the scope from the road and up the path that he had marked on the map which Frick must now be holding inside the Cadillac. Lawrence pulled a fine linen cloth out of his front pocket in the gray sweat shirt he wore, and carefully wiped down the Marlin rifle, storing it in the leather case which he shouldered on his back. Lawrence had to make a decision on whether or not to take down the pit bulls before they reached the mine entrance. He had an edge. Frick and his men had no idea that Peter Lawrence was hunting them. Nor did they realize that he was a well-honed hunter with an advantage over them they could not even conceive. Lawrence could not rush the kill and give away his place in the hunt. To do so precipitously would scare them off, let then fall back, contemplate what their enemy's true ability was, and they would return better prepared. Lawrence could not let this happen. There could not be another day. He must not change his sortie because to do so would absolve any advantage his hunting experience gave him on this day, in this weather. The dogs were a major problem. His strategy centered on the mine. The dogs eliminated that strategy.

Lawrence heard the loud barking, snarling, and human cries of pain. He turned away from watching Frick reading the map, to see that the dogs were no longer in the kill equation. The dogs were attacking their two handlers and so ferociously that both men had let go of the leashes, kicking at the dogs, and trying to reach the safety of the Plymouth. One almost made it, but got trapped just inside with the crazed black pit bull's jaws at his leg. The white pit bull, who had ignored the other pit bull up to now, ripped out his it's throat. The dog saw an advantage and went after the black pit bull that was half into the rear seat of the Plymouth savagely attacking the man inside. The white pit bull ripped out a chunk of another dog's hind leg and when the dog went belly up, proceeded to rip out its intestines. Satisfied with his attack, the killer white pit bull began running around in circles howling. Lawrence heard a gunshot and saw the killer pit bull dig deeply through the accumulated snow, trying to bury its snout into the frozen ground. Unsuccessful, it howled loudly and spun itself around until dizzy, attempting again to bury its nose. Another shot rang out and the white dog leapt high into the air and fell onto red blood stained, snow covered ground. The gutted pit bull was whining in pain and trying to bury its face into the ground.

Lawrence heard the third shot that finally killed off the last pit bull.

Lawrence could not understand what had made the animals go berserk. It did not matter. For whatever reason, their death leveled the playing field. As he watched through the binoculars, he realized he was in an even greater position. Having planned to face at least three, possibly four attackers, Lawrence saw Frick jump out of the Cadillac, slam the door, and grab the man standing at the Plymouth by his throat. Frick's driver had to pull Frick away from the man or Frick would have strangled him. Frick backed off from his driver and slapped the other man across the face. Frick began gesticulating with his hands, pointing at the dead man lying on the front seat of the car. He shoved the other man into the Plymouth. The others helped get the body into the rear seat of the Plymouth alongside of the injured man. Once in the Plymouth, the driver backed out and headed back down the state road.

The Cadillac circled Lawrence's car now with Frick inside. Lawrence had no idea what Frick would do. What just happened was totally Frick's stupidity in using pit bulls as hunting dogs. They are too volatile to maintain the poise needed to hunt Lawrence's note and map inside of the Ford station wagon had made it very clear to Frick that this would be his only chance to get the drugs back. Lawrence had written very precisely where to go, what to expect, and the consequence of altering the circumstances. Frick knew that Lawrence sat on a lot of cash, too much money to write off. Still Frick could back off, give up and find another drug deal to gain back the amount of money Lawrence stole from him. Frick could not tolerate what Lawrence had done to him. It would damage his reputation enough to give second thoughts to his suppliers. It would embarrass him on his turf. Frick knew that he ran a big risk following Lawrence's demands. Frick was not used to being lead around like some Uncle Tom. Giving it up might be best and the most intelligent decision but Lawrence had taken that possibility away from Frick. Lawrence made it very clear in his note that should Frick give it up, cede the drugs to Lawrence, that Lawrence would turn them over to the FBI, not the locals, or the state cops. This Frick could not allow. It did not take long for Frick's decision.

Masabi Frick and the thug took weapons out of the trunk of the Cadillac. Lawrence was pleased to see they carried shotguns and revolvers. Where Lawrence planned to ambush them was not a good place to have to reload. He guessed correctly that Frick saw the situation as two against one. He and his crony had enough shots to take down Lawrence face-to-face. This Lawrence knew would be true only if they were facing off in the streets.

They weren't on the streets.

***

It was getting dark and Uncle George took a break from Lawrence's story to start up a small wood fire in a circle of rocks surrounding burnt coals. As he was igniting the kindling, he spoke. "Did you ever find out what happened to the dogs, why they went berserk?"

"I more or less figured it out when Frick and the black man walked into the mine shaft."

"How's that?"

"From the smell. Both of them smelled like skunk."

"So the dogs went crazy smelling a skunk? Damn that was a pretty lucky break for you Petey."

Lawrence smiled and shook his head because he could not remember who wrote the words that followed, "sometimes you make your own luck."

"How's that? You were what? Two miles up at the mines? How'd you get the dogs to attack a skunk?"

"There was no skunk. When I set up my trap, I knew that there'd be a chance I might not see Frick and his men as they walked through the forest or even if they got as far as the mines. I needed more of an advantage than my eyesight to know just how close they were to the mines. I especially needed a way to sense them when they got into the tunnel. Black men have a distinct camouflage advantage in the dark. Skunk smell travels, travels pretty damn far as anyone who's ridden by a dead one on the highway knows."

"When Grandpere George and I hunt deer, we spray the area around our blind with skunk spray. Deer have a keen sense of smell, can detect human smell extremely well. Deer, like every animal, are overpowered by skunk and while they don't like it, they know the skunk isn't about to start shooting them."

"Where do you buy that stuff?"

"Don't need to. Grandpere George bottles it. He used to catch skunks when he was a kid and sell the fur. Don't ask me who 'cause I never wanted to know. Anyhow, he learned how to descent them. Nobody I'm sure wanted skunk fir, smell and all. So he trapped them live and anesthetized them and removed the anal sac."

"Anal as in ass? He dissected skunk's asses? Christ, I'm gonna nail his ass next time I ..."

"Come on, Uncle George. Don't do that to me because he'll know I told you. Besides he was so good at it that vets and pet shops still call for it to descent pet skunks. I watched it once. It's amazing but damn difficult. Once you scrape away the tissue and free up the gland, which is not much bigger than your thumbnail, one little nick, and the whole house is doomed!"

"So you scented the trail up to the mine?"

"Yep, I just found which way was up wind and backed away, as I sprayed it from a bottle. Started it about twenty yards up the trail. All I needed was Frick's dog handlers to do was to get the pit bulls' noses into the spray. Pit bulls go insane, which is what happened. They broke from the leashes and went running Couldn't find any skunks to tear into, so they went after each other and the men behind them. The dogs were beyond control and wanted to kill anything."

"Yeah, I've been to close to that scent myself. It'll do that to you."

"Best part was that I was worried that Frick would smell the scent on the trail and go around it. Instead he just held his breath and nose and went right through the scent."

***

Frick and the big black man tried as best they could to ignore the smell along the trail, hoping as they went up hill, the scent would decrease. It did, but not by much. Lawrence had no problem following them from the hill top since they were using the flashlight retrieved from Frick's Cadillac. It was almost too easy. Lawrence guessed it would take them 45 minutes or so to reach the chain link fence around the abandoned mining company. He had already set up the "T" for the showdown with Frick. If Frick had brought more men with him, there would have been a danger of a flanking group trying to find the other entrances to the mine shaft where Lawrence had left the drugs. There were no other men to find those entrances unless Frick split off from his cohort, one of them going down the main entrance and the other searching for a side entrance. This Lawrence knew was doubtful.

Frick was being very careful, which made him dangerous. If this were to be a simple sight, shoot, and kill, Lawrence would have been finished already. It could not be that, though. Eventually someone would find the dead men and Lawrence would never always be looking over his back for the law. Frick's slowness was sure to burn out the flashlight, which happened not less than 50 yards from the boarded up mine entrance. Frick cursed and swore and threw the flashlight. The batteries were dead. It had lasted long enough though to make Frick's journey to the entrance easy to finish. The night's ambient light was barely enough for them to find the torn fence, crawl under it, and negotiate through the small crawl space that Lawrence had created in the sheet metal nailed over the entrance to the mine shaft. As soon as both were in, Lawrence could detect the skunk smell and he lit up the Coleman gas light that was sitting on top of the canvas bag with the drugs.

Masabi Frick had no fear of the dark. The skunk smell took some getting used to but he could not let this punk ass kid scam him for so much. Worse than that, Frick could not go back to jail. If he had enemies outside of prison, he had twice again as many enemies in jail. Frick's life was on the line. He stood still at the front of the dark mine shaft thinking he had been taken. There was total darkness, no cache waiting for him, nothing but blackness. The note said it would be there. The thug held the ransom money Lawrence had demanded. It was in a tote bag similar to luggage carried onboard an airplane. It was a ruse. Lawrence had baited Frick and tricked him. Frick was a fool, standing in a black hole in an old mine, truly getting the shaft. Frick grimaced at his thoughts, but smiled when a light rose up from the mine shaft. It was a flicker, not much bigger than a match.

"Okay, White Meat. We're here! You coming out?"

Lawrence had the drug cache and Coleman lantern at the "T" junction of the mine. There were three arms of the "T." Frick and the huge black man stood at the bottom off the "T"; Lawrence occupied the right arm of the "T". Frick could not tell whether Lawrence was right or left because of the echoing effect in the mine. This did not bother Frick since there were two guns ready to fire. The black man would shoot down the left shaft and Frick the right. One of them had to get Lawrence.

"Jesus! What's the damn awful smell down there? I know you niggers use that damn lotion on your bodies, but damn if that isn't bad!" Lawrence stood with his back to the right shaft aiming his voice directly at the junction where the three shafts met.

Frick gestured for the huge black man to start sneaking down the left side of the shaft as he replied, "you one lucky, white fucker! I had dogs, that'd been down this shaft by now eatin' out you liver. Fuckin' skunk got to 'em 'fore they get to you."

"Skunks? How many did your dogs get?"

Frick didn't know the reason behind the question, "they didn't get none, asshole. Why are you asking?" "Because skunks are extremely rare in these parts and at this time of the year. Most of them have hibernated by now," said Lawrence. He made loud sniffing sounds that echoed off the walls.

"I think your dogs are about as dumb as you are, Frick. That smell all over you comes from skunk scent I sprayed along the trail that you took. Hey, it's getting ranker down here. I hear a little scuffling along the north side of the mine shaft. Do you see that light, Frick?"

"Yeah, I see it!"

"It's right next to your drugs. It's a kerosene lamp. I shoot it, your drugs will go up in flames and the whole tunnel goes black. How's your flashlight? I got some extra batteries back in my car."

Frick did not need to tell the black man to come back because he was already next to him. Lawrence had them in a perfect set up. Frick had no idea where the other two shafts went. If they rushed Lawrence, not only would they lose the drugs, they would never catch Lawrence without any light.

"We are here, White Meat!" yelled Frick. It echoed over all three shafts. "What goes down now?"

"I'm obviously in one of the shafts. Even if you guess right, when you swing to fire at me, I'll see you and I'll gun you down. So what you need to do is bring the money down, leave it, and pick up the drugs. Nice and simple, isn't it?"

"You're out of your fucking head, White Meat! How'd I know the goods is in the bag?"

"Good point, Masabi. You don't mind if I call you Masabi, do you?"

"Anything you want, White Meat."

"Either you or Blackie," said Lawrence who heard the huge black man grunt, "need to check the bag, don't you?"

"How we do that? You'd shoot us."

"Why? It's a standoff position. I shoot one of you, the other shoots me if I go after the money."

"So what we do, White Meat?"

"Got to know if your chips are good in this game, first. Send your boy," again Lawrence heard the growl, "down with the money. Got to feed the pot. He can check the bag and leave the cash in front of it."

Lawrence hoped he did not have to lead Frick by the nose into the ambush. If he had to, then either Frick or the huge black man might catch on to Lawrence's set up.

Frick knew it would be a total waste of his or his cohort's life to attack and there not be any drugs in the bag. Besides, if Lawrence was going to ambush somebody, Frick would make sure it was his man, not him.

"You ain't so dumb, White Meat. Okay, my man here's gonna walk down to the light with the money. He'll hold it up, show it down both shafts, right and left. Then he'll put it next to the lamp. Drugs goes up, so's the cash. He'll check that you'se got all the drugs there. Okay?"

"Send him."

Frick called the huge black man over. There was very little light at their end of the tunnel but Frick could see the man was very disturbed. It was near freezing inside the cave but the man was covered in sweat.

Whispering, Frick spoke to him. "What's matter with you?"

"I go down there, what's keep him from shootin' my ass?"

"Cause we gonna kill him."

"How we gone to do that?"

"Sssh, keep it down. He's right. We need to know the drugs are there. Useless if they're not, ain't it?"

"Yeah, all three us could get killed."

"He's got to know we got the cash, don't he?"

"Yeah, or he'll start shooting. So he's got to see it."

"Right now, he thinks he's got control. Well, he has until we know the drugs are there. Same plan we went in with. You go down with the cash. While he's watching you check out the drugs, I'll inch my way down to you but stay in this shaft so he can't see me. There's only two shafts down there where he can be."

"Maybe there's three?"

"We are fucked then. You're right. He might be lying about that. Don't make any difference from the get go."

"Why?"

"When you check the drug bag, you'll be able to see how many shafts down there, won't you?"

"Hey, that's right!"

"If there's more than two, we back off. If there's only two, when you back off hold up two fingers. As soon as your back up this shaft so's he can't see you, we charge in blastin'. I got a pistol and you the shot gun. We just fire our asses away. How's that sound."

The thug had some doubts about checking the drugs since he was not an expert on the subject, but figured it would do him no good since Frick was basically a chicken shit.

"Yeah, how'm I goin' carry a shot gun down the tunnel without him seein' it when I get there?"

"Here, take the pistol. You right-handed, so when we go firing, you take the left tunnel. I'll use the shot gun down the right."

Lawrence's yell echoed down the shaft, "hey, you guys still there? Somebody bringing some watermelon or fried wings?"

"We here White Ass! You keep your finger off the trigger, understand?"

The huge black man stuck the pistol in his waist band so he could draw across his body. He eased himself down the shaft. It was a long slow path, but as he neared the "T" crossing, the light filled the area so he could see more of the three shafts. "So far, so good," he thought. When he was ready to cross to the drugs, he spoke, "I'm coming across to check the goods. You don't shoot, hear?"

Lawrence said nothing. He was listening to see if he would have to abort the face off.

The thug eased his face around the bend, first looking to the left, then to the right. Both ends of the tunnels were too dark to see anything. He now knew there were only two tunnels. He pulled out the carryall with the cash from behind him, opened it up, and held up the cash, stacking it on the opposite side of the Coleman lantern from the drug bag. When he finished, he opened the drug bag and took out all of the contents. By this time Frick had almost noiselessly navigated the length of the entrance shaft. In two steps he could make the "T", turn left, and open fire with the shotgun. He could clearly see his man carefully going through the supply of drugs.

"Okay, man. They all here. So's the money. I'm gone back now. I'll go slow," said the thug as he raised his hands in a surrender gesture, two fingers up.

Frick was ready and as soon as his thug was back in the entrance shaft with his pistol drawn, they both turned to the "T" and opened fire into the darkness of the two shafts. The entire cave light up with gun flashes and reeked of gun powder smoke. Nothing could be alive now in either shaft.

The last sounds from the weapons were the clicks of hammers on empty cartridges which continued well past the time that all of the ammunition had been spent. Frick stared down the right shaft and the huge black man down the left. Nothing. Frick went over to the Coleman lantern, picked it up and directed the light down one shaft, then the other. Still nothing. Lawrence was gone; his body was nowhere in sight.

The huge black man walked over to Frick. Neither of them thought to reload. Lawrence did not need to count the gun fire even if he could have from the chaos of sound reaming throughout the mine. Lawrence just waited until he heard the two hammers clicking and dropped out from the air shaft in the right tunnel. Lawrence put two bullets into the huge black man's head first because Frick was looking the other way. The 30.06's tore off the back off the man's head as one went through his left eye and the other clipped off his right ear; taking most of what was left of his skull ten feet beyond the fallen body. Frick turned and in an insane moment when he knew his gun was empty, tried to chamber new cartridges into the shotgun and shoot Lawrence.

Lawrence laughed, dropped the aim of his rifle to Frick's legs and blew out both his knee caps.

***

"Holy shit," said Uncle George. "That's right. I remember when your mother almost killed you over the black bear. You told me about the air ventilation shaft. You were up in it."

"Bingo. I had some luck. They were stupid and would just keep firing away. I probably could have nailed them both even if they had reloaded their weapons. But they didn't. I could take my time. I was lucky they were smart, or at least one of them was. Damn, I forgot to ask Frick which one of them realized I was out numbered because there was only two shafts!"

"Ask Frick? Didn't you kill him?"

"No, not then."

"But why? That's what you were after, wasn't it? To get back at him?"

"I wanted more than revenge ... Listen, Uncle George. You know how I got to the point of killing him. You know that Frick disappeared from the face of the earth. Are you sure you want to know the details?"

Uncle George was not sure. He could not climb into his nephew's mind and therefore he could not pass judgment on Lawrence's soul. He could tell that Lawrence went farther than most men would have gone. He had Frick, had him cold and down. He was a bullet away from retribution, but something else had been driving Peter Lawrence and Uncle George did not want to know what it was or what Lawrence did.

***

When Frick woke up his back was against the tunnel wall and his hands were tied tightly behind his back with rope, covered by duct tape. Frick did not like that he could not feel his legs and when he saw them, he fainted.

When he woke up the situation had not changed. His legs at the knee cap were blasted apart, showing mostly broken white bones and bloody tissue. He wondered why he felt no pain until he saw the two tourniquets of rope where his kneecaps should have been. He fainted again.

When Frick woke up the third time, the pain was so bad that he fainted once again.

Lawrence woke him up.

"Well Frick, I think you're going to have trouble playing basketball again."

Lawrence fed Frick some water, which despite how slowly Lawrence poured it into the man's mouth; it still came back up a yellowish vomit. Lawrence had a wet towel and washed Frick's face. He used a dry towel to wipe off the moisture.

"I've been cleaning you for two days now Frick. Can you get something down? No, don't look at your legs. You'll just drop out on me again."

Frick kept his head back, "what you got?"

"Little whiskey, my friend. It'll help you over that river."

"River, what river? We're still in the mines."

"River Styx, Masabi. You're going to catch that good ferry to hell, but not quite yet," said Lawrence and poured a few ounces of whiskey into Frick's mouth.

The alcohol went quickly to Frick's head due to the fact that he had lost so much blood. It did not make him sick, for which Lawrence was glad. Frick tried to not look at his legs but gradually his chin brought the eyes down to gaze upon his destroyed lower body. There were flies eating at his exposed muscles and broken bones, but oddly he felt no pain. He tried to run his thoughts back to the shootout. They had Lawrence dead to rights. Only two shafts and he had filled the right one with scatter shot. Nobody could have escaped that range. He shook his head, cleared away cobwebs and remembered Lawrence dropping out of the ceiling.

Where? How? He turned his eyes to his left, starting down the entrance shaft; the only light in the tunnels was the Coleman lantern, but Frick caught an umbra shadow, like a quarter moon in the ceiling. There was another shaft going up the south tunnel's ceiling. How could that be?

"Ventilator shaft," said Lawrence. "Pretty big or else I'd had to try something else."

"My legs? My legs, why did you only shoot my legs?"

"Pay back, Masabi. See the rope and tape where your knees used to be?"

"Yes?"

"Keeps you from bleeding to death. Take a good look at your toes. Almost as white as mine. Know why?"

"Where's my man?"

"Down the north shaft. Got him in two Glad trash bags for now."

"Why are my toes so white? Why are all those flies eating at my ..."

Frick fainted again. When he woke, Lawrence was sitting cross legged in front of him, drinking a beer.

"Gangrene, Frick, you got gangrene. Turns your flesh pale at first, then brown, but they'll get back to black. You're rotting like a corpse, my friend."

"Shit! My pants all wet!"

"Pissed yourself boy. Oh, I'm sorry, shouldn't call you a boy, should I?"

"Fuckin' White Meat! Why you lets me piss my pants?"

"Be kind of difficult to get you standing on what's left of your legs."

"Want another whiskey?" offered Lawrence and poured a small trickle into Frick's mouth.

"Smells like shit down here."

"You're sitting on it, Frick."

"I shit myself, too?"

"Just enough, Masabi."

"Enough for what?"

"Give yourself gas gangrene. Those two days you were out, you couldn't help yourself. You were incontinent. Gun shots made you lose control of yourself, not much, at least not yet. Just enough."

"Just enough fer what?"

"Bacteria infection, worst kind of gangrene. My guess is you've got E coli and some streptococcus running through those muscles. Necrosis, my man. The legs are dead and those dead legs are going to kill the rest of you."

"Why you doin' dis?"

"Want to see how good your memory is."

"What da' fuck youse talkin' bout?"

"Rusty, remember Rusty?"

"Ain't know nobody named Rusty," said Masabi. Lawrence could see Frick struggling with pain that the little bit of whiskey could not hide.

"Rusty was a dog, Masabi. Red dog that you and a couple of your cronies kicked to death."

"What's a crony?"

"A buddy, a friend that emulates you. Oops, tries to act like you, follow your lead. Don't remember five, maybe six years ago, stomping to death a red dog at a playground, and then beating the shit out of the dog's owner?"

"I ain't never been there, White Meat," spoke Frick, sweat running down his forehead and mixing with the tears of pain running down his cheeks.

"Might as well let you in on something I've never shared with anybody else. I sort of have this sense, a sense of knowing when somebody's lying. You know how you can intuit that the phone's going to ring and sure enough it does?"

Lawrence knew Frick was close to passing out but he still responded, "yeah, I know what you mean."

"Well you get a free pass on lying, but just one," said Lawrence and walked over next to Frick. He put his left hand to Frick's forehead. Frick backed his head away but still Lawrence was able to run his fingers over the scar Tony had put on Frick's head with the rock he had thrown.

"I always wondered what happened to Tony. Probably is in jail somewhere. He put that scar on you Frick. How's your memory now? Remember kicking the dog, kicking Rusty?"

"No, you're fucking crazy," was all that Frick could get out before Lawrence sent a right jab below Frick's left eye, using his palm so as to not hurt his knuckles. Frick went out cold from both the blow and the fever that was running through Frick's body, excepting his legs.

While Frick was unconscious, Lawrence used his jack knife to cut away all of Frick's clothing. Before rolling Frick over and pulling the clothing away, Lawrence took his canvas water bag down the hill to a stream and filled it. Slowly trying to avoid a new round of defecation from Frick's body, Lawrence rolled him over, yanked away the cut clothes and rinsed off Frick's filthy body, using the canvas water bag pour spout. Finished, Lawrence built a small camp fire close to the ventilating shaft but not too close to attract attention from above the mine shaft. He tossed Frick's soiled clothes into the fire. Lawrence righted Frick's body and waited for what would be five hours for Frick to regain consciousness. Lawrence slept on the other side of the small fire.

Frick's screams woke Lawrence.

"Here Frick, take some water," said Lawrence holding out a canteen, ready to tilt the opening to Frick's mouth. He gave Frick only a small swallow.

"Where did you get that name Masabi?"

Frick was incredulous. This man, this white man had him bound and tied in an old forgotten mine, near to death and wanted to know how he got his name.

"You fucked man! You just fucked! Ain't telling you nothing!"

Lawrence moved next to Frick's body and spoke, "see that red line just above the tourniquet where your knee used to be?"

Frick saw the red line and looked to his other leg, finding it had one that was just a little narrower, "yeah, I see it. What's mean?"

"See the skin below the line? See how it's getting kind of pale? The skin above is just your normal brown skin. That skin is still living. The line shows where you are dying. Watch what happens when I poke the skin below the line," said Lawrence and using his jack knife barely touched the dead skin, making a clump fall off. Frick was seeing his body rot.

"Didn't feel a thing, did you?"

Frick shook his head and screamed in pain when Lawrence did the same to the skin above the red line. "You talk or I poke, your choice."

"Why am I all naked?"

"Makes you smell better. You should notice something else Frick. See how I'm not only fully clothed but have a fire going? I'll bet you're not cold, are you?"

Frick shook his head, "why's that?"

"Bacteria are eating you," said Lawrence and put his finger tips at Frick's throat. "You're sweating like a pig and your pulse rate's slow. Toxicity's got you. Germs are running around your whole body. Sssh! Be quiet a second. You hear any ringing?"

"Yeah, there's like a bell won't stop ringing, not a loud bell, small one. Can I have some more water?"

Lawrence made a mistake holding the canteen above Frick's mouth. As the water poured, Frick nudged the canteen with his chin and a large flow of water washed into his mouth and over his face. Lawrence backed away from Frick and shook his head.

"Hey, White Fuck, what's matter givin' me more water?"

Lawrence just smiled and watched the answer to Frick's question. Frick started squirming slowly, then the twitching started. Vomit erupted out of his mouth in a green yellow flow of bile. Lawrence had tried to keep Frick from taking in too much water at one time but had not been able to stop Frick's madness. Frick's whole body was now twitching and struggling. The legs did not move since they were dead and could not, but instead were rug back and forth like tendrils of a squid trying to crawl. Frick was having trouble breathing and his chest rose and fell in huge spasms as he tried to exhale the stale air and inhale the fresh air. Lawrence could do nothing except watch, hoping his mistake did not kill Frick prematurely. The convulsions finally slowed and Frick lost consciousness again.

Frick did not die, yet. Passed out for nearly another day, he awoke with a burning fever that in the conundrum of life left him shivering and cold. Lawrence put a blanket over him, dragging him closer to the small fire. Slowly the spasms slowed and the fever shakes abated.

"So how did you get the name Masabi? Some African name?"

"My momma named me after that desert out west. The Masabi desert. She like the sound of it, almost African."

"How far did your mother get in school?"

"She ain't never said. I know's she gave birth to me when she about twelve, maybe thirteen. Why?"

Lawrence toyed with telling Masabi that the desert out west is the Mohave, a native American name, but decided to let it go, "how about your father."

"My grandfather."

"No, the man who's your real father."

"My grandfather. He also be my father."

Lawrence knew there were people who raped their daughters, but he could not really fathom what Frick was saying. Frick had no problem referring to his father as his grandfather; in his world it made little or no difference.

"Frick, let's get down to some basics here. You're going to die. You're going to die either soon or over a few weeks. I'm going to watch you die."

"Why man? Why you doing this to me? You ain't the kind a person that'd just sit there and watch me go. Just leave man. Call 911 and somebody come and get me to a hospital. Okay, man? Like you can do that, right?"

Lawrence could see the stages unfolding. Frick had started out all fire and brimstone, trying to intimidate Lawrence with his foul mouth and useless threats. Now Frick was in disbelief which Lawrence found extremely hard to accept in Frick. How could the man see his rotting legs, smell that god-awful odor of necrosis, go through a seizure and still think he would or could survive?

"Frick you're a dead man. You can talk, but you're a dead man. You'll get nothing from me. Well, that's not entirely true. You lie to me and you'll get more pain, but never enough to kill you."

"Okay, okay, what's you name?"

"Lawrence, Lawrence'll do."

"Yeah, Arens," butchered Frick as Lawrence just smiled. "What ya' wanna to know?"

"I want to understand how you could so brutally kill Rusty?"

"Yeah Arens, I remember that. I remember that white boy's pretty little dog. Waste, waste of a dog. Couldn't kill a rat one on one. There's something about killing a shit little animal like that. Get's your blood goin' Stupid bitch oozes its way up to you, tail between its legs. You kick once and the animal just lays there like it wants you to kick it. I remember, weren't good kind of dog to have. Oughta be ashamed having a chicken shit dog like that. Got a coward dog, you be a coward."

"You stomped it because it was weak?"

"Yeah, that's it, Arens. You gotta kill off the weak, embarrass they ass when you do it," said Frick. Lawrence almost slammed his fist into the smile that formed on Frick's face.

"What about beating up the kid, the kid that the dog belonged to? He wasn't a a chicken shit. He came right at you."

"He was just fun. I remember, they's three or four of us. It was cool, knocking that short little fat boy around. Had him dancing, never know where someone come at him. We do that a lot. Gang can't let an outsider mess with 'em. Yeah, was fun laughing at him trying to go after one of us, then another of us slam him in the back of the head. Stomp him too, didn't we?"

Frick was getting to where Lawrence wanted him. He was beyond his pain, the fever had run down a bit, and he was catching his stride, forgetting what Lawrence held over him.

"Just like you do on the streets, right Frick? Ever do that to old people? You know, catch one of those old men walking the street. Catch him and circle. Take shots at him when his back's turned. Get him on the ground and stomp away? Then piss on him? You ever do that, Frick?"

Frick grabbed the bait. "No, never do that shit, Arens. Them does that bad, very bad."

Lawrence kicked Frick's right thigh. The pain was beyond the scream of agony echoing throughout the mines. It was seen deep in Frick's eyes as his face went red and his black eyes bulged in their sockets. It took nearly five minutes for Frick to stop screaming.

"Why, man? Why you do that?"

"What did I tell you, Frick? I know when you're lying. Can sense it. How many old men did you terrorize on the streets?"

"I never ..." started Frick but quickly rethought the pain and continued, "... never counted."

"It's not the weakness, is it?"

Frick's face made a radical change. Denying his malicious behaviors would not work against Lawrence. It was almost like talking to God. Lawrence knew a lie but even worse, Lawrence knew the questions to ask.

Accepting his fate, Frick came out with, "Not weakness, White Meat. It's not the weakness of that fucking fat kid's red dog. It ain't the weakness of some old fart in the streets. Fact is, ain't even a white thing. We took down many a brother. It's the power, White Meat. I love that feeling of seeing a dog's ribs bust out his skin. I love hearing that old woman beg me as I stomp my heel down on her face. You know what the best part is?"

"Go on, Frick."

"You white fucks gave us power. Breed us like fucking pit bulls. Some nigger boy born too weak work the fields, white man let him die. Matter fact white fucker probably hung him. Only black kids survive were strong, beating the white folks at their game. Now we gettin' our turn. White people so scared of us now, they pretend like we is one of them. Hell we're heroes to hundreds of thousands white people. Fore you know it, we gonna be everywhere, fuck just look at who runs all the sports in this country. And you white shits be kissin' every nigger athlete's ass, you women want a sniff of our jocks. You all losin', White Meat!"

"Which makes killing a boy's dog right, doesn't it Frick?"

"Fuckin' right, White Meat."

"I guess your true color is showing Masabi."

"That's right, White Fuck. True color is black!"

Lawrence had to back off. He tried his best to think of Masabi Frick as a monster, not a black man, but what he had seen so far in his life made that difficult. He could not rectify hating blacks, all blacks, and judging them by Masabi Frick. He could not pass Frick off as an aberration, nor harbinger of the Negro race. Lawrence wanted to do both. The shame of slavery bore no connection to Lawrence or any relative in the history of the Lawrence family. His heraldry was open to all people and it judged not people of race but people as humans. His racial guilt was the erroneous guilt of a white man. He was not a man or of a man and woman that created animals out of Africans. The only way Lawrence could deal with Frick was to ignore the stigma that to kill Frick made him an exemplar Frick. It was the accusation of all radicals. To treat a Masabi Frick as Masabi Frick would heinously treat another victim, would make you the same as Masabi Frick. It was convoluted and prejudiced thinking. Lawrence could only justify his humanity by taking down an inhuman creature by way of an inhuman destruction. As right as it is that brutal executions serve no lesson to the brutal creatures, the paradigm does not remove the power of watching a berserk animal die a horrible death. Masabi Frick was close when expressing the heinous power he felt mutilating a poor defenseless dog or an elderly woman. It is not a human life force, but retribution in kind is.

"Here," said Lawrence handing Frick the whiskey bottle. "If you drink it fast, you'll choke and have fits like you did before."

"What you going do, Arens?"

"You've brutally mutilated many people, haven't you? And not just white people, right?"

Frick knew better than lie, so he just kept his mouth shut.

"I knew that Frick. The best finish for you would be to face the same fate as those you have defiled. Defiled means made filthy."

"Fuck you! I knew that."

"Remember your huge black friend?"

"Yeah, you killed him. Said he's in a trash bag back down the other way."

"He is but not all of him. You see Frick, you are here in this mine because I baited you to this mine. I knew about it, even nearly got killed in it."

"How?"

"By a black bear. Where we are right now is where a female black bear hibernates every winter. She's really pissed off because she knows we're in her nesting spot."

"Why ain't she come down here and attack us?"

"A couple things. First she smells humans. Most animals hate our smell and avoid us. Natural selection thing, Frick. Animals that intrinsically avoid humans stay alive. They reproduce and the others that don't avoid humans, wind up stuffed, hanging on walls, or being eaten off some human's dinner plate."

"That alone wouldn't stop her but the smoke from the fire I've kept going in here helped keep her at bay. Also she's still feeding. Black bears eat carrion which ..."

"Carry on, what?"

"Rotting meat. They can digest it and the rank smell of rotting meat is easy to pick up. They are also good at detecting the sounds of wounded animals. Your cohort's flesh is rotting, rotting very badly. He's not all in the trash bags in the north mine shaft. I've been using part of him as bait."

"What the fuck you talkin' 'bout?"

"An arm down the back trail one night, a foot a bit closer after that. After I made sounds like a wounded animal using my deer horn, the bear took the bait pretty easily. His arm and foot were gone each morning when I went back with new bait. Not much left after all of these days. But there's enough."

"Enough for what?"

"To get her into the north entrance of the mine shaft," said Lawrence turning to point behind him, "what, maybe fifty or hundred feet down there? She'll probably get there tonight or at least within another day or so."

Masabi Frick began to see what Lawrence had created, a death trap.

"You see my friend, you're going to die, whether it is tonight, tomorrow or the day after. She's hooked on decaying human flesh, meat. You're also right where she wants to hibernate. It couldn't be any better for her. One last feast, nice dark meat ala Masabi Frick, and a long winter's nap. As for me? Won't I get caught when somebody finds your remains? Bears leave no wastes from their kills. Not only do they strip a carcass bare but they break open the bones and suck out the marrow. Your friend has no remains left outside of this mine. Tonight she'll take care of the rest of him. Tomorrow the black bear will come down the shaft and sniff the air. Decaying flesh? Why yes, Masabi, that's all you are right now. When she's finished with you, all that will be left of Masabi Frick is bear shit."

"You mother fucker!"

"No that would be your grandfather, wouldn't it?"

Masabi had no chips left. His game was over. The sweat pouring from him now was not from the fever. He knew Lawrence would not turn sympathetic and at least shoot him.

"So you're no more better then us."

"Us? You mean African Americans or niggers?"

"What's the difference?"

"You got plenty of hours left to work that out."

"No matter, you just an animal like me."

Lawrence pulled together all of his equipment and disappeared down the front mine shaft to the trail. He had spent his first days after the shootout at the Scranton Mining Camp. While Frick was unconscious, he repaired his tires. He had to hitch hike into town for spares, but time was not a problem in his hunt. He loaded up his equipment and hiked back up the two mile trail to the mine shaft. All that was left was his canvas water bag and a lawn rake. Lawrence went down the tunnels and returned walking backwards, raking the floor of both mine shafts.

"Frick, you've got a point there. You took great pleasure in mutilating and killing weaker creatures in front of your eyes. That is horrible and very inhuman."

Lawrence took the water bag and poured it over the fire. For a brief moment the cave was totally dark, then a flashlight came on. Lawrence aimed it down the main mine shaft and turned toward Frick. "In case you haven't figured it out, I've raked all the floors, checked every nook and cranny, and will back out raking the last of my foot prints in the dust. Inhuman? No, Frick, taking down a despicable creature like you is not inhuman. Watching and savoring would be. The bear will be here soon. Enjoy being her dinner, bye."

CHAPTER THIRTEEN

The Cat Eater

Uncle George was stunned, stymied, unable to grasp what his nephew had done. Lawrence saw this and spoke, "I asked if you were sure you wanted to know?"

"You've trusted me with a crime, Peter. Had I known, I would not have asked. Now that I know, I fear I know too much. Frick might have been right. How is what you did right and what he did wrong? I grasp a flimsy difference. I hope that straw for which I'm reaching, separates you into retribution and not into malevolence."

Lawrence responded. "When I was young, very young I once tortured a cat, not much, just tied a shoe box to his tail. It drove the cat crazy because cats are very protective of their tails, will bite at you to hurt you for even just scratching them where their tail joins their body. The cat almost killed himself trying to escape, much to the amusement of myself and my friends."

"Many years later, I heard stories of kids putting firecrackers in the ears of rabbits and I was thoroughly horrified. I remembered my torturing the cat. I was ashamed of myself. I did no great harm to the cat, nothing even approaching firecrackers in a rabbit's ear, but I was embarrassed within my own mind. How could I have done such a thing? My gut reaction when hearing the rabbit story was to hunt down and beat up the boy who tortured the rabbit. Yet had I been any better? No, I had only been younger. It was about this time that I became interested in life, especially natural selection. Evolution has always intrigued me. The second time I read Darwin's Origin of Species, I realized that the difference between me, Peter Lawrence, doing heinous tortures to a small and helpless animal and being shamed years later was that I had gone through a stage in my life. Much like an embryo in the womb, I went through stages where I was a single celled animal, a tissue creature, an embryonic fish, and I emerged a human fetus. Even through my postnatal life I've lived stages of other life forms."

"As a child we have the instinct of an animal, an animal that plays at capturing and killing. Humans grow out of it as we become adults, maybe."

Uncle George caught where Lawrence was going. Lawrence continued to speak, "we play cops and robbers with toy weapons, and then become adults that should not be playing those roles."

"At least, not as fun and games. If you watch videos of wild chimps, you'll see their hunting is much like juvenile animal torture. It's scary how they hunt down the prey, stalk it, mock it, and eventually brutalize it, ripping it apart, shredding its body into pieces. The eating is less enjoyed then the torture."

"But Peter, we're not wild animals."

"Your cat Ivan is not a wild animal?"

Uncle George had visions of the mice, snakes, and birds that Ivan had proudly displayed at the front door, and said, "you're right. When he was a kitten, it was play. Now even though we feed him, he has not lost that brutal role of playing and killing."

"Evolution is unforgiving to those that lose their link to their ancestors without accruing a better one. Chimps are vicious creatures even to their family units. The violence goes past survival. There's a line that humans crossed over, a line where sadistic and cruel treatment of each other had to disappear if we were to survive as a society. Killing Frick showed me that that line is still there and that there are people that cross back and forth because they have not evolved into humanity, despite being a human."

"So that's how you saw Frick. But, what about you?"

"What I did is there inside all of us. Did I enjoy what I did to Frick? Yes, because I still hurt inside over what he did. I don't just mean to Zinni and his dog. Had I not drawn out of him the malicious horror he had done to others, I might not have been able to finish what I started. That sealed it for me. I can never see accepting inhuman behavior without trying to fight it. Sometimes a creature of such vileness deserves the same in return from another human, if only to remind him of what he could have been and thus what he would now deserve. Maybe Hell is where Frick reached and I was only the provider?"

Uncle George could see the logic but not fully understand Lawrence. "It might be that going back over the line of animal and becoming human is the only way to stay alive inside of yourself?"

Lawrence agreed, "Now it is your turn. I gave you Frick. Please give me my father."

"The first time I saw your father he was dead and the last time I spoke to him he was dead. The Vietcong brought him into the prisoner of war camp skewered on a long pole, like a beast hanging beneath his tied wrists and ankles. He had a bullet hole in his side that had formed a scab but still invited the hundreds of blood sucking flies that filled the air of Vietnam's tropics. It is a tale, no a story, no not even that. I don't know all of it, but I will tell you it goes like this ..."

***

Vietnam 1967

George thought they had brought in an injured VC except as they got closer, he could see the man was too tall and his hair was totally white. He wondered why the VC would bring in a dead American. They carried him to the medical hut and came for George. Of the dozen American soldiers captured and imprisoned at this POW camp, George was the only one free to roam over the VC hamlet. He had no idea where the camp was located, except it was many marched miles north of where he had been captured, closer to the China Sea than the site of the night attack on his outpost four months ago. He could see the stars at night. He noted his higher latitude by sighting on Polaris and he could smell the ocean. He has these freedoms which the other imprisoned Americans did not. They were pilloried to their prisoner hooch, their rear ends hovering over a small diameter hole for personal evacuation of their feces and urine. This prohibited smelling anything not excrement. George's quick but devious thinking when the American outpost had been overridden by VC gave him this modicum of prisoner privilege. Seeing a corpsman's head ripped off by AK-47 blasts, George had slinked out of his mud filled, camouflaged foxhole to quickly remove the corpsman's Red Cross armband, attach it to his bicep, and hold both arms up in the universal sign of surrender. Captured it had gained him special privileges at the VC camp. George was confined to the medicine hooch and not pilloried. The VC gave him unwanted responsibilities. George was considered to be able to remedy all wounds and diseases because of his red arm band. He had been able to deceive the VC capturers despite his lack of medical training, by acting like the MDs he had observed in the United States Army.

The VC took the wounded American into the hooch, followed by what looked to be a family of Vietnamese, an older man and woman, and a young girl new to this hamlet. Maybe the American was still alive and they were going to torture information out of him before he died, thought George. He could hear a loud argument erupting from the medical hooch, soon followed by the VC in charge of the hamlet's infirmary coming out of the hooch looking for George.

"Corpsman George, Corpsman George," he yelled, followed by a slew of Vietnamese which George did not understand and probably never would. George could speak Spanish and some German, but contrary to what the VC thought, George was not a Eurasian from the Philippines. George made sure the Vietnamese did not think otherwise. They were that he had been forced into the Philippine Army as a direct result of American tyranny to subjugation in order to rule the world. His gesticulations when first taken prisoner and the Red Cross arm band, kept George alive and not rotting his ass over a hole in the floor of the prisoners' hut. George had learned to move and move quickly when called by the VC leaders.

He was waved into the hut to find the prisoner, now released from the pole and laying on a bamboo platform that passed as a bed. George was sure the man was dead, and for the man's sake, hoped he was since the VC would torture him until he was dead. Unfortunately the man had a weak pulse at his neck and was exhaling a slight wisp of air out of his nostrils. George was considered a lord inside the medical hooch. While growing up in Texas, he had spent many years as an orderly in a hospital in order to keep his family from poverty. When he was drafted, George made sure this learned semi-profession was not known by the United States Army. What he did not want was extensive service on the front lines. A corpsman could expect just that along with less training in the use of weapons. Corpsmen fixed wounds, they did not make them. George knew that from the many corpsmen that had wound up in his hospital back in Texas.

George cut off what was left of the soldier's clothes. The man was very muscular. Had it not been for his shock of white hair, he was dark skinned enough from the Southeast Asian sunlight to pass for a tall Asian. The man's chest rose and fell better than George had expected. It appeared that the wound now festering on the man's side had not been deep enough to cause internal damage. George took a bottle of alcohol from the shelf and with a sponge wiped off most of the decayed skin, exposing the wound. It was not dark purple yet, which was a good sign. George could see that debriding could probably clean up the wound if the bullet that hit the man was not still inside. He had to find out. Believing the man was unconscious enough to not feel pain, George took a scalpel and scissors to the dead tissue, cutting away infection to let new skin grow. He was still unable to see if that was all there was to the wound. As he cut into live flesh, the man let out a scream and opened his eyes, as he tried to push himself up. George waved two VC attendants over to hold the man's arms and keep his chest down. The man was strong but injured enough that they could keep him relatively immobile.

"No! No, I can't be caught! Who are you?"

"Most just call me George. My full name is Sergeant George …"

"No, I don't want to know your name. Why am I in a hospital? Are these my guards? How come they just didn't finish the job? How come I'm not shackled?"

"Where do you think you are?"

"Army field hospital?"

"No soldier, you're in a bamboo hooch somewhere behind North Vietnam lines. What's your name, Soldier?"

The man passed out and George spoke to the VC orderlies. "What's going on here? You want me to fix this man?" George realized they had no idea what he was saying. The only VC that had any grasp of English was the field commander's attaché, and he was out in the field.

"Excuse, please," said the young girl that had followed and maneuvered through the orderlies to be on the opposite side of the wounded man, facing George. "He name, Arens. Help Arens, please?"

"You speak English?"

The girl shook her head and spoke the few broken words that Llewellyn Lawrence had used when around her. She had listened to him enough to be able to grasp a bit of their meaning. She reacted to George's use of the word English, "no, English, maybe little?"

George was glad that Arens or whoever he was had passed out. There was very little morphine available at this camp and it was used for the VC. He cut away more of the flesh wound and exposed the ribs. One was cracked beneath the wound but no bullet or fragments. George could see the path the bullet had taken out of the front of the man's chest. He finished debriding all the dead tissue and applied the only antibiotic available, alcohol. The man stirred but did not awaken this time. Using only a few stitches, since the debridement needed air to heal, he smoothed a

Vaseline-like cream over the wound, covered it with a thin layer of gauze, and taped it. George noticed that the back of the man's head had oozed some blood onto the bed cloths. Gently turning the man, he saw a missing section of scalp just behind the man's left ear. There was only a small blood flow. The wound needed only cleaning and a bandage. Whoever this man was, he had been very lucky. George still did not understand what was happening.

"Arens, good man," came from behind George along with a pull on his shirt sleeve. George turned to face the old man who had come in with the wounded man. The old man turned to the VC still in the hooch and spoke to them. What he said to them George had no idea, but they a cleared the hut. George looked at the one VC remaining, an officer in charge of the camp when the commander was in the field. George picked up the tie straps on the side of the bamboo bed as if to tie the man down so he could not escape. The old man put his hand on George's forearm and spoke the universal language of shaking his head slowly back and forth. George looked back to the VC in charge who motioned George away from the bed. George had no idea what was going on. The wounded man was an enemy soldier in the middle of the VC camp and he was going to be unfettered with no guard. It made no sense, but to George nothing made any sense in Vietnam. He just shrugged and let them run their war.

"Trong trãìng con khang ði lang thang! Trong trãìng con khang ði lang thang!"

George woke up to the entire hamlet screaming words that meant nothing to him. Before he could get off his crude bamboo bed, the commander's aide, who spoke English, came running into his prisoner hut, "Doctor George, Doctor George! Your patient gone!"

Damn, he's dead thought George. "When did you find him?"

"Find him? Find him? No, find him. Arens gone!"

George dressed hurriedly and followed the man to the medical hooch. It was that unavoidable stupidity of automatically looking where someone else has already found nothing. You know it's not there, you've been told it's not there, but you go there anyway. Arens or whatever his name was, was gone. The VC commander was there and the aide translated, "why you not tie him down, Doctor George?"

George turned to the VC who had waved him off yesterday. He could make his life easier by passing the blame, but the man treated George with respect and a new overseer might not. "He was unconscious and his wounds should have kept him from even getting out of bed."

The old man, his daughter, and whom George correctly took to be the old man's wife, entered the hooch. The old man was very quiet and spoke only a few words to the commander which were difficult to hear.

Through his aide interpreter the commander spoke, "Doctor George, the man you tended to is an American ..." "Yes, I know! Why did you bring a wounded man here? Why didn't you leave him to the Americans?"

"They would kill him. He is ...," there was a pause, as if the commander could not find a word to describe the wounded man. "Excuse please, Doctor George. In Vietnamese the man would be difficult to label? Yes, label. He saved many lives at My Lai hamlet. This family was the first he saved. The Americans murdered many, many people, my people. Arens saved them."

"Why do you have trouble saying that?"

"I have no trouble saying what Arens did for these people. To do what he needed, he turned against his own country. The Americans went after the Quyens. The soldiers followed them. They had no weapons, no way to stop the soldiers. Arens lead them to Ba Quyen's son, a leader in our army. To do that, Arens had to stop the soldiers following them and the other families seeking sanctuary in the north. During the escape, Cho Quyen kept his family close but not close enough to escape the Americans following them. Arens turned on his own people and brought enough American soldiers down that they turned back. We have no word for what American call Arens."

"Does it sound like traitor?"

The aide and the VC commander shook their heads.

"That explains how he acted when he became conscious yesterday," said George. "He saw me as an ..." George had to be careful here since they still thought he was a conscripted medical man from the Philippines. "He thought he was captured by the United States Army. It's too bad. I'm sure he's dead now. He could never survive ..."

George watched the old man's face as the aide translated. The man smiled and shook his head. Speaking to George what was said by the old man was echoed aloud by the aide.

"You, do not know Arens. My village was destroyed by American's many months ago. He has survived many more bullets than those you saw. He is out there. My son said we must find him. The commander agrees but you must come with his soldiers to help Arens. His wounds are not healed. You will come?"

There was not much choice left for George. This American traitor, this Arens or whatever the hell his name is, is a hero to these people. To George he is a patient, or is he? The man killed United States Army soldiers. He had killed them while protecting the old man and his family. If the VC can be believed, Arens helped other families as well, families that Americans were targeting and slaughtering. George had heard the stories, mass murder of hutches, babies thrown into the air and gunned down. He had seen the ears from the heads of villagers hanging by a string around the necks of U.S. Army soldiers. He chalked it up as military bravado. Was it?

***

"So how long did it take to find my father?"

Uncle George smiled, "three days and he made us find him."

"That'd be sort of stupid, wouldn't't?"

"You mean because he thought we were American forces? Yeah, except his memory came back a day or so after he escaped. We thought he was crazy when we found him."

"How's that?"

"Like I said, he made us find him. All we had to do was follow his smoke. He knew he was deep in North Vietnam territory. There was no chance of American forces being this far north. So he hunkered down and built a fire to cook some food."

"What? How did he get food? Damn, how'd he get a fire started?"

***

Vietnam 1967

One of the Viet Cong regulars saw the smoke first. It came off a hillside ridged with crags and old caves, many leading to connecting caverns. The VC were worried that Lawrence would attack them if they tried to approach. George asked them what a lone man could do against a squad of soldiers, added to the fact the man was wounded. They only laughed at George. "Aren's" predatory abilities had spread. During the time that he led the Quyen family north to their son, Arens had learned how to survive in the rain forest from Hoa and his family. They showed him which flora to eat, which would make him sick, and which would kill him. They had pointed out animals that were good food. He had to track them down. It was like tracking and hunting back home, they ate well. Only Arens was armed. The Quyens could build huts quickly and break them down even faster. They were much like Native American wickiups Lawrence had learned about in his youth. Danger from VC and the NVA was their worst problem. Arens knew how to stalk the most alert of all prey, which meant he knew how to stalk or avoid potential attackers if necessary. Word of the massacre at My Lai spread fast through Vietnam. North Vietnamese were expecting many escapees along the trails north but found only a few who spoke the message of the dead. The Quyens knew how to greet North Vietnam forces and could judge whether Arens would survive their scrutiny. If not, he remained a shadow whisking an invisible trail parallel to but on course with theirs. In the south, Llewellyn Lawrence became the traitor, turning on his comrades. The North Vietnamese were learning of the American who saved a family and was leading them to sanctuary in the North. By the time the Quyens met up with their son, Cho, their story had already preceded them.

George was sent to the campfire first, ostensibly because he spoke English. In reality nobody else wanted Arens to swing a trappers short noose about their throat and yank them to their death.

"Arens? Soldier? G.I.? You around here? I'm at your fire. You got something cooking here. The end of the spit's starting to burn."

George saw a bush move slight to his right, about twenty degrees above his line of sight. There was a ledge on the side of the hill which could not have been seen with the bush still there.

"Take it off the fire then," said Llewellyn Lawrence as he crawled out of the small opening of the cave. George could see that he had no weapon. Lawrence's bandages were fresh but he kept his arm tight to his left side where the bullet had entered. He got to the fire, reached for the meat speared on the spit now held by George and took it. He ripped off a small leg, took a nibble, decided it was edible, and took a bigger bite. He handed it back to George.

"There's men out there."

"Twelve men and Hoa. Bring them in," answered Lawrence.

George called to them and soon the small fire was surrounded. "When did you realize you were in North Vietnam hands?"

"I woke up somewhere in the middle of the night. Didn't know it then. All I knew was that an American doctor had treated me. I was still groggy, thought I was a prisoner. I know what happens to turncoats, so I left. Got outside the camp without waking anybody, including the guards. Couldn't tell where I was because it was drizzling, no stars to see. Actually the coldness of the rain felt good, helped the fever go down. Slowed me up a bit but the resting was good. I got pretty far, didn't I? Knew when I stopped to catch this guy," said Lawrence holding up the charred body of what was an unidentifiable medium sized mammal, "that I was north and out of U.S. Army range. I had no reason to run and needed the rest anyhow. I started going through your taking care of me and figured you were some Navajo that the VC captured and was practicing voodoo on me."

Both of them laughed, "I don't do voodoo ... Just who are you? What kind of name is Arens?"

"Llewellyn Lawrence, formerly Sergeant Lawrence. The Vietnamese have trouble with my name. They drop the "L" which is why it sounds like Arens."

George could see that Llewellyn Lawrence was not as stable as he thought he was. He was dizzy. He turned to the VC leader and was trying to explain in sign language that they should stop for the night when Lawrence tapped him on the shoulder.

"Let me. I do okay with Vietnamese. I'll tell them we need to bivouac here until morning."

They understood Lawrence easily and slapped him on the back, laughing at some inside joke between the VC and Lawrence. He hugged Hoa Quyen for a long time with tears in his eyes. When Lawrence turned back to George he could see Hoa's tears.

"How about taking a look at my hurts, Doctor George?"

***

"My father had that much character? That's hard to believe," said Peter.

"No, I'm glossing over him pretty good. What he did was very daring. You got to remember that he was pretty well trained as an outdoorsman. When I got back home and met your grandfather, heard the hunting and fishing stories, I realized that

Lew was just a man whose love was nature. He knew how to live in the wilds, but best he knew how to survive under conditions that would leave the average man dead, starved to death or the meal of some predator. Lew lived a life learning how to be self sufficient. You're almost like that. Are you unique? Couldn't some of your buddies do as well as you?"

"You're right Uncle George. I'm a good shot, but Grandpere George can out shoot me by a mile. Zinni always got more fish than me. First times I went out with them up into the hills and back deep into the forest, I would have scared myself into a heart attack without them."

"Lew ... I guess I kind of slipped into calling him as I did in Nam. Lew had trouble surviving the army. No, not the army like the army that fought WWII, the army that began changing with Korea and fell apart during Nam. He was a nobody on base or in the field as a soldier. He did what he was told and like the rest of us counted off the days from FNG to discharge. He was learning the art of army camouflage. If they don't see you, they don't send you out to be killed."

"FNG? What's an FNG?"

"Fucking New Guy," said Uncle George. "There's more to your father."

***

Vietnam 1967

George had no idea how to perceive Llewellyn Lawrence. Lawrence was a very quiet man. He would exchange small talk, ramble off a couple jokes, but whether he was verbose before My Lai or not, he kept to himself now. On the return trip to the POW camp, George pitched and prodded. Within sight of the camp, Lawrence stopped, realizing George desired an explanation; he had been wrong to judge George as an enemy. He told the VC troops that he and George would catch up. When Hoa went past, Lawrence gently held her shoulder. George heard words, gentle words, and she smiled. Turning to the troops, she spoke, waved, and came over to take Lawrence's hand. Lawrence apologized to George for not telling him the whole story of the Quyen family, from the early days to the villagers being thrown into pits and machine gunned. He asked Hoa to tell George what she saw while he translated. Lawrence had not heard the complete story and it hurt him to hear it now. Numerous times during her telling, Lawrence had to stop her and walk away as tears came to his eyes. George was stunned. His brain locked, fought to disbelieve, but lost. His stomach churned, creating fluids of bile that he could not swallow. His country made him sick to his stomach.

Hoa's descriptions of the U. S. Army's fighting heroes - - being all they could be by inflecting violence, brutality, rape, infanticide, and horror no human mind could dare imagine, nor accept. It was too much to handle and forced George to tears. They were not tears for the victims, but for him. He should not be hearing this, but there it was. He could not ignore this. The taste of horror etched like mild acid at the chapped ridges about his lips. The tears, these could be avoided by not seeing, not hearing, by going back home and not acknowledging your country did this. Back home it was just a news item, a passing news item that you need not heed. Not us, not USA, ran through minds.

***

"Peter, your father killed Americans. He killed them with no respect. They were vermin, worse than sewer rats. Rats infest to survive. Tossing a baby in the air and ripping its head off with bullets is worse than any rat. There is no name for a creature lower than a sewer rat, but God calls him man!"

George stood. His eyes were watery, maybe from the cheap whiskey, but Lawrence did not think so. Lawrence had worried that telling Uncle George how he killed Frick would be dangerous. A moral judgment by George could have sent Lawrence to jail. This would not happen. George had been part of a crime equaled only by human exterminators called American soldiers. He did not see what Llewellyn Lawrence saw that day, but the hearing brought back what he also had witnessed and done nothing about - the ears around soldiers necks, the murderous orders from commanders to off all civilians, the trenches with bodies of grandmothers and babies, photographs of papa sans and momma sans with faces ripped by machetes. And the worse was his own firing at creatures he could not recognize by their shadows in the night.

George went into his house and returned with two glasses of whiskey, straight up. "Here, you might as well put some down. There's more. Let me continue."

***

Vietnam 1967

"Trong trãing con khang di lai," echoed as the search party returned and the villagers saw Lawrence walking into camp. He had helped many escape the American soldiers. They ran to him, shook his hand, and bowed. Lawrence returned their bows.

What are they saying? It sounds like what they said when we left?" asked George.

Lawrence bowed a few more times, spoke to the silent soldiers surrounding the villagers, and turned to George, "trong trãing con khang is a joke they hold at my expense. They are calling me the white cat and welcoming me back. My hair went white in a matter of months while with the survivors from the killings. They call me the cat because like the civets here, I use the night and shelter myself during daylight."

Lawrence and George were prisoners of war in fact but not treatment. There were other American POWs at the camp who were the prisoners of war. They were confined to prisoner huts with leg irons in place unless freed for exercise and bodily functions. This was the extent of their imprisonment. George tended to prisoners, made sure they were eating and getting obtaining enough nutrients to sustain their lives. He represented them to the camp commander, a rather unique Vietnamese; he was very plump, "fat as pig" as his troops described behind his back by his troops. His troops made fun of him only because he was a leader that gained respect because he returned it. The same was true of his handling of George and the POWs. George had earned the commander's loyalty in spite of his being the enemy. His Red Cross training gained him recognition deserved and acknowledged by his talented care of the VC soldiers, villagers, and POWs. It placed in a unique position in the VC camp. Short of the weapon arsenal, George had access to anything, everything, and everyone. The commander put George into a privileged niche of the enemy out of necessity.

Llewellyn Lawrence walked into the enemy camp unfettered, head up. The commander had been alerted to Lawrence's arrival through Ba Quyen's son, Cho. Cho had the rank to keep Lawrence a prisoner, but more an exile than a prisoner with freedom of the camp. Despite protests to the opposite, George coerced Lawrence into spending his first two nights in the medicine hooch. George tended to Lawrence's wounds, fearful of infection, stunned by the healing. After two nights, Lawrence took up residence in the jungle just outside of camp. The commander, in a rare pique of leadership, threatened to incarcerate Lawrence upon hearing of his desire to live outside of the camp. Lawrence spoke abruptly but with respect to the commander in front of George. Whatever Lawrence told the commander was grudgingly accepted, but night guards followed Lawrence out into the night. The guards returned within an hour, but not Lawrence. The commander went berserk, ready to attacking the two guards, but settled down knowing he would not send more men out into the jungle, just as he himself would not lead a search in the dark for "Trong trãing con khang."

As the sun rose the next morning and the commander's aide was marshaling VC troops into a search party, Lawrence walked back into camp. He had a wild boar over his shoulder, two hares, and four squirrels tied and dangling from his left hand. He woke the commander, holding up more fresh meat than the camp had seen in a week, and instantly assuaging the commanders doubts about Lawrence's future habitat.

Llewellyn Lawrence was a taciturn man, mostly keeping to himself. He spoke only once to the other POWs, seeking no secrets but asking whether they had any reading material. One had a ragged copy of <u>Lolita</u> which generated a smile from Lawrence's face when the man offered it to Lawrence on loan. Lawrence thanked the man, but after reading the book and finding there were no others, Lawrence removed himself from contact with the POWs. George asked him why.

"Two reasons, George. A man that's a prisoner needs human contact. He'll talk, and keep talking to just hear his own words, trying to make them last. My opinion is he's trying to invade you with his life. Maybe if he does, you can help him keep it, take his living on. If he gets inside of you and harm comes to him, it makes you sort of responsible. You've accepted a piece of him and now you've betrayed him."

"I can see that. It's going to affect you badly if he gets … Shit, if he gets killed, you'll feel it."

"George, that's not the worst of it. His words turn to his actions here, in Nam, on the village fields, in their rice paddies. They could be words of bravado, macho killing machine garbage from training camps. His words might become challenges. Here I did this, there I killed them. I can't let that be."

"How do you mean? What could you do about it?"

Lawrence turned and stared directly into George's eyes. In a voice soft as a whisper Lawrence told George "I'd kill them and make them suffer."

Lawrence lived somewhere out in the forest, in a place where nobody visited. He maintained his foraging function and thus kept peace with the commander. Periodically the commander and his officers would ask Lawrence to discuss sorties with them. Lawrence owed nothing to his home country. The United States had become his enemy. He freely gave advice and recommended changes in the VCs terrorism attacks. Their night assaults were the best techniques for unnerving the enemy. He told the VC how every American grunt was deathly afraid of the Vietnam night. Take away their sleep, and you take away their alertness on patrols the next day. He recommended that more civilians be used to infiltrate the Americans. Sell them goods, sell them that god awful rice wine, but above give them all the drugs they wanted. He laughed at their amazement and explained that nearly every ground soldier, grunt, could only survive in two ways, by counting days until their return to the States and by being shit-faced every night they could and staying high before going out.

The commander found Lawrence's description of the American fighting man near impossible to accept. How could the generals allow the drunkenness and drug stupors to destroy his troops? Here a man found with drugs was instantly shot. He could not accept a soldier who would pose such an extreme danger to his compatriots.

"No, Lawrence that would be a waste. No drugs to the enemy."

Lawrence shrugged it off. Initially Lawrence saw duty around the camp, in the village. His engineering abilities helped the Quyens build a new home and set up a dyke system for rice fields. Soon others came to Lawrence and he was glad to help. He enjoyed the people much more than back in the south. Here they were not the enemy as they had been treated in South Vietnam. They shared meals with Lawrence, told stories of their lives with the French and now the American's, and laughed at his tales of living in the United States. George talked little with Lawrence but learned much about Llewellyn Lawrence by the repartee between Lawrence and the Vietnamese.

Lawrence did not avoid talking about his family. By the time the United States withdrew the troops from Vietnam and George made it back to America, he knew Peter Lawrence's father

Llewellyn and his wife Evelyn very well. George knew that Llewellyn Lawrence probably would never meet his son, Peter. To the world of America, Llewellyn Lawrence was dead even without a body bag arriving at Dover Air Force base.

***

Peter spoke as George finished his knowledge of Peter's father. "I guess that would be me?"

Uncle George just kept his eyes down on the empty whiskey glass. There was nothing he could say or do.

"I'm surprised my father didn't go out on patrol with the VC."

Uncle George looked enigmatically at his nephew. Peter had come to a conclusion that put George at a chasm once crossed never to be regained. Evelyn would kill him if she found out. Both men stayed quit. The air was calm, the stars fully uncovered, where there should have been winds and the threat of a storm. Evelyn knew it all. She had forbid George to tell anyone the truth of Llewellyn Lawrence, had his pledge on it. George's place between a rock and a hard spot was squeezing the honor out of him. Evelyn did not know that Peter had killed Masabi Frick, killed him in a horrible and nearly inhumane fashion. She would never know unless Peter told her. If he tells Peter what has been forbidden, would he also tell on Peter? Where would he stop? George lit another cigarette knowing better than to offer one to Peter. Despite the darkness, he saw in Peter's eyes apprehension. Peter Lawrence knew there was something else. He knew that Uncle George a story resting on the edge of his lips. Lawrence feared that it might be too much. George told him anyway.

"Lew, your father, could not shake the horror of what the Americans had done. Had it been unique, one patrol, one squad, one platoon, maybe. He knew that this inhumane treatment of the Vietnamese was rampant across all of South Vietnam. Before his flight from the body-strewn rice fields, the stories had weighed on him, but imagine when he saw the bodies in front of his eyes, peoples' guts spilled out, flies eating human livers, maggots infesting dead eyes. The ears hanging around soldiers necks were as real as the horror stories these soldiers boasted about in camp. Where he could not believe before, he now knew the stories were real."

"Peter it ate at Llewellyn, festered inside. He spoke little to me but I did have contact with him. Villagers would come in to camp sick or injured. Of course Lew brought them in to Doctor George. They had been hurt helping him shore up a levee, or cutting timber from the forest for an animal shelter, any number of hurts and cuts and once in a while a missing finger or two. I thought this vocation of his would replace the hatred he felt for American soldiers, but it didn't. I heard the unhealed wound whenever we talked. He'd get into discussing this pig farmer or that old woman's rice fields, but he lacked conviction. One break from the domesticity of the hamlet and he would get quiet and soon leave."

"One day he couldn't keep it inside of him. He came to me with it is or it isn't an order, one from the commander. A company of Americans was using the dark to penetrate the south west military combat zone surreptitiously under cover of darkness. They were taking advantage of the monsoon weather now beginning to blow in from the China Sea. Already they had hit one village, leaving no survivors. They maintained strict camouflage encampment during the darkened stormy days and moved once the village was confirmed asleep. They were Green Berets and under the orders LNL. Lawrence told me that meant Leave Nothing Living."

"I still did not understand what that meant for me," he told Peter Lawrence.

***

Vietnam 1967

"The whole company of VCs here must go George. If you don't go, they'll kill you."

"Shit! That's not right! I'm the enemy. How can they expect me to fight against my own ..."

George stopped and his eyes widened, "what about the POWs?"

Lawrence stared him down.

"I've convinced the VC that you're like me, that you've turned. You do not have to kill anybody, but we'll need you as a corpsman. There's no choice. Think, George! What do you think those Green Berets are doing to these people in those villages they attack every morning?"

The Americans had attacked a second village the night before, using the same night cover tactic. This time people escaped. The reports showed an American pattern that could go one of two ways. The choices were difficult. They could select one village as a Green Beret target and set up an ambush, catching the Americans during the night. If they chose correctly, they could defend the village and stop the furtive night attacks. If they chose the wrong village, not only would the Green Berets wipe out another village, but once the word got out to the Americans that the VC force was sitting around twiddling their thumbs, they would know the night raid strategy was flushed and would probably return back to base operations.

There was only one thing to do: do not defend either village, but send spies to the borders. Whichever village gets razed draws an almost certain path to the next village. The commander was reluctant to do this. He felt that with three successes the Americans would probably cease the night attack strategy knowing they were pushing the limit of a successful operation. Lawrence disagreed; Americans beat every success into the ground. The best football coach in America advocated that you run a play until it no longer works, then you run it again. It is the same here, they will continue to attack until they lose. The losing part turned the decision to waiting for the next hamlet to go down, then setting the ambush for the next one. "Never under estimate the overconfidence of an American, especially a General in the U. S. Army," Lawrence told them.

The Green Berets had gotten sloppy. The third village was attacked but more than half the people escaped. Those that did not were all slaughtered, most after being visibly tortured. None of them were military people, no VCs, no NVAs, and very few even old enough to fight back. Spies, who circled behind the Americans, returned describing bodies of old men and old women, crippled people, a blind man with his eyeballs lying on the ground next to his body. The eyeballs had a boot print on them. Most of the children, now orphans, had escaped into the forest.

The commander and Lawrence arrived at the next village to survey their strategy for the assault and ambush. The commander figured catching the Green Berets in a moving double hedge position. Americans were notoriously arrogant. If there was a clear road to walk, they took it. As they marched towards the village, they would cover most of the trek on such a road. Half of the VC troops would ambush the Americans from the north, the

American's left side, and then immediately scramble east, parallel to the road. If the Green Berets took the bait, they would stay on the road opening rifle fire at the VC fleeing through the tall reeds on the north. On the south side and down the road, would be the other half of the VC company, waiting. As the Americans chased the north enemy leaving their rear unguarded, they would be attacked by the south VC army once in range. Thus would begin the moving double hedge. North attacks and runs, Americans fire and pursue. South ambushes and runs, Americans about face, attack, and chase, only to have the north force waiting ahead of them for a rear attack. It was an excellent plan if the Americans walked up the open road.

Lawrence walked the route through to the village, noticing bridges that took the troops over an open swamp, filled with clumps of sedge. The bridges saved troops a quarter mile hike through the swamp water with its leeches, snakes, and even a crocodile or two. It could work, but the Green Berets knew what a moving double hedge attack was. The VC could not rely only on this plan. If the Americans smelled it out and circled north or south, they could rout one half of the forces. The commander agreed and said that he would send a patrol to insure what the American strategy would be. Lawrence broke off a stick from a dead tree about four foot long. Wading through the swamp waters, he probed the depth of the swamp close to the bridge while also scattering any vipers lurking for a strike. He thought "Indians, I remember reading of an Indian attack of a cavalry troop. They had … Yes, that's the fall back."

He returned and talked to the VC commander; the man agreed and sent two squads to blow up the three bridges before the Americans could get close enough to hear the explosions. Lawrence told him to have the squads warn the villagers about a possible attack. The commander was reluctant to do this since the Green Berets might send out scouts to check the village before they attacked. Lawrence reminded him of the American arrogance.

The Americans were headed to the road ambush. Scouts returned by mid-afternoon to report that the Americans had split their company, sending half north and the remainder south. They did not walk the road and appeared to be ready to fire on anybody who did use it. Lawrence asked them how close the Green Berets were to the swamp in front of the village. The Green Beret company would make it to the swamp nearly an hour too soon. The VC commander remedied the situation. He sent three snipers out to the forest surrounding the road. They were to form an "L" and use automatic firing from each of its three points until the sun met the horizon.

Lawrence knew they would not need the whole VC company to ambush the Americans. Half would be targeted by their own men. The commander selected VC soldiers he knew would follow orders and kill until killed themselves. He did not want Lawrence with them because he knew the men in the swamp would be committing suicide. George agreed but Lawrence overruled them both. It was his plan and he would see it through. George believed that this was Llewellyn Lawrence's chance to end it all with an honorable suicide.

They heard the sniper fire far down the road as the swamp ambushers finished covering as much of their AK47s as possible with grease. They had to survive being underwater and still have firing power. When the sniper fire was replaced by M 16 return fire, Lawrence knew the Green Berets would continue their march. He looked west and as the sun touched the distant mountain, the VC sniper fire ceased. Soon the M 16 fire would start. Lawrence and the men waded out into the swamp waters. They made a lot of noise, swished much water, and slapped their AK 47s on top of the dark swamp water to scare off reptiles. Hopefully the only enemy they would face would be humans. Each soldier found sedge clomps to nestle inside. A few men had to choose new ones that hid them better while another man ran out of his sedge screaming as a cobra zigzagged in the opposite direction. The man shaking his fist futilely at the viper found a new sedge. The wait was excruciatingly and ridden with terror. The men in the swamp knew a company of U.S. Army Green Beret soldiers with automatic weapons would be wading right past them. Lawrence watched the sun.

As to be expected, the Americans were arrogant. They had already raided, raped, and killed three villages without any return fire. They had the procedure down pat. They would go over the three bridges, make camp in the forest about five miles from the village, and wait until early morning to attack. Guards would patrol the bivouac, killing any human going toward or away from the village. No guards had been at the other villages, but still they were set. One quick swoop in the dark, and the village would be sanitized. Sanitized, a word only an American would apply to reducing a human population to zero. For the officers, the best part was payback for the sorties the North Vietnam forces used at base camps against the Americans during the night. Killing them with their own tactic had been used at many a meeting setting up this attack force.

"Halt," yelled the first Green Beret as he noticed the bridges were not there. "There's no bridges!"

A Green Beret Lieutenant cursed, "what da fuck you talkin' bout? There's three fuckin' bridges there!"

"Where? Don't see any. Might have been, but all we've got now is rubble. No bridges."

A Green Beret Captain cursed, "why da fuck you stoppin'?"

"No bridges!"

The captain cursed again, "those stupid slopeheads blew up the fuckin' bridges."

"Sir," said the first Green Beret, "not too stupid. Only way to their village is to go around this big swamp."

"Can't do it soldier. Ruins the whole plan. Can't make a change like that. Won't work. By the time we get around, it'll be light. See, the sun's halfway set behind us. Gotta go through it, Lieutenant. Get 'em marchin' and yeah, get 'em to unload their rifles and wrap them up. Don't need no rusty weapons or misfires. Now do it. We're wading through."

The Green Berets were waist deep wading through the swamp waters to the north of the destroyed bridges when Lawrence rose inside his sedge. He opened fire with his AK 47 on the Green Berets in front of him, a little less than half the American military company. His firing signaled the VC snipers to rise out of their sedge clumps and with the sun behind them open fire. The Green Berets were hit with bullets in the back. Their bodies fell face forward. Lawrence saw American soldiers panicking and popping up out of the swamp and shooting their own soldiers. The rear Green Berets got their M 16s functional fast but once they opened fire, the VC and Lawrence dropped down under the swamp water.

The VC disappeared and the Americans at the rear realized they were shooting their own men who were aiming at them. They waved for the front soldiers to stop but it was useless. It could not be seen. The Green Berets that were not wounded or floating dead on pond scum now unlocked and loaded, returning fire. The return fire into a blazing Southeast Asia sun, did not take out the VC, but mowed down their rear troops faster than the sun could set. They continued until there was no return fire. Still facing the glare of the sun, they waded back from where they had come to count VC bodies. Instead, they found their fellow Green Berets dead. None survived because their compatriots were under order to LNL and had shot anything that moved. The sun had just set. The bodies were stilled. Lawrence came up from his sedge, followed by the VCs and opened fire. No Green Beret raided a village that day, none raped old women, and none shot a baby in a well.

Uncle George had reached the point in his story where if he continued, he would sanction Peter's killing Frick. For it was in the aftermath of the swamp ambush that Llewellyn Lawrence confronted George with abetting a traitor. From the start Lawrence had made it implicit that George was a non-combatant. George was a POW and present at this massacre for one purpose only, to tend the wounded. Llewellyn Lawrence held an AK 47, he set up the swamp ambush, and opened fire, killing many American soldiers. Of being a murderous traitor, he was guilty and if captured would face a firing squad. George witnessed this as did the few survivors in the Green Beret ranks. The swamp was gorged with floating dead bodies. The VC commander sent his troops to pull the living to shore. Wounded Green Berets were scattered throughout the reeds surrounding the swamp, guarded by VCs. George was now forced into being a traitor or a corpsman prisoner.

***

"Peter, your father did not force me to be there. If I had stayed behind, though I didn't know it, my fate would have been that of the POWs we left behind. I would probably have been killed. Lew brought me to the swamp but did not allow me to engage me in the fight; he never even offered me a weapon."

Peter Lawrence was churning inside, not able to fully understand what his father had done, nor able to either condemn his father's actions or sanction them. Llewellyn Lawrence had lead a cadre of Viet Cong fighters against a United States Army company and successfully destroyed them. He was a traitor to his country and a revolutionary leader to the North Vietnamese. His Uncle George had been part of that battle but Peter did not know what part he played. He did know that Uncle George had never revealed what had happened over there, nor had anybody ever challenged Uncle George's loyalty to the United States Army. For it to have been kept a secret for these many years could only cast a shadow over Uncle George's military service. The thought that

Uncle George could be charged with a war crime ran through Lawrence's mind.

"I'm telling you anyway Peter. Lew grabbed me by the arm at the scene. He held his AK 47 in one hand and grasped my upper arm like a vise with the other. He knew I was scared shitless, could see it in my eyes. I tried to not make eye contact but he kept yanking me in front of his face, nose to nose. I might have been crying, but I sure as hell was sweating. It ran off my face and under my collar. I thought he was going to shove what happened down my throat, force me to go along with it. I kept running over and over what I saw, the wounded around me, and the floating bodies being dragged out the water.

"Your dad's face was not angry, nor smiling. It was serious, his eyebrows knotted into a frown. His eyes stopped scaring me as a sensitivity came over them, easing my fear. I started to mumble some unimportant begging words, but he shushed me with his lips. I'll forever remember what he said. He said 'you're a good man, George. You're a prisoner forced here to help wounded Americans, that's all. Those alive know this. I told them. They're watching me shove you around, get you moving. I am the enemy, always tell them that.'"

"He took me over to the bodies lying on the ground and told me to take a good look at each one. He didn't need me for the VC troops because none of them were wounded. Before I could start, he pulled me away. He made it very clear that I must make a decision about each wounded Green Beret. If the man's wounds were life threatening and I could not help him, I must tell him. I knew why and said I couldn't do that. He said that if I chose to not make that decision, he would decide the same fate for every wounded soldier. My jaws dropped and I wanted to walk away but he turned, loaded a fresh clip into his rifle and headed to the bodies scattered along the edge of the swamp. I knew he would kill them all. I caught him up to him. It was the worse decision I'd ever made in my life but the only one I could live with. He let me go through the wounded troops. When I had tended to all, I told him I had put a smudge of black clay on the foreheads of those who would die."

"And he went back and shot each of them? Jesus that's horrible."

"No, Peter, their being there was horrible. I saw it for what it was. None of those marked would ever survive imprisonment more than a day, or even less than a few hours. Llewellyn

Lawrence didn't put them there. Our country put them there. They were dying, could not be saved. Lew did what the United States expected. Make war and people die. I heard the pop sounds going around the swamp and hated him. He did not hate those men; he did not know those men."

***

Vietnam 1967

When the VC, Lawrence, and George got back to camp, there was a new company of Viet Cong waiting for them. The commander greeted their commander and they disappeared into the camp headquarters. Lawrence nudged George and told him to get on his Red Cross arm band. Lawrence put his hands behind his head and followed the new POWs to the prisoners' hooch, a place Lawrence had never visited. George followed. The VC that had been at the swamp ambush did not understand why Lawrence was acting like a prisoner but left him alone. George followed Lawrence into the prisoners' cell. He asked Lawrence what was going on. Lawrence could see that the new troops had stopped staring at the POWs and himself. He told George that he could hear them talking. There was going to be some big change in the camp and these new soldiers were there to make it happen. George, as well as Lawrence, must act completely like a POW until the dust settled.

***

"Your father saved my life here. The leader of the new troops of Viet Cong had ordered his men to imprison all Americans not already shackled. They had rifles trained on us and I was sure they would open fire. Lew put his hands behind his head and subserviently bowed his head in submission. I followed his lead, including dropping to my knees as he did. Others were not as quick and AK 47s bullets took down maybe five or six captured Americans. The noise was loud enough that the camp Commander came out of his headquarters hooch screaming at the new troops. All I could guess was that he was telling them to stop. The VC leader came up behind him, grabbed his shoulder, and started yelling at him. I thought there would be blows exchanged but fortunately for us they began to settle down. Nobody paid attention to Lew and me kneeling on the ground less than five yards away. Lew picked up on the altercation between the two leaders. The camp commander was a superior officer but the VC commander kept waving papers in his face. The camp commander grabbed the papers; and I thought the other man would pull his pistol and shoot him. He did not and the camp leader stared him down. The man turned and ordered his troops to back off, which they did, but with their weapons still unlocked and aimed at the prisoners. The camp commander pushed the VC man out of the way, walked into the middle of the new troops and barked orders at the men. They looked at their commander, which caused the camp commander to grab an AK 47 from one soldier and butt stroke him in the face. The rest of the soldiers locked and lowered their weapons, slinking off to the parameter of the camp. Since Lew kept his head down through the whole incident, I followed his submissiveness, realizing that had I not I would have been shot. The VC leader followed his men, ordering them to set up camp about a quarter mile north of our camp. The commander walked over to us and very softly and politely asked us to please get up and follow him into his headquarters hooch.

"As the Camp commander spoke, Lew translated for me and it became clear we were in dire straits. A force of US commandos had launched an attack on another POW camp less than 25 miles south of us. For whatever reason, Americans called it Operation Ivory Coast. It was a total debacle. US intelligence had been compromised by VC sympathizers in the area to believe the camp held nearly a hundred American POWs. The American forces were getting a lot of bad publicity about rescuing POWs and this seemed like an easy opportunity to capture a small camp and save imprisoned soldiers. Fifty or sixty air borne rangers swarmed in behind an attack force of twenty or thirty Air Force planes to find the camp empty. Counter Intelligence had made a fait accompli that more than embarrassed the American forces. An American helicopter had crashed in the middle of the camp, another one misread the terrain and landed a quarter mile away, slaughtering more than a hundred civilians, and their third team, which landed dead center inside the complex, claimed victory over nobody. The facility was empty."

"The commander could not help but laugh, even though it seemed very out of place. The American radio broadcasts were claiming a complete success for the mission, stating that its objective of seizing the POW camp had been accomplished in less than a half hour with only one American wounded and one injured. They blamed the lack of American POWs at the camp on the flooding of the Ve River flooding. The broadcast did not explain how that forced the VC to move the 65 prisoners nor did the radio mention that the first Air Borne soldier that landed accidentally shot himself getting off of the crashed helicopter and the other broke his ankle in the same mishap. It was totally unbelievable to the camp commander that Americans could write off such a failure by words not deeds. The United States was using the press media, bringing attention to the inhumane treatment of American POWs. They claimed this attack would help change how prisoners were housed and treated. The raid was doing just that and Lew and I would be the immediate recipients of that change. Hanoi had decided that the imprisonment of enemy soldiers in scattered POW camps had to stop. The exposure to random raids like that at Son Tay made North Vietnam bases too exposed. Instead, the North Vietnamese would move all camps closer to Hanoi. No more small POW camps out in the forests. Prisoners would become inmates in large city based prisons, most having been built by the French for Vietnamese prisoners. Control was important but not the only reason. He told us that the United States president had begun massive bombings of North Vietnam cities, especially Hanoi. Moving the prisoners of war north to Hanoi meant that Nixon's nearly secret bombings would jeopardize his own captured soldiers. It wound up being a psychological victory for North Vietnam since Americans now knew that their country would also be bombing their own imprisoned soldiers."

"He had not told us directly but we both knew what it meant. We were moving. Typical of your father, he asked the commander directly without equivocation, when, where, and who was going. The commander did not hesitate with his response. Every unwounded officer would be transported out tomorrow. I didn't catch what he said at first but your father did. He asked what about the wounded and non officers? The commander told him that they would be killed. Lew just nodded his head, knowing the answer before the man spoke it. Again your father was on top of the situation when he asked if the commander had a list of all prisoners. Lew smiled when he was told yes and that his name, Major Arens as well as Colonel Doctor George's name were on it. I realized that the commander had just saved our lives. He told us that while the other prisoners would be shackled until the trucks came tomorrow, that Lew and I would not be since he was putting together the prisoner transfers and needed our assistance. After the face off on the camp grounds, the Viet Cong leader had decided to leave well enough alone until he had the prisoners completely under his command."

"Lawrence and I walked out of the command hooch knowing today would be the last day of what little freedom we had here. We also knew there was a good chance we might never see each other again. While I was running these emotional thoughts through my head, Lawrence was contemplating other strategies. The commander roughly knew where they were taking us. The prison was on Song Da River at Hoa Binh, was about 30 or forty miles from Hanoi. This seemed to bother him. Though the troops going there were not wounded, he doubted that half would ever reach the prison. It was a 450 mile trip at minimum. He guessed at least two days, maybe three or four. I had not even thought about that. He told me two things to keep very clear in my mind. First was that I am a doctor. As long as the North Vietnamese thought that, I would not only be safe but would receive preferential treatment. I knew this and had been putting on an act since my capture. But fear entered, since we would be riding right into the middle of the enemy's capital. I did not know if I could keep up the charade but I had no choice if I ever wanted to return home alive."

"The second thing he told me was to not let anybody know that he could speak Vietnamese, that he was in fact an expert at translation. I thought he was making a mistake since the North Vietnamese would also show him preferential treatment if they could use him to translate for them, but I soon grasped why he did not want them to know. If they spoke anything around him, he would know what they were saying. Their believing he did not understand Vietnamese gave him a great advantage. On the way back to the medical hut he asked me to get him a scalpel, one with a plastic safety guard covering the blade, and some adhesive tape. I asked him why he needed a scalpel. He put his hand on my shoulder and told me I did not need to know."

***

Vietnam 1967

George gave Lawrence the scalpel and the adhesive tape that night. After examining the scalpel and seeing that the adhesive tape was very coarse, he went back to the medical hut and asked

George for some petroleum jelly. George gave him a small tube. Lawrence was very sure that they would be rousted very early in the morning since that was the usual procedure when dealing with prisoners. Scare them, kick them out of bed while still asleep, search through their belongings. Harass them into animal obedience. It works with prisoners and trainees. Fear is a great motivator to prisoners and a great pleasure to those producing that fear. Lawrence cut one very thin strip of adhesive tape and wrapped it around the plastic tube that covered the extremely sharp edge of the surgeon's scalpel. Next, he smoothed on a medium-sized dab of petroleum jelly, making sure none of the roughness of the adhesive tape abraded the surface of his palm. Stripped down from the waist, he laid on his side, bent his knees up to his chest, and probed his anus with a petroleum jellied middle finger. Once his sphincter muscles were relaxed, he slowly and gently inserted the petroleum jellied end of the scalpel into his rectum. He could not wait until tomorrow to do this. If indeed the prisoner transferees were hustled into trucks in the early morning, he would have no chance to stow the scalpel where nobody would search. He slowly rolled over unto his knees, swaying his hips and flexing his rectal muscles to accommodate the scalpel. Other than feeling slightly constipated, he could function normally as long as he did not have a bowel movement. Considering the food received at the camp and probably even less on the trip, he did not anticipate any problems maintaining his continence for two or three days.

He then took out his jack knife. He would be taking a chance because if caught with it, he would be executed on the spot. Still, he could not toss it away. The scalpel was a utility and would not be much of a weapon under any circumstances. The jack knife was. Lawrence knew how to use it in a fight and to dress kills for a food source. Without it he would probably die, yet if caught with it, he would surely die. Knowing where he was going and the fact that he was not really an officer and thus not a negotiable asset to the North Vietnamese, he was probably a dead man right now. He stripped off a long piece of adhesive tape, ran the adhesive side over the folded jack knife, and adhered it into the tissue and muscle to the inside of his left thigh, where his leg met his loins. He used two crosspieces to provide extra support. The two things Llewellyn Lawrence knew that would prevent the VC from finding the jack knife was that they never searched a prisoner's crutch area and they are repelled by nudity.

Lawrence was tired. The battle was now days behind him. The strain of tomorrow would have made another man sleepless, but Llewellyn Lawrence knew how to fight it; he dropped off to sleep quickly.

***

"It was really bad, Petey. I awoke to gun shots. The VC commander walked through the prisoner hooches unshackling officers, ignoring the enlisted men. When all the officers had been sent to the trucks, the VC soldiers went back into the prisoner huts and gunned down the enlisted men. They next went to the infirmary and shot every GI in sick bay. I was so shocked that I shook, just shook like I had a fever. They hustled me out to the trucks. I didn't see your father again for a long, long time. He was gang-shackled with the other officer prisoners. The trucks were flatbeds with pipe frames. Canvas covers hung over the top, which would be pulled down and fastened. The heat was bad enough outside the trucks but inside it was suffocating. The prisoners were bound in a circle. Each man was a shackled to the man on his left and right, ankle to ankle. A slip knot noose ringed the throat of each soldier. One end of the rope was knotted to the wrist of the man on his right, the other to the man on his left. I didn't know until later why they did this. Any movement tightened the noose around the adjacent man. This in turn would set the man off, screaming that he was choking. The VC would stop the truck and beat both men. It meant no escapes and no rest. Not being able to rest or fall asleep reduced the prisoners to swine, animals riding to the slaughter house."

"Lew saw me as he was led up the tail gate into one of the trucks. He did not acknowledge me."

***

Vietnam 1968

Lawrence waited two hours before he killed the two men tethered to his sides. It was easy. He just wrapped the noose tightly around his hand, put his head firmly against the man's head, and jerked down. Since the rope was over the man's trachea, there was no sound. The man on his left had passed out from the heat and never gained consciousness before Lawrence killed him. Lawrence leaned to his other side and broke that man's neck without waking him. He did the both men a favor.

The trucks made three stops for refueling. Only on the second stop did they open the back and sides of the trucks to let air in and pull dead bodies out. Unfettering the prisoners to get to the corpses, the VC allowed the living to relieve themselves in the forest by the road. There was a small stream in which the prisoners were able to scoop up relatively fresh water to wash themselves. One of the trucks was no longer needed and seeing the emaciated condition of most of the prisoners, the nooses were no longer used. Instead, the prisoners were tied cross armed to the men on either side. None of the survivors even knew who Lawrence was, which was good for Llewellyn. The man on his right started up a conversation which Lawrence ignored. The man became obstinate asking what his problem was, only to be chastised by the guard sitting in the driver's cab to not speak. They had no concept of where they were and had only experienced the one stop to know that the truck was traveling over forest roads and through territory that seemed to be untouched by the war.

Eventually Llewellyn Lawrence fell asleep like the rest of the prisoners. The stop of the truck in pitch dark was so sudden and the riding rhythm so abruptly interrupted, that all but two of the soldiers in the truck awoke. Those two would never awake anyway since they had died hours ago. As Lawrence watched the canvas being lifted, he knew he was truly a prisoner. The aged brown concrete walls of the prison could give no other message despite the covering ivy. The windows were miniscule, rectangular slots no more than two or three feet wide and six inches high. Each was covered with a metal plate. The sustained muscle fatigue due to nearly twenty hours without benefit of movement caused the prisoners to trip over their numb legs and fall. Those that did not right themselves were kicked by the 50 VC surrounding the tracks. One prisoner spit on a VC and had the butt of an AK 47 rammed into his mouth, teeth crumbling out of his face in the flow of blood. He fell unconscious to the ground. The same AK 47 butt now crashed his skull and he was quiet forever.

Lawrence understood the soldiers and their leaders. They were the prisoners were ground troops, not pilots. They were almost worthless, very low profile. They would be worth very little in negotiations with the Americans. If any caused problems, they were to hurt them. If they stand up to you, kill them. Lawrence kept his head down, his body posture condescending.

They were unshackled, shoved by rifle barrels through a double-hung steel door with streaks of rust covering the bolts and squeals of friction yelling from the hinges. The hallway was narrow and a cell door stood on each side. All the doors were open and as the prisoners were marched down the corridor, one was shoved through a cell door. The cells were built by the French to imprison Vietnamese and the size accommodation made each door much lower than the height of most American prisoners. Their heads were slammed against the portal as they were pushed into a cell. The VC laughed when one man's head bounced off the portal and he rebounded backwards onto the corridor passageway. They kicked him as he crawled back through the door, blood running down the side of his face. With the row now filled, the next group went through a steel door opened at the far end of the first set of cells. The hallway tilted here, as if built on a down slope, and Lawrence was pushed into the last cell as the remaining prisoners filled the cell he had already passed. As soon as the door slammed shut on him, Lawrence stripped. He had been lucky to be the first in his cell. It gave him extra time. The hall lights remained on during the imprisoning of the soldiers. This would not happen very often once everybody was contained in a cell. He looked for a place to hide his weapons. He would be shot on the spot if they were found. He looked for a drain and found it. He quickly took off his clothes, ripped the jack knife adhesive tape from inside of his thigh, and started on the floor drain grate. He had guessed correctly that each cell would have a drain. With time against him, he dug away the years of human grease and fecal matter locking the drain plate around the sewer hole, pried the grate up with the knife blade, and despite the nausea of the offal smell rushing into his face, reached down the drain to find the side pipe coming from the cell behind him. The jack knife went in the pipe and Lawrence quickly squatted, pulled his cheeks apart, and grabbed the bottom edge of the scalpel inside his anus. It came out smoothly just as the cell door opened. He rolled on top of the drain, stuck his index finger from his other hand down his throat and began retching. He expected a bullet to enter the back of his head, but instead heard the VC guard call him a fucking American as he shut the cell door to let Lawrence finish vomiting. Lawrence put the petroleum jelly and feces covered scalpel up the drain pipe next to the jack knife, replaced the drain grate, and sat back on his naked haunches. He could hear outside the door that it was not his retching that repulsed the VC guard but his nakedness. The door opened and he was lying in front of three VC guards totally bare, with his front parts exposed. He understood they wanted him to put his clothes back on but he feigned ignorance. While one kept a rifle aimed at his head, the other two punched his head, rubbed his discarded clothes in his face, and he punched his head until they let him get dressed. They did not leave immediately but looked over his body both in disgust and to prove to the prison officer that he had been strip searched. They thought nothing of the red abrasions inside of his thighs where the jack knife had been held with adhesive tape.

When dressed, he was shoved out of the cell while they searched it. They ignored the drain grate covered with vomit bile. The soldiers came out of the cell and knocked him down. Lawrence quickly assumed a fetal position, covering his head and drawing his knees up to protect his sensitive loins. They kicked him repeatedly in the back around his kidneys. There was nothing he could do to protect them. One of the guards produced a machete and inserted it along his back under his shirt. Turning the blade back and forth, Lawrence thought the man was going to slice him, but instead the guard positioned the blade against shirt and cut all the way up and through the collar. The other guards spun Lawrence over, faced up, and ripped the remains of his shirt from his body. Lawrence kept his forearms over his face, knuckles against his forehead, but he could see that one of the guards had prison clothes for Lawrence to wear.

The guard with the machete was much larger than any of the other guards, but still quite shorter than Lawrence. Lawrence had learned early on in his imprisonment that Asians detested that the Anglos, as they called Americans, were taller. It debased them and usually sent a guard off on a melee of punches and kicks. Lawrence always stooped when around the Viet Cong to prevent being beaten. This guard was well muscled and had nothing to feel inferior about. Lawrence did not falsely evaluate the man's large girth with obesity and acknowledged that this man could probably hurt him in a physical match up. The machete point was drawn now from the cuff, lifting it off Lawrence's leg slightly and slowly navigated, the point exerting pressure, up to Lawrence's crotch. The man started smiling, an Asian's smile of brutality, but Lawrence knew that as an Asian, the man would never use a weapon or brutality on another's exposed genitalia. The man did not but instead inserted the machete point at the waist of Lawrence's pants and slowly let the blade cut through the side. Lawrence had never seen a machete blade so sharp. Once stripped of all clothing, Lawrence was given the prisoner clothes made of what Lawrence guessed was burlap and shoved into his cell. The door lock set. Lawrence could hear the big guard bragging about his daunting of the American. Lawrence had to remind himself to never let on that he spoke and understood Vietnamese.

Lawrence put on his prison garb and took stock of his prison. He had to smile at his first actions as a confirmed convict. Like every man ever imprisoned, he counted off his space. The cell was about seven feet long from the door to outside wall, with a concrete bed along one side. The bed had an iron bar at each end, one with two ankle slots on the door end, the other a neck groove. At each end of both iron bars, were bolt holes; another bar probably went over the bed iron bar to fasten the prisoner's feet and his head and maybe both. There was no light either in the room or in the hallway outside the door. Lawrence guessed it was early morning from the light he saw at the end of the hallway when they were beating and stripping him. Little of that light fell into Lawrence's cell. He ran his fingers over the shackle grooves in the cement bed and contemplated the denouement of the cell. The iron bars were obviously made for a man much smaller than Lawrence. Neither his ankles nor neck would fit into the grooves, but he paused in his thinking when he came back to their size. Made by the French to imprison the Vietnamese, the tortured would now become the torturers. Lawrence would be the victim and the big guard would make sure Lawrence fit into the shackles.

The distance between the bed and the parallel wall was two hand spreads and in measuring that distance Lawrence became aware of just how filthy the cell was. There was a fungus growing over the wall. He pulled some of it off in sheets as he sat on the concrete bed. It was rubbery and musky smelling. Holding it closer to his nose, he slowly inhaled as he squeezed it. It was very moist and his nostrils recognized the moss to be living in mutualism with an acid smelling fungus. He could feel a bit of cement particles along the runners of the moss and put his hand back up to the wall where it had lived. The synergetic pair of organisms were slowly eating away the concrete walls. It was a jungle, this prison. What more could Lawrence expect than life eating at the inorganic. The room was very tall especially considering that the door was not much higher than four or so feet. Lawrence had about an eight foot reach but could only touch the ceiling by standing on the cement bed. He guessed it to be a ten foot ceiling made of chain link fencing. The building probably was two stories tall with guard access to the second floor to observe the prisoners.

Lawrence put his fingers through the rusted chain link fence ceiling and pulled to see how strong it was. As soon as he grabbed the chain links, hundreds of insects fell through the links on top of him. While this would have scared the daylights out of most people, Lawrence was not fazed by their scurrying. It would be a rare deadly or poisonous insect that freely roamed so blatantly. He guessed the bulk of bugs to be cockroaches. He grasped a few of them in his left hand while shaking the fence again , getting another wave of falling insects falling. Despite the lack of light, Lawrence could feel their crusty shell and leathery wings flittering while trying to escape. Lawrence worked one of them between his left thumb and index finger. Standing on the concrete bed, he held it up toward the transom between the door sill and ceiling. There was just enough light that he could see the creature writhing in terror, unable to do its natural selection dance of run, stop, run, stop, and flit through invisible gaps. Lawrence pinched off its head, pulled off the wings, and ate its thorax. Its bitter taste was nasty, but after seven or eight roach snacks, his hunger subsided a bit. Lawrence spit out the leathery shells that he could not digest and carefully pushed the remains through the drain hole. He would have to save some of the carcasses for bait.

Lawrence gave in to sleep and managed a good ten hours, much to his surprise. He had guessed wrongly that the guards would be back on the attack much sooner. When he woke, he could hear voices from other cells. The voices were tinged with pain. Guards had taken prisoners out of their cells for interrogation. Evidently the Viet Cong had not particularly liked what the American prisoners had to say. Lawrence stayed on the bed, his knees bent to make himself into a comfortable five foot body. Light eased through the edges of the door transom and Lawrence noticed that the light crossed the cell from the ceiling, down the outside wall, and across the floor. This meant that his cell faced east and that it was probably around ten in the morning. He would not get much more of this light as the sun passed overhead of the prison building. A new light shone in his face as the slot, a peep hole, opened in the great iron door. The eye looking through it kept its stare on Lawrence, the man behind it telling Lawrence not to move, which Lawrence intentionally did. This was not to cause trouble but to ensure the Viet Cong belief that Lawrence could not understand Vietnamese. The man banged on the door, yelling loudly until the great iron door swung open. The two men standing in front of Lawrence, one with an AK 47 aimed at his head and the other waving his palms at Lawrence who gestured for Lawrence to back up and sit down on the concrete bed. Lawrence acknowledged the message with his hands up in surrender.

With one guard's aim always on Lawrence, the other brought in an enameled jar and a cast iron bucket. Lawrence took the jar, feeling the swirl of a liquid in it. The guard motioned with his hands that it contained water for Lawrence to drink. Lawrence guessed about a pint or maybe a little bit more. The guard set the bucket over the drain grate and motioned to Lawrence that it was to be used for urinating and defecating. Lawrence dared not smile for fear of a beating as the man ludicrously held the bucket up to his groin like he was taking a leak, then faked sitting on it like he was taking a dump. The man gave Lawrence a brown paper bag. A bag that could have come straight out of a grocery store back home to use as toilet paper.

Lawrence spoke, "I'd prefer plastic if you don't mind."

The man with the rifle raised it to Lawrence's forehead and Lawrence chastised himself for violating his first rule as a prisoner, keep your mouth shut. The first guard grabbed Lawrence by the front of his shirt and instead of getting a beating; Lawrence was pulled over to the excrement bucket. Still holding Lawrence by the throat, he motioned to the drain The man would take off the grate and find his scalpel and jack knife and Lawrence would be caught. That was not the case. He pulled the bucket overtop of the drain and made like he was going to pour it into the drain, then turned to Lawrence and shook his head not aggressively, while shaking his finger in Lawrence's face. Lawrence got the message to never flush anything down the drain, especially feces or urine. Lawrence pointed to the drain and shook his head back and forth. The guard let go of Lawrence's shirt.

The two guards backed carefully out of the cell, closed the great iron door, and Lawrence heard the heavy clang of the solid iron bar falling on to its cleats. The peep hole stayed open meaning the guards wanted to see how fast Lawrence used his new conveniences. Not to disappoint them, he took a sip of the water, turned to the peep hole and smiled, gaving the eye of the watched a gracious and ceremonial bow of thanks. When he picked up the bucket to piss, the room darkened as the eye hole closed.

Lawrence looked above him, waiting for the first sight of guards using the chain link fence ceiling to look down upon their prisoner. It never happened nor did he hear any noise above the wire ceiling. He guessed maybe the heat of what would obviously be an attic would be insufferable in a place like Viet Nam during any season, but he would be wrong. He never did find out why the upper room was not used. At about two or three in the afternoon, Lawrence again saw a light and then an eye in the peep hole. Hearing the same tirade about staying put, Lawrence sat on the bunk as the door opened. It was the same two guards, both assuming the same roles. The one kept his rifle aimed at Lawrence's head, while the other brought in a metal dish. On the dish was bread covered with dull gray gravy. The guard handed it to Lawrence and took Lawrence's water jar. Lawrence made a note to himself to always use up his water since they would refill it to the brim. When the man came back with the jar, he handed it to Lawrence. Lawrence gave him a smile and bowed to both men. They looked at each other, not knowing whether they should respond with a bow, as was Asian custom. They did but with a very snappy nod. Lawrence smiled as they closed the door and he kept the smile on his face as the eye came to the peep hole, once again before it closed, putting Lawrence into near dark. The bread was very hard, so Lawrence poured a bit of water on it. The gray gravy at first put him off. He was not sure what they used to create it but then it couldn't be any worse than cockroach. They gave him no utensils. The gravy was actually quite good, or else he was much hungrier than he thought. The water did not soften the bread and he didn't want to waste his water. It was crunchy but edible. Once adapted to his routine and food regimen, Lawrence would take a try at putting some of the fungus on a piece of bread to see if it made him sick. A very small bite at a time would not probably make him sick. This was a time to minimize risks, not avoid them. Gaining strength increased his ability to survive. The worst that could happen was death and he was close enough to that to accept any risks.

There were three conditions facing Lawrence, if he was going to survive at Song Da prison. First and most important was acknowledging the prison as a life force and adjusting himself to it. Nothing else could precede mastering the life of the prison since anything else could run against the prisons laws and operation and be detrimental to his survival. Unlike the other POWs, Lawrence knew he needed patience in order to learn how the prison would let him live and what the prison would do to him if he violated its existence. Lawrence gave Song Da three months of his dormancy. Other POW's pushed the prison and paid dearly for it. It took less than one week for one of them to announce he was the SRO, senior ranking officer, and to begin a communication line between the cells throughout the prison. The U.S. Air Force officer, a Phantom jet pilot, started the communications by tapping out Morse code against the walls. The message was simple. Who are you, what is your rank, and have you been interrogated yet?

Every cell was occupied but only one gave no response, Lawrence's. The U.S.A.F. pilot increased his bravery by whispering to the cell next to him, asking that the message be passed along. Lawrence knew what would happen. The Viet Cong were fishing for information to be used against the prisoners. They were allowing communication to a point even though it is a violation in any POW camp; the violation is ignored in order to gain intelligence information to be used against the prisoners. Lawrence guessed the pilot, SRO as he appointed himself, would be the first taken down by the VC. In less than three days, the prison cell block had become a dormitory of bragging rights by each POW. They discussed bombs dropped, napalm burning villages, and laughed about the Vietnamese people trying to outrun cannon blasts from the fighter planes. For this, SRO was taken from his cell and the prisoners in every other cell were beaten and told to make no noise, no talking. The order was not necessary order since after the beatings; the cell block became quieter than a prayer at Mass in Rome. After one sun had gone past his door and another was slipping through the next morning, Lawrence heard the guards bring in the SRO pilot. He was still alive although he might have wished otherwise. Lawrence heard one guard tell another to not lift his head or he might strangle. The guard told the other to lift the prisoner's chin slightly so as to not rip out his throat. The guard laughed and said the man looked like a chicken being bound to a spit for roasting after tying the pilot's hands to his feet and knotting the other end of the rope around the his neck. "Yes", the other said, "he even clucked like a roasting bird" and then made imitated noises that set the other guard laughing. Lawrence was even taken aback when one guard asked the other if they were supposed to remove the ropes, ropes that would tightened around his neck if he relaxed his legs. Neither guard knew but both feared reprisal should they do something without direct orders. They left the man, his throat damaged for the rest of his life, stretched out like poultry on a cement bed in the cell. Soon after the guards left, the prisoner in the cell next to Lawrence's started tapping in Morse code to see if he could arouse the pilot, not knowing as did Lawrence that the man was bound, tied, and broken beyond repair.

The verbal communication ceased but for some strange and ridiculous reason the prisoner kept at the Morse code. Three days later the guards returned to the pilot's cell and unfettered him. In that time maybe the man had been able to reach the water, but bound he could never have eaten or used the toilet can. It was another two days before the SRO regained enough sanity and freedom from pain to Morse code to Lawrence. Lawrence kept to himself but guessed that his time would come. The discussion prior to the torture of the SRO had been the ludicrous advice to give the Viet Cong nothing but name, rank, and service number. But pilot's raspy voice and slow Morse coding changed many a brave soldier into a missive serf. Some held firm that the VC would not get anything out of them while others voiced a need to live. The former were the first to be removed to the interrogation room. Unlike the SRO, most came back beaten but not on the verge of death. The meat hook in the room, hanging like the one used in dressing deer in an abattoir, seemed to be their nemesis for each torture. The VC used it to hang prisoners so their body weight would put stress on their limbs. Thumbs were used as a joint attachment, ankles were bound and hanging a man upside down gave ready and fully used exposure to the prisoners chest and abdomen for beatings. The beatings produced the subsequent vomiting, but bound elbows forced behind the back and hanging the prisoner off the floor seemed to be a favorite. All of these tortures were used on any prisoner who would not answer questions or write confessions for the VC. If you did not sign a document attesting to your crimes, they would yank your shoulders out of your shoulder sockets. It did not take long for the soldiers that wanted to survive to realize how stupid it was to reach death in extreme physical pain for lack of making a ridiculous acknowledgement that he was a war criminal.

Lawrence had somehow beat the path to torture. All others were called down to the room, and unceremoniously dropped back hours later in to their cell, the horror still fresh in their minds and now a war criminal and violator of the U.S. Code of Conduct for a soldier.

Lawrence waited another two months before he began working on the other two challenges. He guessed that his service to the previous POW camp commander had followed him as had been promised. He did not expect freedom or even better treatment, but was relieved that his record had circumvented torture, no matter how minor this would have been. He had no qualms about admitting or and signing anything. After two months, he was not asked and had indeed been such a model POW that few VC even knew he was there. A shadow in the lea of the forest can make the predator almost invisible, and that was Lawrence.

Bread and water would reduce him to near death if he let that be his only nutrition. He knew this was POW camp protocol for the Viet Cong. A victim reduced to skin and bones was not a foe and he only use of such a life would be for propaganda and tradeoffs, so nutrition was kept at a minimum. Lawrence would not allow that to happen. After two months, he knew they were going to leave him alone, feeding him minimally, allowing him a five minute exercise period, and a bath once a week. The exercise and bathing protocol he could live with but he needed more nutrition, so he went back to catching roaches. Eating them provided a minimum of what he needed most, animal protein. Using them as bait could catch him more animal protein.

The pattern of cell life dictated his hours. Since nobody paid any attention to him, he could sleep when he wanted and even mumble or sing silently to himself. The first darkness became the best time for his hunt. He had saved some crusty Vietnamese bread and mixed the soft parts of the roaches with it. He unseated the drain grate so a space of about three quarters of an inch made an ellipse open to the cell floor. The roach bread bait was placed but inches from the opening. It only took two nights before the bait was gone. Unfortunately Lawrence never saw it go. Whatever took it visited Lawrence's cell quickly and quietly, mocking Lawrence. Lawrence made a new mixture for the very next night but placed it a few more inches away from the opening. This night enough moonlight entered the cell through the door transom that Lawrence saw movement, a claw he guessed, them a body slinking out, moving the drain plate a bit to grab the bait with a slim arm and quickly pulling it back into the drain. Lawrence knew he must be patient. He guessed the creature was either a mouse or small rat. Rushing at the creature would insure its escape, and probably insure a long wait before it would return again. It was time to use another weapon.

He gave the creature a week before he led the bait path away from the drain toward the wall opposite the cement bed. Lawrence had the jack knife opened and firmly gripped as he heard the faint scratch of the drain grate moving just below his position on the bed. The gray fur permitted some visibility to Lawrence as the rat shuffled to the bait, sniffed it, and rotated back to the drain. Lawrence jabbed once down through the fur. The rat's head turned to attack his predator, but could only nip at the jack knife blade before it collapsed dead. Lawrence knew animals well. He had nearly been gored to death by a deer when he assumed it was dead. Keeping the rat pinned to the concrete floor, he waited. The rat twitched a few times, but still Lawrence waited. Wiggling the knife blade a bit got no response and he dropped off the cement bed to attend to his meal. He cut off the head first, and then skinned the rat, not being too careful with the fur meat zone. Lawrence would only eat the meat off the rat's legs; the meat on the side of the mammal would be loaded with bacteria since that was where the fatty tissue layer insulated fur from skin. The legs were a constant source of rat cleanliness and thus posed less possibility of infectious disease. Lawrence stripped the fur from the legs and gnawed at the sinews of muscle. He had eaten raw meat many times and had not gotten too sick. There were two parts he needed the most. The first, the liver was the easiest to find in the dark. This would be loaded with the nutrients that his body needed to survive. He had anticipated catching vermin in a prison which was why he had asked George for a scalpel. The scalpel would give him abilities to whittle through just about any surface or wall with its sharpness and steel strength, but he could also use it as he had in the wilds to dissect small animals. Many a small mammal had become both a pelt and a meal because he knew how to dissect them. Now he would use that talent to feed himself. His fingers blindly bisected the rat's chest with the scalpel, cutting two doorways through the lower chest and abdomen. He could feel the blood warm and still pumping from a heart that had not acknowledged death. The liver was behind and slightly below the lungs, which were easily felt with his fingers. The liver, when lifted, felt like congealed pudding. After smelling it and getting that slight whiff of bile, he poured some of the water from his enameled jar over it and ate it. The taste was excellent, a delicacy to be enjoyed by a starved prisoner of war.

His hardest task came next, carving away the skull to expose the brain. Since he had to use the jack knife to bust through the head bone, he botched it and in the process nearly ruptured all the brain tissue beyond use. Its taste was a bit tart, but palatable. He would perfect brain dissection on future kills. He had not realized how long he had been at his midnight snack. A bit of light appeared above his head and he knew soon a guard would enter exchange his water jar, and remove his feces bucket, replacing it clean. He doubted that the guards sloshed through his feces to see if he was hiding any rat morsels, so he tilted the bucket and slide in what remained of the rat. He had not needed to rush since the guards were late, after having had difficulty removing another pilot from his cell. Lawrence leaned back on his cement bed, knees pulled up so his feet were not hanging over the edge, and felt his stomach's first roiling at this new organic matter now digesting inside of him. He listed to the growls and gas bubbling, hoping he could hold on until he got a new feces bucket.

The new food supply gave him an increase in energy, enough to start him on an exercise regimen that probably every prisoner in history performed. Lawrence could tell time by the sun shifts along the outer wall of his cell. He knew he could run in place, but needed the challenge of setting a mark of endurance. He tracked his time by the path of the sun increasing the duration as a challenge. This combined with pushups, sit ups, and his new diet, solved his physical disparity. The boredom from long dark hours locked in cells has always been the bane for prisoners. He could feed his physical system but the mental boredom sneered at him from the dark corners of his cell.

Lawrence began to challenge his memory with the many books he had read. He brought to mind the image of the cover and saw himself turning the pages. This he was easily remembered. The words, what about the words? Where were they Llewellyn? You saw them, you read them. They have to be inside your head, so bring them out. He needed to se the words. He had read them so they had to be inside his head; he needed to bring them out.

This he did by starting with an easy one, <u>Of Mice and Men</u>. He could remember the faded brown cover when he pulled it off the shelf at home when he was only a kid. It had that smell of its age, 1937. In his mind Lawrence had read the right book first and had even smelled the right book first. He loved reading from that day forward. It was a small book, maybe a hundred pages more or less. He wondered how many chapters, but as he saw the pages being turned, where there should have been chapter numbers, there were only chapter breaks. It began with George and Lennie hiking near a stream.

"Stop, that will not work", Lawrence told himself. Steinbeck wrote it as a story. From page one to page one hundred, it was a story. If the book is going to help me now, it has to be as the story. What happened, line by line, from page one to the offset beginning of page two? I know the story. I know George kills Lennie, but that's not what I need. I need the whole one hundred pages. It will stop the disease of ennui that this solitary, dark cell infects. Chapter One with no number, George and Lennie are …?

He knew then that the book began with, "A few miles south …" of somewhere. Where? Had to be California and Steinbeck's Mecca, Salinas.

Lawrence had found his panacea for surviving. He knew in his mind that he had read every word so his brain had to hold those words. He had to let them free. This he did. He read the book out loud from memory. It did not matter if the words were even close. As long as he read Steinbeck's story in his mind, he stayed alive and well.

***

Lawrence lived alone as a prisoner for six months, reading only a few books since the words from his memory rarely made sense. The reading, right or wrong, was his savior of sanity. He still kept away from the other POWs. They signaled each other, daring not to speak, that a mute or a corpse must be in Lawrence's cell. This was what Lawrence desired. It gave him autonomy within the prison. The United States Air Force pilot prisoners, excepting the SRO who still suffered from his tortures, were the first to discern the B 52 bombers going over head. Even Lawrence stopped to listen. Their sounds were weak but their bombs made deep, thud like wallops. While Song Da POW camp was too far from Hanoi and Route 1 to feel the impact, it could be appreciated if not for the killing sound traveling so many miles, then for the tremendous numbers of bombs dropped. There must have been thousands of bombs hitting and destroying the Ho Chi Minh trail. Every morning they came, and while their noise was not enough to shake tired POWs awake, those it did felt duty bound and obligated to wake those who slept. All believed that freedom was near at hand. It was not. It would be years away.

To Lawrence the bombers and their payloads meant more prisoners and maybe a firing squad. Freedom was no option for the defector. His avoidance of the other POWs succeeded in preventing recognition that Lawrence was getting special treatment. The enigma of a human being in his cell was now ended since the other prisoners heard Lawrence speaking to himself. Special treatment in Lawrence's case meant that he was not interrogated nor tortured, and allowed to speak aloud in his cell, reciting the phrases from books that most of POWs could probably not even remember. Lawrence kept his voice to a whisper, and the mystery cell prisoner stayed just that to the others. Some found release from the boredom by following Lawrence's rather fractured readings of Steinbeck and Hemingway, and requested to whomever the reader was a list of other books they would like to read if they could. Lawrence ignored these requests but the guards did not. The requesters were taken from their cells and beaten.

The Morse code and dark of night whispers concluded that Ho Chi Minh would soon agree to a truce now that we, America, were blowing up his industries and cities. Thousands of bombs and tons of explosives that were rocking the earth, turning over buildings, and laying flesh across miles of rice fields, would force North Vietnam to agree to a truce. The prisoners saw it in the guards. There were fewer tortures; less demand to sign confessions of war crimes, more vegetables and even fruit in the hope with their meals to combat the insipid scurvy that racked some prisoners.

"Yes," they thought, it's almost over. We'll be marching out of here soon.

They could not know that all the bombs did was force people to dig deeper holes, find better bomb shelters. One of the bombs would kill the Song Da Camp commander.

Lawrence had baited the grate and laid on to his back waiting for the triggering sound of the scurrying rat. Maybe tonight he could nail a snake since he had included more wet bread in his mixture. The small pythons seemed attracted to starch and made an excellent faux chicken. He would have to keep his ears attuned if he was to hear a snake. Instead, a small rat knocked the whole grate off of the drain, jumped onto his concrete bed, ran over his chest, and leapt to the chain link fence covering the ceiling. It could not get through. The flight of the rodent happened so fast that Lawrence could not react fast enough to grab his jack knife and have at him as the rat was trying to wedge through the impossibly small gaps. While grabbing the knife, another furry body landed on his stomach and launched upward toward the other rat. Its claws swatted at the rat, knocking it hard against the cement wall surrounding the locked steel door. Lawrence realized it was not another rat but a cat. He stopped moving, watching as best he could with his night vision what the cat would do. The rat was bleeding from a wound in its side. The cat walked over Lawrence's chest, staring into Lawrence's face with his green eyes, almost daring him to move. It seemed to be ignoring the rat. Just before reaching Lawrence's head, the cat jumped off the cement bed, turned to face the wounded rat, and squatted. Neither Lawrence nor the cat moved. At first Lawrence thought the cat was light in color, but with the light spilling into the cell as a prisoner was now taken away for interrogation for talking. He discovered the cat was a very dark grey. Lawrence knew that cat's eyes did not really glow in the dark, that it had to do with some type of reflection, but he was mesmerized by the green glow and the slight smirk of the cat's lips curled upward in a scary smile. The cat was waiting. Lawrence knew what was happening and could not decide whether he enjoyed the cat's arrogance leading to a kill or that it scared him more than it scared the rat. The rat decided to make a run for it. The only egress was the drain and to get there it had to make it past the cat. It did not and found its head buried inside the mouth of the cat. The rat pawed and clawed at the cat, but to no avail. The cat crunched down, breaking the rat's neck and grasping the body. With a quick yank, the rat was decapitated. Ejecting the head from his mouth, the rat's body became dinner for the cat. Lawrence reached down to pet the cat and was rewarded with a swipe that ran three scratches down the back side of his hand. So much for a pet.

***

The other POWs were unaware of the change in camp until it turned on them with a fury that broke many of them. Lawrence had learned about it from listening to guards. The American bombs were doing the job Nixon wanted, killing. Very few industrial destructions occurred because the North Vietnamese had very few industrial complexes to destroy. The VC did not have a sophisticated army but instead ran a terrorist guerrilla front. Their weapons of war were hand held and hand delivered. They did not need great Naval yards to build a great Navy because they had no Navy. They did not need airplane manufacturers for their Air Force, because they had no Air Force. Little warfare materials were made in North Vietnam; most originated in China or were shipped in from Russia. The United States could run bombings on infrastructure but little of it was hit. North Vietnam ran a silent and nearly invisible war front. Not one VC had ever been trained in fighting with a bayonet. A VC was more likely to cut your head off with a machete while you were on night duty smoking a joint. VC did not smoke joints. VC did not drink themselves into stupors. Bombs did not destroy the VC fighters, only their homes. VC fighters fought from the soil where their toes first touched and in the niche that raised them. A bomb from a B 52 was most likely to kill a soldier only if he was honoring his home with a visit. This is what happened to the camp commander.

The guards held on to their jobs, and for two days little changed. Lawrence knew better than to maintain his routine. Regardless of whom would now take command, that person's first task would be to establish discipline. It was SOP, standard operating procedure, for armies, industries, and businesses. In the Army it meant tight discipline and no lax behavior. In a military prison it meant hell for the prisoners.

On the third day after the bomb that killed the Song Da POW Camp commander, three prisoners were marched out of their cells and tied to three crosses in a rice field slightly uphill from the prison. All of the other prisoners were led out to the rice field under armed guard and stopped facing three prisoners. A dozen or more guards stood behind them with unlocked and loaded AK 47s aimed at them. It was a windy and very humid day. Lawrence guessed it was late April or early May and that soon the monsoon rains would blow in and blow over the prison. His eyes had trouble adjusting to the sun. He kept them shaded as did the many other prisoners, wanting to believe that what they were going to see was not really going to happen. A man tried to speak to Lawrence but Lawrence kept his eyes on the ground and maintained his subservient meek slouch. A guard rifle butted the man on the side of his head. The man went down. Lawrence saw the blood rushing out of his right ear and knew that man would never get up again.

The prisoners stood watching the three men tied to the three short white crosses for more than an hour. The three had been beaten about the face. Lawrence could see their mouths open and close, in need of water which they would never taste. None of the men had teeth, just a bloody gaping wound that used to be a mouth. From behind to his left, Lawrence heard a VC officer call his men to attention. A very tall man wearing formal military clothes walked slowly from prisoner headquarters out to the rice fields. Lawrence tried to keep his head down but could not. The man generated attention as he walked stiffly in military fashion, a tilt to his head was off military. The front of his uniform was covered by a cloak, like a serape interwoven with dark green and dark brown wool. At his waist was a leather holster buckled, containing a pistol. The heat and humidity was getting to everybody. One prisoner collapsed and as a guard helped him up, the tall man turned to him and spoke very quietly. The guard let the prisoner drop, and bowed deeply, begging forgiveness, only to be ignored. The tall man scanned every prisoner on the rice field. No one, not even Lawrence, dared to return his gaze. Done with his intimidation of the prisoners, he spoke to his troops and the prison guards not looking at them but instead gazing deeply into the eyes of the prisoners. No prisoner would understand but Lawrence.

"I am Colonel Tora Togo. I am the commander of this Prisoner of War Camp. You, the soldiers of the National Liberation Forces of Vietnam, must never end this war. It will never be over until there are no more Americans killing our women and children. Look at these prisoners!"

None of the guards looked. They were too scared to lose eye contact with Colonel Togo. "I said look at them! They killed your people, as they did mine. They do it from airplanes, unleashing explosions that rip apart your children's bodies. Look, do you see a brave warrior here? No, Americans are cowards."

He walked to the three men tied to the crosses. "See this man? He is a pilot. He dropped napalm on children. How brave is he? You, look at me!" Colonel Togo switched to English. Lawrence could detect a slight inflection that was more Japanese than Vietnamese.

The pilot did not lift his head so Colonel Togo put a pistol to his head and blew his brains out. Togo repeated the same challenge to each man's crime, blowing out their brains after receiving no response.

Colonel Togo walked among the prisoners, "Americans are cowards, all of you. Who here dropped bombs? What, no show of hands?"

Togo stood next to Lawrence and Lawrence kept his head down and mouth shut. "You," he said in edged English and pointing to a man in front of Lawrence, "did you fly a bomber?"

There was no response. "I have asked you a simple question." Togo was smiling, trying to catch the man's eyes. He stooped down, knees bent, and even in that position Lawrence noticed that Togo was indeed very tall. From the back Lawrence could see that the cloak partially hid a very light yellow protuberance going up Togo's neck. It looked like rubbery meat with red veins paralleling each other up and down the neck. Togo neither favored nor tried to hide the disfigurement. "Come on, soldier, I know you were a ground trooper. It's easy to tell. Like us you're dirty."

Togo repeated what he told the soldier in Vietnamese for the guards and they laughed. "So there is no one in this pack that flies airplanes, huh? How about if I make a deal with you? If you are a pilot and you have dropped bombs on Vietnamese, my Vietnamese, Ho Chi Minh's Vietnamese, raise your hand and I will send you home."

Togo looked around. There were no hands being raised by the prisoners. In Vietnamese he told his troops that that they must think I am sending them back home in a body bag, and he and the guards laughed. He went back to English, "I do not break my word. I am an Asian. If you admit to me right now that you have dropped bombs on Vietnamese civilians, you will be sent home unharmed."

Still there were no takers and Colonel Togo shook his head. As he started to walk back to the prison camp, several guards went to untie the dead bodies but he stopped them.

"As they have left my people dead to be picked apart by scavengers, so I will let their souls rot in the bellies of vermin. Leave them."

The change was immediate. Within hours all prisoners were marched under guard from their cells and stripped naked. The cells were scoured with high pressure hoses, dissolving any and all nooks and crannies gouged by prisoners to hide contraband. Anything found drew harsh punishment and torture. One man had been scratching the days he spent in prison with a small nail. Caught, the guards broke all of his fingers in both hands. Lawrence had sensed what was coming, warned by his ability to translate and interpret the language. His last feces bucket carried with it both his scalpel and jack knife. He had almost thought about hiding them back in the drain but gave them up. Colonel Togo sent soldiers under every building, pulling pipes and inspecting them. A cell containing anything other than water and slime in the pipes, gained that prisoner punishment and torture. Lawrence was surprised how many other soldiers had used the same manner of concealment.

Lawrence had gone many months without interrogation but now his time was up. Three days after the camp was thoroughly searched and prisoners shuffled to other buildings, Lawrence was yanked out of his cell and dragged to the headquarters building. He was to face Colonel Tora Togo.

***

"Sit down. Major Arens," said Tora Togo, "it seems that somehow you've managed to flow through our camp here without ever being interrogated? How's that?"

Lawrence was flanked by two guards, their hands placed firmly on his shoulders. He kept diminutive, face down, acting subservient, "I don't bother people."

"Bother people? You don't bother people? There's no record of you even existing here. None at all. Are you really a soldier? What's your name, rank and service number?"

"Major Arens," said Lawrence giving Togo a fake number.

"There's something strange about you, Arens. What outfit were you with when captured?"

"I don't have to give that to you."

"Ah yes, the Geneva Convention. You of course know my response to that?"

Lawrence knew but would not answer.

"You're a war criminal. You've committed civil crimes against the people of North Vietnam," said Togo not loudly. Togo let the accusation settle in, sat back, and observed Lawrence.

Lawrence made eye contact with Tora Togo and did not flinch. It was obvious after the rice field executions that Colonel Togo was playing by his own rules. Togo no longer wore a serape or cloak about his shoulders and Lawrence could see his disfigurement clearly now. Togo caught Lawrence eyeing his scars and thought Lawrence would avoid more contact. Lawrence did not.

"You see my scars, Arens? Keloids, the strips of tissue are keloids produced from burns."

Lawrence still kept quiet. Togo was trying to lead him somewhere and Lawrence knew to never willingly let a predator bait you.

"I am not a killer, Arens. I am not even a Vietnamese. I am Japanese, Arens. Do you want to know why I am an officer in the North Vietnamese Army?"

Lawrence brought his eyes up to and directly staring into Togo's and said not a word. Togo would not drop his eye contact, nor would Lawrence. Keeping eye contact, Togo finally stated the situation very clearly to Lawrence.

"When your country destroyed my country, Japan, it left us without ever being able to have an army, or for that matter a navy, air force, any military force. It left me as a mutilated ten year old boy with massive keloids covering his face, walking the abandoned streets of Hiroshima, but worse than that I was an outcast, pariah to my people. We that survived were scorned and despised by our own people, normal people. They spit on us, ran us out of their communities because of our deformities. I hated America for doing this to me, but also Japan for making me a homeless mutation."

Lawrence had had enough. "If you're trying to justify torturing me, don't. Just do it."

Colonel Togo smiled. He was beginning to like this man. "Arens, is that your name?"

Not waiting for an answer he continued.

"Despite our surrender conditions to have no military, there was an intelligence police, notice the word police. They were called the Kempei Tai and existed in Manchuria during the war and stayed. By the time the war ended the Kempei Tai had refined torture to a fine art. As an outcast in my own country, I was sent to live with relatives in Southeast Asia. There I learned about the Kempei Tai and joined them. The organization stayed active but not visible for much of the post war era. Ironically, they trained Trinh Minh who would become a revolutionary, fighting the French and Viet Minh in Vietnam. He was killed in the early 50's after successfully leading attacks and personally assassinating a French general. The Kempei Tai were responsible for me going to college in England where I got a degree in epidemiology. Do you know what that is?"

"The study of pathogens, usually those that cause epidemics."

"Very good Arens. I left the Kempei Tai because I really didn't like the politics. I got a doctor's degree in medicine and pledged myself to South East Asia. I saw what was happening in Vietnam with the French and joined against the French as a medical officer in the VC army. It didn't take long to see that the hated French were no better than the United States puppet governments. This was an opportunity to return the pain I suffered. Ho Chi Minh himself swore me in as a Colonel in the NLF."

Toro paused, walked around the room a bit and kneeled in front of Lawrence. "Too much, I am giving you too much. There's something about you Arens."

They were interrupted by a soldier carrying a food tray. In Vietnamese Togo asked if Lawrence would like a bite to eat before his torture. Lawrence passed the test by not responding until Togo apologized for slipping into Vietnamese. He told Lawrence that he was fluent in six different languages and sometimes one or the other would just erupt out of his mouth. Lawrence knew it was a lie. He always knew when somebody was lying to him. Lawrence passed the test.

"What we have here is a delicacy that you snobbish Americans seem to gag on even at its thought," said Togo removing the cloth from the plate. Lawrence had wondered what happened to the grey cat.

As Tora Togo began to eat he spoke again in Vietnamese to the guard who held a rifle. The man was behind Lawrence. Togo told the man that when he said the word 'now' in English that he was to hit Lawrence in the back of his head with the rifle butt.

"There is something you need to know, Arens. Need to know about America's highly flaunted CIA and military intelligence. It is full of holes, especially in South Vietnam. My guess is that one out of every three South Vietnamese military personnel is an agent for the PLF. We know nearly every move your troops make. The United States unknowingly shares nearly all of its troop movements with the South Vietnamese. More than that, we know every KIA and MIA that your Air Force and Army registers. We know them by name, rank, service number, and whom their relatives are in the United States. As soon as an American is killed or captured, you send telegrams and chaplains to the relatives. Guess what Major Arens? There is no Major Arens."

Silently while staring Lawrence in the eye, Tora Togo whispered to the guard behind Lawrence, "now."

Lawrence never flinched, and took the base of the rifle butt at the back of his skull as the black world followed.

***

Lawrence awoke to a new cell much like his old except now he was shackled to leg irons attached at the end of the cement bed. There was more light than in his previous cell since the transom above the door was without a shutter to close. His right rear side of his head hurt but the pain could be ignored. The dizziness stayed with him for another day. Being shackled meant he could not maneuver to the defecation bucket; he had to lay in his urine and feces. That did not bother him as much as not having water. The injury to his head throbbed and he knew that taking in some fluids would help ease the pain. Trying to force the pain away, he lifted his head a few inches at a time until he could almost sit supported by his hands. The dizziness lessened but was replaced by nausea as he vomited alongside the cement bed. While unconscious he had urinated himself adding to the foul smell of his miniscule prison cell. Smell was the least of his troubles if the rifle butt head injury did not convince Tora Togo that he could not speak Vietnamese. He had not even closed his eyes in anticipation of the blow to his head.

Lawrence was troubled by Togo's comments about Viet Cong intelligence infiltrating the United States Army. After My Lai and Lawrence's disappearance with the Quyen family, he was most probably listed as MIA. He seriously doubted that any officer in the field after witnessing what American troops had done could claim that he had defected. Lawrence was a small stain that could be removed with paperwork. Still it concerned him. If he was identified as a deserter, or even worse as a defector, not only could he never return home but his wife and child would not be eligible for any benefits including his life insurance. This haunted him but Togo had nearly erased it. If indeed the VC had access to American KIAs and MIAs, then surely they would have access to deserters or defectors. Togo would know Lawrence's name, rank, and service number. He apparently did not. No matter what, Lawrence must remain unidentified. Should the war end and he survived, America would court martial him and probably send him to a firing squad. As bad as that would be, Togo could do worse by using Lawrence as propaganda. After smearing the reputation of an American traitor, the North Vietnamese would set Lawrence up as one of the most hunted defected soldier in United States history. His family would be left dirt poor and living in shame. He knew that Evelyn would be fired from her job and his son would become the target of every loyal American's revenge.

The cell door's rusted hinges groaned and despite the clouding of his vision from the rifle butt, Lawrence saw Tora Togo standing in the doorway.

"This is a rather odiferous place to live, Arens. It seems you lack any bowel control and I'm glad you declined my offer of food. This mess on the floor would be almost beyond countenancing with cat meat regurgitated," said Togo

A guard came in carrying a water hose, larger than most garden hoses but not quite as big as a fire hose. A steady stream of water with considerable force flew out of the nozzle, first spraying Lawrence, then washing down the entire cell. When finished another guard came in and unshackled Lawrence.

"Take off your clothes Arens. Give them to the guard. When we have you washed up, he will give you some clean ones. Here's a bar of soap. I would have left you unshackled after the guard hit you except I was concerned that you might hurt yourself once you awoke."

The guards being squeamish about nudity looked to Togo for further directions. Togo ordered them to wash Lawrence. The verbal force of his order left no hesitation. Lawrence saw the water run down the drain without backing up.

"Yes, the drain is clear Arens. It will be interesting when I find out who gave you a scalpel and the jack knife."

As he left the cell, Togo told the guards to bring the prisoner to his office once he was cleaned and dried. As he was going he loudly added that if the prisoner was harmed in any way, both guards would be put in prison. The guards were very condescending to Lawrence, demonstrating Tora Togo's power. They led Lawrence, now clean and fully attired with what appeared to be brand new prison garb, to Togo's office where Lawrence had been rifle butted. Togo was sitting at a conference table to the right of Lawrence.

"Arens have a seat, please."

Lawrence sat down at the only vacant seat which was directly across from Togo. In front of Lawrence were plates of food.

"There is no cat or dog here. Most American's like eggs for breakfast so I had some made up for you. The meat is pig meat from the hind quarters, ham I believe you would say. The juice is from local grapes and the coffee I import from South Korea."

Lawrence knew to go slow, protecting what was left of his depleted stomach and intestines. The food was excellent, especially the ham which did not have the heavy saltiness common to American hams. The juice was pure without added water. Only the coffee was disappointing since Lawrence liked the brutally harsh American coffees imported from Columbia. He did not know what was happening, but would not pass up a chance to bolster his energy.

"How's your head?"

"Hurts but it'll go away."

"Arens, do you remember our discussion about the Kempei Tai, Japan's military police?"

"Sounded like the Gestapo."

"Very close, Arens, very close. The Gestapo had an edge on the Kempei Tai because they were more likely to torture then kill. When you do that, the reason for torture is masochism, not intelligence, and also not very intelligent. That doesn't mean that some officers did not thrive on the masochism, since many did. I border on both sides. Torture works. I hope you will not have to experience it. I've had very few failures getting what I needed. Despite what you find masochistic, I am enamored with the effect on certain prisoners."

Lawrence finished his coffee and Togo poured him another cup. The longer he kept Togo talking, the more nutrients and fluids he could add to his body.

"We use basically six tortures here. Do we kill many during these tests of loyalty? A few, but sometimes it's hard to distinguish when a man is close to death and might only be faking unconsciousness. Actually the person is only endangering himself. Prolonged pain leads to death. I rarely use it. I believe it is the anticipation after three or four times of torture that turns the prisoner, giving up what I seek."

Lawrence leaned back in his chair. He had no idea how much torture he could take but since he had no control over it, he was better off ignoring it.

"Arens, I should probably just kill you, get it over with. You irritate me. Why won't you admit who you are?"

"Maybe your network of espionage doesn't work as well as you think."

"That's a good possibility. I have seen something in you that I rarely see. You won't cede to death. You'll take whatever I give you and die. Or will you?"

Togo stood up and walked about the room, "I rarely lose my temper. It is dangerous to let your R complex run your brain, that reptilian …"

Lawrence was getting edgy, "I know what the reptilian complex is. You're a doctor, a doctor whom specializes in epidemics. How does that fit into what you are doing here?"

"It doesn't Lawrence. I grew up in Manchuria, a pariah from my home in Japan. The Kempei Tai thrived in the area where I lived. I studied them and saw they could put me into a position to rectify what happened to me." Unconsciously Togo ran his hand up and down the keloid scars at his neck and continued, "I give in return to the United States invaders the pain and horror they gave me. The Kempei Tai saw in me a recruit with both great intelligence and a bitter need for revenge. They sponsored me."

That did not answer Lawrence's question but spoke to Togo's reason for living.

"I need to know who you are and why you keep it hidden, Arens. I have tortured many Americans during this war which is why I am here now. None refused the standard name, rank, and service number, not one out of hundreds. Why now? Why you? Will I be able to draw it out of you? You do not communicate with your fellow prisoners. Why?"

"It's against the rules."

Togo walked directly to Lawrence's chair, put his hands on the arms of the chair so his face was not more than inches from Lawrence's. "In America you have a term for what you just said. Bullshit. I think you don't want your country to know who you are."

He backed off and walked to the double window facing the valley where a storm that would soon flood the Song Da River was generating. "I have my favorite ways. The basest is to perpetually beat you, rifle butt you like yesterday. But it knocks any sense out of the victim so his information is not very good. The Kempei Tai basic five is usually the best. How would you like the water torture Arens? We tie you down and stuff your nostrils with cotton and mouth with gauze, then pour water into you through the gauze until you pass out. The beauty is the inherent fear all humans have of drowning. We've mastered it. We know how to bring you back to life. The problem is that in pumping your abdomen by jumping up and down on it does too much damage so we have to be very careful and do it slowly."

"With many of the pilots we get here, finger torture works quite well. They watch as their hands become almost useless, perhaps forever. We take pencils and jam them between fingers, right into and through the membranes between each finger, and then we wrap them tightly together, as tight as we can. This works good during interrogation. You know why?"

Lawrence smiled but it was a weak one.

"The body adjusts to the pain. It becomes numb, the fingers become numb, but not completely. If you ask the prisoner a question and he refuses to answer or lies, you squeeze his hand. I've seen men literally jump out of their seat into the air when their hands were squeezed. The wrist torture is a lot like this also. Have you ever noticed the hook in the ceiling of some of our rooms? No, you've never been in those rooms have you Arens? They are there for hanging animal carcasses and prisoners. The simplest is with handcuffs, long chained handcuffs. We shut them as tight as possible around the wrists. We then lift you, putting the chain over the hook. Underneath we put a chair. The toes barely touch the seat of the chair so that the strain on the wrists begins immediately. It's interesting to watch a prisoner's face. At first, there's a bit of disbelief, as if this isn't much of a torture. In a few minutes the pain increases and we see the agony in the eyes. I know when to start, right at the point of fear. Fear Arens. When fear shows, then the torture starts. The first time, nearly everybody is brave. You know honor your country, and don't give them anything. I ask a question and get no answer, except maybe name rank, and service number. That's okay because then I kick the chair out. It's almost immediate, Arens. You watch their eyes bulge as the pain runs down their arms, through their shoulders, and to the chest. I have been told that it is very much like a heart attack. Eventually they lose consciousness. We raise them back up on the chair and douse them with cold water. It takes a while, but waking with less pain brings the knowledge that more pain will come again."

At this point Lawrence was no more than a spectator, watching a crazed maniac put on a theatrical performance. Tora Togo had gone over the edge, was wrapped up in his description of tortures and his mania.

"Stop," said Lawrence, "you are past your purpose, Doctor Togo. You are worse than those that haunt you. You have lost control, which you said you don't do."

Togo turned on Lawrence and Lawrence steeled himself to be hit.

Togo responded, "how perspicacious of you Arens. You are correct. I have to back off, which at times is difficult. You see very well the inside of me. I have an anger that will never be assuaged. However, I will not use it on you."

Togo called a guard into the room, told him to take Lawrence back to his cell, and as Lawrence was being removed Togo said, "you see better than most Arens. Dr. Tora Togo? I haven't been called that for many years. Can you also see that I will not stop until I have what I want?"

"You've lost your soul, Dr. Togo. You are here for the people of North Vietnam, but you are after what you want. It is no longer the same."

***

The torture started the next morning. Lawrence was handcuffed behind his back and forced to kneel. A thick bamboo stalk two inches in diameter was shoved behind his knees. Immediately his knee joints roared in pain, the force running down his lower legs and up to his thigh muscles. A guard stood behind Lawrence keeping both hands on Lawrence's shoulders to prevent him from rising up from the pain. After ten minutes, the guard moved away since Lawrence's knee joints no longer had the power to raise his body. He rested in a squat. Another ten minutes passed before Tora Togo came into the room.

"Arens, your knees should be nearing numbness now. How about a little stretch? We'll lift you up to get some circulation back into those knee joints," said Togo waving to the guards and ordering them to lift Lawrence up, grabbing him under his arm pits from both sides.

At first Lawrence's legs would not straighten and he dangled with his knees still bent as the guards lifted him. Gradually the legs relaxed, easing some of the pain. The guards continued to hold him since they knew from previous victims that he would fall over if they let go of him now.

"Arens? Arens is not your name. What harm would there be giving me your real name?"

Lawrence gave no response.

"Let go of him," said Togo.

Lawrence went down, his legs squeezed thigh to calf with the bamboo pole between them. He screamed . When he fell over, Togo cursed the guards in Vietnamese telling them to keep him upright.

Togo stooped down in front of Lawrence and spoke, "you helped me yesterday, Arens. You've made me see that I cannot go over the edge using the torture for my own reasons. Isn't it in all of us? Isn't it begging that we want from other human beings? That absolute control? Your name, just that, and we're done for today."

Lawrence said nothing. He hardly paid any attention to what Tora Togo was saying. The pain in his knee caps was horrible but he noticed a numbness setting in, a numbness that started not in his knees but in his toes and continued up to his calves. When Tora Togo saw the lessening of pain he stood up in front of Lawrence, raised his left foot, and stumped downward on Lawrence's upper right thigh. The pain that shot through his knee knocked him unconscious. Togo had the guards untie Lawrence and return him to his cell. He also told them to make sure the man had fresh water and meals until tomorrow's torture.

***

Lawrence woke up in the middle of the night believing that he had no legs. He reached down quickly, fearing he would find stumps but was rewarded with finding his legs still there. It took over an hour for him to loosen them up. He noticed the fresh water and tray filled with food. He felt like the fattened calf, but ate anyway. Lawrence tried to deal in reality. How long could he last? Could hold out until death? Togo had chosen a torture that would not physically kill him. If he thought that he would give up, concede to Toro's questions, how could he force Togo to kill him without an answer to his question? Using some of the fresh water, he ripped off his shirt and washed his face.

***

"Arens, another day? Do we need the bamboo pole?"

Lawrence stared into Togo's eyes and spoke, "I have lived a short life but I have learned an ability many others do not have. For some reason I can tell when somebody is lying. What do you have to gain here? Why do you need anything from me?"

"It is my job to learn the name, rank, and service number of all prisoners so that when the war ends, I can help them return ..."

"You're lying Dr. Togo. Try again."

"Let me finish," said Togo, now a bit riled. Lawrence noticed this and stored it in memory. "During a truce there is usually an exchange of information about prisoners of war to insure that both sides are acting in good faith ..."

"Dr. Togo, you are a liar."

Togo smiled at Lawrence, motioned to the guards to get the bamboo pole ready and spoke, "propaganda, Arens. Pure propaganda. We use information about prisoners to show the world the kind of imperialists that are attacking Vietnam. With enough torture we can actually get some prisoners to testify in front of cameras or tape them for radio broadcasts. Does that satisfy your talent? Am I now telling the truth?"

"What about you Dr. Togo? Why do you do it?"

Tora Togo had not lost his composure completely. Lawrence rattled him. Togo gave Lawrence credit for guessing his lies.

"I do it because I hate Americans. It is rather interesting contemplating your country, Arens. The commandant before me used to tape prisoners that talked. He would use it against them as a reason for punishment but also he would find that sometimes the prisoners gave away very valuable information. You never talked with your neighbors, which I found surprising. Even more surprising was when you did talk, nobody knew what you were saying. Nobody knew what to make of it. I did. Every prison commandant knows the hardest trial for a prisoner is boredom. You didn't communicate with anybody but you talked, read out loud as if you had a book. What the previous commandant didn't know was that you did have a book. It was in your head. I believe the first one was <u>Of Mice and Men</u>. Am I correct?"

"Yeah."

"You went through a couple other writers but you came back to Steinbeck. I've read Steinbeck. It would obviously be impossible even for the greatest mind that ever lived to be able to repeat from memory a book, but you tried. You weren't even close."

"Maybe not the words Dr. Togo."

"Yes, amazingly you got many of the chapters down to what they were about. Right now you are on Chapter Ten in <u>The Grapes of Wrath</u>, where the Joads have packed up the truck and headed west. Am I right?"

"I thought I was on Chapter Nine, but as you're checking on me, you must have the book. I guess I missed a chapter."

"Did you know that Steinbeck wrote another version of The Grapes of Wrath before his 1939 book?"

"No, what one?"

"<u>In Dubious Battle</u>, in 1936. Title's based on a line from "Paradise Lost". Here you are fighting to stop communism from clacking like dominoes falling into democracy's world and John Steinbeck himself was a communist. It's very clear in <u>The Grapes of Wrath</u> and obvious in

<u>In Dubious Battle</u>. Don't you find that rather ironic, considering this war?"

Lawrence knew Togo judged him wrong and for some odd reason felt an empathy with him.

"You don't understand me Dr. Toro. What I will tell you is that I'm here through no choice of my own. Probably half of the

Americans in Vietnam did not choose to be here. What you want from me? I refuse you but not for my country."

Tora Togo smiled. Lawrence had broken through the silence. It was a step. The guards stared at Togo. He directed them to administer the bamboo pole confinement.

"Then it should mean nothing to you to tell me your name."

Lawrence did not respond and four hours later was carried unconscious to his cell. Again he woke up in pain, this time taking much longer to abate. Serious and possibly permanent damage was being done to his knees. To get to his food and water he had to roll off the cement bed and lean on his side to eat and drink. He crawled back into bed using his arms, his legs feeling like dead slabs of meat dragging behind him. He could not feel his toes, so he reached down and began kneading his body with his fingers, starting at his thighs and going down to his toes. At first he thought he had made a mistake since the massaging not only brought his extremities back to life, but came with great pain. He had to stop something, either living or Tora Togo. He knew the torture would continue. Togo's was a method designed to break him, using the pain of torture and creating the horror of anticipating the next day's torture.

***

Tora Togo kept the torture the same, choosing not to switch to other methods of the Viet Cong. Those came too close to death, especially the water torture. Each day Lawrence was brought into the interrogation room, his hands shackled behind his back and his ankles shackled with a two foot span of chain. Once in place, the bamboo pole was brought out and positioned behind Lawrence's knees. Tora Togo had only one question for Lawrence, his true name. Lawrence refused to answer and was left on his knees, thighs flat against the back of his calves. Periodically Togo increased the time by fifteen minutes, using it as a mental challenge to Lawrence's ability to accept the torture. Lawrence had fought the pain well for up to two hours, but heading into the third hour, it had become unbearable. Not only was there direct pain in the center of his knee, the pain was shooting up the back of his tibia to his hamstring. Worse was what happened when the torture ended. Where initially he could stand when lifted off the pole if given a few staggering moments of gaining his sea legs, now he could not unbend his knees enough to walk. He had to be carried to his cell. It would take hours of agonizing pain for him to slowly ease forward and draw back his lower legs. Tora Togo was a master of mind torture. First, he kept Lawrence physically well by providing him with nutritious meals and all the sleep he needed. Next, he started each torture session with small talk, picking away at Lawrence with miniscule questions about his home life and family and what he did back in the United States. Lawrence did not respond. Finally, the poles would come.

Tora Togo knew that he had to prod Lawrence to speak. He was irritating Togo with his silence, pushing Togo dangerously close to losing his temper with Lawrence. Tora Togo wanted Lawrence to lash out, as every other prisoner at Song Da River Camp had done. Sooner or later all of the POWs erupted, except Lawrence. Togo would get in Lawrence's face, accuse him of crimes against humanity, call him a baby killer, but so far Lawrence had not flinched. Togo would keep at him.

Lawrence had to force Tora Togo to either kill him or write him off as confessing his true identity. He would not die from the torture that faced him here every day. His mind was wandering day by day. The more the pain flooded his tendons, ligaments, and muscles, the more likely Lawrence would pass out. Lawrence hoped that it Tora Togo would lose his temper and execute Lawrence or he would find Lawrence's unconsciousness intolerable and give up on the interrogation.

"I have asked you numerous times if you have any children Arens," said Tora Togo. "Surely admitting to being a father offers no compromise in your reticent attitude?"

Lawrence had to push, either execution or relief from the torture. Once down on his legs, the pain was immediate. "I don't understand why you hate me so much, Dr. Togo? Is this some kind of personal vendetta against me?"

"Arens, Arens, you take us in circles. I have told you my history. Does it not let you see my hatred?"

"No, it's a cute little story seemingly designed to draw me into accepting your Hiroshima tale as a reason for you to become a masochistic voyeur."

"Are you saying I am a liar? Doesn't that invalidate your claimed ability to see the truth in others?"

"I only sense people lying. Most people have that ability to some extent." Lawrence tried to ease the pressure off his patella by raising and shifting his buttocks. It did not help much and Lawrence was feeling dizzy.

"But you are saying I use my pain to inflict pain on you?"

"That's true."

Togo did not know how to react but continued. "What would it take for you to see ..."

Tora Togo stopped when he realized Lawrence had tricked him into an angry state. He could not lose control. He walked over to a table against the far wall, the only wall with a window. The monsoon season had spent much of its wind but the rain was unceasing. He brought over a high back chair and told the guard to get the other one. He then directed both the guards to lift Lawrence up so that his arm pits would rest on the chair's backs. This eased Lawrence's pain greatly since the pressure reeking pain in his knees abated once he was no longer squatting. Togo pulled over his personal desk chair and sat directly in front of Lawrence.

"Read the truth in me Arens. I will tell you my tale as you call it, and when I finish then you call me a liar."

Lawrence stayed quiet, enjoying the respite from the pain in his knees.

"Do you remember when you were ten Arens? Still quiet? When I was ten, I got these flesh scars on my neck," said Tora Togo. To Lawrence's disbelief, Togo took off his shirt, exposing his entire side of massive scar tissue as ugly as that on his neck. "They are keloids, keloids that come not just from the flash but the radiation that followed, not allowing my body to heal. That day lives forever, that day, August sixth nineteen forty-five. I was up early. I went outside and played soldier. I'm sure you used to play soldier Arens?"

There was no response so Togo continued; "only if you ever played it, it wouldn't be as scary as it was to a little Japanese kid. I was practicing how to die, to die honorably for my Emperor. As ten year olds, what do you think we were taught to practice during war?"

Lawrence needed this rest so he looked for questions that could do him little harm, "I guess you had to play war and practice shooting the enemy?"

"That is a good guess but a wrong one, Arens. We were taught in elementary school how to hold a land mine and jump in front of one of your tanks. Not very heroic, is it? But let me continue. I was practicing blowing up American tanks when I saw two small silver streaks cross the sky at the same time my mother called me inside for breakfast. She saved my life by 45 seconds, because as I was walking into the wash up room, ready to close the door, the flash ran through my house, blowing the door of the wash room closed. It seared this side of my body."

"This side of my body was charred by that flash. I tried to push open the door to get to my family but thirty seconds after that flash, a blast blew away most of our home. The roar was like a large animal growling over your head. I did not need to open the door because there was no door. It had been ripped off."

"Now try to imagine who I was trying to see? Who, Arens? Who would I seek after that?"

"Your family, probably your mother."

"Good, Arens. Consider yourself. Your mother is only a door away from you, your father in the front room reading a newspaper. Suddenly no door, no house, only a huge pile of debris that was once the kitchen. There was no longer a front room, no father. Under the remnants of the kitchen I saw my mother's back, I could identify her clothes. At least I thought what I saw were her clothes. I went to them and pulled. They were only pieces of what was left of her clothes, shredded rags. Underneath these rags was my mother's naked body; her clothes had been burned off. When I tried to lift her, my hands came away with folds of skin so I was only able to turn her. Her face was covered with blisters and swollen to twice its normal size. Strips of her skin were stuck to my hands. Her right eyeball hung down on her cheek. An eyeball, Arens, my mother's eyeball was just hanging there. I was so naïve that I tried to fit it back into the socket."

Tora Togo stopped and walked away. His blood pressure was rising. This would not be good for either him or Lawrence. He poured water out of the carafe on his desk into two glasses. He brought one to Lawrence but since he was still shackled the guard had to dispense it. Toro drank the other glass of water.

"I had been burned once, small flesh burns, and I remembered how my mother treated them. I tried to find the cupboard where my mother kept cans of food and other items, but I could not find it. It was crazy. Here I was, alive with burns on my side, but still able to move, function. My father had been totally incinerated, my mother was probably near death, and I was searching for olive oil. And I found it under some boards that were still smoking from the aftermath of the flash. I poured some into my hands and applied what I could to her skin. It didn't help. Every time I smoothed the oil on, strips of her flesh were wiped away. I stopped when I realized that during that whole time, my mother never stirred, not one movement. I wanted to shake her, make her come awake, but was afraid of ripping more skin off her body. I refused to accept she was dead, but I knew she was."

"I walked toward the area where my father had been reading his newspaper, like he did every morning. He was a cripple and had not been called to duty during the war. There was nothing left of him, I thought. As I went through the rubble I got my last sight of my father, his burnt shadow imprinted on the living room wall that was now lying on the ground. At times I wish I had saved at least a piece of that shadow, the last remnant of the Togo family."

"What I saw that day is burned deeper in my mind than my father's shadow. Dante would add another layer to hell with what you Americans did."

Lawrence spoke, "I was four years old."

"You in the plural Lawrence. See, you can give me information can't you? I know how old you are now. There are two smells that nobody ever forgets in war, Arens. What do you think they are?"

"One is death, the other rotting flesh."

"Yes, it was everywhere but covered at times with what might even be worse, burnt flesh. I went to the river, the Honkawa River. I was not alone. Thousands of victims were there, trying to wash away the burns. They did not know better, that the water only hurt them more, so much so that most died as soon as they entered the river. Bodies on bodies floated down the river. Bodies scraping off their own flesh whenever they rubbed against the trees in the water, or the refuse floating near them, or if they hit the shoreline, this was my world. Skin and peoples scalps stuck like adhesive to anything it touched and the odor made me vomit, over and over it made me vomit. Bodies with open wounds had intestines hanging out, blinded eyeballs hanging tethered to their face by sinews. On the shore I saw an infant crawling over its dead mother's body trying to nourish itself from the dead mother's nipples."

Lawrence was mesmerized by Tora Togo's story. He had read books about the war, none better than John Hersey's Hiroshima. Here was a man, a mere boy at ground zero of one of the deadliest bombings in history.

"Wasn't there anybody alive?"

"There was a man, maybe a boy, that walked along and who kept repeating, over and over again "where's the sunrise that his family never saw." He had pleats of face skin falling off his cheeks and forehead, exposing the raw muscle below but he kept talking about the beautiful cobalt blue sky being filled with a massive cloud of red, yellow, white, blue, and purple colors swirling like a monsoon above his head. I could not believe that he saw beauty in the killer."

"These, Arens," said Togo pointing to the exposed keloids going up the side of his face and ending at his ear "these keloids were to be our badge. Not a badge of honor or bravery or duty to our country, but a badge of your country's inhumanity."

Tora Togo had nearly forgotten that Lawrence was there. Togo had never gone into such detail with another human. Maybe he should have. Now the anger exploded, more anger than he ever felt before. "The flies did not get killed. The flies swarmed to the dead and the living almost as fast as the bomb ran its course of destruction on Hiroshima. I was only ten but the pity I felt hurt me. I tried to help others but felt like I should just let them die. As I roamed about trying to find a place, any place to be safe, to get some drinkable water and maybe some food, I came across a man lying on the edge of the river with massive burns and flaps of dead skin. I could see lumps under his skin, lumps that were moving. I thought I was too tired and therefore was imagining things. I looked closer and his skin was so thin that I could see the moving lumps were not my imagination. The lumps were maggots under his skin, eating away at his body. I ran away but could not run the reality. I came to another man whose face was badly burned, pus oozing out of his eyes and nostrils. I scooped some water from a rain barrel into an old glass that had survived the explosion and tried to drip some into his mouth. The pus seeped out from his eyes and nose; it was teeming with maggots."

"Did you check your burns?"

"No, after seeing the maggots, I avoided my burns. My keloids developed later. The victims I saw as I roamed Hiroshima had both of them. Some were black, some red. Most of them would erupt, seeping either blood or pus."

Togo turned and slammed his fist on the desk behind him. He had proven that his hatred of Americans was justified but he had taken it too far. After a couple deep breaths he asked Lawrence if he wanted another glass of water. Lawrence declined.

"I do not blame you for Hiroshima. You were but a child, then. But you, an American, are here, here in Vietnam where you don't belong. It was bad enough to see the victims of America but the worse was later, months later seeing the survivors become victims of their own country. We were pariahs, outcasts.

Hospitals, especially prestigious hospitals turned away victims of the atomic bomb. They turned away their own people. I lived as a refugee but I was only a ten year old. I was asked to help, to work with people that had been burned or harmed in other ways. I was allowed to live in a German hospital. I remember a baby was born around Christmas. He was running a fever and needed help that the German hospital could not give. Another hospital refused to see him. After some officials put pressure on them, they agreed to take him in, saying it was only because his fever had dropped. He became deaf and blind. He could not defecate and had to be given enemas for his bowels to be evacuated."

"That doesn't make much sense," said Lawrence. "Why would a hospital avoid handling a child in such poor health?"

"There was a fear that the victims of the blast now had tainted blood. Nobody knew what the radiation would do. People, other people besides the bureaucracy, would not consort with the victims. They stared at us, told us to keep away. What they saw well after the bombs were dropped were sick people dying from the radiation, its own weapon within the bomb of flash and wind. The radiation began taking lives. A person would feel fine but then get a fever, become nauseated, and gangrene would appear on their toes or near keloids. These infected people would rise from their bed and leave a halo of hair on the mat."

Togo stopped and walked about the room, knowing he had gone too far but after thirty years, knowing he could no longer allow the pain and anger continue to fester.

"Why did you do it Arens?"

"I didn't bomb Hiroshima or Nagasaki."

"But you are here, a prisoner in a country that has created no Pearl Harbor for America to use as an excuse. You are here killing people, villagers that just want to live their lives like my family in Hiroshima. Don't try my patience with the Republic of South Vietnam being a reason. We are a nation divided by the United States' need to own the world."

"I'm here because I got drafted. I was sent here without any choice."

"So like General Tibbets, you have been ordered to kill these people and you obey?"

Lawrence was starting to get angry. "There is no choice, Dr. Togo."

Tora Togo was smiling. "Do you know who Tibbets is?"

"Yes, he was the pilot of the Enola Gay who dropped the bomb on Hiroshima. Yes, he was ordered and when asked years later said he would do it again if he was so ordered."

"General Tibbets was asked about the 80,000 plus people he killed on that day or who died years later because of his bombing Arens," said Togo. "He said it didn't bother him because he was 32,000 feet up and never saw them die. Is that how it is with you, Arens? Can you shoot a man at 300 yards and feel no compassion?"

"I didn't make that decision. The United States made it and forced me to obey."

"Yes Arens. Like the Japanese people who blindly followed the orders of the Emperor and fought the war, you are a member of a bigger force than yourself. You can be blind and worse, you can be inhuman without any compunction."

"Or I could become a masochistic torturer trying to prove he's more than a mere human. I could be a coward and tie up people already broken, just to extract pain from them."

Tora Togo could feel the heat rising along the back of his neck. If he let Lawrence get to him, he would kill him. That would just prove that he was indeed a terrorist masochist.

"I perform a function Arens," said Tora Togo but Lawrence could hear the grit in his words.

"You're Kempei Tai. You watch people die in horrendous pain. You're not even after anything of any value when you start to take apart a prisoner. You're not interested in what you ask from the prisoner. The answer's not your raison d'être. You live for the pain, to see the agony in the face of the victim."

Tora Togo sent his chair flying backwards. The two guards on either side of Lawrence backed off in fear. They had never seen Tora Togo lose his composure and were not sure whom would suffer at his obvious displeasure. Togo ordered them to take the chairs from under Lawrence's arm pits, putting him back on bended knee, the bamboo pole forcing the tibia away from his knee cap. As soon as they did, Tora Togo put his face scant inches from Lawrence's. He smiled as the guards backed off.

"Let me see how much I enjoy yours Arens. Does it go up your back when I do this?" Tora Togo put his foot on Lawrence's right thigh and pushed down. Lawrence screamed as his knee cap felt hot and moist.

He could not lose consciousness. The situation was unraveling and unplanned. Togo had lost control and was using force to regain it. Lawrence had almost pushed him past intelligent thought and into random violence. That was what Lawrence was after, a slip from procedure in Tora Togo's situation. Togo already recognized that Lawrence had taken the protagonist position from him and knew he had to regain it. Losing his demeanor meant that Lawrence had controlled him. Togo did not care since the ultimate control remained his here in his interrogation room.

"You have proven my point Dr. Togo. I accuse and you act as the guilty. You're less human than Tibbets," said Lawrence. Lawrence had to make his play now while Togo's aggression was overriding his intelligence. He had to force Togo to kill him or make a mistake which could be used to Lawrence's advantage. "You are a schizophrenic animal that would not want to be 32,000 feet away like Tibbets. You would want to watch the skin peeling off your mother's burning face up close. You'd laugh at her, you'd spit ..."

Lawrence did not have a chance to finish his verbal attack. Tora Togo grabbed the back of Lawrence's head and jumped with both feet, landing on Lawrence's right thigh. Lawrence lost consciousness, despite trying to fight it. Togo had become a mad man and needed no more prodding for a kill. He had made a serious tactical mistake when he lost his façade of control. The blackness and nothingness for Lawrence lasted only a shorter. He awoke slowly his right leg totally numb and the pain was past senses. He did not move or open his eyes, but listened. Tora Togo was behind him yelling at the guards, trying to pass blame onto them for the failure with the prisoner. The first thing Lawrence sensed was that his hands had been unshackled but his feet were still chained together. They were waiting for him to regain consciousness. The guards had assumed that what Togo did to Lawrence's leg would keep Lawrence out much longer. Togo assumed that the weight put on Lawrence's thighs had caused enough pain to render Lawrence useless.

As Lawrence regained consciousness, he realized he had one shot at taking down the prey. The only people afraid of the anger and violence thrown off from Tora Togo had been the two guards. They had backed off toward the only door out of the interrogation room. The guard with the AK 47 had been helping hold down Lawrence in the chair, and had left his weapon against the window wall, less than two feet away from where Lawrence lay. Togo had turned his back to Lawrence while attacking the guards. It was not a question of could he move, just as there was no doubt his right leg would have nothing to do with that movement. The leg was virtually dead. Shoving off with his left foot, he lunged toward the window, grabbing the AK 47. By the time he turned, Togo and the guards were standing in front of Lawrence stunned. Quickly he injected a round into the rifle's chamber and aimed the AK 47 at Tora Togo. Lawrence now controlled the situation.

Tora Togo thought otherwise, "you won't shoot. You'd never get out of ..."

Lawrence shot the guard standing closest to the door through the front of his head.

"... out of here? I don't care. Your guard won't leave here alive now will he?"

Lawrence's head was muddled and his eyes were having trouble focusing. Inside this small room, he could open automatic fire and kill everybody within seconds.

"Before I die, I want you to understand something. I care about those people who died in Hiroshima and Nagasaki. No matter what Truman, Stimson, or MacArthur said, it was murder. What we did to your family and to you was worse than the Gestapo at any of the concentration camps." Lawrence was slowly losing it and could barely keep the rifle aimed at Tora Togo.

"You know why? Because it was faceless. None of those men could see their victims. It was a cleansing of the earth under a silver plane. It was more heinous than executing 6 million people because they did not see your mother's skin peeling off in folds or your father's burned image. To Truman and Tibbets and every American that cheered them, your people were squashed like vermin in a sewer set afire with gasoline. These Americans could not hear the screams, see the scorched, disfigured corpses, or even taste the smell of seared and rotting flesh. Impersonal genocide of hundreds of thousands of people to stop the war is a sin Americans must carry, a sin that is as horrible as Germany's shame. How many actual enemies of America were killed? A couple thousand, maybe ten thousand?"

"Two hundred and fifty thousand Arens."

"Why? How could anyone do that? Kill innocent people by incineration and radioactive poisoning, just to ..." Lawrence's eyes closed but he reacted to Togo's movement, raising the AK 47 to Togo's chest.

"Truman's toy Arens. The United States had a new play toy and had to use it. Like kids with a pellet gun, my family were shot down like small birds at the mercy of kids with a toy."

Lawrence pushed with his left hand, sliding his back against the wall. His initial dizziness passed and he laid his head cleared back. "If the people knew, maybe ..."

"Wrong Arens. Your people knew what was being developed, knew the potential death toll. Einstein told the world that it was a horrible weapon and the world, your world, did nothing. Even Henry Stimson said that there was something wrong with a country that could kill people like the A bomb did. Stimson was one of the leaders involved with dropping the bomb. Why did your people, the people of the United States, not even feel shame at this crime? Ruling the world, Arens, it's all about conquering and walking over the dead bodies."

"I can't accept that Doctor Togo. People in the United States were horrified by the German holocaust. I can't believe ..."

"Come on Arens. Had Germany won the war, would the world have ever seen the horror of the concentration camps? You know better than that. If your country is so shamed by the nuclear deaths in Japan, then why have you built over ten thousand more nuclear weapons, weapons even more powerful than Hiroshima's leveler?"

"If I say to maintain a weapon's balance, I would be wrong. I know that, Doctor Togo," said Lawrence. "Give me a drink of water from that carafe on your desk, please."

Tora Togo told the guard to sit down and Togo personally filled a glass with water and brought it over to Lawrence.

"You are correct Arens. I wish I knew."

"I've not got much longer to stay conscious Doctor Togo. You know what you do; the tortures you ran me through. They are the same malevolence as Hiroshima or Dachau."

Togo started to disagree but knew he would be lying to Lawrence and to himself. The tortures gained no valuable information. All they did was bring revenge into Tora Togo's life, a revenge he needed.

"Yes Arens, when I remember seeing the rack of pain flowing in frightened eyes, hearing the loud screams, wiping away the bloody tears, yes it is pure revenge. I feel no shame in it."

"You tortured me not to gain information. I am a nobody. You torture me to avenge your dead family."

"No Arens, I torture you to avenge the people of Vietnam. You think what America is doing now is any better than Hiroshima? Your armies attack this country for absolutely no reason. Is it because you want to flex your capitalistic muscles to the rest of the world? No one in the world believes that communism will topple over the Great American. That is political rhetoric, propaganda for the illiterate. The world wants to know why you are here killing innocent people. These villagers are no threat to you. Why do you napalm their hamlets? Why do you gun down the farmers from your helicopters? Every night you hear the bombs falling east of us, very close to here. Why? Our military suffers little compared to the thousands of civilians you blow apart …"

Lawrence knew Togo was right. "I have killed VC. I have killed in defense of my own life. I did not come to this war of my own volition."

Lawrence had to calm the situation now before he lost consciousness completely or the confrontation escalated.

"Doctor Togo, I am telling you what will be your death warrant. I have killed Americans. I have gunned them down as an enemy. Why have I killed my own brothers in war? You are completely right Doctor Togo. The Vietnamese people that live in each hamlet, work fields to support their families, and raise future generations, are the innocents. I know what America has done to them. I have killed to keep them alive. Your torture would never get it out of me, but your death will seal who I am. I am not only a deserter from the United States Army, I am also a defector. That Togo, you cannot know and remain alive. You have asked me under the duress of pain who I am. For me to tell you would bring shame and ostracism to my family. I will not let that happen. Know as you face death that I am not the enemy."

Tora Togo walked to his desk, lifted the desk chair, and brought it over to Lawrence. Sitting down, and following his habit of putting his fingers together at their tips in a pensive gesture he spoke, "You are a defector? You have actually fought your own army? Where Arens?"

Lawrence described his escape from My Lai, joining up with the Quyens, and fighting side-by-side with Cho Quyen whom Tora Togo knew to be a VC officer. Tora Togo knew about the swamp defensive near the previous POW camp but did not know that Lawrence was part of it.

"Why not make it known? Arens, the people of the United States are right now protesting the country's involvement in Viet Nam. Marchers are descending nearly every week on your capitol trying to stop this war. You're coming out with what you have seen could help us …"

"No! I fight but I do not bring my family down. No matter what the country thinks, Americans will do to my family as Japan did to you. They will be scorned pariahs, looked down on as the family of a traitor, the Benedict Arnold of the Viet Nam War. I owe them too much to face being the family of a traitor."

"When you kill me, you have signed your own death warrant Arens. No sooner am I dead then others will raid this room and kill you."

"But only you know," said Lawrence and fainted.

***

"Peter, your father told me as much as I could handle about his time in the Song Da River prison from the time he was taken there to his waking up in the hospital bed. I had not seen him for a very long time. Myself? My false medical credentials got me a cell in the Song Da River Prison hospital. Luckily I was able to fake my way through just about every wound or illness coming into the ward. The VC didn't care too much if I couldn't help American prisoners. Still I did the best I could. You can imagine how surprised I was when Llewellyn was brought into the ward and put on a bed," said Uncle George.

"Tora Togo wanted special attention given to your father. I had no idea why, but Togo had a surgeon brought in from Hanoi to look over Lew's leg. You father was unconscious for almost a week. In that time, the surgeon not only diagnosed the knee injury but operated on it. I even got to attend to the doctor during the operation. It was incredible that so much care was being given to an American soldier by the VC. I almost caused your father even greater pain when he finally woke up."

***

Vietnam 1969

Lawrence was very groggy as might be expected for a man who had been unconscious for six days. Add to that his being anesthetized for a four hour operation and was now waking up to believing he was in the torture room of the prison. He thought he was dreaming since Doctor George was sponging off his body in a hospital bed and neither of them was shackled. Lawrence tried to speak but fell back to sleep. When he awoke, Tora Togo was standing next to George.

Unfortunately George spoke first, "gonna stay awake this time Lawrence?"

Before Lawrence could clear his fogged brain, Tora Togo had already asked George how well he knew Mr. Lawrence. Lawrence could not believe George responded that he had known Lew back at the other POW camp. Lawrence tried to force what was happening back into being only a dream.

"Lew Lawrence? Is Lew short for a longer name, Doctor George?" asked Tora Togo.

Lawrence reached a hand up to quiet George but it was too feeble and too late.

"Yeah, Llewellyn. Don't blame him for wanting to be called Lawrence."

Tora Togo smiled at Lawrence, " relax, go back to sleep. Nothing would change yet, and Togo left.

Despite wanting to strangle George, Lawrence was very glad to see a familiar face. George finished the sponge bath and brought him some soup and tea. Lawrence would not look at his leg for fear it would not be there. George told him about the surgeon from Hanoi and Lawrence reached down to double check that the surgeon had not removed it. Tora Togo returned shortly and asked George to leave them alone for a while.

"Llewellyn Lawrence, Sergeant Llewellyn Lawrence. The "L's" do not work right with the Asian vernacular, do they? Arens is just a brutalized pronunciation of Lawrence."

"Why didn't I kill you?"

"Because your pain finally exceeded your strength. You're a remarkable man, Arens. If you don't mind, I'll continue calling you Arens?"

"That's fine. What did you do to my knee?"

"You had a tear of the anterior cruciate ligament. It connects your femur to the tibia at the center of the patella. As I told you, I am a doctor. Even though my specialty is epidemiology, I could diagnose it and maybe even have done the operation. But instead I chose to give you a chance to walk in the future. I brought in a specialist from Hanoi."

"Thanks."

"Not only do I have your name, rank, and serial number, but I reached Cho Quyen by radio and he told me that you're a hero to his family. He verified everything you told me."

"What good does it do me?"

"I know that you were very sincere with me. You are a traitor and defector to America but you are a warrior to the people of the villages. I cannot ignore that. If I had learned this earlier, I would have exposed you for propaganda purposes. I admire your honor. I believe you had intended to kill me, then kill yourself to save your family?"

"That's right."

"That Arens is a very Japanese attitude. I bow to you," said Tora Togo as he genuflected. "I think we can honor each other in this new situation. I am the only person who knows you completely. What I have to offer will keep it that way."

"Why? Here's a great chance for you to smear the United States."

"Yes, I said that. But you have earned a respect from me that will keep your family unexposed. Like you, I have no desire to harm the innocents. What I do want is for you to take down another American prisoner for me."

"Why should I do that? You want me to kill another man?"

"No, I am certain your killing only comes from forced combat. No, it would be very wrong of me to ask you to be an assassin. Instead I want you to attack the man's beliefs. I want you to uncover them, rip them to pieces, and regurgitate their putrid remains. I believe that you will appreciate, and maybe even look forward to the task. The man is the American Senior Ranking Officer."

Lawrence did not need much time to ponder what was being asked of him. In the time since he had been brought to Song Da River prison, Lawrence had repeatedly been chastised and threatened verbally by Lieutenant Colonel Gilbert Logan, the SRO and, per U.S. military rules and regulations, was now Lawrence's commanding officer. Lawrence had ignored every one of Logan's communication attempts and orders to the point that Logan had threatened to have Lawrence court-martialed once released. Logan would have a problem doing that since, like everyone else, he had no idea who the man in Lawrence's cell was.

"If I agree, I remain Arens for the rest of my time here?"

"Yes Arens, but you better tell Doctor George to quit calling you Lawrence or Lew. And yes, get him to never call you Llewellyn. Sounds like we're fighting the British here," said Tora Togo. He started to leave but turned and came back to Lawrence's hospital bed. Leaning close to Lawrence's face, he spoke, "as much as I hate America, I must remember you. Are there more like you back home? No, don't answer. You would not have been ready to give up your life if there weren't. I will not renege on what I have told you. Do you believe me? After all, you do have that ability to know when somebody's lying?"

Lawrence said, "You're not."

***

"Peter, you know from what I've told you that your father was a quiet man. Despite Tora Togo finding out just who Arens was, Lew didn't change much but for one exception. In all the time he was at Song Da River, he never communicated with anybody else being held as a prisoner. It's obvious why he couldn't, but regardless of his defection, Lew would have stayed silent."

"What changed after his meeting with Togo?"

"I can only go on what Lew told me. First, I had to keep his true identity secret. That was no problem since after our initial meeting back at the other camp, I had gotten used to others calling him Arens. The only other thing that changed was his acceptance of Lieutenant Colonel Logan as his ranking officer. Your father did not take orders very well which was why he had ignored Logan up to this point. He didn't explain to me why, all of sudden, Logan and he communicated. It wasn't long before Colonel Logan was brought into the infirmary to visit Lew, while he was recovering from the knee operation. Your father specifically asked that I be present and of course Tora Togo was there."

"Did you know about my father and Togo's agreement concerning Colonel Logan?"

"Not until later. I'll explain but not now. The meeting was strange for some reason I couldn't fathom. It was total fabrication which was obvious to anyone that knew Lew or Tora Togo. Remember your father had never acknowledged Logan as SRO and had not even spoken to him through the prison grape vine during his imprisonment. Now all of a sudden, here was Lieutenant Gilbert Logan at your father's bedside."

"Did my father actually hate this man, Logan, or was it just that he was an officer?"

"Both. Logan was not well-liked by anybody. He was relatively small with a very narrow head and one of those bulging asses that swayed like an old whore's when he walked. I'm tempted to say his eyes were beady but that's way short reality. He had the eyes of a rat, physically and spiritually. He never held your gaze once he caught your sight. Those rat eyes would search over your body like a vermin looking for a place to gnaw at your flesh. Rat only describes his eyes. If you add the rest of him, Logan was more a weasel than rodent. A lot of it had to do with his jet black hair and its gleam, oil-like. Slick, that probably describes him better. I learned later from your father that Logan's father was Irish and his mother was Armenian, which accounted for his face being dark colored and his nose more snout-like, one that made you think it would eat out your intestines if you were beneath him or sniff up your ass if you were his superior."

"Jesus, why did my father change his mind about talking with this jerk?"

"Your father was very perspicacious and patient. He was also a very good hunter."

"Yeah, once in a while when Grandpere George is a bit juiced with Scotch, he'll talk about my father's hunting, especially about how my father started at a very early age going off by his self. It bothered Grandpere George a bit but it also let him unfetter the attachment that he seemed to need for Grandpere George."

***

Vietnam 1969

Lawrence's knee hurt like a bitch. There was no position that gave him relief for more than fifteen or twenty minutes. Tora Togo could not be seen giving Lawrence pain killers and still maintain his absolute image of terror amongst both the prisoners and guards. Tora Togo would surreptitiously pass along a minimum dosage to Doctor George, who was often in the hospital ward. It helped. Lawrence told Tora Togo to give him a week before bringing Lieutenant Gilbert Logan into play. As Lawrence pulled his back up against the small straw stuffed pillow between his back and the wall, he saw Tora Togo bring Logan into the ward. They walked to Lawrence's bed.

"Major Arens, I don't think you've met your commanding officer here at Song Da River Camp? Allow me to introduce Lieutenant Colonel Gilbert Logan. Colonel Logan, this patient is Major Arens."

Logan stood at attention expecting a salute from Lawrence which never came. Lawrence said nothing.

Logan eased out of waiting for a salute and walked up to Lawrence's face. "No need to salute in your condition, Major ..."

"Major John Arens," said Lawrence and then gave him a false service number.

"Commandant Togo here has told me about your accident," replied Logan, his eyes scanning Lawrence from head to toe, looking deeply at Lawrence's bandaged leg with the cast over the knee. "Said it might have to come off, the leg I mean. Commandant Togo won't do it unless I agree. He says I got to put it in writing so as the VC don't get blamed for mutilating a soldier or even killing one."

Lawrence smiled, realizing that Logan had fallen for the ruse Lawrence had concocted between him and Tora Togo. He spoke, "it's my leg and some asshole like you gets to decide if they saw it off. That's bullshit."

"Major Arens," barked Logan, "I'm an Air Force Lieutenant Colonel and you will address me properly soldier! I am your superior officer! Do you understand soldier?"

"How do you figure that? I'm a Major and you're only a Lieutenant? I'm the superior officer here, not you asshole."

Logan turned to Tora Togo and spoke, "what's he on some kind of drugs?"

"We give no drugs here, Colonel. I think Major Arens has no respect for you."

Lawrence silently waved his hand at Logan, motioning him to come closer and when Logan approached, Lawrence spoke, "the war's over here. You're out of it. I'm out of it. How long have you been here?"

Logan spoke, "going on six years, Major. The war's never over, regardless of being a prisoner."

"Regardless, Colonel. There is no word irregardless. Got your college degree by correspondence school, didn't you?"

"Listen boy. You're still in the United States Army. Even though you're a prisoner, you owe your duty and life to our country."

"I'm lying here with a leg that might have to come off and you want my allegiance to the flag? Do you want my virtue, too?"

"What are you talking about?"

"I like to read, Colonel. Doctor Togo will tell you that," said Lawrence and Togo smiled. "You know who T. E. Lawrence was?"

"Didn't he write that dirty book about Lady Chatterley?"

"No, wrong writer. That was D. H. Lawrence and if that book turned you on, you better not look at any "Playboy" magazines or you'll have midnight sperm emissions. No, you might know T. E. best for Lawrence of Arabia. I'm good at remembering what I've read. Helps keeps me sane here, and in that damn boring cell. T. E. Lawrence wrote in a book called The Mint that "soldiers are parts of a machine and their virtue is in subordinating themselves within their great company.""

"Yeah, that sounds right. Obedience to your superiors, subordinating yourself."

"You miss something, Colonel? What is drilled into every trainee at basic and even at OCS? What is your duty when captured Lieutenant Colonel?"

The rat eyes were rolling side to side, and Logan's mouth had spit edging toward the corners of his lips. He knew what Lawrence was after and needed to get out of this situation, "I think you need some rest and ..."

"Doctor Togo, Colonel Logan said he's been here five or so years? That true?"

"I've just taken over as Commandant here, Arens, but I believe when I read over his dossier that he's been here about that many years," said Tora Togo.

"Just a second? Five years? You look pretty good for a POW living up to the United States Code of Military Service. How many times did you try to escape?"

"I don't have to take this harassment from you. When this war's over, I'm going to report you and have you court martialed for insubordination. You can't talk to me like that!"

"None, right Doctor Togo? He's never even tried to escape. Isn't that one of the oaths you pledged when you became an officer? Where's your virtue, Colonel Gilbert Logan?"

Logan turned to march out but Tora Togo blocked him, "he's asked you a fair question, Lieutenant Colonel. Maybe it's time we recognized you for what you are. A coward can't lead men, nor represent them as prisoners."

Lawrence kept repeating Logan's full name over and over again, "Gilbert Logan, Gilbert Logan, Gilbert ... Isn't Gill short for Gilbert? So in civilian life you would be Gill Logan. Gill

Logan, Gillogan, Gilligan? Hell, Gilligan, Bob Denver, damn if you don't even look like him! A rat, a little rat or weasel, that's you, isn't it? You see Doctor Togo, there used to be a television show called "Gilligan's Island" back in the sixties. The main character was this really stupid ship's mate who kept fucking up everybody's life on this stranded island. How did that theme song go?"

Lawrence whistled a few notes trying to grasp the starting cadence. It didn't take long for to have the song down pat.

"As the Senior Ranking Officer, I demand this man be silenced and brought up on charges, Commandant Togo" said Logan.

"I'm afraid, Colonel Gilligan, this is not your island. In fact, Arens has my sympathy for having you as the SRO. In the military there is no word more horrid than coward. Are you?"

"I resent that!"

"It makes no difference to us, Colonel. Think what you must think, be what you must be, but you're still a prisoner here. Arens will make the decision about his life and his leg. In order to save his leg, though, he will need medical care for which I do not have staff to provide. He needs nursing, daily nursing. He cannot be moved and probably will be that way for many months, at least six. He is under your command. Since you are responsible for the imprisoned Americans here, you will be his nurse."

"You haven't the authority to make me his nurse, sir!"

Tora Togo called to a guard standing at the doorway to the ward. The man marched over to Lawrence's bed and Tora Togo spoke to him in Vietnamese. Lawrence understood every word and wondered why Tora Togo was asking the soldier if he thought the monsoons would ease up soon.

"Lieutenant Colonel Logan, I have just told this soldier that he is to march you out of this hospital and out to the field where he will shoot you through the head for disobeying a direct order from the Commandant of this prison. Leave with him now!"

Lieutenant Colonel Gilbert Logan fell to his knees and begged Tora Togo to rescind the order, that he would do whatever he was ordered to including being Lawrence's nurse.

The nursing care started that night. Tora Togo sent guards to escort Logan to the medical hut. As soon as Lawrence heard the men bring in Logan, Lawrence started whistling, whistling over and over again the theme song from "Gilligan's Island." Logan had the responsibility to help Lawrence defecate and urinate, then remove the wastes from the bed pan and then clean bed pan. When finished he had to give Lawrence a sponge bath and check the bandages around Lawrence's cast. Lawrence whistled that same song over and over again. He could see the fury rising in Logan's face.

"Does my whistling bother you, Gilligan?"

"I am an officer in the United States Air Force and expect to be treated as such, Major Arens."

"Come on, Gil, relax. How can you stay so tight when you've gotta clean up my shit? Didn't you say you were a southern boy? Came from some pig farm in Norfolk?"

"What unit were you with?"

"I'm not supposed to tell you that and you know it. But I don't care," said Lawrence making up a U.S. Army division and company, knowing that Logan, being Air Force, would not have any idea if it was true. He also concocted a story of how his capture bore no resemblance to the horror that turned Lawrence into a defector. It got Logan to relax and take his mind off of his menial tasks and embarrassing ablutions.

Logan had this need to talk, to put him back in time. "The hell of this prison is the darkness. Here I am, a man trained to fly extremely high technology machines worth millions of dollars and I got to clean up your feces. You ever flown an airplane Arens?"

"Nope, never even wanted to even when I was a kid. Don't particularly like heights although I'm not afraid of flying."

"In my plane I'm soaring at incredible speeds at heights near outer space. You feel a rapture so strong that it's dangerous. You lose control at those speeds and you go down fast, very fast. Now as a prisoner what do I see, what feelings run through my mind? No more at the edge of space, I live in a windowless closet, no suns bursting through the high clouds, never see the moon when returning to base, there's nothing. Five years of a black room and torture."

"Did you do napalm runs?"

"Yeah, you zoom down near ground level, let'em go and you can see the balls of fire lighting up behind you. You even think you can hear the swoosh of the napalm burning everything into a crisp ash."

"You forgot something that you miss."

"What's that?"

"Sitting in that tiny cell, you've got no more people to incinerate."

Lawrence's comment ended the conversation for the day and for two more days. Logan needed communication and therefore could not keep from conversing with Lawrence. As typical of a conceited man like Logan, he quizzed Lawrence at first but quickly turned the discussion back to his own concerns and braggadocio.

"You a religious man, Major Arens?"

"No, my father ..." Lawrence avoided the trap, although he sensed Logan had not really meant to interrogate him, "... and mother took me every Sunday, but after all those years, you know what I realized?"

"What's that?"

"It's all repetitious. In December it's Christmas and Jesus is born. Come spring, it's Easter and Jesus is crucified. Kind of like reruns, isn't it?"

Logan had been regaining his supercilious attitude by ignoring Lawrence's remarks and just continuing with what he had to say, "faith Major, look at the smartest and bravest men in this war. Look at yourself, the other prisoners here. God knows our faith and will reward the way we live."

Lawrence felt a knife jab at his soul, "so America is God's country?"

"Of course, Arens. Jesus will not fail us; only we can make ourselves fail by not having faith in our way, the American way."

"America is God's way? Thank Jesus and drop napalm, right?"

"How do you expect to stop communism in this country?"

"Gilligan, I don't care if this country is communist. It's not our country. It's the Vietnamese people's country. How many Americans are going to live here when this war's over? Few, very few, if any. So Johnson and Nixon are going to decide how they live?"

"You don't see it right, Arens. We can't let the people go communist."

"Why?"

"Look at them. Do you really think they know how to run a country?"

"You know, there's something familiar about those words, Gilligan."

"Yeah, you see it now?"

"Do you know why we have an electoral college in the United States?"

"Because we couldn't count votes back when this country was formed. People didn't have any way of communicating who they voted for. They sent representatives with their votes to Washington."

"Then why do we still have the electoral college?"

"I guess it's …," Logan was stumbling, "… well it's just there like your appendix or something."

"Those noble leaders that set up the government of the United States put it there to insure the common man could never put people into government that the leaders of the country did not want. George Washington himself said we must oversee the minions and prevent the humble but unintelligent masses from ever taking power. People were cattle to Washington."

"You're crazy, Arens. That's not true. The people elect our leaders today and have forever."

"No, they don't. If they did, we wouldn't be here. The electoral college was specifically created by Washington and those other merchants, traders, businessmen, and bankers, to prevent their people from being voted out. How did anybody over a hundred years ago know for sure that one man got this many votes and another this amount? They couldn't. Read your Jefferson. He knew. He was against it and his antipathy caused him to lose power in his later years."

"I don't believe that Arens. You read too much. It doesn't mean anything today and especially here in Southeast Asia. These are common people. They need our guidance. They can't rule on their own. It's either us or the commies. With the commies, there's no God in this country."

Lawrence had about enough of justifying the blowing up and burning of people in the name of God and country. He knew the self-righteous and arrogant man that was Gilbert Logan, was one name out of a hundred million that were just as self righteous and arrogant and living back in the U.S.A.

"It's a bit facetious of you to claim the intelligence of God and ability of Jesus to save the people of Vietnam, isn't it?"

"Why? Look at them. They send women and children into our camps, into our mess halls to blow themselves up to hurt us. How stupid can you be? How can a God fearing person, a God driven country, allow these people to commit such horror? Sacrificing your own children's lives …"

"For what, Gilligan? For their right to live their lives as they choose? Would God sacrifice his child to bring peace to his world?"

Logan was stunned. Lawrence had lead him into a trap that sank its steel teeth into the pedagogue of all religions.

"How do you justify violence when God speaks of love thy enemy."

CHAPTER FOURTEEN

The Beast

"That's the end of it, Petey."

"What do you mean, Uncle George? Did my father get better? What happened with Logan? It can't just stop there?"

"War ain't a movie, Petey. There's no plot, no beginning no end. Stories start and the tale has no ending, no getting a rescue of the hero. You know that, Petey. You're an English teacher. Life is no tale spun by writers."

"I'm not a teacher yet."

"You go to upstate New York soon. Gonna be damn cold up at the Falls. Guess it's not much worse than our winters. Kind of shook your Mamma you going up there, but a job's a job."

"She's not that upset. Might even move up there herself. Got that French Canadian blood in her. There's just something attracts me to Canada. All the times I've been up there, always been taken in by the people and the atmosphere."

"Should've just got a position there, Petey."

"You're beating around the bush, Uncle George. I've been over it with you before. Get back to how my father's story ends."

"The truth, Peter. It just ends. One morning when he was near recovered, he was gone."

"That's it? He just disappeared?"

"Not quite. So did Gilbert Logan. Both went in the middle of the night. Best I can guess, Lew badgered him so much about being a coward, that Logan stood up to him and busted out of camp with Lew. It wasn't difficult to do, especially for Lew. Hell, Tora Togo gave him full rein of the camp and overlooked his night time forays into the jungle since Lew always brought back food. Might have been your father dragged Logan by the neck out of camp."

"There was no trail, no soldiers trying to capture them?"

"The Vietnamese knew how good your father was at survival. It'd of been a waste of time and it would have left the prison camp poorly guarded. Your father had turned. He was more Viet Cong and very little U.S. Army. As for Logan, we all hoped Lew killed him and fed him to the alligators."

Lawrence had always held on with desperate hope of finding what happed to his father, Llewellyn Lawrence. His mother ended Llewellyn's life at his being MIA; she would not even discuss Uncle George's. Why? What George had told Peter bore no stigma to Peter's father as far as George was concerned. Lawrence had been a soldier witnessing horrors as horrendous as the German atrocities during World War II. His alleged anti American actions were fully validated by the horror America's military visited on the people of Viet Nam. Llewellyn Lawrence would have been close to overstepping his own atrocities by his treatment of Gilbert Logan, but Logan's horrors over the bombing of villages of families drew a patina of blood and visceral gore far more horrible than Llewellyn's personal attacks against the killer pilot.

"Uncle George, you're leaving something out. Don't do it to me. You're not giving me the full story. How do I know? Because everything you've told me offers no reason for Ma Mere's silence. She could have told me these tales. What shame do they bear? Why has she kept Mon Pere from me? He was a brave man who stood up to a government underhandedly encouraging its warriors to brutalize and slaughter innocent families. Do I have to go to her and force her to tell me the final chapter? Does she feel shame for her husband, Llewellyn Lawrence? I love her but I must force from her ..."

"Stop," said Uncle George. "I have gone where I promised I would never to revisit. Let me get another Pabst and I'll finish your father's story. You want a beer?"

"No, I'm fine."

When Uncle George returned Lawrence could see how sallow his face had become. If it was the alcohol, the beer was winning at eroding George's life. Yet during their conversation, George had knocked back many less bottles than usual. No, thought Lawrence, his grey face has not due to chemicals, it was conceptual. Uncle George's alcohol abuse had opened doors in his past that he had thought were closed and sealed. The ghosts rushed out, taking advantage of his alcoholic stupor. Lawrence saw the fear in George's eyes, a fear of knowing you are about to lose someone you love. What could he tell Lawrence that would make Peter no longer love him?

There was no ceremony. George knew no way to forewarn what he was about to show Lawrence. If Peter covered his uncle with a blanket of guilt, it would be because of the newspaper George now handed to him.

"Read this Peter," said Uncle George, the paper folded into quarters exposing a photograph of a military man with a face not much different from that of a weasel.

The first read through gave nothing to Lawrence. It was an obituary, ironically an obituary for Colonel Gilbert Logan.

"So? Logan's body was found? Doesn't really say much. His remains were to disposed by cremation at …"

"Unfold the paper to the Community News page. Read the first story."

Lawrence gasped. He was stunned at the cruelty of the article being in the same newspaper on the same day as Logan's funeral. What happened to Colonel Gilbert Logan was not a war crime by the enemy. The Viet Cong had no need to execute and commit such horrors. The article was a follow up to Logan's remains being shipped to his family from Saigon. No warning had been given, no sender identified. A box inside of another box was hermetically sealed and labeled Biological Materials - - Open Under Total BioChemical Isolation - - when it arrived at the home of Logan's parents. It was taken to the police who took it to their crime lab who took it to CDC in Atlanta. It was very easy to identify the remains since the inner box contained a large jar with the head of Gilbert Logan staring out through the formaldehyde and glass in horror. At the bottom of the jar appeared to be his testicles.

"Ma Mere knows this was Llewellyn's doing?"

"That's why she does not speak to you about your father. The military authorities investigated Lew's family thoroughly but what was there to find? Nothing, and nothing leaked from it. Why should it? I knew it was Lew. Your mom knew it was Lew. That's all. The military only knew that Logan escaped with your father from a POW camp. There was … There is no reason to think your father did this. But he did."

Uncle George sagged on the porch steps. His shoulders shrugged. The burden that was lifted drained him every second he spent with his nephew. He feared Peter's reaction to what his father had done but feared more that the relationship between the two would be destroyed.

"Ma Mere is a good woman. She knows?"

"I told her only the story I told you."

"She knows," said Lawrence a slight smile forming on his face.

"Yes, Petey, and—like you—she smiled."

Lawrence sat next to his uncle on the porch step. He knew what happened today was so intense for Uncle George that it could well have killed the old alcoholic even before his Pall Mall's finished him off. Lawrence saw the tears and brushed them from Uncle George's face with his fingers. He smiled at the old man, grabbed him gently behind his neck and pulled him into a gentle hug.

CHAPTER FIFTEEN

The Falls

The Falls High School has one place from which you just might be able to view Niagara Falls if it is a clear day in the fall when there are no leaves or better still, if it is winter. The rest of the view is of urban city mixed with tenements not much better than ghettos of other economically despoiled cities. The city's share of tourist finances are miniscule. The ugly United States side is an easy walk across Peace Bridge from luxurious accommodations on the Canadian side. An hour, maybe two satisfies the curiosity of tourists since there is little to offer money spenders on the USA side. The pity is that to take the time to visit the USA side makes for a thrilling walk through the islands leading to Turtle Rock and the gigantic precipice of Niagara Falls. So exhilarating are the sonic currents of the upper river dumping into the gorge, that most people are scared to go near the rolling waters surrounding Niagara Falls National Park. It is these trance-like mental rides one feels when watching the speeding waves and currents that take your breath away more so than proximity of the view. The best view is the natural mural of seeing the Falls a quarter of a mile away when you are watching the flow from Canada. Maybe being on the American side is fear, the fear of the currents of power?

It was a week before the start of school and Lawrence was parked in the Falls High School parking lot finishing a cup of coffee from the 7-11. He had not been to the school since his interview a month before. Right now, Lawrence could care less about the famous Wonder of the World. He had driven straight through from his home in six hours, arriving in the dark and in this same parking lot only to wait another three hours for his interview with Ms. Mosse, the principal. He had not been early. She had been three hours late for the 8:00AM interview. Lawrence realized very quickly that her interview was not the one that counted. She had little time for him, glancing at his college credentials, and giving him a quick overview of what would be expected from a new teacher. Her veracity and intellect flowed through the cracks in her perspicacity when she introduced him to the Chairman of the Science Department; Lawrence was being interviewed for an English teacher position. She left Lawrence with the science teacher, who limply shook Lawrence's hand and welcomed him to Falls High School. The deed was done without need for protocol; he obviously would be hired.

When Lawrence began to beg her indulgence so he could explain to her that he was not a science teacher, the science chairman grabbed his shoulder slightly, put his finger to his lips, and gently shook his head. Once Ms. Mosse was out of hearing range the man explained to Lawrence that Mosse's lack of intelligence was not relevant since she justified her presence and position at Falls High School by virtue of racial accommodation. Falls High School was composed of city kids. The city kids were mostly black. Ms. Mosse held the credentials of an administrator but she wore the color necessitated by the school board and superintendent to be the school's principal. Color and lack of intelligence not withstanding she could shut down a pack of black kids with a strut and a "you listen to me baby, get yo'self out dese halls, now!"

The science chairman took Lawrence to meet the English chairman, Doctor Belafont. Again, it seemed moot that he should be here. Belafont asked a few personal questions, explained the curriculum to Lawrence, and told him that the students fell into one of three categories. They are black and if you're lucky, absent most of the time. They are Italian and sleep in class most of the time. Finally, one or two might head for a community college after graduation since they have the ability to read a comic book. Follow the curriculum exactly, do nothing out of the ordinary, get at least half of them to pass the State Regents, and if you're on hall duty don't let anybody out or anybody in. Lawrence asked what English he would be teaching and was told the kind intelligent people speak. Daring to go one step farther, he asked what books are required reading for the students. With a menacing stare, Belafont told him The Color Purple. A pregnant chasm of silence opened between them. Belafont stretched his neck as he lifted his chin, eyes boring into Lawrence's. He was a tall man, but slight. He wore a red striped tie, inexpertly knotted and not pulled tight to his neck. His shirt was white with light blue stripes. The pants probably had not been ironed for years and had one cuff, on the left leg, inverted as if it had just exited the dryer. He moved his eyeglasses up to his forehead and spoke.

"Mr. Lawrence, I expect you meant more than one when you said books. There is no more than one. That is the one. If you think my comments to you are sarcastic, then you are better educated than I credited you. You have been hired. Nobody actually interviews you for this school. Why? Because nobody with any intelligence wants to teach here."

Lawrence was about to ask the obvious.

"So you surely have enough brains to ask it," spoke Belafont, "why am I here? Because I needed to get my doctorate in English and needed a job where I could give kids busy work while I do my research. That is why I came here five years ago. Two years doing a Masters and three years to finish my PhD. If you can survive the year out, you will probably do the same thing. With luck I'll move on to a college position."

Lawrence had known bitter people. This man could rise to the top in any pudding of bitterness. He was hired? He had sent his application, sent references, and had his transcript mailed. The personnel director called him and interviewed him once. In less than a week he got a phone call from the personnel director asking him to visit the school district for some interviews. These were not interviews. He was being introduced to what was expected of him. He still had not met with the Director of Personnel. Belafont's phone rang; he listened and responded, "Yes, he's right here. Yes, I'll send him over." He hung up.

"You need to go to the district offices. I'll give you directions. But first they want you to stop off at the city hospital and get a chest x-ray. You're to take the results with you to personnel. The hospital's been contacted and they are waiting."

He stopped long enough to take a 3 X 5 index card from his desk and draw a rough street map of Niagara Falls showing Lawrence where both the hospital and the district offices were located.

"Here, this should do. Listen, Larry ..."

"No, my last name's Lawrence. Just Lawrence will do."

Peevishly, his eyes now raised above his properly placed eyeglasses, a large gasp of sardonic air spoke, "and your first name is?"

"Peter, but just Lawrence will do."

"Peter, Lawrence, whatever. This is all new to you. You'll be like any new teacher, ready to blow away all us old salts, want a chorus of "To Sir, With Love" playing as you walk into the building. Maybe even do a great Glenn Ford imitation like in that movie … Can't for the life of me get a handle …"

"Blackboard Jungle. Want to try Robert Donat? Actually Peter O'Toole was better."

"Mr. Chips, yes. Goodbye Mr. Chips. Is that what you want to be? Mr. Chips?"

"No, potato chips would be fine."

"Yeah, Larry, you'll be one of those. I'll wager it. On the kids side and good pals with them. It doesn't work that way. You got hired because for the last three years we've had overloaded English classes. Nobody would take a teaching position here. These are hard kids, tough kids. They know one kind of obedience, in your face obedience. The one thing going for you is you look tough. You've got to be tough. Mosse and her staff will back you up. Our discipline room is the lock up, downtown. These kids learn it fast. Now you better get going."

Lawrence saw a slight breakdown in Belafont's demeanor. His speech to Lawrence nearly begged for a bit of empathy. Lawrence got up and turned to leave the room.

Belafont spoke, "Don't like The Color Purple? Have you seen the state's reading list?"

"Yep, I'd a picked Les Miserables."

Belafont continued, "State won't let us do condensed versions."

"Good for New York! I'd make them do all 1,463 pages."

Lawrence got no laugh. He seriously doubted the man had laughed in years.

He found the hospital, found the district office, had a quasi-interview with the Director of Personnel, and signed his contract. He was back home in time for a very late dinner.

Today was the first day for teachers. He had no schedule, he knew no classes, and his association with other teachers was limited to Belafont and the science teacher of whose name he did not even know. The science teacher arrived at the parking lot the same time as Lawrence. He was followed by a woman driving a yellow Shelby Mustang. The science teacher walked over to the Mustang and opened the door for its driver. Many a man has been laid astray by the smile of a beautiful woman and Lawrence would not be any different. She was tall, at least two to three inches above the science teacher. Her hair was auburn bordered with slight streaks of near red that could be seen as she turned and the sunlight refracted through the strands. Lawrence now knew the definitive meaning of buxom. She was buxom. She walked with an n athletic stride, paces that forced the science teacher to quicken. She had on a dress that was tight enough to validate a figure worthy of admiration by any healthy man. Yet it was loose enough to contain her sauntering walk. The closer she came, the more enamored Lawrence became. If all of this glimmer had not won him over, her blue eyes above the thin red lips sealed his fate.

"Oh, hello," said the science teacher. "I never did catch your name. Sam, I'm Sam Watson. I teach physics here. Let me introduce you. This is Eileen, Eileen Ledger. She doesn't teach here. She's the director for SAIP downtown. I forget Eileen. What does SAIP mean?"

Lawrence was stirred, nearly close to aroused. The woman carried herself like a woman who knew she could love you until it hurt. "My name's Lawrence, Peter Lawrence. I'm a new guy. Gonna to teach English."

"Mr. Lawrence, nice to meet you. I'm in charge of the Substance Abuse Intervention Program. Thus SAIP. Are you new to the Western New York area?"

Lawrence told her where he came from and asked, "you get many kids doing drugs?"

"As surprising as it may seem, not as many as you would expect in a city like Niagara Falls. We only deal with those actually caught on school property. Kids bringing pills from home, mom's little blue and white friends. Every once in a while a school catches a student selling pot in the bathrooms. If you have a student who gets caught, then you'll hear from me. I see that he keeps up in his classes while he's attending SAIP."

Lawrence knew he had to have this woman. She was beyond all he had ever met. Just by seeing her, he judged that she would affect pleasure better than anyone else.

"Well, Mr. Lawrence, I've got a presentation to do this morning for you teachers, if you'll excuse me. I'm sure we'll get together again," she said, her blue eyes and challenging lips, with the tongue provocatively moistening her lips serving its purpose and more.

I hope we meet again but not because of a referral from one of your classes. Bye."

***

With the exception of Western New York, April is a most refreshing month. Buds form on stark naked trees, promising life and streets suffering salts from snow plows are washed with clean rain from clear skies. Not so Niagara Falls, New York. Filthy piles of snow still blocked two lane streets, making for a slow drive from home to the high school. Even the mountains of his home did not fight the change to spring as bitterly as Upstate New York. Lawrence had learned to live with the dreary. He also lived pusillanimously as a new teacher. This he learned from his mother. Herself, Evelyn Southern Lawrence had recognized the initiation that forms the obsequious three year tenure for a new teacher. Knowing her son's fortitude and insipient aggressiveness, Evelyn had coerced Peter into becoming a teacher despite the disparate anger and the strength of his convections that he held dear when faced with people and situations that rankled his sense of honesty and integrity. Not liking to bow to Belafont as English department chairperson, he none the less still called him Dr. Belafont. Appalled at the basic objective of the system's educational process, Lawrence wrote stereotypical and innocuous lessons in his plan book, telling his Chairperson and Principal Mosse once every two weeks that "the students will be able to …" So puerile were these mandated objectives that Belafont and Mosse let all teachers merely write TSWBAT in their lesson planning books in an effort to save paper.

Lawrence wrote his TSWBATs using pure Bloom taxonomy and handed them in every other week, as he had done for the past three years, or rather almost three years. Today was tenure. Tenure meant three years. Whether you were deficient in your teaching or the epitome of a Plato, the school board could fire you without just cause within that space of time. April of your tenure year posed a dilemma for principals and administrators since state law mandated every teacher had to receive a contract by April 1st. Thus a neophyte teacher technically gained tenure with almost three months to go before the three year completion. Lawrence knew this was a shady period for both the employee and employer, and heeding his mother's advice, vowed discretion so as not to put his career into jeopardy. It had rankled his brain for over two years to give doctoral credit to Belafont and laud him with the honor of being a superior teacher. The man was a tyrant and a racist, but smart enough to hide both faults. No longer would he call Belafont, Doctor Belafont.

Lawrence noticed the yellow Shelby Mustang with the administrative decal on the windshield in the visitor's space of the high school parking lot. This meant Eileen Ledger was visiting the school today. It was a rare day, almost as rare as a sunny and mild day in April, when Ledger visited. It meant she was dealing with drug problems at the high school. This was unusual. Most students were sent directly to her. Lawrence hoped to see her but doubted there would be an opportunity since his classroom was miles from the main offices and guidance department.

Lawrence kicked the grey, salty snow off his shoes, used his pass key to open the windowless double doors on the east side of the school, and entered, pulling the long steel bar tight once inside. The school smelled. It was not a pleasant smell nor was it a rancid one. It was more antiseptic which would be expected, but contained that faint whiff of rat poison. The school was overrun by rats. In Lawrence's first year, he had been helping his homeroom students open their lockers at the start of school when one student flipped through the three dial turns, lifted the latch handle and screamed. Old clothes and stale food from last year's locker holder had been built into a snug nest and food supply for a growing family of rats. The rats tried to scurry through a hole in the back of the locker that Lawrence thought was not large enough to let a spider penetrate. Most of the rats got out but two of them ran out the front of the locker into the hallway, one of them biting a student along the way. Lawrence learned to kick doors in Falls High School before opening them, thus avoiding rats and roaches.

Lawrence kicked the bottom of his classroom door, turned the same pass key and let himself into the room. The room was sweltering and Lawrence opened two of the windows to cool it down. Taking off his coat, Lawrence kicked the storage closet door before opening it, listened for any scurrying, and allowed that his coat would be safe here while classes were in session. He checked off the big red star on his large desk calendar signifying today was April 1st and then reluctantly wrote his objectives for the day on the faded blackboard as the bell rang to let the students into the building.

It did not take long before a fight broke out in the hall. The crowd amassed, surrounding the combatants as Lawrence rushed from his room. The mob was at the crossing of two hallways allowing for a large battle. Shouts of "get that mother fucker! Fuck his face up. Rip out his whitey fuckin' eyes!" carried down the hall.

Lawrence started yanking students away to form a path to the fighters. The path sealed behind him as he neared the battle. He found Belafont in the middle of it. He had encircled his arms around a toe headed white boy. A corn-rowed black boy jumped into the duo of student and teacher and was throwing jabs into the contained and defenseless white boy's face which now had blood pouring out of his nose. Every blow the black kid made drew screams of "get that mother fucker" from the crowd. The black kid was a good six inches taller than the white kid, but scrawny. The black kid was well known by his classmates as a gang member and a vicious fighter. Despite the blood that covered his face, Lawrence recognized the white boy as one of his students. Even though the boy outweighed the black kid by a good fifty pounds, he had no chance with Belafont's arms wrapped around him. To fight back and stop the assault tearing his face apart meant, he would have to physically disengage Belafont thus assaulting a teacher and being automatically expelled for the rest of the year.

Belafont kept yelling to the black kid to stop fighting. The black kid just laughed at him. As usual, the altercation had now gone on without any help from school security. Lawrence shoved his way between the two combatants and raised his hands to separate the two.

"Stop! Stop now!"

The black kid was on a high, both emotionally and by the look in his eyes, chemically. The crowd, now all black, roared "fuck that white asshole teacher!"

The black kid danced and laughed, beckoning Lawrence to come on. "You want a piece of me, white fuck?"

Lawrence smiled and shook his head slowly back and forth. "I don't fight anybody with their zipper undone. Zip up and let's go at it!"

The boy looked down at his crotch discovering too late that his zipper was fully up. With his arms down and chin to his chest, Lawrence caught the boy's throat with his left hand, wrapping his fingers around the windpipe, bringing the boy to his toes. This gave the boy no balance to lever a punch at Lawrence. Fear showed in the boy's bloodshot eyes as he gasped for air. The kid knew any struggle could force the teacher grasping his windpipe to tighten his grasp and cut off all breathing. The boy could not speak; he did not need to. His wide eyes with yellowish fluid seeping out the corners and the dropped fists told Lawrence the fight was over. The crowd screamed obscenity after obscenity but in cowardice it did not rise to perpetuate their "mother fucker killer."

Security arrived and pinioned both kids against the wall. As the school police officer went to handcuff both students, Belafont stopped him when he tried to cuff the white boy.

"Officer, this student did nothing. I saw the whole fiasco. The Negro boy attacked the other boy from behind and wouldn't stop pummeling him until I broke it up."

Since he was Doctor Belafont, he was held in reverence so his description was accepted without question. The police officer looked to Lawrence who only a shrugged. The mob dispersed and went to their first period classes, as did Peter Lawrence.

***

"Mr. Lawrence, do you know why you're here?" said Rolanda Mosse.

Lawrence thought he did. "About the fight this morning?" It was now his planning period, soon to be followed by his lunch hour.

"No, the fight didn't have much to do with you, thanks to Doctor Belafont. But thank you for being there in case he needed help. You're here ..."

"Excuse me a second. Could you tell me what happened to those two students?"

"They'll both be suspended for fighting. The white boy is why you are here." Mosse handed Lawrence a red covered trade paperback book with a drawing of a man and woman aiming weapons at some object or persons to the left of the book.

"Danny Costini had this book in his book bag when the police officer searched him. He claimed he's reading it for your English class?"

"Never heard of the book. The Turner Diaries? That's a new one to me."

"So he's lying?"

"I didn't say that. I gave all my students a chance to read whatever book they wanted for the last marking period. It was his choice."

"Mr. Lawrence, you really don't know what this book is about? It's published by Barricade Books, a white supremacist organization. It advocates a war to eliminate all non-whites and Jews from the world population. It tells readers to get ready for a great war where whites will kill off all blacks and other minorities. You can't even buy it like a normal book. You have to order it through mail order houses like Barricade or pick it up at a gun show."

"I didn't know that. I sort of expected kids to read a Stephen King novel or James Patterson book."

"Didn't you check what books they were reading?"

"No, I didn't. That would sort of be not trusting them, wouldn't it?"

"The State of New York has a very comprehensive reading list. The students can chose from it. Let Costini do that. Actually, you've solved a problem for us by allowing this to happen. The book explains why Costini started the fight this morning."

"How's that?"

"Costini has been in fights before, always with Afro-American young men. This boy is just following what these racists want, violence against minorities. We asked him where he got this book. His father bought it for him when they were at a Niagara Falls Convention Center gun show. He said the man who sold it to him fought in the Iraq War. Desert Storm. He sure won't want to have it with him where he's going."

"Where's that?"

"I'm going to recommend he be brought up on charges of assault and battery. With his record ..."

"When will that happen?"

"The courts like to jump on these juvenile cases; don't want violent kids out free roaming the streets. My guess it'd be next month."

Lawrence's mind was racing. Danny Costini might be a racist but he did not precipitate the fight nor did he fight back. Lawrence knew his job might be in jeopardy. He had no contract yet. Knowing what his mother told him about the self righteous administrators of school districts and their attitude that they were above the rules and regulations, without a written contract in his hands they could still sing and dance around terminating him. Would his conscience allow him to ignore the truth of Danny Costini? He knew Danny and liked him. He was a wild kid that seemed to migrate toward trouble. Usually it was innocent misdemeanors putting him in Saturday detentions, or in-school suspension, or at least once this year already thrown out of school on suspension. This punishment would go much farther than a minor punishment administered by the school system. It might seal Danny's future.

"Where are these two boys now?"

Mosse glared at Lawrence's use of the term 'boys' but since it also meant a white boy, she let it pass. "They're both in the hospital."

"Let's get something straight, here. I don't care what you or your security people or Belafont say. Danny Costini was never in the fight. The black boy was beating the shit out of him while Belafont held Danny. The black boy's eyes were hazed, bloodshot, and had yellowish fluid tearing from them. That boy was on drugs."

Lawrence stood and walked to Mosse's door. Opening it, he was going to ask Mosse's secretary to come in for a second as a witness to what he had to say. The secretary was not at her desk but much to Lawrence's delight Eileen Ledger was.

"Mrs. Ledger, I thought that was your car out in the parking lot."

"My Shelby. How you doing Mr. Lawrence?"

"Not bad. You here to see Ms. Mosse?"

"Sure am. Got a couple of her students I had to boot out of the program and need her signature on the paperwork."

"You mind coming into her office for a quick second?"

"No problem," said Eileen Ledger as she picked up her handbag and a stack of manila files. "You sure Mrs. Mosse won't mind?"

"Just need you to be a witness for something I've got to tell her."

Lawrence held the principal's clouded glass front and gold labeled titled office door open. He gestured to Eileen Ledger to enter. As she walked past him, he noted her lovely, athletic body and silently sighed. She entered and went to the seat that Lawrence gestured for her to take. Ms. Mosse's eyes opened wide and she started to speak, "I see no need for Mrs. Ledger ..."

Lawrence did not let Mosse finish. "This won't take long. I have just told Ms. Mosse that an Afro-American young man who was engaged in a fight this morning had blatant signs of being on drugs. In front of you as a witness, I am telling her," continued Lawrence as he paced back and forth ending less than two feet in front Rolanda Mosse. "if he is not tested for drugs at the hospital, I will go to Danny Costini's family and tell them that Ms. Mosse was advised of the boy's drug condition and refused to have him tested. You understand, both of you?"

"Mr. Lawrence, I find your behavior insubordinate and ask that you leave ..."

"Ms. Mosse, I am not going to debate with you. By school board regulations and state law, if an employee of the school system suspects drug use of a student, that employee is legally mandated to report his suspicions. Legally, Ms. Mosse I don't report it and I am violating the law."

Mosse knew Lawrence was right. "Fine, Mr. Lawrence, you've done your job."

"And Mrs. Mosse, you are legally liable to report that employee's suspicions to the police. If you don't, you are violating the law and school board regulations. Mrs. Ledger, I don't want to involve you in this but ironically, you are the school district's substance abuse director and I'm sure you know what the regulations are and what the State of New York has to say about drug use in its schools. Am I current in saying the boy should be reported?"

Lawrence did not like involving Eileen Ledger in this confrontation. It was putting her job on the line.

"He's right, Principal Mosse."

"I know that, Mrs. O'Hara. I think you can leave now. I'll be with you in a couple minutes."

Eileen Ledger got up, and with her back to Principal Mosse, gave Lawrence a smile that conveyed surprise that he had opened this hornet's nest but also one with an alluring twinkle in her blue-green eyes. For some unknown reason, Lawrence ran his tongue over his very dried lips which caused her to broaden her smile.

"Mr. Lawrence, I have a little gift here for you," Mosse said opening her drawer. She pulled out an envelope that was clearly school stationery. "This is your contract for next year, already signed. I'm going to do one of two things. Either I'm going to give into your threats, report the Afro-American child to the Niagara Falls Police Department, and tear up this contract. Or, I'm going to drop the discipline assessment against Danny Costini and give you the contract renewal. It is your choice, Mr. Lawrence."

Lawrence liked dealing with stupid people. It usually produced the easy goal he had in mind. Mosse was stupid. There was no way the notoriously ignorant and lazy Niagara Falls Police would arrest the black kid and test him for drugs. The police had a strong phobia for doing paperwork on juveniles especially considering that the courts rarely produced any judgments against offenders more severe than assigning them to the school district's drug intervention program. Danny Costini was another issue. A white racist could not be written off. Lawrence had no idea if

Danny was indeed a white racist but he did know that Danny's beliefs had nothing to do with the beating he took in the hall.

"I want the book."

Principal Mosse was about to rule that out but caught herself. She was as ignorant of <u>The Turner Diaries</u> as Lawrence and was acting on the claims of Dr. Belafont. Was the book white racist propaganda? She probably had no idea, which was Lawrence's hope. Mosse sat down behind her desk. Taking a key from the middle desk drawer, she opened another drawer on the bottom right side, the only one that could be locked on her desk. Lawrence saw the bright red cover of a book as Mosse put it on her desk and pushed it toward Lawrence. On top of the book she put the envelope with Lawrence's renewed and tenured teaching contract. The deal was done. Lawrence was not stupid enough to smile. He picked up the book and letter. He knew saying nothing as he was leaving was best. At the door, Principal Mosse spoke.

"You better be careful what you let your students read, Mr. Lawrence."

CHAPTER SIXTEEN

Beast To Beast

"You Mr. Lawrence?"

"That's me," said Lawrence looking at a man very close to his own age. If Lawrence had a military crew cut, they might be brothers. Lawrence guessed that the man was slightly taller at 6 foot 2 inches. The visitor was lanky with a prominent neck drawing attention to a long face holding a nose slightly aslant not broken. Unknown to Lawrence the nose took its slight turn due to a wrestling injury when the man was in junior high school. He had been intentionally shoved face first into the wrestling mat by his opponent, an obvious foul ignored by the referee and the focus of verbal ridicule launched by his foe. The man never wrestled or played school sports again.

Wearing a light tan short sleeved collared shirt over a white t-shirt, he was not muscular, but sinewy like a fine trained athlete who relied on technique and maneuverability instead of brawn. His eyes were narrow with dark, almost feminine eyelashes. His posture was pure military, stiff and erect, ready to drop and give you fifty push-ups. His was young, easily in his early twenties but with an aura almost childlike.

"I'd like to shake your hand, please sir."

Lawrence could have done without the "sir" but smiled and squinted at the request to shake his hand. Lawrence's first thought was that the man represented one the few religious sects that roamed the streets of Niagara Falls soliciting donations. Lawrence was prepared to tell the man he was not going to buy anything or make any donation. He was not given a chance.

"My name is Tim McVeigh. You helped out a friend of mine's son, Danny Costini?"

"Yeah, Danny was one of my students this year. Just how did I help him?" Lawrence was still not ready to allow McVeigh inside. There was an atmosphere of set-up here. Maybe McVeigh was a door-to-door salesman using Danny Costini as a hook. Maybe he was being set up by the school district and Principal Mosse.

"You kept him out of jail."

"Actually I got him to read, which was why he almost wound up in jail. Hey, come on in."

McVeigh walked military. He kept upright, his back taut. His arms swung in rhythm and were positioned properly at his sides. McVeigh scanned Lawrence's apartment like a sniper looking for insurgents.

"How well do you know the Costinis?"

"Only from gun shows. Danny's dad is a collector. I sold Danny The Turner Diaries which is what he said got him in trouble."

"It didn't do much for me either."

"Have you read it?'

"Yeah."

"That's good to hear. Quite impressive, isn't it? Where did you get your copy? Gun show?"

"No, I read Danny's copy."

McVeigh was not sure where to go with Lawrence. His ostensible purpose for being here was to thank Lawrence for standing up for Danny Costini. Down deep though, McVeigh was seeking sanction for his beliefs. This man might be another contact, one outside of the hunting and guns community. It was rare to find someone outside of these arenas who might have similar emotions to America's decline.

"It's a tough book to discuss with an English teacher, sir."

Lawrence noticed again the addition of sir it being perfunctory considering their similar ages. "You are definitely military."

"Not since the end of '91."

"Didn't like it?"

McVeigh was not a talker, he was more a preacher. Lawrence was controlling the discussion and McVeigh did not know where it would go. He was not even sure where he wanted it to go, why he was even here. He avoided Lawrence's question as if it was rhetorical.

"I know The Turner Diaries lacks a lot of literary ... It's a bit difficult to follow at times."

"That's because it's poorly written."

"You know the author was a physicist?"

"Andrew Macdonald?"

"That's a pseudonym, made up name. His real name was Pierce, William Pierce. He taught at Oregon State during the 60's when Vietnam was killing the drafted students he had taught. He saw the anti-war movement as a communist Jewish conspiracy. It never registered with him that those students of his needn't be sent to Vietnam to die."

McVeigh was taken aback. He knew the book, and reveled in it. He never bothered to look into the heart of the man who wrote it.

"The book is what's important. He got a handle on who's breaking down this country."

"Want a beer Tim?" Lawrence had no desire to get into a debate with McVeigh. He had been there before. Discussion with fanatics was pushing rocks uphill. Lawrence did not wait for an answer. If McVeigh did not want the beer, Lawrence would down a second one. He took his time. McVeigh was trying to sell something, but it was not religion or encyclopedias or home siding. Lawrence had seen the same effect in Danny Costini when he handed in his report of The Turner Diaries.

Returning with two bottles, Lawrence shifted the conversation. "Gun shows, huh? Danny said he got the book at a gun show. You do a lot of gun deals? New York's got to be tough, what with its anti gun laws?"

"Yeah, I get by. Don't make much on the book though."

"You get into guns when you were a kid?"

"Sorta. Just after I started school my Grandpa let me shoot his .22. Grandpa was a crazy old man but a loving one. We were kind of this farmer like family, only not really farmers. The early McVeighs were but that was long ago." McVeigh did not gulp his beer, just took a small sip. Lawrence did not react well to this. Here he had a possible white supremacist, gun toting ex-soldier in his second floor flat, and the last thing he needed was for McVeigh to get drunk.

"He had this garden out back of his garage. You know … grew corn, tomatoes, the like. He, Grandpa, and I'd go in the garage and shoot varmints out of the back window."

"I don't think your neighbors were too happy about that?"

"Not at my Grandpa's but neighbors where I lived got the cops on me for shooting ground hogs."

Lawrence could not sit. There was a nervous quality to this discussion that made Lawrence uneasy. He walked over to the bay window of his flat. He lived on Maple Avenue, just off the Robert Moses State Parkway, north enough from downtown to avoid tourists and the rapidly encroaching low income city dwellers. In time he knew this area would probably turn into slums but Lawrence had no intention of staying in Niagara Falls. The view from the window was excellent. Looking west he saw Canada and smiled every time he thought of the view the Canadians had looking east, old tenement housing. While he could not see to the bottom of the gorge, the cutting erosion of the Niagara River over millions of years had left a enthralling panorama of rocks and eskers topped by the beautiful Whirlpool Golf course only 2,000 feet from Lawrence's home. In summer he could see golfers going up and down, back and forth. Today was gray, the commonest of colors for Western New York from November through March. Even today, in the month of April, skies were gray and a fine drizzle of sleet pelted his windows, the wind rattling the panes. Niagara Falls and its sister to the south, Buffalo, existed physically on the edge of geologic depression and their people huddled for half of every year in psychological depression. It was a challenge to survive six months without dying or winding up insane. While it was not quite true, your skin might turn just as gray as the sky during late Fall through early April. Yet this might be the challenge, a gift to produce courage and survival ability in its people. You waited, you started waiting in October, for days when you thought you could hike down the parkway trail or bike the Robert Moses but instead were greeted by the wind and cold blowing off Lake Erie that locked you at home. Still you woke the next day hopeful the weather would change, and in two, maybe three more weeks, it would. As time passed, the outdoors not only flaunted your leaving, but Lake Ontario drew in its gusts and clouds and snow, ripping down from the northeast, to stop any adventure, be it a drive to the Rainbow Mall or to the movie theaters below Niagara Falls International airport.

"Where did you go to school?"

"Starpoint Central, Junior High and High. You know where that is?"

"Out as you go to Lockport. Kind of an interesting area out there, almost rural farm life, but don't most people work at the GM plant?"

"Yeah, my dad did at Harrison Radiator. I quit the Army and thought they'd have a job for me. Couldn't believe they didn't. Damned if they didn't hire blacks."

Lawrence paused, ignored him, and stared out of the window. In a week, maybe two, he could clean and oil his bicycle and do the weekend jaunts down to Niagara Falls State Park, two and half miles down the parkway and usually into the wind coming off the falls, and the remaining of his daily five miles back up Maple Street. When tourist season brought in the money and arrogance of the rest of the world, Lawrence went north, past Niagara University and the Niagara Falls Country Club. Rarely did he have to skirt ignorant tourists and lost travelers running him off the road into a ditch.

McVeigh wanted something. What? The conversation was strained. McVeigh was working on Lawrence like a traveling salesman selling magazines. No, thought Lawrence, it was more like a traveling evangelist selling bibles and seeking pledges and donations for the cause. McVeigh was not good at it.

"Listen, Tim. Why are you here? I mean I'm glad I helped your friend's son out of trouble. I appreciate you stopping by to thank me, but it seems you got something on your mind?"

"I got the impression you might be interested in guns and hunting. Also Danny said you speak out against authority a lot, give them reading to do about fighting for people's rights."

Was he recruiting me, thought Lawrence as he spoke? "Grandfathers seem to have this affinity with grandsons for teaching them outdoor life. Did yours have a monthly mailing of Field and Stream magazine?"

"Yeah, you're right. I used to go through it every time I visited," said McVey.

"You obviously got a lot more into the field than the stream. Mine taught me about hunting and how to use a rifle, but I never thought of it in an Army way, as a weapon. I hunted for food. Unlike most of the hunting population, I was not after the kill," said Lawrence.

"But I'll bet you liked it? Come on, Mr. Lawrence, wasn't it exciting?"

"McVey, you know how many deer I've killed? Three. Yet I stalked hundreds."

"Couldn't get them?"

"No, didn't need to. I did it like a game. I had no need to kill them. What I did get was learning, learning how to survive like they did. More than that I could trail them, and the better I became at learning from the prey. Are you trying to sell me guns?"

Lawrence's question was so abrupt that McVeigh's head jolted back as if he was avoiding a punch.

"No, I can't sell guns in New York."

"How about that book? You trying to sell me <u>The Turner Diaries</u>?"

"No, what makes you think I'm selling something?"

"No, I think you are trying to sell. You're trying to sell yourself. What I can't figure is, why me?"

"Look, I'm sorry I took up your time Mr. Lawrence. And thanks for the beer," said McVeigh taking his half empty bottle into Lawrence's kitchen, pouring out the remains, and zipping up the camouflage parka as he headed for Lawrence's door.

"The irony? No, irony doesn't work. Enigma maybe? No matter, how old are you Tim?"

McVeigh stopped, "I'll be twenty-four this month."

"That means you're only a half year younger than me. Yet for some reason I get the feeling you're trying to find some wisdom in me. I'm just a kid, really. Do you want me to validate what you are somehow?"

"I don't know what you mean by that?"

Lawrence knew McVeigh was smart. Lawrence could usually sense that in people as soon as he met them. Smart did not mean learned or being able to use that smartness.

"How long you been out of the Army?" Lawrence remembered that McVeigh told him this initially. Lawrence needed to back track McVeigh some.

"About four months," McVeigh opened the door slightly, preparing to leave.

Now Lawrence was more than curious. "You were in Desert Storm?"

"I was in the First Infantry Division, Charlie Company, Bradley tanks, sir."

"You drove a tank?"

"No, I was straight infantry but we worked with the Bradleys."

Lawrence remembered the Iraqi War as a joke, "what'd you guys do, wrap the war up in a couple weeks or something?'

"Seven days, sir."

Lawrence was going to repeat his request concerning McVeigh's obsequious use of sir but sensed McVeigh's obvious military personality was surfacing and Lawrence was being treated like an officer. Maybe this would get McVeigh to elaborate on his reason for the visit.

"Seven days? In seven days you guys ran the Iraqi army out of Kuwait?"

"Actually, it only took four days to rout them sir. They just could not fight, had no training. Their weapons, those that had them, were ridiculous. Smart bombs blew them to bits before we even got to where they were, sir. It was like a high tech turkey shoot.

Missiles were targeted and launchers watched it run right into their buildings ..."

"Why the pause? And what buildings? Did they have time to establish positions out in the desert?"

"I meant in Bagdad."

"Okay, I remember that. Didn't one of those high tech missiles kill off about 300 women and children?"

This hit McVeigh's weak point, cracking a part of that wall he boarded up when they first met, and he stood back a bit to attack, "It's war. That fucker Saddam Hussein had no problem executing thousands of his neighbors. It's how a fucking bully works. Son of a bitch looks for some weak little kid ... er, country and beats the shit out of it."

Lawrence went to the door and shut it. "Little hot in here for that camouflage jacket. Why don't you take it off, hang it on the chair. Getting a little agitated, aren't you?"

McVeigh was looking about the room, avoiding eye contact, the same non-contact he made with Lawrence when defending the U.S. Army's slaughter of civilians. McVeigh was right. Hussein wanted control of Arabia, specifically oil rich Kuwait and Saudi Arabia. A monster like Hussein needed to be caught and exterminated. It was a war. Innocent people died as happens in war. Innocent people have no choice but to face death when they are ruled by a tyrant. That Lawrence could not fathom.

"I'm sorry. I basically quit because of what happened there, sir. In my entire life I have hated bullies, been the brunt of their displeasure ..."

"Brunt of their displeasure, that's good Tim. I like that phrase, brunt of their displeasure. How did you do in English in school?"

"I passed."

"Did okay in writing?"

"Yeah, wrote stupid stuff. Some of the reading was okay," Lawrence went to the refrigerator, held up a Pepsi and asked if he wanted one. He grabbed a second bottle out of the refrigerator and handed it to McVeigh.

"What did you like to read?"

"Any book that I'd seen the movie of, especially like Planet of the Apes and Omega Man."

"You read Pierre Boulle's Planet of the Apes? You know what other book he wrote that was a great movie? The Bridge on the River Kwai."

"Yeah, but I didn't read it. And I know that Omega Man comes from Richard Matheson's short story I Am Legend."

This information reshaped Lawrence's vision of McVeigh. Both leading characters were put into survival situations as individuals and had to rely on their own abilities without any help.

"That's a very interesting concept Tim. Watch the movie, then read the book. More I think about it, the more I know that's how I became a voracious reader. Trouble is that it's rare for a teacher to use books from which movies are made."

McVeigh enjoyed the praise Lawrence provided and began to relax, "oh, also Treasure Island, read that because of the Disney movie."

"That's a great book. I really liked Stevenson's use of Young Jim Hawkins hearing the pirates' secrets. It was almost a contrived mechanism, but so scary you ignored its use. Great plot twist, the kind a teacher wants a student to recognize," responded Lawrence.

"It worked better in the movie, though. We got all these barrels of apples around my Grandpa's farm from harvest time. If I had been younger when I saw the movie, I might have tried to hide in one like Young Jim did and see what the pirates in my life had as secrets."

Lawrence saw the opening. "Did you kill anybody, Tim?"

McVeigh's head came up and both eyes stared deeply into Lawrence's. He started to talk but got hung up in his thoughts before they could be formed into words. He paused so as to not mumble.

"Yes."

Lawrence eased back in his chair, stretched out his legs putting the right ankle over top of the left while interlocking his fingers behind his neck. "Yes, that's it? Yes?"

"Am I supposed to brag about it?"

"It was what you were there for, wasn't it Tim?"

"No, I was there to stop an enemy that threatened our allies. Schwarzkopf, Bush, the Army told us Hussein had weapons that would wipe us off the face of the earth. One day we were told about nukes, next about biologicals that put us in agony for hours, only to die of asphyxiation as our lungs were eaten up like they had breathed in sulfuric acid. The general himself said even though we will win, thousands of American personnel will die, the war will last 6 to 7 months, maybe a year. None of it was true."

"How's that?"

"I killed. I was a sniper. I positioned myself about two thousand yards from an enemy with weapons that couldn't kill a dog at a hundred yards, and I nailed him center head with my sniper scope and rifle. All I saw was his head disappear in a red mist. Boom! His head was gone, body still upright looking for its fucking head! Guys in the platoon were all screaming, slapping hands, shaking me like some kind of celebrity. Did it again and again. Here I was, a fighting machine manufactured by the good old United States Army and I was assassinating helpless human beings. I got a fucking medal for it. It was like in Lee Marvin's movie "The Big Red One" when he said 'these are your enemies. They're animals. We kill animals!"

McVeigh was calm, a surface calm. Lawrence knew it was time for him to keep his mouth shut.

McVeigh continued, "we had to get rid of them. Put 'em in a sack and throw 'em in the pond."

"What?"

"When I was a very small kid, a family lived next to us sent their son out to the pond where I was fishing. He had a sack. I could hear sounds in the sack, meowing sounds, kitten sounds. The kid, with tears running down his face, was drowning kittens. Once I had a similar thing happen to me. One night I was driving going to Amherst and I saw eyes reflecting on the road in front of me. Deer were crossing and I barely missed running into one. I had to pull off into the other lane but a pickup truck in front of me hit one, sending it flying up into the air. Destroyed the pick-up and the guy had just bought it. The deer was an awful mess, laying in the ditch with its head half submerged in water, gasping for air through its nostrils. I got a hold of the pickup driver and offered him my 9mm Taurus pistol. He didn't move. I told him that he hit the deer and he needed to put it out its misery. He refused so I had to do it.'

"That's how brave my job was for Charlie Company. Innocent poor workers, slaves to a country, thrown into a pond. Kittens, like kittens but it was women, children, gunned them down. Officers said "no prisoners. So that's what we did. No prisoners."

Lawrence could taste the tang of remembrance - - Uncle George's description of Lawrence's odyssey in Viet Nam.

"No self-defense here, none. Hundreds of deserted Iraqi's abandoning Kuwait, walking a journey of miles over miles back to their poverty in Iraq. I stopped popping off people from a half a mile. Me and others just followed them. They had no food and rarely found water. Bodies laid in the sand, vultures gnashing away at flesh during the day, predators growling at each other for a leg or liver in the middle of the night. The eyes, the women's eyes were the worse. We were the evilest beings they could imagine. I'd offer some of the mothers candy and they fell down, fear sweating out of their bodies, not knowing I was trying to help, waiting for their last seconds on earth, hoping my bullet would not take her child with her."

So like his father's battle in Vietnam.

"Every one, sergeant, lieutenant, captain, Schwarzkopf took no prisoners. Add to it the enlisted men. It was a joke, a big party. I could hold on to what I did as war. I could accept my orders. What I could not hold or accept was when I saw other soldiers intentionally slaughtering weaponless men and helpless families. It was a fucking joke to them. An Apache helicopter wanted in on the action and raked the field with machine gun fire and rockets. Didn't even have to bother sighting. Killed two GIs leading the refugees out of the desert. Ground company threatened to return fire on the Apache, their own army. I heard the radio commands blasphemously shouted back and forth, eventually blaming the friendly fire on Iraqi hit teams. Iraqi hit teams? The ground commander sent the Apache after the long trail of Iraqi deserters with one order. Kill the Iraqi ragheads."

Lawrence was starting to seethe, not at McVeigh, but at the eruption of his own demons. He choked back the rising bile, glad he only had a bagel for breakfast. Why? Was it really the same? Maybe not in terms of motive but identical in horror. The dead were innocents. Saddam Hussein's troops were charades, facades with no backbone, no weapons to fight. The slaughter was the people.

"How many innocent people were killed?"

"They never knew. Iraqi soldiers? It was a stupid statistic. There were no soldiers, no fighting core trained. Hussein sent thousands of people out of Iraq with either no weapon, no ammo, or no sense of combat. He ordered his soldiers to take women and children. The Iraqi army used them as shields. Saddam was a blood thirsty tyrant, creating a wall of innocents to balance off the United States storm of weapons and soldiers. Saddam guessed the shield of children and women would stop the Americans from wholesale murder. They were shoved in front of the United States Army and we knew it. You would have had to be blind to think these people were an army. And we weren't dumb. Here was a chance to show off to the world the deadliest. strongest military force in the world. Who would know it was a fish barrel shoot? Nobody. This was the feel good war. No prisoners, that child could be carrying a mortar, that robed Iraqi grandmother might be hiding an RPG. No prisoners, kill the ragheads, kill their women, kill their old men and children. We need a tally, a score card to show how strong we are. A company commander would say thousands of enemy soldiers were killed, the battalion commander jocked it up to tens of thousands, and eventually the generals claimed hundreds of thousands."

"A couple months ago I looked it up in the library. The deaths of civilians and damage to civilian areas was specifically avoided by coalition forces as I remember the news after the war," spoke Lawrence. "The United States military seems to have it right, deaths from 10,000 maybe 20,000 or could have been 200,000. They did know that only about 150 Americans were killed in action and admitted that most were from friendly fire."

Lawrence did not explain to McVeigh why he had researched the Persian Gulf War. Following it on television had riled him. The whole show, and Lawrence started seeing it as a well staged media event, had familiar overtones that gnawed at his consciousness. It kept picking at him, a sand mote irritating his tear duct that could not be rinsed out, and feared rubbing would cause more harm. Similarities abounded, but was it trite, maybe ridiculous, to see war with Iraq as a Vietnam debacle, refought with a new perspective? The gain, where was the gain but as usual in its proper place, domination. Was this the answer to both wars?

"So you quit? I can see it, Tim. Trained to kill doesn't mean you accept the killing."

McVeigh was reluctant to continue, "yeah, yeah that's part of it. They gave me a medal and sent me to Special Forces. I couldn't pass the physical tests."

"That sounds hard to believe."

"You got to have your heart into it. It was like basic but with respect. You are a killing machine. They didn't care what you killed. Then came, why they didn't care. The country needed people like special forces that trusted in their leaders. They did not just need them for places like Iraq and Afghanistan, but on the home front. Ragheads are everywhere. They run the streets of America, killing for drug money, armed because of the Second Amendment. Someday I might be asked to ..."

McVeigh stopped, alarmed that he might have gone a bit too far with Lawrence.

Lawrence saw where he was going, "you better be careful where you go with what you think you see."

"What I see every time I show up at a gun show is a police force waiting to close you down. What I see is television with criminals holding up pizza joints at gun point and citizens not allowed to defend themselves."

McVeigh had been close to Lawrence's vision but at an obtuse angle. McVeigh saw the urban war as not being able to defend yourself. Lawrence saw a country strengthening itself as a military force from ground level police on the streets to using flimsy wars and international conflicts to create the dominant world power.

"Tim, I think you see government demons in the shadows. Are you really that worried that the government will take away your power to defend yourself?"

"Yes."

"Do you believe the government might actually invade your home to strip you of protecting yourself?"

"Yes."

"Why would they want to do that? Where's the gain? Do you legitimately believe the answer is in The Turner Diaries?"

"You're a hunter. You want to turn over your weapons to the government?"

"They're not out to take those kind of weapons from civilians, Tim."

McVeigh was riled up and he knew it. He could not explain to Lawrence how he felt as a soldier, having the professional ability to defend himself and yet knowing that right was being challenged. He had killed for his country and knew the sin of murder. How could they strip him of this ability and throw him into a world where a gun brandished by a criminal infesting the streets could murder him, unprotected? Why was he not allowed to protect and nourish his loved ones and property, insuring their safety that was provided by his ability to control and fire a weapon? Who were these people that were going to put him at the mercy of killers and thieves? Were they so powerful that they could not be stopped?

"Mr. Lawrence, I'm sorry to have run you through all this. To be honest with you, Danny was an excuse. This country needs people who stand up for the rights of other people. I was hoping to get you involved with Second Rights protection, maybe encourage it in school?"

"I'd never do that, Tim. It's very dangerous to prejudice a young person's mind before they have a chance to learn."

"No, I wouldn't do that. I don't do that to Danny or any of the other kids that visit the shows with adults. I'll go now. You've done me some good, though. Wished I'd had at least one teacher like you growing up."

"Tim, you grew up the same as me only a couple months later. Don't make me feel so old."

"Look if I run across any guns you might be interested in, like good deer rifles, I'll get a hold of you, okay?"

"You know you're right about the guns that are out there. The criminals using weapons in Buffalo are making the city look like Deadwood anymore. You'd expect Wild Bill to come walking down the street any minute to square off in a gun fight."

"That's part of the trouble. The porch monkeys have the guns. They drive down south to Virginia, and buy them at hardware stores. Only good thing is that most of the time they shoot each other."

Lawrence let the racial profile go, "guess the old gunfighters wouldn't be drawing Colt's from holstered belts now days."

McVeigh had the door opened but still had that long drawn and weary visage which had been prevalent all day, "that's my business, Lawrence. Want to get into a gun fight today, you best be carrying Colt M1911A1s in the Miami Classic II shoulder holster system developed by Galco."

Lawrence had no idea what McVeigh was talking about, but he waved and half saluted McVeigh as he went down the stairs. It had been a long afternoon, and it was now near evening and it was still Western New York ugly outside.

CHAPTER SEVENTEEN

A Beauty

Lawrence looked out of the faculty room widow toward the east. A clear weather front faced him and was predicting the same for tomorrow, Saturday. Should he prepare for a bicycle trek up to Lewiston and across the Niagara escarpment, maybe camp overnight in one the wooded areas just south of Lake Ontario? Not if it rained. Today it was 46^0 F and clear. It had warmed enough for an overnight bike trip but not if there was a chance of rain, if he was miles from Niagara Falls and home. The weather forecast was for the 50's and clear. He thought he would just have to decide in the morning using his own forecast which was the only true weather prediction if you lived in Western New York. Wake up, put your head out the window and if it doesn't get wet, it will be a clear day in Western New York.

After the loud crash of a telephone receiver on the telephone cradle in the faculty room, Eileen Ledger administered the coup de grace to her conversation, "fucking ass hole!"

There were only three others in the room when Ledger voiced her profanities. She sat, still fuming, on the Goodwill, early American sofa commissioned to the faculty room. A rather mousy math teacher who took Polaroid photographs of children sleeping in her class as a way of reporting them for administrative discipline was out the door before Ledger even sat down. The math teacher could not handle the blasphemy. The other teacher in the room was the Chairperson of the English department, Belafont.

"Mrs. Ledger, I find that bit of language rather inappropriate for …"

"Belafonte, why don't you just cool it?"

Mr. Lawrence, how many times must I implore you to call me …"

"Asshole?"

Belafont was now at Lawrence's mercy. Having tenure, Lawrence had already faced down Principal Mosse with his failure to address Belafont or any other Doctorate of Education holder as doctor this or doctor that. Lawrence had shown her the research proving that it was incorrect to address anybody as doctor unless they were medical personnel. Otherwise these pseudo doctors were boosting their ego in a fatuous manner. As Belafont prepared to fume and fulminate, two other teachers walked into the faculty room. Lawrence did not know their names, but one was a physical education teacher, the other a social studies teacher and friend of Eileen Ledger's.

Eileen Ledger spoke, "anyone care to see the Sabres play tomorrow night?"

Lawrence did not know Eileen Ledger as well as the other people in the room. Yet he was surprised that she got no response. Lawrence spoke up, "it's a playoff game, isn't it?"

Lawrence had followed ice hockey a tad when he was younger and lived only a train ride away from the Spectrum in Philadelphia. The Flyers games were a near impossibility for getting tickets.

"Yep, they're up two games to one on the Bruins. I've got two seats. Now I've got one for me and one for whoever wants to go with me."

The social studies teacher spoke. "What's wrong with Zig?"

"He's going to Rome tonight. Just like that, he's off to Italy. So I'm available. How about it Ned?"

"Nah. Got a softball tournament tomorrow. Means booze and beer tomorrow night."

"I'd be glad to go with you."

Eileen turned to look at Lawrence,. "You sure? Starts at 8:15 and runs late?"

"I'm sure my mother will let me stay up," said Lawrence.

"Well great, Mr. Lawrence. I never did get to learn anything about you. We'll have a chance to get acquainted. Where you live?"

"Here in the Falls, about a mile north of the high school near the Robert Moses Parkway, on Maple."

"I live on Grand Island, down River Road. I'll make it easy to find me. When you pay the toll take the first right onto River Road. You'll go toward the Niagara River and there's a parking area just at the bend that goes south alongside of the river. It's a picnic area that'll be empty this time of night. I'll meet you there. Say about quarter after seven tomorrow night?"

"Sounds good."

Ledger smiled at him and Lawrence, as he did every time in her presence, felt a bit scary inside and nervous.

***

"What is this, a 1970 Shelby?" Lawrence stuck his head inside the passenger side window of Eileen Ledger's mustang.

"No, '69, same body, same engine. 70's were just left over 69's. Ford Motor chased Carroll Shelby out of the engineering department and in '71 built the worst Mustang that ever existed. My sweet little pony became a 1970's compact car. Iacocca gave the world a smaller Mustang, cheaper, fuel-efficient. By the middle of the 70s Mustang become a sporty, oh how I hate that word, Ford Maverick, a small size and small power almost a Falcon."

"This beauty had to cost a bit."

"Thirty-six thousand and another two thousand for body restorations. Get in, Mr. Lawrence. Mind if I call you Peter?"

Lawrence slid into the passenger side and was engulfed by the posh bucket seats. He hooked up his seat belt. "Most people just call me Lawrence. Lawrence is best."

"Okay Lawrence, we're off to the Aud."

The hockey game was like any hockey game, slow but with those moments of violence that made it all worthwhile. Lawrence remembered the Flyers games back home when he would be doing busy work and wanted background noise to keep him alert. The Sabres were not Philadelphia. When they started a fight, it was pedantic for the most part, the players sort of saying, "look we can mix it up if you want." The Bruins on the other hand, had their Boston reputation to keep up which came close to the violence of the Flyers. The Bruins were up two games to one on the Sabres in the Wales Conference playoffs and could run themselves to 3 to 1 with a victory in Buffalo, leaving two home games in Boston and needing only one win. The Sabres were terrible away from home and had a losing season record of 31 to 37. A loss at the Aud would mean having to win two games on the road in Boston plus one at home. Ironically, the Sabres had one of their most penalized seasons in history serving over 2700 minutes in the box, nearly a thousand more minutes than the aggressive Bruins.

At the buzzer it was a tie and that meant overtime.

"Want another beer, Eileen?" Lawrence did not especially like beer, but to be a considerate guest of Eileen Ledger, he drank two LaBatts during regulation time. Eileen was an enigma. Until this night she was only an attractive, well-educated and stylish proper school employee. Adding to those traits, Eileen now showed a more aggressive and down to earth person inside the hockey arena. Eileen booed the refs as loud as any redneck in the stands, cheered as loud as the next fan when Buffalo scored, and put away six beers and most of two large, heavily salted pretzels. If asked about eating pretzels, she would reply that she only have some bites from Lawrence's.

"No, time to stop. You want one? I'm buying. Come on, it'll do you good."

"No, it'll put me in line at the men's room before we can drive out of here."

It had been a strange hockey game, not because of the two teams, but because of Lawrence's relationship with his date. Eileen and he could only talk randomly because of the contained volume of noise inside the ice rink. The seats, being tight, had given Lawrence considerable body contact with Eileen during most of the game but not all the contact was due to the seats. Their shoulders would abrade as she wiggled to comfort during the hockey match and she would turn toward Lawrence with a smile both of apology and acknowledgement. She wore a Buffalo Sabres team jersey that hung loosely over her more than mature chest. Lawrence did not see her as stacked, but as bountifully healthy. Eileen had a flickering foot that beat to a semi fast rhythm as it dangled over her right knee. At times she let her toes innocently oscillate against Lawrence's calf. He could not say that she was flirting with him, but would not deny her effect on him.

"You really get into this don't you?"

"I used to play field hockey in high school. Never could get into skating. Of course ten years ago no female would strap on pads and a helmet and go out onto the ice. That's changing though."

"Girls are playing ice hockey up here?"

She stared directly into his eyes, "Mr. Lawrence, just what do you mean by that statement?"

Her facial expression was one of either slight anger or slight teasing, until she let up on him and smirked, "of course girls play ice hockey up here! You Southerners can't handle your women doing battle?"

"Eileen, I wouldn't go out on that ice."

"What are you, a golfer tennis player?"

"Both way beyond my family's standard of living."

"You didn't play any sports in school?"

"I did track."

"High school and college?"

"Yeah, both. Did the high jump and in college the javelin."

"No team sports?"

Lawrence got uneasy with people asking about his personal life. His life was no embarrassment, but his reaction to people when discussing his life was one of caution. The less people knew about you, the more protected you are. His family was close knit, free with each other in the sharing of their lives. His family, and especially his mother Evelyn Southern and grandfather George, interacted with outsiders by keeping it close to the vest. This trait was inherited by Peter. It was a very predatory attitude, which Lawrence recognized most during times when he was stalking animals.

There was no predation in Eileen Ledger's intercourse with Lawrence, but why did he feel like the quarry?

"I've always kept to myself. I learned it as I was growing up. My father was not there to raise me, so mostly I grew up as a prodigal of my mother and my grandfather. No, before you ask, my father didn't abandon me. He was an MIA in Viet Nam. My mother was sort of an outsider back home, being a French Canadian and all. She taught me games and led me to reading. Grand Pere helped to acclimate to growing up as an American kid with Little League, Boy Scouts, both of which were okay. I had friends. I just didn't like being judged as part of a team. Track worked great. In high school you made the basketball or football team because the coach took you in. It wasn't a matter necessarily of your being better. You just had to hope you got a good chance. I had friends that played Babe Ruth league baseball but they never got a chance in high school because they were ninth or tenth graders. Coaches already had their teams set. You'd play JV for a year or two and maybe you'd move up."

Eileen had her arms folded and legs crossed, signs she was focusing on Lawrence's response, "so track was a good choice for you. I'll bet the coach put up the high jump standards, leveled the bar, and if you leaped the highest, you were entered in the track meet?"

Lawrence felt less guarded. He had already spoken more about himself to any human being outside of his family. There was an aura about Eileen Ledger's eyes and smile that made him not only comfortable, but attracted him both sexually and intellectually. Lawrence knew without ever having seen her work with students that she was very good with young people. Eileen gave you an intense feeling that she cared and wanted to hear your story.

"Yep, that's me. I could beat everybody in the school."

"And you carried it over into college?"

"That and the javelin. Both had an intensity to them."

"How good were you? How high did you jump?"

"Did six nine in college. Got a silver medal in the high jumps at the MAC Championships my senior year and a bronze in the javelin."

The buzzer blasted loudly. Fans were rousted from rest rooms and refreshment stands as the overtime period began. Lawrence and Eileen turned from each other to square themselves into their seats. The Bruins came out to boos, the Sabres hit the ice to wild screams, and Eileen Ledger rested her right hand on Lawrence's left thigh squeezing it just enough to be familiar but nothing more at least for tonight. Her grasp took Lawrence out of the ice hockey game. What had been a risky liaison with a very attractive but married woman was becoming more than a social outing of two people who worked together and were out for the night on a "we are just friends" activity.

The Sabres lost. The Sabres were now 1 and 3 in the playoffs. With three more games to go, the chances of them winning the playoffs were slim to none. The rush out of the Aud was bizarre, not because the Sabres had lost, but because it was drizzling outside. Eileen had parked in a lot under the thruway, reducing the wetness somewhat. It was after midnight, people were tired, and the traffic was horrible. Finally they got to the onramp and headed north toward Grand Island.

"You asked me about athletics, how about you? You do seem the type."

Eileen Ledger chuckled a bit and spoke, "are you saying I look like some dyke Russian shot putter?"

Lawrence laughed, "you know I'm not. But you did say you played field hockey. That's not exactly like making feminine jumps during figure skating while wearing a tutu."

"I've always been sort of a tomboy. Used to beat up Sammy, the Jewish boy next door, once a week just for the fun of it. I liked sports and aggressiveness, the fight. Got me into college."

"You played field hockey in college? Where did you go?"

"No, I did not play field hockey in college and I went to Canisius College right here in Buffalo. I could have commuted since I grew up in Kenmore but my father had some crazy idea that since I was so good at sports ... by the way, I played basketball and softball at Kenmore High School ... that he'd pay for my college if I majored in physical education and lived on campus. Those were two mistakes he made."

"How's that?"

Lawrence handed a quarter to Eileen as they neared the toll booth noting the irony of Buffalo. When you drive into the City of Buffalo, there is no toll. The toll booths are set up to make you pay to leave Buffalo. There is a kind of humor in one having to pay to leave Buffalo. Eileen down shifted the Mustang, kept her knees holding the steering wheel while rolling down the window with her right hand and tossed the quarter out the window and into the machine. The gate rose, allowing them to escape Buffalo, New York. She never looked at the booth and hit the toll machine with the accuracy of Whitey Ford.

"First he assumed that since I screwed up most of my grades in high school, except gym class, that the only program I could handle in college would be phys ed. He assumed it was easy. He was very wrong. I nearly flunked out twice. Second he insisted that I live on campus because I was sort of .. wild might be a good word for it."

"Your father never went to college, did he?" Lawrence laughed gently.

"Nope. Canisius is tight assed but saying you're a dry campus and actually cutting students off is just talk. I got into booze pretty heavily, even some pot which I didn't really like."

Lawrence could sense Eileen was getting a bit embarrassed, "enough said. So you became a gym teacher."

"I also grew up. Went to Buffalo State and got a Masters in Counseling and left physical education behind me."

"Had to surprise your father."

There was an awkward moment of silence and Lawrence caught Eileen rubbing at the corner of her right eye. "It was the proudest moment of his life. I didn't know how much he loved me until the day I graduated with that Masters. Never saw the man cry."

Lawrence could see the brilliant and dazzling lights out the windshield as they went over the south Grand Island Bridge making the night time view of Niagara Falls a hallucination in the northwest clouds.

"So you teach English. You don't look much like a Belafont."

"Sometimes you get lucky."

"An outdoorsy guy and an athlete, why English?"

"Jack London did it. My mother read to me every night until I could read myself. It became such a ritual that I just followed in her footsteps. It's rare when I go to bed without doing some reading."

"I know what you mean. I do a couple books a month myself. I really love Stephen King and I've got into Grisham's books. I guess they're not your elite classics."

"King is good. When he sticks with basic horror stories like Cujo and Pet Sematary, there's no better. I like Grisham's books, too. Classics are classics. They don't make you elite or any smarter. Most of us started out with Where The Wild Things Are anyway."

"Listen Lawrence, I want you to forget about my little explosion at school."

The Mustang was going under Whitehaven Road and Lawrence looked out the passenger window and barely seeing the darkened amusement park, Fantasy Island, now closed for the night. "Your words didn't bother me. It was what happened to you that was scary. I wouldn't have guessed from just meeting you that you had that amount of anger in you."

"It wasn't just about the hockey game alone. My birthday's April 30th, Thursday. You kind of like to have your husband with you for that kind of occasion, you know?"

Lawrence saw no tears, which made no sense unless she had already written off her husband's neglect. "You miss class room teaching?"

"No, what I do now is very small groups with very diverse students. I don't teach them peer say. I work with their problems. In some ways it's easier than the classroom. Other ways it's an emotional nuclear war. Initially I had a lot of trouble handling the diversity that came to me."

The Mustang pulled off I190 to River Road, Eileen made a right hand turn, and within seconds was in the parking lot of the picnic area. She pulled up on the passenger side of Lawrence's Bronco II. "Like your Bronco?"

The rain had stopped and Lawrence got out of the Mustang and walked around to the driver's side. Eileen rolled down the window and Lawrence squatted down to talk to her. "I'm not big on automobiles. Had my way, I'd never own one or drive one. This one does the job. Gets me to work, gives me room to throw in my bike or skis, and has four wheel drive for this lovely snow you people got up here."

"So Lawrence, Mister English teacher, what book would you recommend I read?"

"Ever read anything by Pat Conroy?"

"No, I don't think I even know any of his books."

"Not even The Prince of Tides?"

"Yeah, that's a Barbra Streisand movie. I never saw it. Wasn't it out just this past Christmas?"

"Pat Conroy wrote the book. Try it. You'll like it. Conroy is a very excellent writer. One more thing," said Lawrence gesturing with his fingers to Eileen Ledger, "lean your head out a bit."

When Eileen leaned out, Lawrence slowly lifted his right hand up and to the left side of her head, gently caressing her long hair. She did not bolt, nor look away, but her eyes held his until they closed slowly as he leaned and kissed her softly on the mouth.

"Thanks for a great night," said Lawrence as he stood, turned and unlocked his Bronco. Eileen looked at him buckling into the driver's seat, raised her right hand, and slowly waved to him as he headed back to Niagara Falls.

***

"Is Ms. Ledger in?" Lawrence stood in the extremely small office of the SAIP program, holding a small stuffed animal and a wrapped package. The secretary barely noticed him and obviously could care less what he had with him.

"Her students go to the busses in five minutes. If you wait here, after the bell rings, you can walk down to the classroom and see her."

"Thank you."

Lawrence took one of two classroom chairs and waited for what seemed hours to hear the cacophonous end of school as the bell rang. It was not much louder than the screams of the secondary students rushing, pushing, shoving, and bullying as they went to their busses. Lawrence did not wait for permission and ignored the secretary's request to stay put. The students were nothing like those he taught. This was the Niagara Falls Rehab Building, euphemistically labeled Second Chance School because the school board received too many complaints from parents when they sent their children to a rehab school. The students here were in trouble and were trouble. Second Chance School was redundant in most classes, since most of these students were on their third and fourth reassignment here from their home school. It was not a question of these students needing a second chance, their assignment here gave the home schools a second chance to get rid of them. They were the dregs of teenage society. They were discipline at its worse failure in a normal classroom situation. They bullied other students, refused to do class work, made a mockery of the school's locker system by stealing from other students without trepidation. With sheer bravado they confronted other students in the cafeteria to either steal their lunch money, or beat up any student who would not use their ID card to buy them lunch. Bus rides to and from school were a traveling holocaust of thug beatings and forced sex while the bus driver turned off the video so as to not have to deal with the violence. Daily the assigned Niagara County Policeman had to physically take down and handcuff predators. None were legally punished since the court system preferred not to deal with juveniles and the mounds of paperwork that came with them. Teachers of these students were hired first for brawn, second for a combative attitude, and in as an afterthought, their academic ability.

Lawrence had a few of these students during his tenure at Falls High School. They wound up at Second Chance. One student kicked him in the back when he broke up a wrestling match between him and another student in the hallway outside of the classroom door. Lawrence turned on the boy, caught him under the chin with his forearm, and slammed him into a wall of lockers, and raising the boy off the floor. The boy said Lawrence attacked him for no reason. He and his bro were just having some fun and Lawrence punched him when he was not looking, otherwise he would have "put him down." Lawrence laughed. While the boy was taller than Lawrence, Lawrence knew he could have put the boy down for the count instead of pinning him to the wall. Ms Mosse got all over Lawrence for physically touching a student which stunned him but taught him a lesson. Do not be a witness; keep out of it the next time. Lawrence had been lucky that time since the video camera in the hall ceiling caught the two boys fighting in the hall, Lawrence breaking it up, and the boy kicking Lawrence.

The boy went to Second Chance School, nicknamed as Sucks by the students and teachers. Lawrence's guess was that the boy was probably in jail now.

Lawrence waited by the door to Eileen Ledger's classroom as the blasphemous bellowing rang out from the school buses carrying a cargo of societies refuse as they sped around the main building and out onto the streets where the students would now become Niagara Falls problem until tomorrow at 7:30AM. As the last bus driver ran the red light, minimizing his time exposed to the Second Chance School detritus, Lawrence saw Eileen Ledger walking toward her classroom's outside door. What amazed him was that she dealt with these misfits each day yet seemed unaffected, as evidenced by the smile that crossed her face when she saw him.

"Decided to visit the zoo today Lawrence?"

"I'm pretty good at handling discipline problems where I teach, but these students of yours are pure animals."

"You're right Lawrence. They are animals, most of them. Mine are a bit less, though. I deal with the "druggies" so to speak. The students you saw as the busses pulled out are mostly dangerous discipline problems of the high schools, more from yours than LaSalle High School."

Lawrence followed Eileen into her semi dark classroom. She did not turn on the lights but went straight to her desk, sat down, and now showed the weariness of seven plus hours, as she offered him a chair while kicking off her shoes. She lounged back in the swivel chair and after gasping a relief breath spoke, "so did you like the hockey game Saturday?"

"Very much, and I didn't forget today's your birthday."

"Am I right that that stupid looking elephant is for me or do you carry around stuffed animals all the time?"

"Stupid looking? Do you know how long I had to search to find Dumbo?"

"Why it is Dumbo! Where did you get it?"

"Niagara Falls Boulevard Mall, here. It fits you."

"I remind you of an elephant? That's not going to get you very far, Lawrence."

"No, not an elephant, the character. With a little faith, you can fly. Isn't that sort of what you're about? I mean from gym teacher to an counseling position?"

"You don't know how much I'd like to go back to phys ed. This job drains you. My kids aren't usually the ilk you saw out in the parking lot. They aren't sent here for a semester or school year. They're here for two weeks, that's all."

"That's not so bad, then? Only two weeks?"

"Yes and no. You don't get the hard criminals that SCS gets, usually. Maybe once in a while. SCS is just bad kids, kids that would spit on you if you fell and couldn't get up. Mine range from some pretty bad, to honor roll students going to Cornell to study astrophysics. How does an honor roll student wind up here? Ring dance, prom, gets caught throwing up after too much booze or worse, one of the local thugs sells here some pot in the home school. Bingo, she's here. Scared to death, but if she doesn't do my program, she doesn't graduate."

"The effect this school has on a kid like that must be horrific. They got to be scared to death when they come here."

"Some are. Some are glad to be here."

"How's that?"

"They're dealers. Every student in my program is a prospective client."

"Ah ha! Makes sense and being put in your class creates a market."

"Got that right," said Eileen as Lawrence handed over his gift wrapped package.

"Is this a mirror so I can see how much I look like Dumbo?" The smile stirred Lawrence. Eileen Ledger was the most sexually beautiful woman Lawrence ever met and it was all epitomized by her smile.

Eileen carefully levered the ribbons off the wrapping paper, finger nailed through the tape, and neatly folded the wrapping paper into a smooth sheet to be used again.

"The Water Is Wide, huh? Another Conroy book? I bought Prince of Tides and am near finishing it. Pat Conroy writes very well. Thank you for recommending it and for this one. What's it about?"

"Teaching, but that's all I'm telling you. Wait. Just one other thing. They ought to make every teacher read this book before they can teach."

"That good?"

"You trying to get me to tell you about it. Not going to."

"I rented the video and I must say that the movie of Prince of Tides didn't do too bad with Conroy's book. Takes a bit to accept Streisand as Lowenstein, but Nolte's pretty good, and I like George Carlin's role. They make a movie of this book?"

"Yeah, I think it was in the early seventies. It's good although I've heard some teachers ram it pretty hard. Movie is called "Conrack" because the assholes that make movies think people would buy more tickets with that name."

"Conrack? Why's it called Conrack? Who's in it?"

"On the first question, I'll let you figure it out. Second Jon Voight stars. Did you ever see Deliverance? Great book, almost as great a movie. Voight's the leading character. Burt Reynold's in it too."

"No, Isn't that the movie with the banjo music?"

"That's it. You got to see it. A real classic. Especially gets to me since I do outdoors stuff like canoeing. Listen, are you doing anything for dinner tonight?"

Lawrence threw the question in fast and caught her eyes looking directly into his. He had remembered her saying she would be alone for her birthday and hoped that she was still in the same situation. Lawrence doubted that Eileen Ledger, a married woman, would agree to go to dinner with him.

"No, I'm not. Are you inviting me, Mr. Lawrence?"

"It' a sad day when a lovely woman has to spend her birthday alone. Have you ever been to the New Schimschack's in Sanborn, out on Upper Mountain Road?"

"I've lived almost thirty years in Western New York and never heard of it."

"Absolute best prime rib in the world. The cheesecake rivals NYC. So can I have the honor of taking you to dinner on your birthday?"

Lawrence had no idea that Eileen Ledger would say yes.

"You may, but it'll have to be a bit late if you don't mind. Every other Thursday, I have a parent conference at 6:00PM here. Kids can't leave my program unless the parents attend this meeting. It only lasts about an hour, rarely more than an hour and a half. Is that too late?"

"Not by me. Where should I pick you up?"

"You know, it might be good for you to sit on in this meeting? I doubt there's any classroom teacher in the district that knows what's going on in this program. How's about it? Are you up to meeting the moms and dads?"

"Yep, I'll make it back here by six," said Lawrence, his mind trying to grasp the situation he was entering. "They stop serving at 9:00 on Thursdays. If we're done with the parents by 7:30, we should make it there. Being a Thursday, I don't think we need reservations?"

Lawrence got up from the student seat and slowly started for the door. Eileen Ledger met him at the door and shut it. She was a tall woman, five feet eleven inches, so that when she gently put her hand behind Lawrence's neck and pulled his head towards her, Lawrence barely had to lower his mouth to meet hers. It was gentle but firm, her tongue stirred him, and her hips swaying into his abdomen stirred him even more. Lawrence had never been kissed with so much passion in his life. If she had not slowly eased off, Lawrence would never have let go.

***

"The French onion soup is great here. You ought to try it," said Lawrence.

Eileen put an enigmatic smile across her face, a malicious yet friendly smile and said, "really? I was thinking of maybe the charbroiled ostrich."

Lawrence had sat in the back of the classroom through the parents meeting. True to her word, it took only a little more than an hour due to Eileen Ledger's abrupt but needed intrusions when parents got off target. She shut them down, politely, but often aggressively. They had talked little as Lawrence drove his Bronco II to Sanborn, leaving Eileen's Shelby Mustang in the fenced school parking lot for which she had the security code to re-enter when they returned. Lawrence could see that she was tired and caught up in the aftermath of various parental complaints and attacks. He left her to her thoughts and headed up the Niagara Thruway toward Queenstown, headed east on long Saunders Settlement Road, took a left turn on 429 at the community college, and was soon in the parking lot of the New Schimschack's Restaurant in Pekin New York.

"It had to rain. Can you see those few house lights out the window?"

"Yes, but not very far."

"They actually go on right up to the shores of Lake Ontario. On a clear day … I will not sing this … On a clear day you can see across the lake to Toronto. It's even better at night. You can see the lights at the top of the CNE tower."

"Funny, I've spent my entire life in Western New York but never ate here before. What else do you recommend besides the French onion soup?"

"I always get the king's cut of prime rib. Might be too much for you but the queen's cut is not that much less. And don't say you want to order the char broiled filet of ostrich."

"I'm not much of a beef eater. The chicken Rolundo sounds great."

The waiter came and asked what they wished to drink.

"What would you like Eileen?"

"There's something hypocritical and duplicitous about ordering an alcoholic beverage after having a meeting with parents of students having substance abuse problems. I'll do a vodka gimlet, please."

Lawrence laughed and ordered a Dewar's on crushed ice, double, "not going to feel guilty are you?"

"No, the problem my students have is not the substance, but the abuse of it. So what did you think of the group?"

"I found myself thinking in stereotypes which is wrong but true."

"Wrong but true?"

"Yeah, the upper class soccer player who made only one mistake when she was at a party and somebody slipped drugs in her diet Coke. Her mother probably used the same excuse when she got smashed in high school."

"You're right, she's a stereotype. Too real to believe, right out of a bad movie. Except she does drugs and alcohol. I assume you heard her mother's remark that her daughter never touches alcohol except some wine once in a while with dinner?"

"Can't get more stereotyped than that,"

The waiter returned with their drinks and Lawrence held up his scotch toward Eileen who reciprocated by clicking her gimlet to his as Lawrence wished her a happy birthday. Lawrence ordered French onion soup for both of them and chicken Rolundo for Eileen, medium well-done prime rib for himself. Being a Thursday night, there were only five other tables with guests.

"If the soccer player was only the abuse I see, my job would be more than simple. Did you notice the scrawny tall blond boy who wouldn't sit with his parents?"

"Henry Hawkins?"

"How did you know his name?"

"I had him for English two years ago. I didn't want to say anything while we were there. I don't think he wanted me to remember him."

"That would be Henry alright. He's done about everything, booze, every kind of pill, loves marijuana which is his downfall whenever he gets close to quitting."

"I take it those were his parents he walked in with but sat a mile away from?"

"His mother yes, but the man is his … Can't really say step father since I don't think his mom married him, but you know what I mean."

"All I remember about Henry was how quiet he was," said Lawrence. "Did his work, was fairly smart, but just before spring break he disappeared."

"What I tell you here, I shouldn't. It would cost me my job if anybody knew I told you."

"Yeah, I understand that."

"Henry got busted in school, busted selling pot. School police officer got him in a rest room selling."

"Did he go to court?"

"No! And this is the problem I have in doing my job. Kid sells marijuana in school, gets caught, and the school handles it, not the authorities."

"Public relations would be my guess. Heaven forbid the community learns their kids go to school with these bad guys. So what happened to Henry?"

"Second Chance School."

"But isn't SCS for behavior problems?"

"It's for anything school administrators want it to be. Somehow Henry got sent to Second Chance School and has been there since you last saw him. Technically, he's a senior and should graduate. First he's got to get through my course, though."

Their meals came. "Wow, this looks great!"

She cut a piece of the boneless chicken breast and smoothed some of the white sauce over top of it, "you've got to try a piece of this. The spinach mixed with ham is excellent. I was leery about it, but damn does it work. Here, try this little piece."

"You see what I've got in front of me don't you?," said Lawrence opening his hands in front of his prime rib.

"Yeah, could you get anymore of the cow on your plate? You need a chain saw just to cut it," said Eileen after scraping some Chicken Rolundo onto Lawrence's plate.

Lawrence ate the proffered chicken breast and asked if Eileen wanted to try some prime rib, which she did not.

"Is Henry going to graduate?"

"Got me, I told you that I get them for two weeks and rarely see them again. Even though Henry's in the same building as my program, the school keeps their students away from my classroom. Believe me, that makes my life easier. When Henry leaves, I doubt I'll see him again."

Lawrence remembered Henry as a sleeper, a student who would doze off in class, head down off in dreamland, solid as a block of concrete. He was a smart kid but out of place in school. The waiter came and took away their plates.

"Before you say no, they have excellent desserts here. I go for their hot apple pie with brandy sauce," said Lawrence.

"That's a bit much for me. They have cheesecake? That's one of my favorites."

"When I don't do the apple pie, the cheesecake's the choice," said Lawrence and when the waiter came back, Lawrence ordered the cheesecake plain for Eileen and a coffee to go with his hot apple pie with a scoop of vanilla ice cream.

"The way you eat, I'm surprised you're not overweight. You did say you bicycle, didn't you?"

"Yep, but I don't do skin tight latex, Star Wars helmets, and skinny tires. My bike is a trail bike and I keep a pace that lets me enjoy where I am. Winter, I do cross country skiing but usually on my own. I didn't cross country ski until I moved up here. I thought it was kind of lazy and stupid looking. Art teacher talked me into doing Allegany State Park one weekend with a couple of his friends the second winter I was up here. I learned fast just how wimpy cross country is. I lost sixteen pounds that weekend and slept twelve hours the night I got home. Next week I bought my own skis, and now I try to get out two or three times a month before the snow slows up."

"Zig, he's my husband, has us do an Aspen trip every Christmas vacation. Downhill skiing. He's pretty good but I'm still only one step up from the bunny trail."

Lawrence felt a clenching in his stomach at the mention of Eileen's husband. He remembered the husband's treatment of her from their hockey game a week or so ago. Lawrence was here with Eileen because Zig was off on business somewhere, somewhere Eileen had told him but which he forgot. Was the reality here that Lawrence was just somebody to take up Eileen Ledger's loneliness until her husband came home?

"You weren't kidding me were you? There they are," said Eileen Ledger as she looked out the window. Schimschack's was built on an escarpment of basalt and below the restaurant was a plateau of flat land that lead to Lake Ontario. Their seats by the window were like a stage view from a balcony of Lake Ontario. Once the rain stopped and the clouds evaporated, Eileen and Lawrence could see the lights of Toronto across 50 miles of water just northeast of them.

"Amazing, isn't it?"

"It's very beautiful and quite romantic. I'll always remember you giving me this for my birthday."

Lawrence savored his hot apple pie, reveling in the exquisite combination of warm and sweetly tart red apples covered by Schimschack's vanilla bean ice cream. The dark and aromatic coffee capped off the excellent dessert. He noticed Eileen's quietness and knew it had little to do with the cheesecake that she was only nibbling and poking at with her fork.

"I canoe when the weather's good. Ever canoed the Allegheny Reservoir? River's kind of tame but the camping and fishing are excellent."

Her smile was barely perceptible. It faded at the edges and was only a charade. Lawrence knew he had lost her but he never really had her. Still Eileen, was a woman to behold and admire even though she could not be his.

"I've never done any camping. All I'd need was some snake crawling into my sleeping bag and I'd have a heart attack."

"Never will happen, Eileen. Not many snakes up here. Too cold for reptiles. Not many insects either. I grew up camping and hiking, fishing and hunting. It's a world that brings back your sanity. Hearing what you go through, that might be something that'd be very good for you."

"Why do you say that? You think I have some kind of personal problem? Is it that obvious?"

"You are the sexiest women I've ever met. You not only have a great body but you're a bold, aggressive, and extremely intelligent human being. That you took me to the hockey game last week and celebrated your birthday with me tonight, doesn't mean we're just buddies."

"How long have you lived here, Lawrence? Isn't your three years' goal coming up? I believe you've got the school system by the horns now. You're tenured, aren't you?"

"That's right."

Eileen Ledger was changing the course of their discussion. "Aren't you involved with somebody? I mean like a girl?"

"Is that your rationale? Both of us are spoken for?"

"No, it is not. But are you involved with a woman?"

"Would that make you the other woman?"

The smile lifted; the charade had ended. Lawrence injected his humor to which she replied, "could I be?"

"Is that a request?"

"Lawrence, have you visited the Erie Canal at night?"

"I don't even know where it is."

"Let's go."

Lawrence paid the check and followed Eileen out to his Bronco II. Opening the door for her, she said, "make a left on to Upper Mountain Road out of the parking lot."

Lawrence drove east until Eileen told him to take a right in Cambria on Shawnee Road. She leaned next to him and grabbed his right arm, swinging it over her shoulder as Lawrence drove left-handed. Lawrence carefully watched the very dark, unlit road in front of him, as she ran her right hand over his chest.

"At the next intersection make a left. You'll be on Lockport Road. Stay there for about four miles," she said. Lawrence stopped the Bronco II for another car going up Shawnee, preventing his immediate left turn. Eileen turned her body into him and kissed him deeply.

"You're going to make a turn at Bear Ridge Road. It's just before a bridge over the canal."

Lawrence was having trouble concentrating on his driving as her hand gently rubbed his loins. "Do I get to see the mules?"

"Okay, see the bridge? Slowly make a left hand turn but don't go far. It's been a while since I've been here, like twelve years or more."

Lawrence saw the bridge and slowly made the left turn. Since they had left Pekin, they had only run across one car. The Bronco's lights lit up the shoulder of Bear Ridge Road where it crossed the bridge approach on the west. You could see a gray stoned road leading down a steep sloop off Bear Ridge Road.

"There! See that old road? It goes down to the canal, but take it easy or you'll wind up in the canal."

Lawrence had better control now that they had reached the destination and Eileen had sat back in the passenger seat. The Bronco shook and sidled sideways going down the sloop but there was no need to switch to four wheel drive. There was another road at the bottom that paralleled the canal. It was only wide enough for a single car.

"Go right under the bridge."

Lawrence went slowly until Eileen pointed to the bridge beams on Lawrence's right and told him to park between the beams. No sooner had Lawrence clicked off the headlights and shut down the Bronco's engine, then Eileen had his pants opened, underwear pulled down, and was stroking his penis.

***

"Jesus! I never had a man do that before!"

Lawrence turned from the basin in his bathroom and looked out into the bedroom. He was brushing his teeth when he spoke to Eileen who was, at the moment, lying totally naked on her back on Lawrence's bed. "Woman?"

"Never went that way, Lawrence." She was covered with sweat. "How did you ever learn to do that?"

Peter Lawrence was in love with Eileen. There had been other women but Eileen Ledger was the best he had ever met. Her well-built and sinuous body was not just a showcase, but an intoxicant to passion. Her body went well past what any lover could ever hope for and brought Lawrence to sexual pain, a pain so intense he could never have enough. He begged her to stop every time they fucked, but would not let her withdraw. She knew how to get that second, third, and sometimes fourth orgasm out of his body. He had never known it was possible.

Despite love and its physical pleasure, Lawrence still remained taciturn when defining his life. Emotionally, he wanted to keep her from his inner self. He could not overcome that weakness of not letting people deep into his soul. It was a defense mechanism, one he lived by all his life. Maybe it was his predator prey psyche.

"Watch this," said Lawrence as he walked naked over to Eileen, knelt beside his bed, and gently with the palm of his left hand, massaged her left breast, cupping and lightly squeezing, and with his right forefinger, tweaking her hard nipple.

"Jesus, stop that," she yelled as she jumped up from the mattress. Her eyes closed with his snap that created in her a post orgasm shock.

Lawrence had learned how to please a woman when he dated a lesbian softball player in college. It had been a challenge to Lawrence and the softball player. They had crossed paths as athletes. He was the track high jumper and javelin thrower and she was a pitcher on the college's softball team. They were exposed to each other daily, the track being at one end of the training fields with the softball diamond adjacent to it. Lawrence had to wait each day for softball practice to end so he could practice the javelin. After the track team finished practice, Lawrence would watch the softball team's practice and joke with them. The shortstop was his favorite and the one he had sensed might go both ways. It was not a challenge to Lawrence's masculine ego to turn a lesbian straight by acting the macho man. It was the opposite if anything. Lawrence wanted to please his mate and the ones he had been seeing were pretty much ten minute missionary interludes with little if any pleasure for the woman. So Lawrence cased the softball team. As a team they were leery of Lawrence and would make fun of him being a track athlete. Lawrence smiled, made no excuses and was one of the few male students who came to their home softball games. Lawrence became a team pet, then a talisman since they seemed to win more games when he was a spectator. After turn downs and more turn downs the shortstop agreed to go to dinner with him.

She surprised him, dressing about as female as a woman could get for their date. She made it clear as soon as they ordered dinner that she was not going to have sex with him and become his conquest for the bragging rights with other male members of the track team. Lawrence did not circumvent the morals of other people to get what he wanted. He faced her with the truth that he needed help with pleasing a woman sexually. The shortstop accused him of lying but she could not respond to his question of why would he lie? They spent two weeks together, intimately. It also included another girl. Lawrence never had sex with either of them but was able to bring both women to orgasm simultaneously. The softball shortstop had so many orgasms one night that Lawrence's tongue was numb the next morning. Lawrence learned to be slow, learned to avoid high pressure, and learned when to stop. He found that edge a woman has. To the amazement of both softball players, he learned the coup d'gras of female orgasm, that final flick of the tongue when his mate bordered on unconsciousness. Both of them would slap him across the face when he did the post orgasm nipple tweak to them, but not too hard.

Lawrence returned to the bathroom, took a small swig of vanilla flavored Listerine, and gargled. Summer was close, close enough that even in Western New York some of the days were hot. The Niagara River finally was ice free which meant the boaters could actually set sail or start their engines on Memorial Day.

Eileen slowly rolled off Lawrence's bed, shook her hair twice, and got up. Lawrence never failed to admire that luscious body, firm but with a muscular firmness that Eileen made every effort to keep from becoming even a little fat. She exercised four or five times a week and watched her diet carefully. Eileen knew how to use her body completely when having sex with Lawrence.

She walked slowly by Lawrence with her teasing, almost childish smile, running the tip of her tongue slowly back and forth over her upper lip, then turning her gaze slowly down to Lawrence's penis. Her smile broadened as she spoke to him, "I'm going to take a shower, unless you think he's ready for another go?"

Lawrence was mesmerized by Eileen's insatiable sexual appetite and despite his youth and prime physical condition; he could not keep up with her literally. "You might have killed it."

Eileen rotated the shower faucet arm until steam gushed out of the top of the shower stall. Lawrence could not believe how hot Eileen regulated the shower water, close to a burn.

"You'll set off the fire alarm when you have that shower so hot."

"It won't be the shower that sets it off, Lawrence."

Lawrence was dressed by the time Eileen exited the shower. There was no rush to shower since Eileen used all the hot water. Rubbing her towel between the swells made by her breast with her right leg up on the toilet seat, she spoke, "remember Henry Hawkins? The boy you had in class that was at my parents' meeting?"

"Yeah, how's he doing?"

"He's in a halfway house for a drug overdose."

"What did he do?"

"Speed in alcohol. Chemically, methamphetamines, also known as chalk."

"What, did he come to school high?"

"No, the police arrested him at home. Henry had my card on him when he was arrested. It seems Henry high balled his speed with vodka at a party, got sick, threw up, started having hallucinations of seeing and hearing his step father fucking his mother. So Henry went home at two o'clock in the morning and took on the stepfather. Henry lost but his mother ended up sending the stepfather to the hospital via a baseball bat."

"Jesus, what these kids get themselves into scares the hell out of you."

"Henry is very typical. I had him getting close to the root of his problem through a CBI plan ..."

"CBI?"

"Yeah, Cognitive Behavioral Intervention. Ironically, his step father's insurance covered Henry enough that he was seeing a therapist once a week, the cost covered by the step father's medical plan. While I can't really tell you what was going on with the therapy, I'm sure you can guess the essence of his problem."

"Sounds like Momma's sex life was too much for Henry to handle. What I remember about Henry from class, he was either falling asleep or aggressive. In fact, when we were doing <u>Of Mice and Men</u>, Henry joked around about Lennie killing animals, like it was cool."

"Henry's in the halfway house for the rest of the year, Lawrence. Amazingly, he's passing all but one of his classes. I've talked to his teachers. With less than a month to go, they'll pass him. He can graduate if ..."

"I gather this is where I come in?"

"He will fail English if he misses anymore classes."

"Even though he's incarcerated?"

"Yep, he'll not graduate. The halfway house is Henry's last shot. He'll stay there for three to six months. His therapist staked her professional life on him. She signed all the papers putting him there and keeping him as a patient. She does once a week therapy with him at the house."

"Which means Henry could graduate if his English teacher tutored him there."

"That's right. Henry cannot leave the house until there's a hearing before a judge with testimony that shows he's controlled his behavior and is no longer a danger to himself or people around him. That he can do. But if he fails English he fails the year and goes back to school in September."

"Belafont's his English teacher, right?"

"Son of a bitch refuses to tutor him. Gave me an earful about ridding the system of scum like Henry. He even said that the best thing that could happen is for Henry to OD and die. It seems Henry did not get along with Dr. Belafont. Henry had two suspensions because of threatening behavior in Belafont's class just this last semester."

"Will Belafont agree to Henry having a tutor so he can pass his class?"

Eileen dropped her towel to the floor and slowly walked, stark naked, up to Lawrence. There was still some wetness glistening off her body and her nipples were rigid. "That's where you come in. Oops, did I just use a double entendre? "

Lawrence was sitting on the edge of the bed. Eileen knelt down before him, running hands up and down his legs. He was stirring.

"If you get him to approve transferring Henry to you as his tutor, Belafont is totally out of the picture. You'll become his English teacher of record. Why Lawrence, I believe it's come back to life."

***

The juvenile detention halfway house was just north of the Robert Moses Expressway as it runs from Grand Island Bridge to Niagara Falls. Lawrence met Eileen there after school, so he could tour the facility and make sure the staff knew he was there to help Henry Hawkins.

"How did you ever get Belafont to agree to you being Henry's teacher? What, did you threaten to beat him up or something?"

Lawrence shrugged, not really understanding why it had been so easy, "got me. I caught him after school and asked him if he'd mind me taking over as Henry's English teacher. He started to get riled a bit, but then asked me if that was the kid that you were handling. I stayed cool and let him go on a little diatribe about these "druggie kids" sleeping through his classes. He returned the conversation back to you and got a little personal about it."

"Got personal about me?"

"I think he gets excited just thinking about you."

"God that's scary. What did he say?"

"Just what I would say, that's one hunk of great sexual femininity."

"Okay, what did he really say?"

"Actually it got to be a little bit uneasy. He said that it seems you and I are very close. Said the whole school was talking about it."

Eileen had nowhere to go with this. It had been one of these dangers that made her relationship with Lawrence both tremendously exciting and precariously fraught with comeuppance should her husband find out. That was unlikely since Zig Ledger had nothing what so ever to do with the school system and had always abstained from attending any related functions.

"What did you say?"

"I told him that I have students with problems that need your, that's you, Eileen Ledger's help. We need to discuss these kids, so of course we get together. He just smiled and said it sounded like a good reason. I haven't seen that buzzard smile in three years. Truthfully I think he just wanted to get rid of Henry Hawkins."

The front doors of the halfway house opened into a small lobby the space taken up by a few chairs placed across from an attendant's counter, where a middle aged, black man was sitting on a stool reading the newspaper. He recognized Eileen but still asked for photo ID. Eileen showed her school district ID and introduced Lawrence. The man looked over Lawrence's identification and filled out a registration card to put on file.

Eileen explained that they were here to meet with Henry Hawkins and the receptionist pushed a button below the counter. Lawrence could hear a metallic click and buzz.

"Go on in through the doors. There's a guard that supervises the recreation room and student study spaces. He'll introduce himself but you've got to show him your identification cards."

Lawrence was surprised at how much the detention house was like the Boys Club recreation center where he used to work during college. It was moderately long but lacking a bit in width, eliminating any type of sports activity. Some boys were playing board games and one or two were doing written work at the study desks located amid several library shelves. There were only seven young men in the recreation study area. Henry Hawkins was not one of them.

"You here for Hawkins, right?"

"You got it," said Lawrence but the man ignored him and spoke to Eileen Ledger.

"He's in his room. He spends most his time there sleeping. Ain't good for him but nothing I can do about it. Maybe you can Missus Ledger."

"Show me to his room. This is Mr. Lawrence who will be tutoring Henry over the next few months."

There was a thirty foot hallway with rooms lining each side. Like the rest of house, the interior walls were concrete blocks. Except for the front reception area, there were no other windows. Lawrence could easily smell a faint bleach odor. Henry's door, like all the rest, was a double door, the top which opened without a key, exposing a steel meshed screen attached to the solid oak bottom door that had a key lock. The attendant pulled open the top oak door and looked through the screen.

"No, he's still asleep. What you want me to do? Wake him?"

Eileen said, "yes, right now." The man pulled out a group of keys on a steel ring, found the one for Henry's room, and spoke.

"Henry, if you awake better get up, you hear?"

Henry did not move. Lawrence passed by the man and into the room. He shook Henry's shoulder.

"Better not do that, sir. Some these boys get a bit angry and start fighting someone waking them up."

Lawrence put his right palm in the middle of Henry's back so if Henry came up at a start, Lawrence could keep him flat faced on the bed's mattress. Grabbing Henry's left shoulder, Lawrence shook Henry's arm until he got a reaction.

"Hey, what the fuck you doing?"

Henry tried to rise quickly but Lawrence gently kept the pressure on the boy's back.

"Time to get up Henry. Do it slow Henry."

"Lawrence! Mr. Lawrence, what the fuck you doing here."

"Come on, Henry. You're not impressing anybody here by using the "F" word. Sit up."

Henry sat up and faced Lawrence.

"Hello, Henry. How you doing in here?"

"Food kind of sucks, place smells like ammonia, but it reminds me of home."

Lawrence laughed, "let's hope not for too long."

Eileen spoke, "Mr. Lawrence is now your English teacher, Henry."

"Halleluiah. That son of a bitch Belafont is a monster."

"You got any books here, Henry?"

"Take a look, Lawrence. This is all that's mine. Three cement walls, pull down ledge they call a bed, and one desk. They say that when I've burned out the little chemical binge in my blood and pass their urine test, they'll leave the door unlocked. Right now if I got to piss, I have to wait for one of these guards to come let me out to the potty down the end of the hall."

"We're not guards, we're attendants. You don't have to wait long boy."

"Yeah, he's right. He's cool Lawrence. Night man? Better watch out. I think he likes being here with us fresh virgin asses."

Eileen spoke up, "let's have a seat over at the table in the study area."

Once they were seated, Eileen continued, "Henry, as I told you, Dr. Belafont agreed to switch you to Mr. Lawrence .."

Both Peter and Henry responded, "Lawrence, not Mr. Lawrence."

Lawrence laughed and shook Henry's hand.

"Okay, we'll agree to that. He's to be called Lawrence." Smirking at Lawrence as Eileen continued, "the deal is that you've got to pass Lawrence's English class as, just as if this were summer school. But you must get through drug intervention too. The district has approved the mental health professional that your step father's medical plan designated. That's one good step. She won't come here though, Henry. You'll be transported by an attendant once a week to downtown Buffalo to meet with her."

Henry spoke, "hey, that sounds good. Get's me out a here for some air."

Now that they were in brighter light, Lawrence noticed for the first time that Henry had a large bruise on the side and top of his left eye.

"Henry, do you realize just how close you are to being in a world of hurt?"

"Let it be Peter," said Eileen massaging the muscles in Lawrence's upper arm.

Lawrence knew Henry, remembered him well. Henry looked at his life as being a big joke. He would laugh off being late for class, falling asleep in class, not having his work finished, or being caught cheating on tests. Henry used his smile to make everybody accept his lack of seriousness in school. Unfortunately for Henry Hawkins, the smile worked and even worked well enough to win over Lawrence when Henry did not do his work in class.

Lawrence let it slide. "Henry, are you good enough for us to start tomorrow?"

"Hey, let me look at my calendar Lawrence. Yeah, seems I can work you in."

Lawrence did not have much faith in bringing Henry Hawkins around. Just looking at Henry was exhausting. He was constantly scratching at the sides of his folded arms, his skin was one degree from being a corpse, and he had trouble breathing. Eileen had told Lawrence that he should be prepared for this. He was not. The boy looked like a walking cadaver. How was he going to get through an entire marking period of English in a couple weeks?

***

"Lawrence, Lawrence, Mr. Lawrence," spoke Dana Nuevello, the Superintendent of Schools as he got up from his desk and motioned Lawrence to have a seat in front of it. "I don't know whether to fire you or give you a raise. Here have a seat."

Lawrence sat in one of the armless chairs in front of the dark mahogany desk while Nuevello walked to the large window behind his desk.

"I've been hoping for years that somebody would deck that prick Belafont."

Nuevello seemed satisfied that the world outside of his office bowed to his presence in the window, and he returned to his desk but remained standing.

"Lawrence, you're a very clever young man, especially for being what, twenty-three?"

Lawrence knew he had to control himself since Nuevello was on the prowl, stalking Lawrence like a panther cornering a lamb, "twenty-four."

Nuevello ignored Lawrence. "Kept to yourself for three years, taught our fucked up curriculum exactly as New York State wrote it, made no waves, let that bastard Belafont push you around, got your contract, know you're protected now from being fired."

Nuevello sat down and interlaced his fingers, putting a smile on his face. Dana Nuevello, the Superintendent of the Falls School System was not a large man, maybe five four or five in height. Regardless of the season, he always wore dark suits, usually pin-striped. He had well groomed hair, dyed pitch black and reeking of pomade that kept his widow's peaked forehead prominent. Nuevello always smiled, whether he was handing out diplomas at graduation or tearing apart an employee before firing him. He was savvy in face-to-face confrontations and a master at attack after wooing his opponent into a lull. During this whole confrontation, Nuevello made minimal eye contact with Lawrence. That changed abruptly as Nuevello's large black almond shaped eyes stared directly into Lawrence's face.

Very gently manner he spoke, "well you fucked up this time boy. Tenure might protect you from being fired arbitrarily but tenure or not, I can axe you for decking Belafont."

Lawrence was caught but Nuevello would have a hard time justifying that what Lawrence did was assault on another teacher since Belafont had made the initial contact.

"I know the school has a video camera in that hallway. Look at the tape. I was just defending myself."

Nuevello laughed. "Bull shit. You call that lame confrontation he made in your face an assault? Belafont couldn't intimidate a kindergartener. No one will buy you were defending yourself. Christ you broke the son of a bitch's jaw Lawrence."

Nuevello got up from his seat and walked around the table towards Lawrence. "What are you, some kind of boxer or something? Damn Lawrence, what'd you do? One, two jab and catch him with a cross?"

"Sounds like you know."

"Yeah, being a small shit when I was a kid meant a lot of getting beat up. My father sent me to work out at a gym when I was eight. Loved it. Problem was I was still small and the big shits would overwhelm me."

"The tape?" said Lawrence. He could not be caught in a brawl here, verbal or otherwise, so he intended to keep his comments to a minimum.

"Funny thing about that Lawrence. Tape got erased. Asshole security guard used it to tape soap operas. Can you believe that?"

"No."

"So I've got you on an immorality termination, except I doubt our friend Belafont will testify in court. I say in court since I'd guess that's where we'd wind up if you challenged being fired."

Lawrence trained his eyes on Nuevello and held his gaze. It was like trapping a deer in the dark with a flashlight. Dana Nuevello's smile ebbed and fearing that this confrontation could seesaw into him becoming the prey, he stated. "Lawrence, I don't want to fire you and there's a way out of this. Belafont will drop his complaint against you if you apologize …"

"Won't happen. You can go all around why I should apologize but it'll never go down. Belafont deserved what he got and if I had it to do again, he wouldn't get back up this time."

"Are you a fucking idiot Lawrence?" asked Nuevello, getting into Lawrence's face. The two men were less than a yard apart. "I can bring this off. I can see that you never get a job in any school in the country. I've got that power, Lawrence. That what you want?"

Lawrence just smiled, "do it. I always enjoy a good fight."

Nuevello's eyes opened wide, so wide that Lawrence could see the red veins pulsating in the tissues in his eye sockets. There was saliva edging its way out of the corner of Nuevello's lips. Dana Nuevello prided himself on his ability to intimidate and scare people and he could see that Lawrence showed no fear at all. He held Lawrence's gaze, waiting for him to back-off and there was none. Nuevello let his eyes close slowly, ingested the saliva from his mouth, and brought his lips up into a shit eating grin. Nuevello also knew how to set up a prey for the kill. Lawrence eyes flickered. This little man had another weapon, another strategy that could take Lawrence down.

"Quite a man, aren't you Lawrence. You don't back off, do you?"

There was no need for a reply and Lawrence made none.

"Forget the apology. I wouldn't apologize to that prick myself. You're a good man, Lawrence, a proud man. Need more people like you in this world. You got high ideals, sound and basic morals. That's good," said Nuevello as he went back to his desk, took off his pinstriped suit coat, and sat down. It was time for the attack. Nuevello rolled up his sleeves, leaned back in his swivel chair, and put his feet up on the mahogany desk, carefully keeping them on the desk blotter so as to not scratch the wood. With his hands behind his neck, Nuevello launched his best weapon.

"You're not a bad teacher, Lawrence. You got fair to good evaluations, enough at least to keep you on contract. Oh, by the way, it seems you've gone out of your way to help others on my staff."

Lawrence could smell the onslaught.

Nuevello paused, feet still on his desk, fingers interlaced behind his neck, stretching out the moment for the kill.

"Let's see," said Nuevello as he dropped his feet to the floor, swiveled his chair to the left, and picked up a folder. "You're doing tutoring of a substance abuse student over at the Juvenile Detention House, aren't you?"

"Yes, I am."

"That means you work with Eileen Ledger, don't you?"

"Yes, I do."

Nuevello hesitated. What he was about to say would either destroy Lawrence's aggressiveness and get him to agree to Nuevello's demands or get Nuevello's nose broken. Either way he would get from this confrontation what he needed to achieve.

"What a nice piece of poontang! God, I'd love to get me some of that."

Lawrence stirred, the face-off was ended and the battle enjoined. Nuevello would bar no holds, follow no rules, and would care less about the people he destroyed. "It's a shame you're such an ugly little shit. Nobody would want to fuck you"

Nuevello stirred from his seat but stopped from getting up. He leaned back. Lawrence was not a typical sycophantic, kiss ass teacher like most. Lawrence showed no personal fear and Nuevello felt a little stir of fear going up the back of his neck. Lawrence had his own ethics and if Nuevello pushed him too far, Nuevello was sure that Lawrence would physically assault and damage him. Nuevello was physically scared but enjoyed it, as did Lawrence.

Nuevello smiled, a gaping smile, one put on solely for the benefit of his opponent. Lawrence recognized it instantly. Nuevello pretended to ignore Lawrence's comment but knew Lawrence had scored, "how'd it go when her husband came after you?"

Nuevello knew what had happened and Lawrence could not retreat. "It's none of your business."

"Ah, but you are so wrong Lawrence. Immorality, Lawrence, immorality. You work in a strongly religious district here. Good Catholic culture. Screwing another man's wife just isn't one of those things we let go by, turn our heads away from. Hell, Lawrence, there's still a state law against it."

Lawrence was trapped.

"You're a smart man, Lawrence. What do you think the school board would say about two teachers shacking up immorally, immorally because one of them is married to another man. Shame, Lawrence. Shame on you."

Nuevello walked behind Lawrence to a secretary desk, pulled out the top drawer and Lawrence could hear a match being struck. Soon Lawrence smelled the easily recognized aroma of a cigar. He did not turn. Lawrence knew his head was in Nuevello's guillotine and he just had to keep still until the blade fell. The smoke got closer as did Nuevello who was now right behind Lawrence. He put both his hands on Lawrence's shoulders.

"Very simply, Lawrence, you're dead. I've killed you. You go down."

Nuevello patted Lawrence's shoulders twice, gripped them firmly, and Nuevello returned to his desk chair, exhaling smoke upwards to avoid smarting Lawrence's eyes.

"Got you don't I Lawrence?"

"No, you don't. I'll just get up from this chair, beat the shit out of you, and leave."

"Yeah, you could do that. Man like you would just write it off, wouldn't you? Walk out and start another path in life. Except for one thing Lawrence. Ledger gets fired as soon as you walk."

Lawrence was stunned. None of this seemed to make any sense. Why was Nuevello making such a big deal about his affair with Eileen? Yes, it was a religious community but not so much that anybody would care about what an English teacher and a drug abuse counselor were doing. Was it for Belafont's benefit? Nuevello admitted he could not stand Belafont so that ruled out Belafont as the cause of this confrontation. Maybe Nuevello was just exerting his power. Lawrence had been very close to insubordination with his attitude and caustic comments. Was that enough to get Nuevello to fire Eileen? She was irrelevant in the total picture.

Lawrence took in a big gust of air through his nostrils, laced his fingers together, engaged his arm and back muscles to tense and relax. He let his mind relax. Nuevello had no intention of firing Lawrence or he would have just done it. Lawrence and Eileen were insignificant in the scheme of things. Was Nuevello just exerting his power? No, it would not have gone this far. Lawrence could not win in a butting heads confrontation, or could he? It was time to attack.

Lawrence got up and walked to Nuevello's desk. Nuevello leaned forward, elbows on the desk, cigar between the fingers of his right hand, his eyes looking up at Lawrence.

"My mother's going to be really mad at me," said Lawrence.

Nuevello saw a small smile on Lawrence's face. It spread to a wide grin which Nuevello could not ignore, so he smiled.

"Your mother?"

"Yep, my mother is French, well mostly French. She, like all French people, hates Italians. I'm going to have to tell her I got fired by a God damned guinea wop."

Nuevello laughed at Lawrence's comment. "You fucking frog, how dare you call me a guinea wop. I oughta punch you in the nose."

Lawrence laughed. "Look there's more going on here than just Eileen and I loving each other."

"Loving each other? Boy, you are in way too deep."

"That's my problem. If you wanted to fire us, I'm sure you could. If you wanted to do that, you wouldn't waste your time dueling here. You'd have just done it."

Nuevello had his turn with a shit eating grin. "Here's the deal asshole. I don't care if you fuck the cafeteria manager, but you've got to agree to the demand that Belafont's made."

"Which is?"

"That druggie you're tutoring, Hawkins?"

"Yeah, what about him?"

"Belafont's pissed that you're going to be his teacher of record. You shouldn't have decked him. He wants to get back at you through the kid."

"You're kidding? Doesn't make sense."

"You're right it doesn't make sense, and you're right that there's more to it then is on the surface. Leave it be. Belafont wanted to press charges against you but I showed him the tape."

"Which is now gone."

"He doesn't know that, and besides, I saw the tape and would never let him go after you for that."

"Why?"

Nuevello swiveled in his chair and avoided Lawrence's eyes, He did not speak for a few seconds, "stay out of it, Lawrence. You're on the edge of a long gang plank here. If you want to get off it, turn around, take off the blindfold, and do what I ask."

"Which is?"

"Belafont is going to be reinstated as Henry Hawkins's teacher. Now, before you blow up, he will not be tutoring Hawkins. You'll still do that. Belafont demands that he grade Hawkins. Whatever you do with the kid, Belafont grades the kid's work at the end of summer school."

"So Belafont can flunk Henry without me being able to intercede?"

"That's the deal."

Lawrence did not like the conciliation at all. Belafont could just nail Henry for sheer spite and Lawrence could do nothing about it. Or could he? Belafont was scared to death of Lawrence and avoided him like the plague. Would he be dumb enough to chance another confrontation with Lawrence? Probably Belafont wanted to stay as far away from Lawrence as he could get. More and more it looked like a matter of honor. Belafont getting his honor back by forcing Lawrence to agree to Belafont overseeing Lawrence's evaluations of Henry Hawkins. Lawrence could live with that.

"I don't like it but let's see what happens."

"Lawrence, you made a good decision. You got a bad attitude about you, Lawrence. You can't handle authority. You're not going to do well with Bruno Scarpetti."

"Who?"

"Your new principal. I've moved Rolanda Mosse out of Falls High School. She's now downtown, an administrator. She's officially the Physical Education Coordinator for the school district. It's something she might be able to handle. At least she won't fuck it up."

Lawrence turned to walk out.

"You aren't going to make it here, Lawrence. To make it here, you've got to be subservient. I don't see you doing that."

"Why should I?"

"Because men like me rule the world."

"The world? That's a pretty big ego, Nuevello."

"That it is. By the way, Belafont told me about you're not calling him doctor. I agree with you Lawrence. Fuck if I'd call somebody doctor just because they got some K-Mart blue light special degree in philosophy of education."

"Then why do you?"

"Cause I use them, manipulate them into thinking they are the rulers of their domain. Don't give a shit if calling them some pseudo doctor is pompous and self aggrandizing. If that's what it takes to get something out of them, than fuck it. We square here, Lawrence?"

"How long do you give me?"

"I don't know? Gone to kiss some ass? If so, and you start calling me Dr. Nuevello, you might make retirement. Damn Lawrence, you'd be a good administrator, boy. Tough ass. I could send you down to a school and let you butt heads with the fucking union reps. What say, Lawrence?"

Lawrence smiled and reached out to shake Nuevello's hand, "I'd say you need to read some John Steinbeck, Mr. Nuevello."

***

Every man must face this world as it collapses, as must every woman. Women seem to face it better than males. In the past weeks Lawrence had watched his world turn to chaos. His confrontation with Dana Nuevello just added more destruction to his world. Lawrence knew better than to let it get to him, but knowing the misery, pain, and upheaval were time controlled and would be replaced by better times, did not make the reconstruction of his world happen. Time may heal all wounds but all wounds need time for mending and attention to removing the scars of total demolition. Lawrence brooked total destruction of his world from nearly every compass point. Patience was needed but patience was the weakest of Lawrence's talents. He was sure that Nuevello would put his head on the chopping block. Despite Nuevello's hand shake, there was a tenseness in their face off that hinted that the problems not over.

Lawrence had reneged on his own knowledge about survival. One had to back off from assault, not take on too many adversaries at a time. You must take your simplest demon to first and begin to work your way through the forage, weeding out minor enemies one at a time until you reached the Satan of your conflagration. He was fighting on all levels and feared losing Eileen Ledger, who had become the target of all his travails.

Less than two weeks ago, Lawrence had returned to the teacher's room after his last class to find Eileen standing in front of the large windows facing Niagara Falls. It was an unexpected treat that turned into poison. Behind Lawrence, Belafont entered the teachers room beaming, a smile that Lawrence knew the man rarely used. Eileen turned from the window to face Lawrence, not realizing that Belafont was also in the room.

Belafonte spoke to her immediately, "That's a beaut! What did you do, run into a door?"

Lawrence could not believe what he saw. Eileen's left eye was swollen, almost closed. She also had a bruise on the upper right side of her face that was partially hidden by her hair.

"Peter, I need to speak to you in private. Is there anybody in your classroom now?"

Belafont continued his sneer as he walked across the room to the closet where teachers kept their coats and boots. Lawrence held open the door for Eileen and she led the way to Lawrence's classroom. As they were leaving he could hear Belafont mumble just loud enough to assure Lawrence heard him, "yeah, that's one hell of a shiner."

No one passed them in the hallway as they made their way to Lawrence's room.

"Who the hell did this to you?" Lawrence asked as he put his hands on her shoulders. She would not face him, even when he gently tried to maneuver her around. She stood weak, bordering on tears, but would not turn.

"Zig knows about us."

"He did this to you?"

"Lawrence, he knows we've been ... meeting. Shit, he knows we've been fucking our brains out."

"How? You've told him we work together, spend time dealing with kids in your program. I thought he knew about Henry and you and me?"

"Yes, but he didn't care, always said I was wasting my time with those drug addicts. All these weeks we've been together, he couldn't care less. Even if he suspected something, it meant nothing to him. The son of a bitch was screwing around anyhow. He's been doing it for years. He goes away to Chicago or Dallas on business, takes one of his staff ... staff as in office whore, and bangs her every chance he gets. Calls me to say he's lonely and buys me little gifts because he's lonely. The asshole actually bought me a present from the Buffalo Airport once and expected me to think it came from fucking London."

Lawrence could see what was happening, "it's okay to get fucked but not to have your property get fucked."

"You're a very smart man, Lawrence. You're right, I'm his property and he's not going to let anybody use it. Including himself, of which I've been more than glad."

Eileen turned to face Lawrence. He could not believe his eyes when he saw hers. Nobody had the right to beat up somebody like that. Tears ran in streams down her bruised cheeks. She started to speak but Lawrence would not let her. Despite the churning inside his guts, he had to step in.

Lawrence gently touched her left, swollen cheek, "have you put ice on this?"

"No, he wouldn't let me. Called me his scarlet letter. Wanted everybody to see the Whore of Niagara Falls."

Lawrence got some paper towels from the classroom sink in the back of what was once a science class room, ran cold water over them, and gently held them to her cheek.

"That's not all. The son of a bitch tore off my clothes, was going to kick me out of the house naked. He actually rubbed his nose in my panties to see if I had that cunt smell I get during sex."

"Jesus, Eileen! I am so sorry. How did you get him to stop?"

"By getting this black eye, he wouldn't let up yelling at me, pushing me around, calling me every filthy name in the book, threatening to toss me out of the house. I couldn't put up with it anymore. Lawrence, it's not you that's caused the death of my marriage. No, don't feel any guilt. You're my life now. I've been dead as a woman for years, but not as dead as Zig. I knew how to stop him. I slapped him across the face and he stood stone cold still. I slapped him again and dared him to fuck me, fuck me like those girls he fucks on his alleged business trips. I got into his face and told him to come on, do it. Guess what? He couldn't get it up. I didn't let up on him, made fun of his tiny little prick, embarrassed him about his poor sperm count which kept us from having children all these years. That's when he smashed me in the face."

"You should've called the police, had the son of a bitch arrested."

"I told him that unless he stopped right now and agreed to a divorce, that I'd do just that. He stopped. It was over. He left the living room, went to the kitchen, and got out his cheap whiskey."

"Damn that could have been really dangerous, Eileen. He could have gotten drunk and killed you."

She put her arms around Lawrence, and keeping the sensitive left side of her face turned away, hugged him. "No Lawrence, you don't know him. He's one of those alcohol abusers where the booze acts as a narcotic. Add in how hyper tense he was, his blood flowing like lava, he took two drinks, mumbled about killing you, and fell asleep. He was totally out this morning, that is until I was leaving. The violence turned into pathos, tears, remorse, crying that he didn't want to lose me. It was really shameful but not sympathetic. When he started begging, I got into his face and said look at this. Look at my face. Don't be here when I come home tonight. If you are, I'll call the police. Stay away from here for the weekend. I'm packing up and going to my parents."

"What did he do?"

"Nothing. I could see the anger but there was really more fear than anger. I think he also started seeing the chance of getting all that pussy without having to hide it from me anymore. Still, his anger for you had not abated."

"I would have guessed as much. How did he find out? Did he tell you?"

"He got a phone call last night, about nine or so. A man asked if Mr. Ledger knew where his wife Eileen was. Zig thought it was somebody who was late for the meeting where I was supposed to be. Told the man I was probably at the school's administrative building. The man laughed and asked Zig if I was the sexy woman who drove that great Shelby Mustang? Zig told him I did. Then the man said that Zig ought to take a little drive up to your address, and hung up."

"Shit, that explains something that has bothered me these last few weeks. Go on."

"Zig did just that, found my car, saw us standing in front of your windows, and knew you and I weren't at any parent meeting."

"Belafont ratted us out. I'm surprised he didn't come banging on my door."

"He was not sure until he …"

"Smelled your underwear."

"Yes. Lawrence come here."

Eileen pulled Lawrence over to the large windows that looked down from the classroom to the teachers' parking lot, "he's waiting for you. That's him sitting on my Mustang."

Lawrence was stunned. Never in his mind could he have predicted this. "Does he have a weapon?"

"No, I wouldn't allow one in the house, thank God. You don't have to go through with this Lawrence. Call the police and have them deal with Zig."

"That won't happen. My problems I deal with. I love you."

Eileen was startled. She had spent too many years with less of a man than to understand the most of a man. She had pictured Lawrence accepting that their affair was over. She had tried to tell herself over and over again that what they did was just sexual release, pleasure for the moment. Never had she thought that her and Lawrence were more than that. Many the night she laid restless in bed, trying to convince herself it was just an affair, but knowing she felt a deep love for Lawrence. Never did she try to draw out of Lawrence whether he reciprocated this love. Even this morning Eileen began to sway at her remonstration of her cuckold husband thinking that Lawrence would just give their affair up now that they had been caught. Given time, she and Zig Ledger could at least maintain a charade of a marriage.

"Do you?"

"Eileen, I want you forever. But now we've got to get through this situation. I want you to follow me down to the teachers' parking lot and to your car."

"He might go berserk Lawrence."

"I doubt it, but I'm going to give him a chance to get around his anger. He will not cause you harm, not today, tomorrow, or ever. You stay behind me and let me do the talking. I will tell you to go to your car, and you should do that as quickly as you can. Do not respond to anything he says. I will protect you. Call me later tonight, after eight or so."

It was a short walk from the school across the narrow one-way street to the parking lot. It was the end of May in Western New York but still brisk and ubiquitously windy. Lawrence walked straight to Eileen's Shelby Mustang. He could hear her rummaging through her pocketbook for the keys. Zig Ledger saw them as they exited the school. He never took his eyes off of Lawrence. When Lawrence was about ten feet from him, Zig spoke.

"So whore, is this your latest client?"

Lawrence was not going to let a fight happen in full view of anybody still at Falls High School, "I've never met you and I'll never see you again after today. You are not going to embarrass your wife out here in the school parking lot. She's out of the picture. It's you and me, now. Get away from her car and let her leave."

"And if I don't?"

"Now!"

The hairs on Ledger's neck were visibly erect but he would not back down, "you and me in the school parking lot?"

"No, we're six blocks from Goat Island. I'm sure you know where it is. Go to your car and I'll meet you there. Park in the big lot at the east end of the island. I'll meet you there."

Zig hesitated, "okay, but I want to say one thing to Eileen."

"No fucking way."

Eileen grasped Lawrence's right arm from behind, "It's okay, Lawrence. He'll make it short. You go on over to Goat Island and he'll meet you there."

"Are you sure?"

Even though Eileen gently shook her head, Lawrence was leery of leaving her alone with Zig. Lawrence had to trust her though. He looked into her eyes and wanted to kiss her right now but the situation was horrific enough. He turned and walked to his Bronco Two and drove the half mile or so to Goat Island.

Eileen's talk with her husband was not short.

Goat Island lies between the Horseshoe Falls and Bridal Veil Falls, just south of the city of Niagara Falls. It got its name from John Stedman who kept a herd of goats there back in the late eighteenth century. The goats did not make it there, a typical Western New York winter, with dramatic freezes and blinding blizzards, killed off his entire herd. By the nineteenth century the island was recognized for what it would become, a tourist attraction. August Porter bought the island and allowed the

Tuscarora Indians to live there and sell trinkets and crafts to tourists arriving by trains and stage coaches. Porter built a few toll bridges for tourists but a bridge over the rapids was ridiculous since the massive blocks of ice raging down the Niagara River every winter just tore any construction to pieces. In 1885 Goat Island became Niagara Reservation, better known as Niagara Falls State Park, the oldest state park in the United States.

Lawrence used Goat Island as the turning point when he bicycled from home. The deafening roar of the falls has a soothing effect on people and Lawrence would often pack a lunch or dinner to eat when he pedaled over to the island. Lawrence told visitors that given his choice, the most beautiful time on Goat Island was in the dead of a severe winter. The falls were fascinating, spectral, and frightful with iced over trees, snow covered grounds, and rapids running under frozen ice. It was a time to admire how beautiful nature can be when it is demonstrating its ferocity.

Lawrence was about to give up and drive back to the school parking lot when Zig Ledger pulled into the east parking lot. This was tourist season and the reason why Lawrence chose Goat Island. The parking lot was about half full with tourists roaming over most of the island. Ledger finally saw Lawrence standing next to his Bronco. He pulled into a spot across from Lawrence. Slamming the door Ledger walked very quickly toward Lawrence who remained leaning against the Bronco's front left bumper. As Ledger neared Lawrence, Lawrence turned and walked slowly toward the Three Sisters Islands, which protrude out into the Horseshoe Falls side of Goat Island. The islands are extremely dangerous since the rocks are eroded heavily from the waters of the Niagara making them very slippery and jagged. The islands are named for the daughters of General Parkhurst Whitney, Celinda, Angelina, and Asenath, who frequented the lush woods and roaring rapids of the island like it was their personal playground. The General built a large hotel just above the rapids. Before white men took over the island, the Iroquois used Goat Island shamans to make sacrifices to He-No, the Mighty Thunderer, who lived in a cave at the base of the falls. It is said that you can hear voices of his spirit if you catch a quiet day on the Three Sisters Islands. It is difficult to repute since the falls and rapids are so loud you can hardly hear somebody talking, even when standing next to you. This was why Lawrence stirred Ledger toward them.

"Hold it there, you son of a bitch!"

Lawrence turned before Ledger could grab his arm.

"Who the fuck do you think you are, fucking another man's …"

"Hey, Buddy," said a father walking behind Ledger, holding his little daughter's hand while his wife was pushing a baby stroller. "You want to watch your mouth?"

Lawrence just smiled and Ledger quickly turned to the man profusely apologizing. Lawrence had made up his mind that Ledger was entitled to one punch.

"Zig, how did you get a name like Zig?"

"What? Why the … It's short for Fitzgerald. It's none of your business anyhow."

"Is Eileen okay?"

"Like you really give a shit!"

Lawrence shook his finger in front of his mouth in consideration of the tourists.

"Sorry. Yeah, she's alright. We'll work it out when I get home after this."

Lawrence knew better. There was no way that Eileen was going back to Fitzgerald Ledger.

"Fitz, kind of sounds like Zits. I can see why you took Zig or is it Ziggy? Never mind. We're in a very public place here Ledger. Park rangers patrol the entire area and do a good job of it. They have to, what with the danger on both sides of the Island."

Lawrence walked over to a paved path with a boulder constructed bridge, crossing a shallow stream, and leading to another island with huge boulders waiting to be washed over the falls sometime in the next millennium.

"Before we get into it, I have to let you know something about my heritage. My mother's a French Canadian, actually one of her distant relatives was an Inuit, a shaman for his community. When I was a kid, I couldn't lie to her. She had this sense about her, still does, knows when you're lying. Got my butt kicked quite a few times when I doubted that she knew I was telling a fib."

"So big deal, what's this got to do with you and my wife?"

"It seems I inherited her ability. I can feel another person's words. I get a strong tingling in the hairs at the nape of my neck if you're lying to me. Don't do it."

"Yeah, like I believe that scum bag."

"Let's see about it. Is Eileen going back to you?"

Zig Ledger just shook his head and laughed in Lawrence's face, "damn right she is. You were just a onetime lark."

"Zits, right?"

"Zig or better yet, you call me Mr. Ledger, Asshole."

Zig was getting braver. They were now on the very edge of the Niagara River, among the huge boulders, where it was rare to find tourists since it was very easy to slip on the damp, moss covered rocks.

Physically, Fitzgerald Ledger was short, much shorter than Eileen, maybe five six at tops. He had a Smith Brother's beard and curly black hair with just a trace of grey at the front. He was also very thin, thin like a runner which Lawrence guessed he was. Ledger was not in poor shape but he was not in shape to handle any conflict with Lawrence, who not only outweighed him by a good fifty pounds, but stood maybe eight inches taller, and not to mention his background in boxing. Ledger was one of those executives who turned from being a little man into being a bully to people who worked for him, people that owed their financial lives to how he ran the company store. It obviously spilled over into how Ledger handled other people whom he did not have a financial grip on.

"You know Ziggy, you missed your chance. I'd made my mind up that I owed you one shot, a punch in my nose for loving Eileen. But when people lie to me, I knock them on their ass. I can sense you're lying right now," said Lawrence rubbing the back of his neck. "Eileen's not going back to your tyranny."

Ledger knew better than to swing at a man Lawrence's size, especially one having obvious physical talents. He looked around and saw that there was nobody to hear what he had to say "You mother fucking son of a bitch ..."

Lawrence leaned back on a boulder and smiled, a smile that said he had control of himself. Ledger unleashed a violent tirade, threatening to have Lawrence arrested, get him fired, and on and on. Lawrence let him vent. None of his verbal assaults bothered Lawrence. Lawrence just laughed.

Never did Ledger reach the violence range of Lawrence.

"You finished?"

"Fuck you, cocksucker!"

"I didn't know you cared?"

Lawrence let the man cool off a bit then spoke, "did you ever fuck another man's wife?"

"What? Why's that mean anything?"

"Tough to accuse a man of having illicit sex with your spouse if you're doing the same thing?"

"No, I'm not that kind of man. I'd never do that."

Lawrence rubbed the back of his neck, dropped his right hand and spoke, "remember what I told you about sensing a lie?"

Ledger had no time to respond. Lawrence caught him with a left cross at the side of the head and with a second blow to his ribs. The man had moved his arm to protect another punch to the face. Ledger came up on his toes as Lawrence threw a right upper cut to his jaw. Lawrence had only put minimal force into the upper cut so that Ledger would not be knocked out. Ledger went down, his face swelling on both sides.

Lawrence was not going to prolong this face off. To him, it was over. He stood over Ledger, lifted his right foot and stepped firmly but not painfully on Ledger's neck.

"You lied. Told you not too. We're done for now. When you wake tomorrow, you're going to have two swollen eyes that won't go down without ice. They'll be black for a week. Did I feel guilty for making love to Eileen? No, never, not once. If you ever touch her again, I will kill you. Understand?"

Ledger did not move.

Lawrence pushed harder with his foot, "you better understand. Nobody deserves what you did to her. Never again, right?"

Ledger shook his head and Lawrence walked off the outer islands to the parking lot and drove back to the school parking lot. Eileen's Shelby Mustang was gone. Looking around the teacher's parking lot, Lawrence noticed that Belafont's Volvo was still there. Lawrence looked up to Belafont's room. It was still lit, even though it was well past the end of the school day on a Friday.

"Good!"

Entering from the single, steel plated door facing the parking lot, Lawrence closed the door behind him, put his keys back into his right front pocket, and slowly walked up to the English department's floor. He scanned the ceilings on the hallway until he found the camera, then walked into Belafont's classroom.

Belafont jumped when Lawrence entered and spoke, "Dr. Belafont, I need your help. This morning, when I first arrived here, there was a fight in the hall I had to break up."

"There's fights in the halls every day, Mr. Lawrence. What's it got to do with me?"

"Just what you said. There are fights in the halls every day but nobody does anything about them. The assistant principal said he'd handle it, but you know better. Two black kids. They'll tell him they were just fooling around and he'll let them go. You've always said we should nail these kids. Is there a camera out in this hall? If so, I could ask to see the video and force the AP to nail them."

"Yes Mr. Lawrence, there's a camera in every hall. You know that."

"Can't find it. You mind taking a look?"

Belafont got out from behind his desk with a shrug and a moan, walked out the door, as Lawrence followed. After a few steps Belafonte stopped and facing the camera said, "see, it's right up there."

Lawrence walked past Belafont and turned his back to Belafonte who was looking at the ceiling. Lawrence was no more than two feet in front of Belafont. Turning a hundred and eighty degrees so that he was face-to-face with Belafonte but with his back facing the video camera, Lawrence put his hands up with his palms gesturing an enigma.

"I don't see it?"

Lawrence had Belafonte positioned where he wanted. The camera would record Lawrence's back, his hands held shoulder high, palms in a questioning shrug, and Belafonte clearly visible standing at arm's length in front of Lawrence. As soon as Belafonte lifted his right arm to point to the ceiling camera, Lawrence threw a full force left jab into Belafont's right eye. The man's head jerked quickly backwards as he slammed into the lockers behind him. Lawrence brought both of his fists up into a sparring position, ready should Belafonte attempt a counter punch. He had guessed right. Belafont was scared and panicky.

"You son of a bitch! What the hell do you think you're doing? You've had it now, Lawrence. You stupid bastard, I've got you on video tape assaulting me. I'll see you in jail and fired!"

Lawrence walked straight into Belafont's body, forcing the man against the lockers, his arms splayed backwards against the wall. Belafont did not even raise his arms to defend himself. Within inches of Belafont's face, Lawrence gestured with his fists for Belafont to protect himself but the man only cringed in fear.

"No you won't, Belafont. You know what that video will show? It'll show you taking a swing at me, a right jab, and a rather poor one at that."

Belafont was sweating in fear, "no it won't be that way. The tape will play back you asking me ..."

"There's no audio on surveillance cameras, you idiot. Now I'm going to ask you a question but I'm going to warn you. I can tell when someone is lying. You lie to me and I'll bust up your other eye. I just got back from a confrontation with Eileen Ledger's husband. Did you tell him that Eileen and I were having an affair."

"I never ..."

Lawrence brought his clenched fists up and Belafonte pleaded, "no, don't hit me. Let me finish. I just told him you two were seeing a lot of each other and maybe he should keep an eye on her. That's all."

"You rotten bastard. That's the same thing. You ratted her out. You damn well knew why she had a black eye today, didn't you?"

"Listen, Lawrence. Everybody in this school knows you two are ... well, an item. You haven't tried very hard to cover it up."

"Nobody else had the gall to snitch on her but you."

"Lawrence, this isn't the first time she's been here with bruises on her face."

"So that means making fun of her is appropriate? Why did you call him. Don't lie!"

"To get rid of you. Zig goes to the school board with the two of you carrying on like you did and they'll fire you."

"And her!"

Belafont had no response.

"You ever do anything to cause her pain again and I'll kill you."

"Jesus, Lawrence. You're crazy! You'd kill a man because ..."

"No, you're special to me, Belafont," said Lawrence as he put down his fist clenched arms. Lawrence had his say and turned to leave. When he got to the stairs, he turned back toward Belafont.

"Hey! By Monday when you get to school, that eye of yours is going to be a real beaut!"

CHAPTER EIGHTEEN

Beauty's Beast

CRACK!

Lawrence heard the crack and instantly rose out of his sleeping bag. No animal would break a branch like that. Lawrence knew there was a human outside of his tent, but he realized too late. Hearing the snap of a round injected into a shotgun, Lawrence rolled to the side of the tent as scattered shot burst through the flap on his side of the tent, catching the back of his left shoulder and tearing flesh away. He had avoided death. The blast had not only ripped his sleeping bag to smithereens, but tore the back off of the two man pup tent. Forgetting his wounds, Lawrence scurried out the back and headed into the forest. He heard another shell being injected into the shotgun as Zig Ledger called Lawrence a mother fucker. A second shot blasted the silence of the forest and Lawrence feared the worse. He had to gain the safety of the woods to retaliate. On ground level, Lawrence would be dead of a gunshot wound within minutes. Ledger was fully prepared to hunt and more than prepared to kill. Lawrence guessed from the sound that Ledger was carrying a 12-gauge, pump action shot gun. Lawrence had only one saving attribute.

After he and Eileen Ledger had fucked their brains out in the tent, both of them had fallen asleep. Lawrence woke soon after and had to urinate. Stark naked, Lawrence had pulled on his canvass shorts and sneakers, pissed against a tree yards away from the tent, and exhausted, fallen on top of his sleeping bag, instantly going back to sleep, still clad in his canvas shorts and Reebok's. Not being trapped inside the sleeping bag had enabled him to flee. Wearing his black Reebok classics let him move quickly through the forest. Wearing his Khaki shorts meant he had a weapon, his nine inch folding jack knife.

Lawrence had gotten a good fifty yards into the forest when he saw Zig's flashlight searching the forest floor.

"You're next Asshole!"

Lawrence went toward the trees. He was a dead man if he stayed on the forest floor. Pulling back limbs of a large pine tree, Lawrence quickly pulled himself behind the pine needle and scaled the trunk limb, by limb. Finding a thick branch of an old oak tree, he leaped onto it, grabbing it firmly, and swung up to another smaller branch. Quickly putting the oak tree's thick trunk in front of him, Lawrence turned to find his pursuer. He was a good twenty five to thirty feet above ground.

"So where can you hide, asshole? You got no light and your rifle's back in the tent. Make some noise! Come on, Lawrence. One large scream and it's over. Want to fuck another man's wife? Well are you up to it? Up to getting fucked?"

Zig Ledger was obviously no hunter. He was randomly lighting all the floor areas of the forest searching bushes for traces of Lawrence. It was a pine forest. The floor was covered with needles and since it had been a dry and warm month, there would be no tracks. Lawrence could very easily lower himself through the trees, make ground level, and escape through the forest. Allegany State Park was huge, giving Lawrence a great advantage, especially considering he had spent many days camping all over the park. Lawrence knew how to find his way and could reach safety, but it would take many hours. This he would not do. He could not leave Eileen to Zig's violence.

Questions arose in his mind. How did Ledger know Lawrence and Eileen were camping off the reservoir? How did Zig find them, considering they were so far down river from their canoe launch site? The questions were meaningless and he put them away. Zig was following a path taking him twenty degrees from Lawrence's lair in the oak tree.

"You idiot," thought Lawrence. "You'll get yourself lost."

Lawrence did not want that. Ledger's back was now to Lawrence. The man still flashed his light, looking down traceless paths for some sign of Lawrence. Lawrence had almost forgotten the shotgun had ripped off flesh from his left backside muscles. He reached back and felt the wetness. It was not a deep wound but his hand still came back wet from blood. All his pursuer had to do was keep the flashlight at body level and he would increase his chances of tracking Lawrence. Zig obviously did not know about deer hunting in the dark and the revealing exposure that reflected light made when bouncing off a prey's retinas.

"Look at this, blood! I got you, didn't I, asshole?"

Zig was under the pine tree that Lawrence had scaled. Lawrence had put himself up into the heights of the forest. Lawrence needed the man to move out of the pine trees made it difficult to attack because of all the branches. Waiting, Lawrence knew it takes waiting to snare the prey. Yet Lawrence could not risk too long a wait before getting back to Eileen.

"Over here, Zig! Flash your light behind you."

Ledger spun quickly and fired off two shots, blasting apart a bush and a pine sapling. Would he use up his ammo, thought Lawrence? Was he stupid enough to give Lawrence that advantage? It made no difference since Lawrence could feel the adrenaline rush through his body. He crossed from one oak tree to another, farther away from Ledger but downwind and in his path.

Ledger came into view as the beam of light flashed from the flashlight. He was practically handing himself to Lawrence as he walked on a wide open path, the flashlight scanning back and forth. Lawrence realized that Ledger must have seen the blood and thought he was too wounded to become arboreal. Lawrence moved to a higher branch but still directly under the path Ledger was taking. The drop would be about twenty-five feet but Ledger's body should help break the fall. Lawrence flipped open the jack knife, gripping the hilt so the blade was aimed down, and squatted on the branch. Breathing through his nostrils and ignoring the pain of his gunshot wounds, Lawrence turned, putting his back to Ledger's traveled path. While he could not see his protagonist, the light increased in intensity below him as Ledger neared Lawrence's perch. Lawrence needed Ledger's back to him when he leapt. He got it.

Ledger passed directly under Lawrence, stopped and scanned the flashlight in a half circle, ignoring anything above him, and took that fatal step.

Lawrence came down feet first on Ledger's shoulders, breaking both of the man's collar bones instantly. Lawrence rolled off the man's body which was now lying flat face down on the forest floor. Ironically Ledger's flashlight had not broken and had spun so that Ledger's upper body was fully lit. The shotgun was pinned under Ledger's body and his arms were splayed outward like he was taking a dive into a swimming pool. With each collar bone having a compound fracture, the fight was over. Lawrence squatted on the man's back, forcing screams of pain from Ledger. He grabbed the man's hair and pulled his head backwards. Ledger nearly passed out from the pain. Lawrence put the jack knife to his throat.

"You'll not die now. You'll only wish you had."

Keeping the jack knife to Ledger's throat, Lawrence rotated off his back and yanked the shotgun from under Ledger. Making sure that Ledger was totally incapacitated, Lawrence kicked Ledger in the chest, breaking two ribs and causing the man to vomit blood.

Lawrence picked up the shotgun, chambered a round, and aiming it at Ledger's head, told him to get up.

"I can't! I can't move my shoulders and my lungs are filling with blood!"

Lawrence kicked him in the ribs again. Ledger rolled over, his arms useless, blood spurting from his mouth.

"Get up!"

Ledger came to a sitting position. The blood vomiting had all stopped, a slight trickle still oozing out of Ledger's mouth.

"Stand up or I'll butt you in the chest with the shotgun!"

Ledger swung and swayed and was able to stand even without any use of his arms. Lawrence picked up the flashlight and aimed it back towards the camp site.

"Move! Stay in front of me and follow the light."

It took all Lawrence had in him to not kill Ledger when he saw what had happened to Eileen. The side of her face was blown off, brain matter covering her left ear. Yet she was still alive."

"Lawrence! Lawrence, you're still alive,"a horrendous scream followed.

Lawrence turned on Ledger, kicked him in the stomach, sending him to his knees as he caught him in the side of the head with the shotgun butt. Lawrence quickly grabbed some towels and went to their water supply. Soaked with cold water, Lawrence placed the towels against Eileen's wounds. She screamed again. Lawrence cried, cried-out with a pain that would never die. It was a horror that no one should have to endure. He knew she should be dead. They were miles from any place where other humans could be. Lawrence had seen enough gunshot wounds in animals to know Eileen was dying and could not be saved. That she was still alive was beyond belief. The screaming stopped.

"Peter, why? Why did he do it?"

Lawrence could not choke back the tears. He drew gasps that created spasms in his throat making him cough up bile. He wanted to touch her but feared the pain would be too great. Any movement, any touch was agony for her. Lawrence took her pulse and initially got none. Shaking his hands to revive the sensitivity in them, he tried again and barely felt the blood flow at her neck. His eyes welled up again when he saw the side of her face oozing fluids through the compresses.

"Lawrence, my dear Lawrence. Peter, I love you," and then another scream.

Lawrence thought she passed out but her eyes opened again. They were changed. No pain showed but her pulse was even weaker. The blue in her eyes brightened, just as they did each and every time they made love. She smiled.

"Peter, you almost had one."

"One?"

"A child for us. I will die expecting ..."

... and she died.

Lawrence took his hand away from her and fainted. He awoke not much later and she was still dead. He grabbed a blanket and covered his dead love, then remembered Zig Ledger. Ledger's wounds and broken bones had put him in a state of unconsciousness until now. Lawrence had to control his temper. He could not kill the man until he had answers. Ledger was flat on his back, his eyes nearly dead, with just a twitch of the eyelashes. Lawrence kicked him in the ribs that were not broken. Ledger let out a scream, but the screaming only increased his pain.

"You're going to be dead sooner or later, much later I think. You'll beg me to kill you but I won't unless you tell me what I want to know," said Lawrence this time stepping on the man's shoulder blade and sending him into a paroxysm of unconsciousness.

Ledger awoke in more pain, "do it! Kill me!"

"When you answer my questions, you'll be free of pain."

"What, what is it?"

Lawrence got all the answers he needed, loaded Ledger into the canoe, and paddled out into the middle of the reservoir. With Ledger sitting up against a strut in the middle of the canoe, Lawrence clung to each gunwale and eased his way into the deep water. Lawrence hoped that what he had been told about drowning was true and overturned the canoe. Was drowning the worse death one can imagine? Fitzgerald Ledger was finding out.

***

Of course there were two policemen, one of them understanding and congenial and the other mean as hell. To

Lawrence, the challenge was to keep to his story. He had formed that story during his two hour escape from the camp site. One slip would put him into jeopardy.

"That had to be awful seeing your girlfriend blown to bits right next to you?"

The New York State police detective was working Lawrence over sympathetically, striving to prod at any missing detail in Lawrence's story.

"I told you. I didn't see anything. I rolled out of the tent and fled into the woods. All I know is that I heard shots."

The New York State police lieutenant was a black man, a very large black man. He appeared to need a shave but it was more likely his hirsute face could not be shaved any closer than it already was. It was now inches from Lawrence's face. Lawrence was staring into the it. The man had puffed eye brows and a slightly cockeyed nose, one a man would have gotten from being in the ring, a fighter. The Lieutenant was playing his role, the obvious, his interrogation that of the bad guy.

"I don't buy that shit, Petey! You telling me you ran like a scared chicken ..."

"I told you once and this makes twice, do not call me Petey or Peter or any other name but Lawrence."

The Lieutenant smiled. The Lieutenant felt he had executed his role perfectly. He had riled Lawrence, got him off of his carefully thought-out story as to what had happened at the lake. He knew Lawrence was not telling the correct one. Push him, push him now. This guy was not more than a kid, in his early twenties. He will break if I back him to the wall.

"I don't give a fuck what you want me to call you, Petey," said the Lieutenant using a smile meant to scare the shit out of any witness. It was his forte, his edge in the New York State Police Department. Nobody could stand up to his rigorous interrogation.

Lawrence saw the detective at the window looking out and at nothing, letting the Lieutenant grill the suspect into the ground while not being a witness. He would be able to deny any harassment directed at the suspect, Lawrence.

Lawrence did not flinch but stood erect, himself face-to-face with the black cop. In a voice just loud enough that the detective could not say he never heard Lawrence's response, Lawrence launched his attack on the lieutenant. "You know what the arm's length rule is, I'm sure. You've violated mine."

The black cop had not anticipated Lawrence's threat. Stunned by Lawrence's not backing down to the verbal assault, the Lieutenant lost his composure and reached for Lawrence's throat. He should not have done that. The detective had turned just time to see Lawrence's response. With his palms together, Lawrence lifted his arms up so that they parted the two black arms reaching for his neck. The Lieutenant's hands spread eagled outward and any protection to his face was gone. Lawrence caught him with his left palm, smashing it into the lieutenant's right side of his jaw. All three people heard the jaw bone crack after which Lawrence drove his right fist into the abdomen, doubling up the lieutenant's body in pain. As he went down, Lawrence brought his right knee up into the lieutenant's right side jaw breaking, it too. Quickly Lawrence dropped to the floor, locked his fingers hand-to-hand behind his neck, motionless.

"You son of a bitch!" cried the detective, his pistol pulled and aimed at Lawrence's back. The lieutenant was out cold, and while the detective would have liked to beat the hell out of Lawrence, he knew that the lieutenant had gone beyond the proper interrogation protocol,and that all of this was on videotape.

***

Lawrence avoided the funeral services for Eileen out of respect for her family but also to distance himself from the police that were watching him. A week after Eileen was cremated, Lawrence visited her parents to pay his condolences. They knew Lawrence well in the short time he had been seeing Eileen and they approved of him and had been prepared to support Eileen through a divorce and probable marriage to Lawrence.

As he was leaving their home, the father brought out a large brown envelope for Lawrence. Lawrence thanked him and left. In his car he opened the envelope to find a rough draft of Henry's final examination essay, plus copious notes he had used to write the essay. Belafonte had failed Henry because of the essay but had not provided a copy to Lawrence so he could see why Henry had failed. Belafont claimed he had turned it into the administrative offices and they would not let Lawrence see it. Skimming through the rough draft and notes, Lawrence was struck by the research and documentation Henry had put into his essay. As Lawrence started up his car, Eileen's mother came out to his car.

"You don't know, do you?"

"Know what?"

"That boy? Hawkins? He's dead. He committed suicide."

Lawrence sat, stunned. With everything he had been through, he never had thought of Henry. That was not a fault. Instead of going back to his row home, he drove to the halfway house where he had tutored Henry.

As he walked into the lobby, he could feel the tension.

The man at the desk was either new or had not been on duty when Lawrence had visited Henry. Lawrence introduced himself and explained why he was here.

"Yeah, he's dead."

"How did he die?"

"Hung himself."

"Here? At the halfway house?"

"I don't know all's about it. Let me get one the attendants."

Lawrence recognized the attendant as he approached the double doors leading from the facility and dormitory rooms into the reception area. Passing through the doors, the man turned and locked them.

"How you doin' Mr. Lawrence."

"Very badly. What happened to Henry?"

Lawrence had worked with this attendant frequently. He was a good man and a favorite with the patients.

"Hung himself, Mr. Lawrence."

"How did he manage that?"

The man turned and looked at the reception counter behind him. The receptionist was on the phone. Lawrence realized that soon there would be an administrator arriving, ending any chance for Lawrence to find out what happened.

"You! Get off the phone! There's no reason to be calling anybody. Understand?"

Lawrence knew the remonstrance had been too late. "You're a good man. Tell me quick."

The attendant led Lawrence to the locked facility doors, opened them, and escorted Lawrence into the dormitory hallway. "It'll take a while before anybody gets here because there's nobody on administrative duty today, it being a weekend."

He locked the doors behind them and Lawrence could see only one other attendant in the patient facilities.

"You, go on and take your lunch. I got it covered."

The man was more than eager to leave.

"I didn't find him. A substitute attendant I never seen before found him. He hung himself, Henry did. Least that's what it looked like. Did it in the shower."

"Jesus! I'd never in a life span imagine Henry hanging himself. Overdose, yeah, but hanging himself? How'd he do it?"

The attendant lead him to the shower room. "Ripped up a sheet, took a chair, tied one end of the noose around the shower pipe and kicked out the chair. That shower right over there, in the middle."

"It makes no sense. Henry was never diagnosed with suicidal tendencies."

"Coroner said he was high. Had smack in him. Gave him the courage."

"No fucking courage, no way! It doesn't take fucking courage …"

The attendant touched Lawrence's arm and shook it slightly, "I know man. I know …"

"Know what?"

"Come here a second."

The attendant led Lawrence to the shower faucet to the left of the middle shower where Henry hung himself. He grabbed Lawrence's right hand and fitted it around the pipe stem of the shower head.

"What?"

"Pull on it, but for God's sake don't break it off."

"Don't break it …"

Lawrence pulled slowly on the pipe stem. He eased off very quickly when the pipe started to give; more pressure would obviously yank it out of the wall..

"This is between you and me. This place was locked shut for two weeks. Patients moved temporarily to another facility. Cops went over the whole place. Funny, but when we got back in, the middle shower head looked the same but … Come here."

The attendant gestured for Lawrence to grab hold of the middle shower, Henry's shower. It took less than a second for Lawrence to realize that you could do pull ups for a month on this shower pipe. The actual shower head had been clearly as old as the others in the shower room and would not have taken any weight tugging on it. When Lawrence wiped off the pipe stem behind the middle shower head, he could see there was new pipe and it was obviously better bracketed than any of the others in the shower room.

"Don't Mr. Lawrence. Don't say a thing. No way you can prove anything now. It's been cleaned up. Now you've got a come with me so I don't get in trouble."

The attendant lead Lawrence to a supply room where what was left of Henry's belongings was stored. As Lawrence was going through them, he heard a loud voice in the reception area reprimanding the attendant. There was nothing here but old clothes, no papers or books. Lawrence went back out to the reception area where a tall, extremely pale bald man was castigating the attendant rather vociferously.

"I'm glad to see you laying into this asshole! I'd fire him if I were you," said Lawrence. The man turned to look at Lawrence. Lawrence could see the attendant that helped him was watching. He was stunned by Lawrence's tirade.

"Excuse me sir but who are you? I happen to be the administrator for this facility and you have no business being in here."

"My name is Lawrence, Peter Lawrence. I told your dummy attendant there that I was a plainclothes officer for Niagara Falls PD and needed to see what Henry Hawkins had left after killing himself. I flashed my medical insurance photo identification at that dummy and he thought I was a fucking cop! Lot of good it did me. Takes me into a fucking storage closet that smells like fecal matter and waits outside while I find nothing! Fuckin' nothing! I want you to discipline the son of a bitch. I could hear him laughing out here in the hall."

"If you don't leave immediately, I'll call the real police. Do you understand?"

"Fuck you! I'm out of here," said Lawrence as he walked to the exit, his back to the administrator. A smile crossed his face, a smile no one could see except the attendant that had helped him. Lawrence had returned the favor.

***

Some days you just get lucky. It was an October Saturday in Western New York in the mid-60s and windless, and it made today his second lucky day in a row. Lawrence oiled the axles and pedal ball bearings of his bicycle and sprayed lubricant on the gear sprockets and chain for shifting. It was cold enough to need a hooded sweatshirt. He could tell by the slowly rising sun coming this way via Rochester that he probably would not need it later once he got started up Main Street Route 104 and began working up a sweat. Lawrence was not riding his bicycle to Fort Niagara for physical conditioning and therefore was not out to break a time barrier. He needed to purge his mind and flush it clean; he needed a better perception of what his world had become.

Yesterday he had given up. The death of Eileen, his killing of Ledger, and the suicide of Harry Hawkins had pushed him far beyond the ability to comprehend the reality of his life. Starting out with a quart of cheap scotch, he revisited the past weeks and came to only one conclusion. Let it go. It's over. He needed to stop crying and he needed to stop believing that somehow there was anything he could do. Because of the ongoing criminal investigation of both Eileen's and Fitzgerald's murders, and the fact that Lawrence was listed as an informant and possible suspect, Bruno Scarpetti, the new principal at Niagara High School had met him on the first day back, a teacher day, in the parking lot with a letter from Superintendent Nuevello placing Lawrence on unpaid leave. Because Lawrence was a member of the teachers' association, their lawyer had gotten a court order rescinding the unpaid leave of absence. As soon as the judge ruled to revoke the first leave of absence written by Dr. Nuevello, the attorney presented Lawrence in court with a leave of absence with pay. It was the best teachers' association could do but Lawrence did not care.

Lawrence had gotten drunk many times. It was a catharsis for him. The numbness of the morning brought out his fears and he spent the day fighting headaches, stomach pains, sweating, and fear that he would not be able to survive. He started slowly, mixing the scotch with tap water, built his courage gradually hour by hour, until his glass was pure scotch and he was ready to leave his world and seek out the offenders of his life. Lawrence would clean house physically and metaphorically. He grabbed the letters and folders from his kitchen table and shoved them into the trash can. One more scotch and he probably would have lit up his fireplace and burned everything, burned away his life. Pack it up and cede defeat. As he was stuffing his life in trash bags a single, small task, caused by his now partially alcohol-numbed brain, complied with his tirade. He grabbed the Harry Hawkins manila envelope that he had just received from Eileen's parents and as he grabbed it to trash it, the contents fell all over his kitchen floor. The clasp on the envelope flap had not been locked. Papers and notes fell out.

Lawrence looked at the spill. He still had enough of his sober self to realize he had to stop drinking right now. Lawrence might have rid his mind of Harry Hawkins by trashing the brown envelope but it would take more than Scotch to rid his mind of Harry Hawkins' work. There it laid Harry's work. Work, he never did for any other teacher except Peter Lawrence. More importantly, Lawrence had been only a few drinks short of destroying Harry Hawkins' failed final exam essay.

Lawrence swirled the half inch of scotch around the bottom of the glass. He poured the Scotch and melted ice into the sink's drain. Lawrence went to the kitchen cabinet next to the refrigerator and took out some peanut butter cookies. After eating a couple of them, his mind had cleared. He was still-light headed but not alcoholically comatose. The taste of cheap scotch still lingered as he sat down to read Harry's final exam essay.

He read it three times, each reading separated by a walk out into the dark streets of Niagara Falls. Lawrence had not even considered that what happened to Harry Hawkins could have been murder. His best conclusion was an accident. Why would anyone want to kill Harry Hawkins? The people portrayed in Harry's essay had a lot of reasons to get rid of him.

Lawrence had given up trying to piece together what had happened, that is until today. Once he read Harry's papers and essay, Lawrence could not help but tie Eileen, Harry, and even Fitzgerald Ledger's deaths together, but that made no sense. The night and the booze not yet cleared of his mind fought him into a draw. What he needed was what he invariably fell back on when facing an impossible challenge. So he locked his door, straddled the bicycle, and headed up Portage Road which turns into Main Street and parallels the Robert Moses Parkway. By the time he reached Niagara University and Route 104 which became Lewiston Road, the traffic had disappeared. Through the entire journey Lawrence went over the sequence of events beginning with his tutoring of Harry Hawkins.

***

"Harry, you know that you have something in common with Jack London?"

Lawrence needed only one New York State acknowledged book to get Harry a passing grade in senior English. Lawrence could pass Harry by testing him on a novel from the required list. He could use that book as a basis for his required written composition. <u>The Call of the Wild</u> was the perfect book. Harry said he did not want to read any book written by a little kids writer. Lawrence had heard that story before and used his well-developed snare to lure the complaining teenage students into seeing just how adult Jack London was. He read Harry a story. Of course Harry moaned and groaned and pretended to go to sleep at first but it did not take long before London's six paged "Batard" grabbed Harry like every other listener Lawrence had read to.

"Yeah, how am I like Jack London?"

"Niagara Falls locked both of you up."

"Jack London actually came to this shit pit?"

Lawrence just smiled. Profanity was one of Harry's weapons. It had chased away every other tutor Hawkins had.

"Yep, he rode here on a side-door Pullman."

"Never heard of that kind of passenger car."

"Yes, you have. It's the hobo name for a box-car."

"Jack London jumped a train to come to the Falls? Damn!"

"And he got arrested."

"What'd he do? A protest or something?"

"He didn't have a job. He was homeless. It was the summer of … if I remember it correctly 1894. Got off a freight train and ran right to the Falls to see'm."

"So why did he get arrested?"

"Not that night. You see there was a big round up to jail hobos, what we call the homeless today. The homeless we have in the cities today can't cut the mustard when it comes to surviving not like the hobos did a hundred years ago. He was so stunned at the Falls, that he lingered there until late at night. He knew that cities were catching hobos and putting them into jail so he took off to the outside of the city for the night. Problem was he came back the next day, in the morning, and a cop thought he'd been there all night and nailed him. Put him right into the city jail."

"How come we never hear about things like that, you know a famous writer getting arrested by the pigs?"

"Niagara Falls denies it ever happened."

"I guess since it goes back so far there are no records?"

"Yeah, there are records of his arrest, but when he was taken to the judge they gave him the name Jack Drake. City has that name on record."

"Fuckers, what a bunch of fuckers. So how long was he locked up in the city jail?"

"Just overnight until his court appearance."

"Wow, Lawrence. Big deal. I've spent more time in …"

"Harry, they tried him, no witnesses, no jurors, wasn't even allowed to plead not guilty, and he was denied habeas corpus. The bailiff stood him up, announced the charge, 'vagrancy", and the judge said 'thirty days. Boom, it was over. When he complained the judge told him to shut up."

"Fuck if I would shut up."

"London was smart. Before him, a man from Lockport was arrested for vagrancy and given thirty days. He tried to explain to the judge that he had just been laid off at his job and the judge told him to shut up and added thirty more days to his sentence for quitting his job."

"Jesus! So London spent thirty days in the city's hoosegow?"

"No, they locked him in chains with other prisoners and put him on a train to Buffalo. They marched the chain gang right down the streets of Niagara Falls in front of the tourists. Once in Buffalo, they shipped them to the Erie County Penitentiary. Chopped off their hair, shaved their faces, and suited them in good old black and white stripes. Stuck in a cell with so many bed bugs, that he, as did all the prisoners, took their bread and moistened it with saliva to use as mortar to seal up holes in the prison walls where millions of bugs entered every night."

"Well, I think we're alike here with bugs, except we got mice and rats too. No, keep your mouth shut, Lawrence. They've had inspectors already in here and found nothing. So what you're telling me Lawrence, is that Jack London had to spend thirty days in the Erie County Penitentiary for looking at Niagara Falls. Like that's his fucking crime? Why do they do that shit?"

"You want to know what London did during those thirty days in the county jail?"

"I'd guess he did some of his best writing."

"No writing. Guess what he did those thirty days?"

"What?"

"At the back of the Erie County Penitentiary was the Erie Canal. Each morning the short timers were marched lock step out to the docks to unload canal boats and to carry huge stay-bolts. Think about this Harry. The cops in Niagara Falls and Buffalo rounded up the itinerants in large groups periodically. These people were homeless, couldn't hire a lawyer if their life depended on it. Since the court misreads their names, there isn't even a record of their arrest. Hundreds of them were used all over Western New York, and not just for canal work. They were only there for thirty days. Why?"

"Well that's pretty obvious. Damn people at the canal are getting free workers. I'd guess the cops and judges got some kick back?"

"Yep, and London saw it. He also saw what happened to prisoners making trouble, which is why he kept his mouth shut, his pen idle, and after his thirty days, sneaked quietly into Pennsylvania. If I remember from his short story 'Pinched' all he did was walk on their sidewalk and gaze at their picayune waterfall."

"So he made some money at least by writing about it?"

"That's right. Couple dollars at least."

"That's all?"

"Yes, that's what the old times were about. Now I'll tell you why I got you into Jack London and Niagara Falls. I've read some of the essays you've written for other teachers. They're terrible."

"Hey, thanks a lot! So I'm no Jack London. Give me a break."

"You know why your stories suck?"

"Go ahead, keep fuckin' with me."

"You don't know what you're writing about. Your stories are off in Never Never Land. Why do I remember 'Pinched' so well?"

"Cause it's a good story."

"Why is it good?"

"London puts it together …"

"No! What does he have to do before he puts the story together?"

"Got no idea."

Lawrence poked his right index finger into Harry Hawkins' temple, "you've got to live it right there. How many of those essays and stories that you wrote did you actually live?"

"You don't have to live a story, man. Like those people that write the screen plays for Star Wars have never been in deep space."

"Yes, they have Harry. They have been at points in their lives that parallel exactly or close to what they're writing. Do you think for a second that Jack London wrote "Batard" without ever living in the wilds of the North?"

"So I should get out of here and canoe to Alaska? That's insane."

"Harry! You've got to write an essay. It can be any story, doesn't have to be true. If you got to write, write what you've lived."

"Yeah, right. Like I've lived this great life."

"Harry, you've done things and been places that Jack London could not even write about. You don't have to write what really happened but you can turn events that have been dramatic to you into writing excitement. What you write does not have to be true, just believable and passionate."

"Like why I'm here?"

"Sounds like a good place to start."

"Listen, Lawrence. It's also a good place to get me in trouble."

"Make it fiction, a story. Use what happened and rewrite it so it's only a story. Harry, look around you. This could be Niagara Falls City Prison, couldn't it? Who knows what could happen here or how the other detainees got here? Write what you've lived."

***

Lawrence had reached the Robert Moses water slews coming off of the reservoir and dumping into the Niagara River. He had not gone far in his journey. Remembering of those words to Harry made him dizzy. "Write what you've lived." Those words were what got Harry killed. Lawrence looked across the river at Canada. He always joked how fortunate it was to live on his side of the river since the Canadian side was beautiful and the United States side was so ... there.

He headed up Lewiston Road to the escarpment. This side of the Niagara escarpment was a better ride than it would be on his return trip. The road climbed slowly through the Niagara Falls Golf Course to the escarpment peak, exposing the flat lands running to Lake Ontario. The view, after making that first turn through the hills was always breath-taking - - one flat mass of land, mostly farm land with the leaves of apple trees turning into their Fall demise. Brakes were in order because, unlike the slow rising, the other side of the escarpment down to the plateau was steep and only allowed a bicyclist a return trip if the cyclist used his gear shifts accurately.

As Lawrence coasted, scanning westward toward the gorge a few miles to his left, he could see the Art Park which serves both worlds. Like most of Western New York, the Art Park serves the public mostly in the summer. It caters to families by offering free concerts, off-Broadway plays, music, art festivals, and a wide range of summer camps for the youth of both upstate New Yorkers and their Canadian neighbors. It is most picturesque in the spring when the snow has ended and life returns to Niagara Falls. The slow ride down the escarpment has the danger of drawing a person's eyes away from the road, creating many honking horns by drivers coming up the hill. Lawrence got the honks out about a quarter of the way down the escarpment. His mind was too slow for the cars behind him.

***

All of his thoughts were not directed to the escarpment panorama which he had seen hundreds of times before. Did Henry Hawkins commit suicide? That thought was never far from Lawrence's mind. Was there an obvious reason that the one shower pipe at the halfway house had been replaced while others were deteriorated to the point of snapping off? It did not seem reasonable. Then there was Henry's essay.

Henry was a very smart kid. Intelligent, not just street smart. As Lawrence reached the bottom of the steep decline, he bore to the left on Lewiston Road, made a left hand turn onto Ridge Road and headed through Lewiston. Henry was an intellectual when his intellect was challenged. Breaking Henry out of his disenchantment with teachers and schools had rarely been accomplished in the educational system. Eileen had stressed that to Lawrence, going through records of Henry's school career which was better labeled as a lack of career. Henry had put more time in the school system's in-school suspension classroom then most of the tiles on the floor. Henry sat for seven hours a day, minus the twenty minutes to eat lunch, for offenses ranging from not doing his work in classes or sleeping in class. The latter was a direct result of Henry spending school nights getting high on drugs. Henry liked ISS. He liked being kicked out of the classroom and sitting at a table chair with work sent from his teachers, though Henry rarely did any of the assigned work.

Lawrence knew all of this before he tackled Henry, which was why he put Jack London in front of Henry. "Batard" worked and worked well on kids like Henry Hawkins when being told to read a child's story. He refused to read, smiling at Lawrence, revealing a mouthful of rotting teeth. Lawrence surmised this would happen after having read teacher write-ups on Henry. So Lawrence read it out loud and laid his trap. "Batard" was Lawrence's favorite Jack London short story. It deals with two characters, both sired by evil, the human Black Leclere and a dog whose name Batard translates into bastard. London gets straight to their relationship in the first paragraph - - "when two devils come together, hell is to pay."

Just the first paragraph jolted Henry's head up from his nesting place on his folded arms.

"Hey, you can't say H E L L out loud in here! I'm going to report you for that," said a now attentive Hawkins.

"Damn it! I'm sorry Henry," smiled Lawrence as he continued. "I don't know what the fuck's wrong with me!"

Henry, not Lawrence turned red in the face. Lawrence continued reading and Henry pretended to go back to sleep. Both characters in London's short story were born of Satan. The story has each of them out to give pain to the other, Batard from horrendous beatings and Leclere from carelessness around the Spawn of Satan. Most readers root for the dog in any animal stories, but London is no mediocre writer. Batard was a killer, but he was a wild animal who needed to kill to survive. Batard was very good at surviving. In the end justice is served between the two foes as revenge weeds through Batard's mental ability to perceive Leclere's predicament. Both are abandoned at a hanging.

"Jesus, why did he end it that way Lawrence?"

"Jack London is not Walt Disney. What do you think of London's last words - - "but his teeth still held fast locked?"

"That dog is one mean mother ..." unlike Lawrence, Henry could not bring himself to end the sentence.

"Except what is the difference?"

"Dog's an animal. He's suppose to be a killer."

"Batard is not an animal in this story."

"What do you mean? You read it. I listened. Says he's a wolf dog."

"You know what anthropomorphism is?"

"Yeah, right. Like even the geeks at Niagara High School don't know that one."

"Bugs Bunny, what is Bugs Bunny?"

"Duh! Like he's a rabbit."

"No, he's not. He's a cartoon."

"Wow Lawrence, you are one brilliant man. Man, if I had a teacher like you, I wouldn't be here. I've seen the light!"

Lawrence smiled, "anthropomorphism is defining a non-human in human terms. I don't want to get you upset Henry, but Bugs Bunny is not a rabbit."

"Which means every cartoon is really . . . wait, wait. Cartoons, characters in a book that speak are all anthropomorphisms, right?"

"Almost. How about Leclere? Human or not human?"

"Well he's a man, talks like a human."

"But he's not real. Who's the real human?"

"Yeah! Jack London is. The guy who writes the story ..."

"Or draws the cartoon?"

Henry proved his intelligence and shamed the schools, "that's right. London's putting down letters joined together to make me ... or anyone reading his story, see the man as real."

"By God I think he's got it!"

"Huh?"

"Another Henry, Henry. Henry Higgins in the play "My Fair Lady".

"So writers are all anthropomorphists?"

"Basically that's true. But in this story, London gives you a dichotomy. Think you know what that is?"

"Sounds sort of like dissection?"

"Good, because you see this like very few people see it. The story breaks down the humans and wolves into two groups that are very different. Obviously the dog is portrayed in human terms but what about Leclere, his owner?"

"Yeah, that's right. Leclere is also an animal ... No, London uses animal terms to describe a human."

"Why?"

Henry paused, started to respond but shook his hands, asking silently for Lawrence to give him a few seconds.

"It was how to show that the man was a sinner ..."

Lawrence blinked, screwed his forehead muscles into furrows of doubt, "sinner? How do you see that?"

"The man tortured the dog for no reason. That's not an animal thing. Yet the only way London could describe it was in animal terms."

Henry was more than Lawrence could have hoped. Henry was seeing past where Lawrence took the story. While there were many religious symbols in the story as is the case in many Jack London stories, this concept was one Lawrence had missed intellectually in the dozens of times he had read the story.

"I think you've just went out the door and left my mind an enigma."

"Don't you see it? We're supposed to be God's creation. When you want to describe evil, how can you describe the evil person using religion's definition of why humans are not animals? You can't. What's the opposite of anthropomorphism?"

Lawrence was stuck. He ran thoughts through his mind. What word describes the reverse of anthropomorphism? A word that attributes animal attributes to human? Animalism?

"Henry? They have some books here, right?"

"Yeah but not many. What do you need?"

"Dictionary should work. I'll go ask."

"No, I'll get it."

While Henry left his room to get the dictionary, Lawrence went to the lavatory to wash his face. A warm splash of water and rubbing his eyes always made Lawrence relax, get smoothed. Henry's problem was a public schools problem as it has been since public schools came into existence. How can you teach kids that are slow learners, through no fault of their own? How do you teach easily bored kids that seek and fail to find higher thoughts?

"Here I looked up anthropomorphism and it gives theomorphism as an antonym. It says that theomorphism is the "depiction or conception of humans as having the form of a god."

"Henry, I have no idea why."

"Maybe because we're too much for our own good? Like we cannot except any reference to ourselves except that we are God?"

"That's great, Henry. Think how that works for the story. When Batard kills Leclere, how does London describe the wolf dog?"

"Damn smart! And ... "

"Yeah, the dog's smiling at him ..."

"That is human. That is only human, not animal. That's human behavior in an animal and we can't accept it as humans. We all think we're God. How's that my good buddy? Are you God Come on Lawrence, no response?"

Henry had just changed Lawrence's view of three decades of being enamored by reading, learning, and teaching Jack London's writings.

"Henry I came here to teach you. I have never had such a delicious lesson in all my years. That is one very inspiring view of the human mind. If only Jack were still alive, what could we learn. At least we could ask him if we are God ..."

"I don't think so Lawrence. I think he's telling us we can't understand. Our only knowledge is that of being a human. He proves we can only be what we are - - animals, deviant animals. Animals that evolved horror."

***

Lawrence had too much running through his head and as the cars went speeding by voices yelling profanity at him from their rolled down windows. He decided to stop at the McDonald's in Lewiston for a quarter pound of grease better known as a quarter pound hamburger with cheese. As he filled his blood stream with cholesterol, he thought about Henry's essay, the rough draft which he had only by pure chance.

The assignment, the essay that Henry had to write had been made by Lawrence but graded by Belafont thanks to Superintendent Nuevello. One book from the New York State Department of Education's approved list had to be used as the basis of the essay. Lawrence chose London's <u>Call of the Wild</u>. Henry had read the book when he was in middle school, after seeing the movie on late night television. It turned him off because the 1935 movie starring Clark Gable totally ignored the book. Therefore when Henry had to do a book report on <u>Call of the Wild</u>, he opted to not read it since he could just write about the movie. Obviously, this resulted in a very low grade. The book is an animal story with very few humans. The movie was a vehicle for Clark Gable which Henry realized after he mouthed off to his English teacher that she read the book incorrectly and his version was the true story. While serving another day in the suspension room, Henry read the book and determined that Clark Gable and William Wellman, the director of the movie, were assholes.

Henry told all of this to Lawrence. Lawrence agreed with him and they had a good session at the halfway house that day. Using <u>Call of the Wild</u> proved an ideal choice. When Lawrence came for his next session with Henry, following the mind bending experience of analyzing whether Jack London wrote as an animal, a human, or God, he laid on Henry what his final grade essay was to be.

"I want you to write a story, a made up story with you in it but only you and I will know you are the character in the story. I want you to reread <u>Call of the Wild </u>for next week. But while you're reading it, I want you to use a marker and high light as many incidents as possible where London uses anthropomorphism in describing Buck, the dog."

"Wow, that's pretty tough."

"No, it's going to be a little easier than you think. Here's a paperback version you can mark in."

"That's yours," said Henry.

"Sure is. Turn to page 52. Buck's being sold here. "The man in the red sweater", see where I circled it?"

"Yeah, man's collecting money by selling dogs."

"Below that it says that Buck saw money being passed. What do you think of that?"

"So the dog saw money being paid to buy him?"

"Buck's a dog. Dog has no idea what money is and couldn't pick out a man with a red sweater on in a thousand people standing in front of him. What's London doing?"

"Wow, anthropomorphizing!" Hawkins was one step ahead of Lawrence and was scanning the end of the chapter on page 54. "Wait a second. Let me finish the last paragraph."

Henry found two places to high light as Lawrence watched his eyes scouring left to right. Lawrence had only circled one. "Hey, I only found one on that page."

"Yeah, that's all I found. Saying a dog feels shame is the one. What's neat about it is the theism he uses on the dog. You know the dog doesn't know shame. He's never seen snow before and the onlookers were laughing at him trying to catch flakes with his tongue. That's a human reaction. Yet in the telling of the dog chasing of the snow, London makes the dog very … Like how a dog would …"

"Great, Henry. You're getting what I want. Go through the book and high light where you see human attributes given to Buck. Do that for homework and I'll tell you what your essay will be the next time." Lawrence's words went to unheard. Hawkins was not paying attention to Lawrence as he continued reading and high lighting. Lawrence wanted to rough up Henry's hair like he was his own child. He was getting very attached to Henry.

It was the next visit that became Lawrence' s last session with Henry. The assignment was very simple. Henry would have to write a story using himself as a character and it had to be based on an incident in Henry's life. At first Henry balked, claiming his life had been boring and not worth writing or reading about. Lawrence threw it back on Henry.

"How did Jack London know what to write in <u>Call of the Wild</u>?"

"Because he lived it?"

"No, London never had a dog named Buck and no, he never went through all those adventures with a Saint Bernard. But he did live in the Wilds. He did know winters and sled dogs and miners and a few nasty bastards that someone should have taken down. But he never did any of those things. He used what he knew best to make the basis for a book or a story. Write what you know."

"I don't know shit. Man, I'm just a punk teenager who does drugs."

"Then that's what you write. Use your background and make a story out of it."

"Like why I became a druggie and why nobody should do …"

"No Henry. A story, not a testament. You know, a plot and people and some action, only dress up the real characters, the ones out there you know. Change them, change them to fit your story, to add to your story."

Lawrence saw the wheels turning in the back of Henry's eyes. Lawrence knew Henry could do it. What he did not know was that Henry Hawkins would not change the story very much.

***

He pedaled out of the McDonald's down Center Street Lewiston to 14th Street and followed the signs to Fort Niagara, where he made a left at Oneida Street and a right at North Second Street which became Lower River Road. This route was along the edge of the gorge, as close as twenty feet to the Niagara River rushing full speed to provide energy for two countries. After a tiring three miles up the slopes and a resting as he coasted down, Lawrence came to a vision. Topping a long incline, a cross appeared before him. It drew a smile on his face since he was approaching Stella Niagara Education Park. Lawrence knew little about the school, only that it was for students K-8 and if his memory did not fail him, it was originally founded by the sisters of Saint Francis. As he pedaled by the entrance and its huge and structurally exquisite main building, the dichotomy of teaching at a city public school compared to a parochial school ran through Lawrence's mind. No matter the chastisements aimed at private schools, and especially those affiliated with religion, the private school students got a better education.

Lawrence had been raised as a Catholic by his mother. She had often been recruited to teach at private schools back home but clung to public schools. Lawrence teased her about her being a French teacher in a public school and his being an English teacher. She got the elite and he got the dregs. Except she turned the tables on him by pointing out those were exactly the students Lawrence wanted.

Evelyn Southern raised her son as a catholic, not to imprison him in the religion but to illustrate to him how she had been raised and demonstrate for him the power of belief. She did not force him to participate in the ceremonies attached to being a Catholic but exposed him to the good that religion has engendered in the human mind. She loved her son deeply and missed his father even more. She knew Peter would not worship at an altar nor bow to any God, but she absorbed the maternal warmth Peter brought to her from the first day he faced his own students. She remembered his telling her how every English teacher must spend the first class of the new school year with their students, going over the rules at Niagara High School. Peter gave each student a 50 page student rules book and spent five minutes out of what was supposed to be fifty minutes going over each rule. He stopped after page two, told the class to close their books, and put them in their school lockers. He asked them one question. Who knows what the golden rule is? Lawrence got no answer. He wrote it on the board, "Do unto others as you would have them do unto you."

It produced responses, most students having remembered hearing those words. Evelyn had ingrained in Lawrence from the beginning of his intellectual growth with that one rule, a rule that was the basis on all rules. Evelyn knew Peter was going to be a great teacher as soon as she heard his first day and the abandoning of the school rule book. What she taught him, with her beliefs that had guided her life, Peter was passing along to his students.

Lawrence stopped at Stella Niagara, the Niagara River gorge only about 400 feet behind him. He still had about five miles to Fort Niagara but he had a whole weekend to get there, camp overnight and return home.

Lawrence could not shake that Henry Hawkins was dead. He would never be rid of him. He had known many people that had died but none that may have murdered. The pipe on which Henry hung himself had been replaced with one that could support a body. Had Henry attempted to hang himself on any other pipe, it would have broken and the worse that could have befallen Henry was a few bruises. So did Lawrence accept that the only strong pipe had been replaced before Henry's death or after? Lawrence might have attributed his death to pure numbers of odds except for the story that Henry had written and which had disappeared from the files of Niagara High School.

Back on Lower River Road, Lawrence passed through Jefferson Davis State Park which he found ironic since Jefferson Davis was a Southern rebel but still had been honored with a New York, thus Yankee park named after him.

Fort Niagara spent more time being a base for the United State's enemies in war than as a guardian for the United States. During the French-Indian War, France controlled this very strategic venue and built a permanent fortification there called the "French Castle." Sitting at the exit of the Niagara River into Lake Ontario, Fort Niagara was positioned to control access to the Great Lakes and ultimately the heartland of the continent. During a nineteen day siege, the British took control of Fort Niagara and kept control of it during the Revolutionary War only ceding it back to the United States in 1796. One year after the start of the War of 1812, the British recaptured the Fort and held on to it until the end of the war in 1815. Its strategic importance virtually disappeared when the Erie Canal was completed in 1825.

Despite rebuilding the walls and increasing its strength for the Civil War, the south never came close to attacking Fort Niagara, which later became a barracks for soldiers during World Wars I and II. The only military at the Fort now is the Coast Guard, the Fort and Park now being managed by a not-for-profit organization, in cooperation with the New York State Office of Parks, Recreation and Historic Preservation. The park is heavily visited during the summer season as it offers swimming pools, picnic areas, hiking trails, and many playing fields for sports like soccer and softball. Summer and Western New York do not fold over into crowds once Labor Day arrives. They trickle away with a small entourage of cross country skiers when the first snow fall pelts the area, sometimes occurring as early as October or as late as December. Lawrence had good weather luck on his side - - clear skies, sixty degrees plus temperatures, no snow, and as he glimpsed in approaching the Fort off of Scott Avenue, there were no boats at the launch and only one or two cars in the large parking lot.

Instead of heading straight to the park, he cycled to the Fort. It was a majestic sight and Lawrence enjoyed walking through its turrets and over its walls. For now he had the vision of almost castle-like structure built out over the Niagara River. The building could easily pass for a castle out of Eastern Europe and the Carpathian Mountains. He propped his bike against a tree and sat supported by the other side of the tree, allowing him to see the great expanse of Lake Ontario and the flowing current of the Niagara River.

He could not enjoy the view. Lawrence knew Henry Hawkins was murdered. No amount of sweat during his trip could wash away the story that Henry wrote. It was not the pipe that proved Henry's murder but the essay. Lawrence intentionally left the story back in his apartment in Niagara Falls. He needed to get away from it. It was just a teenage kid's fantasy and Lawrence took this trip to regain his sanity and walk past his conundrum of imagination. But he could not. Even now, late in the afternoon, his mind would not let go of Henry's essay. His mind beleaguered, Lawrence put his body to work. He was going to spend the night here even though there is no overnight camping at Fort Niagara State Park.

Having rested for about fifteen minutes, he headed back down Scott Avenue to Brown Street and the entrance to the state park. Taking the big curve of Old Lake Road, Lawrence entered the parking lot at Riddle Road and saw that there were a few soccer teams playing. He would have to wait until they left to set up his overnight camping. As daylight savings time had not yet started, it got dark very early since Western New York was so far north. The soccer teams and the team moms finished their games and all but one team left the park. Lawrence walked over to Lake Ontario's shore. During the ubiquitous Western New York summers, there are some days when it is actually warm enough to swim in Lake Ontario. There is a thin beach of sand for sun bathers, but most prefer the grassy area behind the sand. The beach expanse is about a half a mile, with the west end merging into Fort Niagara property and a wall of boulders that were dropped at the shore to prevent erosion. The east end shore gradually disappears into a pine tree forest separating Fort Niagara from the community of Fort Niagara Beach about three or four miles away from where Lawrence was going to set up a camp. Police periodically patrol the area, especially on weekends when teenagers are seeking hideaways for parking.

Lawrence walked east along the narrowing beach. About a quarter of a mile down, the shore line was fronted by a small cliff six or seven feet high and built mostly of sand with old dead tree roots keeping the erosion at bay. This would be Lawrence's camp site. Returning to the parking lot, he found himself completely alone as dusk headed toward darkness. Having chained his bicycle to a road sign, he dialed off the numbers, opened the lock, and rescanned the park for any sign of life. Being none, he walked his bicycle down to the sand, headed east, and stopped at the selected site. Lawrence had a small cave dug into the side of the cliff before total darkness. Since the only place a fire could be seen was out in a boat on Lake Ontario, Lawrence gathered kindling and small dry logs which would create less smoke, and using his jack knife, cut strips of thin bark catching the sparks thrown off by the jack knife as he stroked the flint he kept in his backpack. He kept the fire small so as to not draw any light above the cliff where patrolling police might see it.

Lawrence had no real reason to have a fire since his sleeping bag would provide more than enough warmth and the food he had brought food did not need cooking. The fire's purpose was religious; the fire unearthed in Lawrence the same consciousness of safety as it did in his ancestors for thousands of years. Lawrence, like those before him, read in the flames emotion and peace.

Out of his backpack Lawrence took a flask he had filled with St-Remy, Brandy Francais, VSOP. Pouring a double sized shot into his mess kit drinking cup, he begged the gods brandy to forgive his disgracing their fine liqueur with such a unworthy vessel. The first sip was always the best. If the bicycle trip had not done so, the brandy warming his system convinced Lawrence that he had to do something about Henry Hawkins's death.

When he had taught Henry about Jack London and anthropomorphism in relation to Call of the Wild, Lawrence was using a teaching strategy that was very successful in Lawrence's English classes especially with students that did not like to read. By having students try to write a story where they gave an animal a human's mind and ability to communicate, students were able to write stories quite easily. It worked for nearly all of his students. Being able to tell their story as if they were a cat or a fish or an eagle, came easily to them. This is what he had hoped for from Henry. He had wanted Henry to write his essay with himself as a creature like Buck in Call of the Wild and thus pass English.

Henry might have been enthralled by Lawrence's demonstration of anthropomorphism but Henry's essay proved to be based on Jack London's scathing examination of the police and the authorities that were almost criminal in how they treated Jack London in the short story. The story itself was good, but nowhere close to great. Henry Hawkins did exactly what Lawrence had asked of him. Write what you know. That he did. In his story, he was a character caught up in a system much more malevolent than any Jack London wrote about. Henry wrote about what he saw in the drug market of Niagara Falls and its high school. He described how his step father smuggled drugs over the Canadian border. He could do this because he drove a school bus. The school district takes many trips across the border, especially to Toronto. When they return, according to what Henry wrote, the border agents do not inspect the school buses or search the riders. Henry discovered this after being on one trip when his step father was the driver. They returned to the school bus facility next to the high school where Henry had to wait for his step father before they went home. He saw a crew of non-school employees, smartly dressed and well-built, meet with his stepfather. His stepfather escorted the men to the school bus crawled under it, and came out with a grease-covered box. Using a socket wrench, his stepfather removed the top of the box and took out plastic packages filled with white powder. Henry knew instantly what they were. He had been a drug user since elementary school when the security guard at his school sold Henry his first drugs.

Henry's story did not stop there. The step father never knew Henry had spied on him. But Henry did more than that. He watched every time his step father was scheduled for a trip across the border and cut school so he could hide at the school bus facility to see the drug deal. Knowing he had his step father dead to rights, he took it a step farther and followed the drug dealers. First they took the packages, carried in K Mart shopping bags, to a row house behind the school bus garages. Henry knew these houses since he bought marijuana there. He always wondered how they got their supply.

It was the second stop that sealed Henry's fate. After leaving the row house, the dealers got in their cars and drove off. But to where? Henry would have to wait for another trip to find the answer. Three weeks later his step father took an earth science class to the Toronto Museum of Science. Henry cut school again but this time he chained his bicycle to a tree near the row house and went back to the school bus garage and waited. Like clockwork his step father returned and drove the bus into the garage as the dealers showed up. Henry scurried away to retrieve his bicycle. He was second guessing that the dealers would not drive too fast and thus avoid being pulled over and searched by the police. His plan was to follow them in stages, since he could not hope to go too long a distance to track them down.

No plan was necessary. The dealers made a left turn on Walnut Street, another left on Sixth, cruised past St. Mary's Hospital, turned right on Ferry Avenue, and pulled into the Niagara School District Administrative Offices. Henry got there just as they were going in the back door of the four-story brick building. In less than fifteen minutes the men came, followed by a short Italian man dressed in a very exquisite dark blue suit with gray pin stripes. Henry did not know who he was so decided to wait and see what car he got into.

Henry was about to give up, started to get on his bicycle to go home. Just then a Niagara Falls police car entered the parking lot. Henry froze where he stood in the alleyway unseen. It was the first time Henry could remember being really scared. He had a criminal record, albeit a juvenile one. That made no difference since the entire Niagara Falls police force probably knew Henry and would recognize him immediately. But that worked two ways. Henry could also recognize and identify nearly every police officer in the city. There was only one man getting out of the cruiser. It was the Chief of Police.

Had Henry ended the story at this point, he might still be alive.

Henry waited. It did not take long. The police chief walked out of the Niagara Falls School District Administrative Offices with the same short Italian man in the same very exquisite dark blue suit with the same gray pin stripes. The men shook hands and the police chief got into his car and drove off. Henry now knew too much. It was time for him to leave.

So Henry handed the story over to Lawrence and got himself killed? Lawrence could not accept that initially. Even when he discovered the pipe enigmas at the Detention Facility, Lawrence still could not believe Henry was murdered. That view was changing as he drank more of the brandy. Alcohol worked too well on Lawrence and he knew he was near the edge of letting it overwhelm him. When drinking, Lawrence gradually built up his antagonism toward the world. Along with it came a surge of violence which up to now he had been able to control.

But now was here in a cave in a cliff facing Lake Ontario with a small fire and a canteen of brandy. Henry did not kill himself, of this Lawrence was sure. Accident? That was a possibility.

The darkness was complete across Lake Ontario. Lawrence could clearly see the lights of Toronto. It brought back tears and intense pain remembering Eileen and that first night when they made love. Lawrence was tired, more from his thoughts than from the bike trip. His body was fatigued. A last drink of St. Remy's turned his thoughts back to Henry Hawkins. He had no doubt that someone killed Henry. The remembrance of Eileen's death and the last words of Zig made it clear. Lawrence and Eileen had been ratted out by Superintendent Nuevello to Ziggy. Belafont had called Nuevello about the Hawkins essay and brought it over to Nuevello at once. As soon as Nuevello read it he tried to contact both Lawrence and Eileen but was told by Belafont that they were canoeing and camping together in the Southern Tier. Nuevello called Eileen's parents, whom he knew socially, and found out exactly they were. He then called Ziggy and chided him for allowing his wife, a married woman to go whoring in the woods with Lawrence. He told Ziggy that if she were his wife, he would find and kill both of them. Italian men did not let their women fuck around. This was Ziggy's last confession before Lawrence drowned him.

Why? Lawrence had restrained himself from going after Nuevello as soon as he was released by the police. It was the police interrogation that actually held Lawrence back. It was obvious that the Niagara Police Department knew far too much about Lawrence and Eileen's love affair. The challenge to Ziggy by Nuevello and the harassment Lawrence endured at the hands of the police made sense once Lawrence read Hawkins's essay. Henry had hit the school system in the underbelly and Nuevello got rid of him.

Still, Lawrence could not fully accept it. He was down to half a cup of brandy as he walked the shoreline, absorbing the cold night air and the very quiet lake effect waves smoothly lapping on the shore. He decided he had to talk to his mother. Lawrence really needed his father, needed that same rise of challenge that his father had faced in Vietnam. Uncle George could not help at this point but maybe his mother had enough insight into her husband to guide him.

It was late. He was tired. The brandy was gone. Lawrence walked back to his cave, kicked sand over the smoldering ashes from his fire, crawled into inside the cave, and pulled the tarp over the entrance. St. Remy had done its job. He was asleep in minutes.

***

Never take a chance on the weather in Western New York. It will not only rain on your parade but usually blow a snow storm up your ass. Lawrence woke to the sound of rain drops, small scattered ones that pelted the canvas between his warm bed roll and the outside world. With a little bit of luck the rain would cease in a short while. It did not. Because of Lawrence's ignorance of Western New York weather and his arrogance at not covering some kindling before he retired, he not only faced a drenching bicycle ride back to Niagara Falls but he would have to do it without any caffeine in his system.

"I'm fucked," he screamed loudly to the lifeless world surrounding him.

Since Lawrence had left his rain gear at home, he had to cut the tarpaulin into a rough parka to keep him from getting soaked. He did not want to go back by way of Lower River Road since poor visibility on such a winding and narrow road would have made for a dangerous Sunday morning ride. What he did not need was to get slammed by some good Christians on their way to church. There was only one other way to go, the Robert Moses Parkway which did not allow bicycles.

"At least a jail would be warm," he thought as he headed out on to the road.

Lawrence got pretty far before the flashing lights came up behind him. Kicking down the bike stand, he pulled off his handmade hood and wiped his rain drenched face. At least it was a New York State Trooper. Better yet it was a woman trooper and she was not carrying her ticket book.

The trooper looked Lawrence over as she approached him, wasting no time. "Come on, get in the cruiser. You do know it's raining?"

"You're kidding?"

Lawrence took off the sopping wet, self-made parka before getting into the back seat but the officer opened the front seat passenger side door for him. Lawrence knew he was not going to get a ticket or be arrested.

"Got some ID on you?"

Lawrence pulled out his driver's license and handed it to the woman. Yes, she is a woman, thought Lawrence and very obviously a woman as her long blond hair unraveled from the drill sergeant state trooper's hat.

"Got a job?"

She thought he might be a vagrant, "Yep, I teach at Niagara High School. Teach English."

"How did you get caught out here like this?"

"I camped over last night at Fort Niagara. Weatherman said it wouldn't rain this weekend."

"Obviously you haven't been in Western New York for long or you'd know better than to believe what the weather reports tells you. You can't ride a bike on the Robert Moses Parkway. Did you know that? Didn't you see the signs?"

Lawrence did see the signs and before he went on this sojourn he knew that bicycles were not allowed on the parkway, "I didn't get on at a ramp. Came through the woods."

"Look, Mr. Lawrence," she reached down to a thermos, unscrewed the steel cap, poured a cupful of dark, black coffee and offered it to Lawrence who thanked her, "I'm not writing you up. If I did I'd have to write you up for camping on state property. You're not allowed to camp at Fort Niagara. Didn't you know that either?"

She was very attractive, with strawberry freckles, good teeth, and blue-green eyes. Her mouth had one of those smiles that said be good and you will enjoy me. Before he had a chance to respond, she stopped him.

"Don't answer that. Want some breakfast?" She pulled back her hair, the trooper's hat sitting perfectly with the chin strap tucked under a slightly dimpled chin. "Only thing close is Mickey D's. My treat."

She did not wait for an answer but eased herself out of the patrol car, waved him to the trunk, popped it open, and spoke, "stick your bike in here. There's a bungee cord or two floating around back here."

The trooper went back to the driver's seat while Lawrence fitted his cycle into the trunk.

Lawrence had two egg McMuffins and the trooper a fruit salad. They discussed his being a teacher and her being the daughter of a teacher. She was taking courses at Niagara Falls Community College to get an Associate's Degree in education with hopes of becoming an educator for the New York State police. She enjoyed her job as it was but knew as time went by the physical challenges would get to her. After breakfast she asked him where he lived and drove him home. On the way she talked about her family and two kids. Her children were a major deciding factor in getting off the patrol and active duty roster. The way things were going anymore, she believed it was only a matter of time before she got involved in a armed conflict was some drug addict or another felon.

Lawrence decided to take a very dangerous chance. Her openness and the fact she was a state police officer, not a Niagara Falls' cop, made it a little less so. Still he kept his conversation with her under tight reins. "It amazes me when I go up to Fort Niagara, how close we are to Canada. You ever get involved with the Canadian police?"

She popped her truck and Lawrence hauled his bike out. As she closed the trunk, he wheeled the bike up to the front porch which was out of the weather and dry. She followed him, "No I never have. There's some special liaison officers that do a lot with them."

"It would seem to me that as close as Fort Niagara is to the Canadian shore, there'd be a lot of smuggling going on?"

"There's some. Also we get a few migrants sneaking across up there. Be kind of rough down here."

Lawrence laughed at her allusion to the Falls being an escape route. The Falls could be heard all the way to his front porch and the killer rapids were just yards west of his house. He opened up with his story about Henry Hawkins's suicide keeping it at a level where Henry was just a student he tutored. This drew a reaction from her.

"That's one tough scene to handle. I'm glad I wasn't involved in it."

"You mean a kid hanging himself?"

She took off her trooper's hat, wiped the rain drops off the plastic covering, and looked seriously at Lawrence, "yeah that was bad enough but we - - not we - - other troopers and detectives working the case had some strong doubts about how it went down."

She avoided Lawrence's gaze for the first time. "I talk too much. It's gonna to get me in trouble sometime. Let's just say it was kind of a strange suicide, strange case. We didn't get involved in it until well after …"

She stopped but not before Lawrence caught the look on her face. It obviously did not go down as a routine suicide and just as obviously she wanted to talk about it but feared putting her job in jeopardy.

"Yeah, I understand. I knew Henry. Knew him well enough that I couldn't really accept that he killed himself. He was not that hooked on drugs. Go figure. Listen, I'd invite you in but it wouldn't look too good on your part. Your choice?"

"That's okay. I understand. You knew Henry Hawkins that well?"

"Yeah, got him interested in reading. He got hooked on Jack London."

She put her hat back on, tucked the strap under her chin under, and reached inside her jacket, bringing out a small leather case, "here's my card. You get caught out in the rain again, give me a call. Probably I'll have to come scrape you up off some stretch of road on the New York State Thruway."

Lawrence took the card and thanked her.

"You got some doubts about your former student Henry, don't you?"

"If you mean how he died, the answer is yes."

"Let me warn you. Unless you're ready for major trouble, you'd better leave it alone."

"As in you guys are doing something about it?"

Startled, her warm dimpled smile closed into a grim visage, "I can't answer that."

She went back out into the rain, turned to face Lawrence still standing on the porch, and tried to smile but did not make it. She waved, got into the patrol car and drove off.

CHAPTER NINETEEN

Beast of the Mother

Daylight savings had ended and Lawrence was stuck meeting with a parent on a Friday of all days. By the time he hit the road it was already 5:30 and he could see the sun setting in the rear view mirror as he drove east on the New York State Thruway, one of the most boring rides on earth, not to mention the ten signs to Rochester which also makes it the most convoluted roadway this side of Hell. By the time he hit Syracuse and headed south on route 81, the easiest and most enjoyable part of the drive, it was dark. It took him nearly four hours to reach his mother's house south of Scranton in the hills of the Poconos. He knew she would have French chocolate éclairs waiting for him in the refrigerator and her exquisite cabbage soup warming on a back burner. Lawrence parked behind her dark blue Peugeot which was showing the ever present results of the Poconos' weather - - rust. She had heard his car grinding the driveway stones and was waiting for him at the door.

At the age of fifty five, Evelyn Lawrence Southern was still a knockout of a woman. She was tall but not as thin as when she bore Peter's father a son almost twenty five years ago. Evelyn was now retired from teaching high school French but did some substitute work to pay for her golf club dues. She never remarried, but not due to Llewellyn Lawrence's disappearance in Vietnam. Evelyn liked romance with one man, but her romances usually ended in boredom. She did not like being bored and would kindly slough off lovers after a few months. At first this made Peter angry. He never knew who the next uncle, as she called each of her lovers, would be that she brought home. Regardless, they were usually hung over, red-eyed, and still half drunk sitting at the kitchen table when Lawrence got up to go to school.

"Mon fils, you are very late?"

Lawrence was nearly eye-to-eye with his mother who stood only inches below Lawrence's six two frame. He hugged her first, they kissed cheeks, and he noticing the taste of Reunite on her breath. He was thankful it was only wine which would make her sleepy unlike the St. Remy's brandy she had taught him to love.

"Mama, you're looking good! How's the golf game? Seasons nearing an end, isn't it?"

"Non, mon fils, this is not that Antarctica called Buffalo where you live. We've got a good four or five weeks still."

Lawrence would not chide her as usual about Niagara Falls not being another name for Buffalo. "Which Uncle's visiting this weekend?"

Evelyn smiled and spoke, "you are such an asshole, mon fils. C'est Oncles, non! They are rare and far between anymore. I guess I'll have to come live with you to find some better survivors."

They both laughed. Lawrence took his backpack up to his hallowed room which she kept always available for him. He returned back down the stairs to the smell of cabbage soup.

"Mon Mere, I am so glad that you are predictable. I dreamed of your cabbage soup for the entire trip. Can I guess what's in the frig?"

"Oh, I'm so sorry, mon fils! I was so busy substituting at the middle school today that I didn't have time to bake your éclairs. Can you forgive me?"

Lawrence knew better. Instead of sitting down to his steaming bowl of cabbage soup, he walked to the refrigerator and opened it. A smile was on his face as he took out an éclair and bit off one end. Cream filling gushed out the side of his mouth as Evelyn handed him a paper towel.

"Those? Those are not good enough for my son. No more. I bought them at the Food Lion."

"Before I forget, mon fils, some judge has been calling you from Virginia?"

"He's not really a judge, Mon Mere. His first name is Judge. His mother named him that so she could say her family had a judge in it. He's an English professor I took journalism with when I was a junior in college. He's a good man but gullible. He bought into a newspaper in Virginia City Beach and wants to hire me to come down there and be one of his editors."

"A newspaper man, C'est magnifique!"

"No, I'm not taking it. Like I said, Judge gets himself into these little projects and thinks he can make money on them. It's doomed to fail. I've been putting him off. I'll give him a call when I get back. Who knows, maybe I could be the next Clark Kent?"

Lawrence laughed and started on the soup. The time passed as they talked and Lawrence ate two bowls of soup and his mother a small salad. In his entire life Lawrence never saw Evelyn Southern eat more than a small bird's meal at a sitting. He never caught her eating one of her éclairs. The only time anyone ever touched one of her son's éclairs was when some long ago uncle dared take one out of Evelyn's refrigerator. He never finished it or his romance with Evelyn. Discovered in flagrante, she ejected him from her house, never to return.

Evelyn started up the conversation that she knew her son wanted, "so does this mean you'll not be home for Thanksgiving?" It was only a few weeks away and Lawrence always came home.

"You know I'm not here for a visit with Mon Mere."

"C'est la femme? That married woman that was killed?"

"Don't fuck with me, Mama. I know you detested her and our time together but ..."

"Detested? You say detested? You should be ashamed ..."

Lawrence reached over and took her hand gently. He rolled his hands over her skin. She did not like anybody touching the skin of her hands because it was the only physical part of her that said she was aging. Still, she knew her son needed the touch and needed her to listen.

"She's gone, Mon Mere. Let her rest. Let me recover. Yes, I still hurt and no, it's no concern to you any longer. What I need from you now may be too much. First I have to tell you about a student that I was tutoring ..."

Evelyn was in tears by the time Lawrence finished. "That is horrible. How could people, school people, which is even worse, let that happen to a boy like Henri?"

Lawrence had not told her about his suspicions. "I don't think they let it happen, Mama."

"What do you mean, Petra?"

Lawrence was named after his maternal grandfather who died years before Lawrence was born. Evelyn's mother, who was still alive and living in Canada, collected many uncles in her youth. Unlike Evelyn, grand mere married grand pere when she discovered she has pregnant. Grand pere happened to be a Russian immigrant whose first name was Petra. He was a very loving father to Evelyn and while she would not stick her son with a foreign sounding name on his birth certificate, she named him Peter but called him Petra.

"I think Henry was murdered," explaining to her what he had discovered.

"So why do you not turn them in?"

"The evidence is there but people like the Police Chief and Superintendent Nuevello have too much power. If I report what I know, they'll refute it and using their powers, especially their economic power, they'll destroy anything I say. Mama, I know they set up Henry to be killed and then tried to make it look like suicide. They, or I should say one of their lackeys, will say they replaced the shower room pipe after the old one broke when they tried to hoist his dead body off of the old pipe. Damn, there were pieces of the old rusty pipe around the hole when I pulled down on the new pipe. Nuevello knew that Henry was aware of what was going on at Niagara High School. He knew it because Henry wrote it in his essay. I caused him to die. I told him to write about what he knows, tell his story exactly as he knows it. Shit, I practically said he could be the next Jack London. He did write what I asked and he died."

"And no one but you thinks this?"

"Good question, Ma Mere. I met a New York State trooper and mentioned to her that I taught Henry. I asked her why the state police weren't involved. She had no response."

"And you come to me for an answer? Mon Fils, what can I do?"

This was the hard part for Lawrence. "Mama, these people must be taken to task for their crime. They are vicious killers who take lives to make money. They are evil. Somebody must rid the world of them."

"And that is you?"

"I know about my father. I know he turned on his country. I know his vengeance was unmerciful against the armies of the United States."

"How do you know this? How can you judge a man who is gone from us? You accuse your father of being a traitor ..."

Lawrence put his hands on her upper arms and gently rubbed her muscles, "no, mama, he was not a traitor. He was a savior of Vietnamese people being slaughtered by our country, the United States. He chose to fight fought for Vietnam and its people, its women and children. It hurt him tremendously but he knew he was right."

Tears welled in Evelyn's eyes, not because her son knew about his father in Vietnam, but because she still loved Llewellyn to this day. She loved his valor and courage and pain. She had hated him for trading their life together to protect poor, illiterate villagers from being butchered by the world's most powerful country. She hated herself for hating his decision. As the years passed she gave up on her hatred for Llewellyn Lawrence and instead hated herself for her selfishness.

"Georg, Oncles Georg, right Mon Fils?"

"Yes Mama."

"What did that son of a bitch tell you?"

Lawrence repeated George's words about Llewellyn Lawrence's desertion and guerilla warfare against the United States Armed Forces in Vietnam.

"Petra, have you no brain? Qu'est que ces't vous? Georg could not tell you that tale. Georg was lost to your father very early in his tale. Don't you see that?"

"Oui, Mama. Which means he is either a great liar or he learned it from someone?"

"Which, Mon Fils is why you are here, n'est pas?"

"Mais oui. It is you, n'est pas?"

Evelyn Southern held a tablet. She had no idea what her son would do if he read the words. She silently cursed her brother-in-law and vowed to see him in Hell. Her son needed to know more than a soldier's tale.

"Mama, was Uncle George making up a story? I know he was very close to my father and I know my father disappeared. Did he contrive my father as being some hero to the people of Vietnam so I wouldn't think of him as being a coward and traitor?"

"Your Oncle Georg did not lie to you and he did not embellish the story. I did not tell him anything. Your pere told him the story. Actually vous pere told me the story and I let Oncle George read it. Llewellyn sent me letters."

"How? He was a deserter. How could he get letters to you?"

"You forget, Mon Fils, I am not an American. I am Canadian. Vous pere sent them to my sister Alsace in Toronto. Your aunt Alsace received a folder from a relative who lives near Paris in Francais. The envelope was innocuous and got through the mail to Toronto. As soon as Alsace opened the folder she found Llewellyn's letters inside with a letter to her."

"But how did he get them out of Vietnam?"

The time had arrived. She had to tell her son that his father was indeed a traitor and enemy of his country. He needed to know. If he would not accept his father after the truth came out, she knew that Peter would not only lose his father but she would no longer be able to have anything to do with her beloved son, Peter.

"The North Vietnamese had begun peace negotiations with the United States. Llewellyn had now become an agent working for the Viet Cong. Because of his service in ..."

"You mean what Uncle George said actually came from letters he sent to you? My father was leading enemy patrols to kill American soldiers?"

"Oui."

"He was helping the people of North Vietnam survive the horror of American atrocities? Even the fucking bombings?"

Evelyn smiled. She would not lose her son, nor her son lose his father, "oui, mon Fils. He had asked the North Vietnamese government officials if he could send letters to me. By then he had saved so many villages from American assaults that he was a hero in many, many hamlets in North Vietnam. The politicians in those villages had sent letters of support to the North Vietnamese government testifying to Llewellyn's valor and allegiance to North Vietnam. The government knew of Llewellyn Lawrence and admired his bravery. They were reluctant to acquiesce until they realized how much propaganda they could get out of letting your father write home. Vous pere begged them to not use his letters as propaganda since it might bring harm to his family. Unexpectedly, they agreed and helped him set up a route through their delegates in Paris, then to my great Tante in Montreuil ..."

"Montreal, Canada?"

"Non, Montreuil, France. It is about 5 kilometers east of Paris. Mon tante repackaged the letters and sent them to Aunt Alsace. It took many months but it breathed life back into my soul."

"So you have the letters? I can ..."

"I burned them," she broke down into a wash of tears and had trouble breathing. Lawrence feared she would have a stroke. He pulled her gently from the kitchen table chair and escorted her into the living room. Her face was red. Lawrence went to the phone.

"Non, do not. I'm okay. I have dreaded for nearly twenty years having to tell you about your father and his letters. It has happened. It is time. It is also painful, not painful physically but emotionally. Yes I burned the letters."

"Why, Mama? I can't fucking believe that I'm this close to ..."

"Petra, you are much like your father. I see strength in you but I see violence also. I know there is more in the telling of your lover's murder than what you have told me. I suspect that her husband now suffers in Hell thanks to Peter Lawrence's vengeance, bravery, and uncontrolled violence. You must not lose control when I tell you why I burned your father's letters. Petra, Petra, I loved him enough to die with his letters in my hand. But I could not let my life in raising his only son be abandoned, me in a prison and you in an orphanage."

"What are you talking about?"

"Do you remember when you were five and I sent you to live with Aunt Alsace?"

"Yes, you were sick and couldn't take care of me. I was scared, very scared. You had trouble getting me into Uncle Ralph's car to take me to Toronto. I have never cried so much."

"Do you remember what happened just days before that?"

"A little. There was some kind of problem between grand pere and the police. There was a lot of yelling and screaming. Grand pere got arrested and the police searched our house."

"They were after your father's letters, Mon Fils."

"Why? They were none of their business."

"It was mostly my fault. I did not keep my mouth shut about your father. I trusted people that I should not have trusted. Friends I thought which were not friends at all. They reported me to the police, who passed it along to the FBI."

Evelyn watched her son's eyes very carefully. She would stop if the angry stare flickered towards violence. "Your grandfather's union kept me out of jail and you out of an orphanage. I remember that night well. Grand Pere Lawrence came rushing through the front door yelling at me, telling me that the FBI was going to be here at any moment. I had to get rid of Llewellyn's letters. I begged of him to tell me why but he wouldn't listen. He said that if I didn't, they would confiscate them away and arrest me for espionage against the United States. I would be electrocuted as a spy."

Peter's eyes were narrowing, his breathing, through his nostrils, deepening.

"Grand Pere had just received a phone call from the president of the railroad worker's union. He had a tip from one of his contacts that tracked down government spies in the union ranks. The FBI was sending agents to confiscate propaganda being held by his daughter-in-law, meaning the letters I had received from Vous Pere.

"Minutes after your grandfather scooted me upstairs, someone was beating on the front door, yelling to open it up. I stopped at the top of the stairs, not knowing what to do. I remember yelling at him that there wasn't time. He told me he would make the time so I better get my ass moving. He told me get the letters, go into the bathroom upstairs, put them into the bath tub, and burn them. He asked if I had any lighter fluid in the house, which I did under the sink. While the banging got louder, he ran into the kitchen, grabbed the can of lighter fluid, and brought it up to me. I had not noticed he had that rifle you now use …"

"The Remington 30.06."

"Oui, he was carrying it around with him. I took the lighter fluid and ran to the bedroom for the letters. Grand Pere opened the door a bit, keeping the chain lock fastened to the frame and his foot wedged at the bottom. He asked who they were and was told they were from the FBI and wanted to talk with Mrs. Lawrence. He told them there was no Mrs. Lawrence here, to go fuck themselves. The reply was that they would bust the door down if he did not unlatch it and let them in. Grand Pere told them to back off and he'd let them in. They did."

"I was in tears by now. I had the letters in the bathtub but could not bring myself to put the lighter fluid on them. It made no sense. These letters were my personal property. How could they take them away from me? I heard the front door shut so the chain could be released. Grand Pere Lawrence yelled to them it was unlocked and they could come in. I also heard him chamber a round in the rifle as they walked into my home. Chambered, is that correct Mon Fils?"

Evelyn asked this for a reason. The question was irrelevant but she knew it would change her son's angry lips into a smile, "oui, mama, after all these years you've finally learned something about a rifle. Go on, s'il vous plaît."

"I snuck a look from upstairs. Three men walked in, all in light grey suits with fedora hats. I had to stop myself from laughing. They told Grand Pere Lawrence they wanted to ask Mrs. Lawrence some questions about her husband whom had been listed as MIA in Vietnam. He told them I did not wish to speak to them. They said that I had no choice. This was official business and if I refused to speak with them they would arrest me and search the house for espionage material. I would be tried for a war crime and sent to jail. My child would be taken away."

"How many did Grand Pere shoot?"

Peter was still smiling so Evelyn eased up a bit, took a sip of Reunite and continued. "Unfortunately or maybe fortunately, none. He asked the spokesman for the trio if he had a search warrant. The man said no, that he didn't need one. Grand Pere Lawrence lifted up the Remington and told him yes, he did. The man sneered at your grandfather like a weasel ready to eat a chicken. There were three of them ..."

Lawrence broke in, "Grand Pere Lawrence can handle the Remington faster than three suits could draw their guns. I assume that did not happen since he's not in jail right now serving a life term."

"No, they did not even bring their hands close to their guns. They laughed at him, one calling him an old goat, as they turned to leave. He told Grand Pere they'd be back with a warrant and we would be sent to jail. Of course like all Lawrences, Grand Pere had to have the last word."

Lawrence smiled and laughed lightly, "what'd he tell them? To go fuck themselves?"

"Non, Mon Fils. He called out to the leader who turned, thinking Grand Pere had decided to let them do their job. Grand Pere Lawrence told them they would need one other thing when they returned. The FBI agent asked what? Grand Pere lifted up the Remington, pulled back the hammer, and told them a bulletproof vest."

"You're kidding me?"

"Non, that he did and because of that our home ended up surrounded by FBI agents, state police SWAT teams, and every news channel reporter on the East Coast."

"You burned the letters?"

"I had no choice. They came back. Not quick enough to stop me from burning them. They arrested us both. I was very glad Uncle Ralph had taken you."

"You went to jail? Did you have to put up bail money?"

"Mais oui, but Grand Pere's union lawyer took care of all of that. The Union hated the federals and were glad to help us. It all went away within a week. The charges against me were dropped and Grand Pere got a suspended sentence and a thousand dollar fine for aiming a deadly weapon at a law officer. He told the judge it was worth every penny of the fine."

"It is true that my father turned traitor to his country?"

"Yes."

"He did it because he saw the violence against the Vietnamese people?"

His mother paused. She did not want to admit her husband was a traitor. The only proof his father was fighting against his country was vague at best. The letters had been solid evidence. The United States government intelligence network discovered that Evelyn Southern was receiving letters and had hoped to force her to give them up. If that happened, she would stop receiving any assistance from the United States Army.

"Ma Mere! Answer me! Was he a traitor as they said? I've got to know!" Lawrence held his mother tightly at her shoulders. "I see what Uncle George told me in myself. Was it the same with my father? Did violence take over his life?"

"Yes Petra, it did. There was more than just his retaliation toward the horror put upon the Vietnamese people. His letters got more and more one-sided, the anger at his country growing. No one knows this but me and now you, his son. As the months, and years went by, Llewellyn's letters became more and more anti-American. He could see only one reason for the war."

"And?"

"The country needs war. War means a prosperous economy."

"My father realized that?"

Evelyn was crying gently, "yes, and he equated killing with bombs to creating jobs for those that make the bombs. Our country needed the war to rule the world ..."

"Yes, Ma Mere, rule the world by greed. Blow up a village ... open automatic weapons on poor rice farmers ... make profits for munitions factories to flourish in the United Sates. Even better, make the owner a billionaire, a multibillionaire."

There was something more that he could see in her eyes.

"There is one exception to your father's vendetta against our country. Llewellyn began to thrive on his war."

"Thrive? What do you mean?"

"There was great pride in his letters when he described how he helped the people in the villages. Those victories for the people began to change in his letters over the months and years. Where once he held back American platoons with his Viet Cong fighters to keep villages free from violence, the war was ending and his violent methods were not needed. Yet he still wrote about the thrill of taking down the Americans. Violence was running through his body."

Lawrence now had the truth. Did his father kill when there was no longer any need? Did the streak of violence run through Llewellyn's blood beyond fighting the American invaders? Did his father continue his own war and wreak violence when it was no longer needed? Even worse, what was the judgment that his father made that allowed him to keep fighting and killing?"

"Ma Mere, the war has been over for many years now. How did it end for Ma Pere?"

Peter Lawrence had lived with an MIA father, one presumed dead. Evelyn Southern had nourished that image and circumvented any attempt to delve further than his father being a victim of Viet Nam. From a hero of a war to a traitor to his country, Peter Lawrence had only one more source that could unravel the last piece of web.

"I do not know. The letters stopped and so did the government's attacks on me."

"That's it? Just like that my father ceased to exist. Didn't you try to reach him once the war ended and the country accepted Viet Nam as an independent nation? You could have flown there and tried to find him."

She hesitated. Lawrence could read the frustration in her eyes, "there was one letter but not from your father. It was from a priest in China. The priest did not write the letter. He only addressed it to me. It contained just a photograph that had a note on the back with my address. It was a photograph of your father in a casket.

"Did you write back to the priest?"

"No, there was no need."

Lawrence was stunned. Even as a child, he held firmly to the image of his heroic soldier father returning home. As he grew and heard more and more storied accounts from his relatives, Lawrence began planning a trip to Viet Nam to find his father. He needed answers in relation to how he saw his own life. Lawrence needed to know how to resolve this current challenge, Henry Hawkins. The boy was dead. That he could not change. The question was how to avenge Henry's death.

His mother gave him life, every day she gave him life. Now she had given him death, his father's death. Why did she not tell him all of this earlier?

"I am tired Mon Fils. I'm going to bed."

"Why didn't you tell me all of this before?"

"What good is it to you? Is your father a great warrior of the Vietnamese people? Is he a great traitor to his country?"

Lawrence felt a slight burn from the brandy at the back of his throat and the sudden narcotic of its alcohol switching violent thoughts off and on throughout his brain. The anger was brewing, a little at a time.

"Go to bed. I don't trust myself to speaking with you anymore tonight. Let's not end with a fight. Go to bed Ma Mere."

Lawrence had put a deep dent in the brandy bottle that gave rise to more anger in his soul. The television was on but ignored. Lawrence began to drift slowly off in the brandy narcosis when the doorbell rang. With the room spinning, he opened the door. Standing on his mother's porch was an immense bulk of a man, weighing perhaps seventy pounds more than Lawrence and standing a good three inches above Lawrence's six feet two inch frame. The man's face had calluses from obvious fist fights at his eyebrows and his nose appeared to have been broken at least once and poorly reset.

"Yeah, what ya want?"

"I've come to visit Miss Southern. Is she home?"

The man was well dressed, smelled only slightly of booze, which might well have been Lawrence just smelling the alcohol on his own breath.

Lawrence needed sleep; he had earned it, "Mom! Get on down here. There's some gorilla here that wants to see you!"

As Lawrence turned to smile at the man, he caught a left fist the size of New Jersey against his jaw, followed by a right to his left ear as he was fell backwards. He did not wake up for seven hours.

CHAPTER TWENTY

Breast of the Mother

"Judi, his name had to be Judi. It couldn't have been Lars or Otto or Bruno," thought Lawrence, "no, I had to have my clock cleaned by a Judi."

Lawrence should not be driving. He had not slept off his drunkenness from yesterday and his face was a mess. The right side was so swollen that he could barely open his mouth to sip down four cups of his mother's dark and dangerous coffee. At least Judi had not broken his jaw. Lawrence had been lucky in that Judi's second blow caught him as he was falling, the blow only a glance, fortunately not strong enough to send him to the hospital. He would have to visit his dentist to extract one of his back teeth however.

"Hey," Lawrence said to the non-passengers in his car, "at least I didn't cry like Judi!"

Judi was Evelyn Southern's behemoth of a boyfriend whose name was actually a shortened version of his German name given to him prior to his family migration to the United States. Judi was short for Judiah. While Judi appeared to be mildly obese, his size was all muscle, not fat. Judi was close friends with Uncle Ralph and the two currently stood at a draw for the number of boxing matches each had won between them. Ralph had the most wins in the ring and Judi led the series of knock downs and called outs at the bar. Judi could not stop apologizing to Lawrence once Lawrence woke up Sunday morning, having been single handedly carried by Judi up the stairs to his bed in his old room. Lawrence did not care.

While the conflicts of his infrequent visits home to mother ended the same way as always, this visit had out distanced every war between mother and son. Always they started out friendly - - Lawrence talking about school and his students, Evelyn telling the same old stories about her days in the classroom before she retired. The same old stories slowly became the family history along with mother Southern's tales of having to raise a child alone, the child being Peter who like his father abandoned her to live in upstate New York and who never visited her.

This visit went way past the usual guilt trips and mild anger. Peter had not known of his father's letters and the fact that Evelyn had kept them from him enraged Peter. The coup de gras was Evelyn not telling him about the government trying to arrest her. What surprised Lawrence the most was that his grandfather had not told him either but Lawrence knew that this was due to Evelyn's pressure on her father-in-law.

Lawrence was driving the long stretch north on route 81, approaching the signature Indian chief rock formation. Lawrence had never fully understood the message that geology had put into the rock formation. Approaching the rocks along the bottom of the stretch of road they projected a visual and awe inspiring sculpture of an Indian created by nature, an almost religious sight. Yet when you finished the two mile climb straight at the face of the Indian, it no longer appeared as the great chief guarding the other side of Pennsylvania's world. Face to face, with no angle to misinform the eyes, the Indian became a pile of rocks standing precipitously on an edge that thousands of years from now would erode and tumble down into the valley.

Before Lawrence had left, he eaten a dish of oatmeal with his mother and the over apologetic Judi. While his stomach groaned and pleaded with his appetite for a stack of his mother's waffles and sausage, his jaw could not open enough to satiate such a breakfast. Judi's stomach had no such problem. Lawrence kept his mouth shut, which was easy to do since he could barely sip his coffee. He and Evelyn avoided the issues from the previous night, made small talk, and ended with hugs and a promise of another visit soon. Judi shook his hand and for the hundred millionth time apologized for his actions, actions which Lawrence knew he had deserved. Tears shed, momma refusing to uncoil her wrapped arms, Lawrence slipped away and was now on the down slope of the enigma called Indian Head Mountain.

After what he saw in his mother this visit, Lawrence's perspective of the world was one he could not accept. What had happened transformed his thoughts way beyond what they had previously been only day ago when he had driven home. Now on his return the answers Lawrence sought took on a different hue. Evelyn Southern's world saw the wrongs but accepted the way of the world and its people. Lawrence knew that his father was a traitor to the United States and he knew why. There was no need to accept or reject what his father had done or whom he had become. His father had not been able to go into the world of Viet Nam and heinously murder and mutilate its women, children, and men for his country. No sin could be more ungodly than the horrendous obliteration of innocent people through fire bombings or the brutal and barbaric armed holocausts of the old, the young, and every breathing human in village after village. That a nation, his nation, could do the same rape of a people as Germany had done on millions of Jews was beyond any acceptance. But it had happened. During the war Evelyn knew what American troops were doing to the innocent people of Viet Nam when she was confronted by Llewellyn Lawrence's turncoat war on his own country. Evelyn knew the stories, knew them because each and every tale that came from Uncle George had its origin in the letters Llewellyn Lawrence sent to Evelyn. If only she had stood and defended her love, Peter might maybe have respect for her. Yet in the evil of government, of America was a big part of the deception. Lied to, exposed night after night by propaganda on television, it was a false war of Johnson and Nixon to save the innocent villagers of Viet Nam. To win this war America had to slaughter thousands of old and young. To not accept this war was to dishonor America and shake hands with the enemy.

Like every American, Evelyn Southern knew who the enemy was - - the leaders and cowards of the American government. Not one in a thousand, maybe not one in ten thousand young men that let a war-driven government draft them from out of colleges, homes, and families, believed in killing the people, whether a soldier or citizen, of Viet Nam. But they went. What choice did they have? None. What did they do? Killed and slaughtered until it was in their blood, taught by the sergeants and officers that these slope-heads were evil creatures seeking to rule the world and rape your mothers while disemboweling your sisters. You accepted it or went to prison. Accepted it or your family live in shame, was disgraced. Sixty thousand died in fear, not the fear of Asians but the fear that put them in Asia, a government of avarice. Evelyn bore that scar, an invisible slash across her chest, that ripped out what she knew was right and replaced it with survival, survival for her way of life in the United States. Play the odds, let your men go, and the chances were good he'd survive and return, as would your world. Then forget it it ever happened.

Peter was now speeding across the New York State Thruway between Syracuse and Buffalo and had to tap the brakes since he had set his speed control too high and did not want a ticket. Thoughts about what could have been ruled Peter's mind. They could have returned to her home land, Canada. But they didn't. The control exerted over the American citizens was intense. Many fought it and became expatriates but many did not and millions accepted and went to war. Why? Because they had to obey the country's rulers or the soldiers would arrest them. Some had been lucky and you were not called. Or maybe you spent a year of jungle murder and returned, or not or maybe you would return but not in one piece. It made no difference because you were bred to accept what the lords of the United States government ordered. So was Llewellyn Lawrence.

Like his father, Peter Lawrence faced the same challenge. Did he really know that Henry Hawkins was murdered? The authorities, the police, investigated. Suicide, most definitely Henry Hawkins committed suicide. He was found hanging by the neck in the shower room. Yet Lawrence could not accept that Henry hung from the lone shower pipe that could have never tolerated his weight. Even the state police woman, whom gave Lawrence a lift home out of the rain had a problem in accepting the suicide ruling. Was it Lawrence's responsibility to find the truth? Who did he think he was in challenging the city police?

As hard as it was with a swollen face, Peter Lawrence smiled. The pipe does prove it. The pipe had been bought the same day that Henry Hawkins died. That was a fact. Lawrence had called a few hardware stores on the school district's vendor list until he found the plumbing store that sold the halfway house the new pipe. It was purchased the same day. Coincidence? Hardly. Proof of murder? Not a chance. It was a lead, a hair left at the crime that could be put under a microscope and connected to the bearer. In this case there was only one source, somebody within the school system. Which took Lawrence back to Henry Hawkins' essay.

***

Lawrence paid his toll at the Depew exit and headed north on Route 290, making the turn off to the Grand Island Bridge. It was still early afternoon but typical of Western New York, the clouds made it seem like dusk. As to be expected, there were two messages on his answering machine. One would be from his mother telling him how much she loved him and totally ignoring their usual departure fights. He clicked on the message button to hear his mother say, "as usual mon Fils, we battle. Mais oui, it is our scenario. I laugh at it now but will cry tonight. We are nearly the same but mon amour. You make the difference. I love your difference. You have made Judiah cry all day. The poor man is in love with me. He thinks I will abandon him because he hit you ..."

Lawrence laughed at her euphemism "hit you." Judi cold cocked him like nobody he's ever come up against. Definitely Lawrence did not want a rematch.

"... if my beloved Fils approves, I would like to marry Judiah. With this ... What?"

Lawrence could hear Judi in the background and the ear piece of his phone went muffled as his mother responded.

"I'm sorry, Petra, he's such a big baby. Judiah is a Union boss with the railroad, your grand pere and oncles know him well. He has contacts? Whatever that means. He said that he has contacts in Buffalo, union contacts and more, and if you need anything to call him."

Evelyn read off three phone numbers which Lawrence copied down and told him again of her love for him as the message ended. Lawrence waited on the second phone message.

It was woman with a bit of a slur in her voice. He recognized the voice just as she said her name. It was Henry Hawkins' mother and the slur was from booze, a fact which he had no business being judgmental about since he was still getting the alcoholic fuzz out of his sinuses.

"Mr. Lawrence? You're the Lawrence that tutored my son? Henry, Henry Hawkins. I remember you from the funeral. Handsome man, you are. Can you call me back?"

Lawrence started copying the number then realized he already had it from when he was tutoring Henry.

The message continued, "Henry had some books and papers that I think are yours. Do you mind if I stop over your place and leave them off? I know you can't answer me since this is a fucking machine, but look I'll just box them and drop 'em off later. If that's a problem? I'll just leave 'em at your door. I don't know though? Might be somebody'd take 'em. All fuck, who cares?"

Lawrence had to smile. Henry's mother, whose name he could not remember, was obviously drunk and the number he called was not answered. Hopefully she had passed out and could not hear the phone ringing. If she was three sheets to the wind two hours ago when she called, driving over here now could very well end up with her running into the Niagara River gorge which was only a few yards west of Lawrence's house. Before he heard any sirens, the doorbell rang. When he opened the door, there stood Lizzy, a name that came back to him as soon as he saw her.

"You didn't need to bring them over, Mrs. ..."

"Lizzy, just call me Lizzy. It's all anybody calls me," she replied as the smell of booze forced Lawrence to back up. "Mind if I come in?"

She did not wait for his okay as she pushed past him into the living room carrying a two foot square brown box.

Lawrence wished that he could think of Lizzy as a young woman with a beauty, ravaged by old age and older liquor. But she had never been a beauty. Lizzy was skinny. The slight folds of skin draping from her neck came from booze and showed no indication of her ever being more than skinny. Her cheek bones formed ledges, the red splotches common to long term alcoholics. She had long, thin arms with large knobbed elbows. The telltale black pockets under her eyes spoke of narcotic and restless sleeps often seen in drunks and addicts. She was both as told to him by Henry. Lizzy wore hip huggers that were covered with pink poodle dogs. With a body so thin that it was hard to grasp what held her together, there was little hip structure to hold up her pants that she kept pulling upward. The worst was her breasts. She wore a sleeveless white T-shirt with no under garment. If there was anything sexual about her, it could only be her nipples which stood out like mushroom caps. Maybe she had intentionally tweaked them before Lawrence came to the door? This was an ugly woman. This was an ugly woman, a woman who knew she was dirt ugly and tried to forget it by drinking or as Lawrence saw in the pits of her elbows, by shooting up drugs. Her scent was alcohol with a slight odor of regurgitation.

"Here, Big Boy, this is the books and stuff I told ya about.

She did not put the box on the table in front of her but instead shoved it into Lawrence's arms and backed off.

"You sure was good to my kid. Boy liked you a lot. Of course you got him readin' a little too much. Could've got himself a job or something if'n he'd read less books."

Lawrence had no idea what she was talking about. He knew Henry only from the time he was assigned to the halfway house. Lawrence put the box on the coffee table in front of the sofa. When he bent down, Lizzy grabbed his ass.

"Heh! Nice buns! Bet you got it up front too. Ever tangled with an older woman, Mr. Lawrence?"

This he did not need. Lawrence was still trying to rid himself of his hang over and desperately needed to put some ice on his jaw. If she came much closer, Lawrence would probably throw up.

"Listen, Mrs.? Lizzy, right?"

"Yep, that's my name. Don't wear it out. What da ya say Mr. Lawrence? Up for a little pussy?"

The thought of this old sot's vagina nearly set off his gag reflex, "you see my face? See how it's all swollen? I got some kind of virus over the weekend. I need to see a doctor. I got these spots and itches everywhere. Right now I want to get into my car and head for the emergency room. I think I got it from this woman I was with this morning. Bad sores but fuck, when you want to get some, you'll do about anything that has a cunt."

Lizzy looked at his face and got the message. Without any embarrassment on her part, she spoke, "got yourself some bad shit boy. Hey, you got my number. Those sores clear, give this old pussy a shot. Bye!"

Lawrence looked out his front window and saw her crawl into her car. She started the engine but before putting it into drive, she reached under the seat and came up with a bottle. Lawrence had no idea what was in the bottle except it was alcoholic.

Lawrence went to his kitchen and opened up an ice cube tray. He put half the tray into a dish towel, held it to his swollen face, and added a few other cubes to a glass. Lawrence knew that the hair of the dog cure for a hangover was only an alcoholic's excuse so instead of liquor, he opened a can of tomato juice, poured the glass full, and downed three Bayer aspirins as he drained the glass. He needed to sleep. His worry was that the swelling might not recede by tomorrow which left him with two choices: go to school looking like he got ran over by a truck or call in sick. Without hesitation he called the substitute teacher number.

Despite needing to sleep, Lawrence could not put off looking through the cardboard box. While Lawrence had a copy of Henry's essay which pictured the school system and police force of Niagara Falls as smugglers and drug dealers, it was obviously ridiculous to connect the essay with Nuevello's assigning Belafonte to grade Henry's essay. It was a story, a story written by a drug addict kid with vengeance on his mind. There was no way that Henry's essay could be connected to Henry's death. Yet the broken pipe spoke otherwise. Or was Lawrence exaggerating? Maybe a clue could be found if Henry's notes and research were available. None had been found with his remains. His room contained only his clothes, personal articles, and a few school books. That was it, nothing else. That Henry was incarcerated at the halfway house during the entire time of the writing of his essay eliminated any other place where he could have kept notes. Very simply what Henry used to fabricate his essay did not exist. Either it all came out from his mind like an epiphany or somebody got to his notes and probably destroyed them.

"Fuck that, you asshole," said Lawrence to nobody in his living room. "You're just scrounging for a make believe story. Maybe old Lizzy's right. Maybe Henry was like you. Too many stories, too many movies. Gotta be a bad guy and gotta a be a good guy. Except life's not a movie or a book."

Lawrence knew he would not find any research notes in the box. Henry was a smart kid, smart enough to logically write out a tall tale directly from his mind. That's how fertile his imagination was. Henry could have easily sat down and wrote the entire story without any research. The only papers in the box were notes and assignments Lawrence remembered from tutoring Henry. There were a couple of paperback books and Lawrence's personal hardback edition of Papillon by Henri Charriere. Lawrence had forgotten that he had loaned Henry Charriere's classic written during the time he was a prisoner and escaped from Devil's Island in South America. Papillon was a follow up to their discussions about Jack London being in jail when he visited Western New York. Henry had asked about writers who wrote about being in prison. Papillon was one of Lawrence's favorite books and he used it in his English classes to show writing from experience and why movies did not work well as a good source of cheating when assigned a book to read. Steve McQueen's 1973 movie of the same name totally missed the Charriere book and Dustin Hoffman's character was not only terrible, but had no relationship to the book.

Henry loved the book and he and Lawrence had spent many hours of intense discussion on prison life. At times it was almost as if Henry wanted to be a prisoner so he could write a book like Papillon or The Count of Monte Cristo. They joked about Charriere's use of his anus to hide weapons and money. Lawrence remembered Henry saying there were a few security people here that would like to look up his asshole.

Lawrence moaned when he saw the dog eared page.

"Henry, Henry," he thought, "after all those hours, how could you do that to a book?"

Lawrence's neck hairs always rose when he saw people use dog ears as book marks. He would have never believed it if somebody told him that Henry Hawkins dog-eared a book. Yet here it was. Lawrence flipped to the page to straighten out the flopped over corner, knowing it was useless. The crease would always be there. As his thumb folded back the dog ear, he saw the writing on the page - - one word.

Pix

"Pix? What does that mean?" thought Lawrence. He scanned over the page. Charriere was writing about hiding contraband in his cell. He remembered Henry's interest in this since Henry knew that even though they were not supposed to invade his private belongings, the security staff searched his cell seeking anything that might have been smuggled. Contraband drugs were the obvious reason for such a search at the facility. They had also discussed how inmates would dig holes into the walls and use toothpaste plus the grindings from the digging to patch up the holes. The guards would never find weapons or money. Henry did not believe him because he said it would take forever to dig a hole, seal it up, and keep the guards from finding it. Lawrence pointed out to Henry that in jail, time was a tool, a tool that you had plenty of ...

Lawrence heard Henry's voice speaking to him. It might be a ridiculous message, conjured from Lawrence's own imagination. Pix means pictures, pictures on this page, pictures where Lawrence teaches about being a convict. Pix and holes in the wall.

***

If you follow Sweeny Street along the north side of the Erie Canal in North Tonawanda and carefully check the woods on your right after two and a half miles, you will find scattered dirt roads that are impassable during severe weather. You are south of the Park Village Community. It is not a place where upper income people live. Lawrence went down three ravaged dirt and sand roads before coming to Lizzy Hawkins home, a rather poor label to put to her trailer. Coming to a stop in front of the address Lizzy had given him, he would have not believed a human being resided in the sardine can that stood before him. It was a style of trailer that could never be called a mobile home or anybody's home without rewriting the definition of a domicile.

The trailer was no more than 12 feet wide and at best 25 feet long, making it more of a camper. The original colors were barely recognizable underneath the orange brown rust that dominated every wield in the metal construction. The roof eaves and fascia, or what remained of them, showed the greatest damage. Instead there were pink feathers of insulation puffing out, covered with dark brown mold. Lawrence had no idea where to park his car since the entire area circling Lizzy's trailer was covered with three foot high weeds. The front door matched the trailer's outside walls, light blue painted aluminum with contrasting light tan panels, which were most likely at one time white. Lawrence could not identify much else about the trailer and its surrounding area since the sun was barely edging up above the trees in front of him. Morning was just dawning as Lawrence wanted it to be. There was a good chance that Lawrence would get shot knocking on Lizzy's trailer door this early on a Sunday morning. His mother, had she known what he was doing, would erupt at his ignoring the Lord on the Sabbath. Had he gone to Mass as God intended, her sinner son would have a better chance of staying alive.

Lawrence smiled thinking about Evelyn Southern as he carefully circumnavigated the rusted trailer. Much consternation went into his decision to visit Lizzy Hawkins. From his talks with Henry, the bad was that Lizzy was alcoholic crazy and thus totally out of control. According to her son's descriptions of her, she could very easily attack him and create a situation that Lawrence could not control. The good was that Lawrence knew Lizzy's reputation and probably she would be hung over.

Lizzy was the only person Lawrence turn go to. She was Henry's last and most frequent visitor. Pix, what did it mean? Lawrence had never seen Henry with any pictures. The halfway school did not allow pictures. Was Henry's note in <u>Papillon</u> really about pictures, pictures that existed? Maybe Henry was thinking about the movie version or maybe he had wanted to ask Lawrence about renting it for him? The halfway house did have movie times for their inmates, but was the video available? This sounded the most reasonable. But why did he write it in Lawrence's book? Was there a reason for it being on the page where Henry had written it? The movie had no connection with that section of the book. All that Charriere had written was the different ways he hid contraband while in prison. That in itself would have been enough to not let the halfway house residents watch the movie. In fact had the administrators and security at the halfway house known what <u>Papillon</u> the book describe in its pages, how to hide weapons, make tools, plot murders, make escapes, they would not have let Lawrence bring the book into the building.

"Of course that would mean that the people who run such institutions would know how and what to read," thought Lawrence with a smile.

The only link available to Lawrence was Lizzy. Even Lizzy was a stretch, since she probably would provide little or no hope. In every contact Lawrence had with her, she had tremendous difficulty drawing any intelligent thought from her alcoholic brain.

Lawrence started to knock on the metal door but stopped. What if she had a dog or a pack of dogs? Probably not, he thought since there had been no mayhem and barking when he pulled up to the trailer. He knocked gently and the door swung open about an inch or two, by itself. Maybe Lizzy was not home. Of course that would mean that Lizzy had found someone to go home with on a Saturday night. He put his right hand on the door and pushed it open, listening to the eerie screech of the long hinge holding the door to the jamb, both well rusted and never oiled.

"Lizzy? Lizzy are you in here?" Lawrence whispered, but upped the volume without any response. As he stepped inside the odor hit him. The trailer reeked of vomit, a smell captured inside of an aluminum box without ventilation since no window was open.

The door started to swing close but Lawrence grabbed it and looked around, finding a vodka bottle to prop the door open. He was in the kitchen/living combo area of the trailer. Trying not to breathe through his nose, Lawrence went to the windows to pry them open. None would stay open by themselves, since the counter weight mechanisms were no longer able to hold the glass panes up. Lawrence used splints to keep the windows up since there were stays of wood by each window cut to exactly the right length. It was winter in Western New York but the suffocating and contained humidity combined with the heat of Lizzy's home bested the cold. There was no breeze and the trailer was taking its time getting aired out.

The back end of the trailer had a bathroom on the right and a closed bedroom door on the left. The bathroom door was ajar and responsible for much of the smell filling the trailer. The toilet had not been flushed for some time, thought Lawrence. Holding his left hand over his nose and mouth, Lawrence pushed the toilet lever down. Nothing, no water came out of the tank. Lawrence reached down to the gate valve under the tank and found it completely opened, a full 360 degrees counter clockwise. With no alternative and owing to the bile rising up in his throat, Lawrence kicked the toilet seat down, backed out of the narrow bathroom, and quickly shut the door.

"Fuck, I left the window down," he said. Grabbing a handkerchief out of his back pocket, he quickly opened the bathroom door, saw the wood splint, raised and propped the window open, and was out of the bathroom before a gag reflex caught up with him.

The smell was starting to over whelm him. He thought he recognized it but told himself it was not possible. The smell was death, rotting flesh and decomposed meat, just like he had smelled many times when hunting. The closed bedroom door seemed to stare at him. Lawrence instinctively knew that there was a dead body in the room. He went to the kitchen and tried the faucets, knowing they would not work. Obviously the water had been turned off. Lawrence knew if he walked into the bedroom, he would survive whatever he found. It would make him nauseous and maybe he would have to leave and puke outside, but he could accept death and its atmosphere.

The door barely budged. Its knob turned freely so it was not locked, but the door moved only an inch or two, enough to fill the air in the hallway with putrescence. Lawrence backed off, walked outside, and vomited. Finished and bathed in sweat he returned to the trailer, went down the hallway, and put his weight against the door. Whatever was blocking it from the inside was solid but not human. He could move it. As the door opened, the gagging returned but he swallowed it back down and got the door open enough to squeeze through.

A big brown dog, a big dead brown dog was lying bloated in rigor mortis on the floor gases oozing out. Across the bed lay Lizzy Hawkins, totally naked, her back showing a set of ribs so meatless that they looked like a rack of meat found at a butcher shop. They were moving up and down. At least Lizzy was alive.

Few people can handle dealing with death, touching them, moving them, or trying to help them. Those that cannot face death leave, seeking others to deal with death. Lawrence went to Lizzy, felt her back gently rising and falling and turned her over. Lizzy was just shy of being a skeleton. If her body had any meat on it, it would take a bone crunching scavenger to find it. Lawrence lifted her gently afraid that she would fall apart, or a leg might drop off. Her hand made a snapping noise since it had little muscle to support it. If she weighed more than a few pounds, Lawrence would be surprised. He carried her into the living room-kitchen and laid her face up on the couch. Lawrence was astounded. Amazingly her breathing was normal and her pulse was over sixty. She needed some water. Her alcoholic suicide attempt last night, and probably every night before, had left her desiccated. His only option was to get into his car and find some bottled water. Since she was breathing okay and her pulse was stable, Lawrence went down the hallway instead, found the linen closet, took out some towels, and went outside. He had driven over a stream on his way to the trailer. The water would not be potable but it would cool her off and maybe she would wake up enough so he could leave and return with water and food. He saw a metal bucket beside a tree stump and grabbed it.

When he returned to the trailer, he saw that she had rolled over on her side and was still breathing regularly. He had filled the bucket and when he returned immediately poured it into the not flushed toilet. Lawrence smiled thinking of the many who did not realize that all you had to do to flush a toilet was pour water into it. The miasma of putrid wastes ran down the hole and left an empty, crusted toilet bowl. Lawrence went back to the stream and refilled the bucket for additional flushing needs.

He knew he had to get rid of the dog carcass, the smell was ripe and parts of his body had been gouged out by someone with a knife. It looked like the remains were probably eaten. Years of hunting and dressing kills, then eating their remains never bothered Lawrence, but the dog bothered him. He heard Lizzy stirring and quickly wrapped the carcass in a sheet from the bed. Back in the living room, Lizzy was struggling to open her eyes. Lawrence went by her carrying the dog's body, to dump the carcass in the woods. He returned to the trailer.

"Why you horny son of a bitch, you found me out!" As usual she was loud.

Lawrence knew the routine. Being gentle and supportive with an alcoholic is what they want. Forgiveness, acceptance with tears that it will never happen again, all flow as truth from their foul smelling mouths. Soon all parties would be feeling comfortable, enjoying the changed sot. It never works. Drunks are experts at manipulating their loved ones.

"You listen to me you drunken bitch. You should be dead right now. You wouldn't even need to kill yourself, because you're already dead."

"Who the fuck you talkin' to? Get out a here fore I call the cops."

He stared deeply into her blood shot eyes and grabbed her by the throat. Lawrence had mulled over what he needed to do. Lizzy was a dead person now and he needed Lizzy to have life. To mollycoddle this foul-smelling, anemic breathing corpse would resolve nothing. Lawrence was done playing her drunken game. He lifted her up, her toes barely touching the floor. She could barely breathe. She was so light that the slightest breeze could move her to and fro, swaying with Lawrence's grip at her throat. Her alcohol-soaked brain knew not how to react to this man.

"We're going to talk, Lizzy. You lie to me and I'll kill you. That's the only promise you get."

He tightened his grip on her throat. "Do you understand?"

"Yes!"

"What happened to the dog?"

Lawrence recognized both fear and shame. "I ate him!"

Lawrence wrapped her in a blanket that smelled of vomit and urine and told her she was going out to his car. "If you throw up in my car, I'll dump you into the Erie Canal!"

It was a wasted threat. No sooner had Lizzy exited the drab trailer, than she vomited all over the side of it. After puking she fell to the ground. Lawrence went to her and shook her. She was unconscious and her pulse was extremely weak. He picked her up in his arms and took her to his car. DeGraff Hospital was only a few blocks away and hopefully in her unconscious state, she would not get sick again. Still he did not trust her and as he looked around the outside of the trailer, he saw a pile of logs covered with a blue plastic tarpaulin. Spreading it across his rear seat, Lawrence laid her across the tarp, got behind the driver's wheel, and drove off to DeGraff.

In the few minutes it took to get to the hospital, Lawrence changed his mind. If he took her to the emergency room, Lawrence would not find out about her son's time at the halfway house. Undoubtedly she would be hospitalized and difficult to visit since he was not a relative. Worse was the rising fear that others would know she was at DeGraff. This might not be good for her and it could very well destroy any chance for Lawrence to talk with her. His imagination was running on overdrive. Would she be openly exposed to a visit from somebody that might harm her? After all there was a slight chance that her son had been slain by some unknown person. Lawrence was getting paranoid or was he?

Lawrence felt Lizzy pulse. It had improved and was now in the 60s. Lawrence drove past DeGraff to Main, up River Road, caught the LaSalle Expressway, and driving along the Niagara River via the Robert Moses State Parkway, entered Niagara Falls within minutes. Lizzy still did not wake.

Leaving Lizzy in the back seat, Lawrence entered his home, propping open the door. It was early on a Sunday morning and few neighbors were awake. His inclination was to deposit her in his only bedroom but then he thought better of it. Going back to his car, Lawrence gently lifted the still sleeping Lizzy out of the back seat and took her through the open door. Inside he positioned her in a lounge chair while he went back for the tarpaulin. He spread it across his living room sofa and lifted her from the chair, laying her on the sofa, her head propped up with one of his older sofa pillows. At her neck he saw the carotid artery still throbbing. The throbbing did not bother him but her neck did. It had little muscle, only pulsing arteries, flaps of skin, and spotted wrinkles. He did not know how a person could be this close to death yet remain alive.

Lizzy slept for most of the day. She snored. Lawrence was lucky enough to be able to watch the Buffalo Bills on television since they were playing the Eagles in Philadelphia. It was a close but boring game which the Bills took 10 to 7 so it made little difference that Lizzy woke up in the middle of it.

"Where the fuck am I?"

Lawrence turned the sound down with the remote and watched Lizzy try to sit up. She was having difficulty.

"Lay back down before you get vertigo and puke. You're at my home and you smell like a dead rat caught in a trap."

"Why am I here?"

"Because you were headed for the morgue, only I got in your way. Do you remember anything about you and me at your trailer?"

"No ... Yeah, you said you gonna kill me! Fuck this! Where's your phone? I'm calling the cops on you. I bet you fucked me while I was passed out!"

"Phone's hanging in the kitchen," said Lawrence watching Lizzy try to right herself. Instead she laid back down on the tarpaulin covered sofa. "When you tell them I kidnapped you and raped you, don't forget to tell them about the dead dog in the woods behind your trailer."

"What the fuck is goin' on here? I don't understand why you're messing with me?" Lizzy's head was swarming and she was having difficulty getting upright, "You got anything to drink here?"

"Yep, but you got to sober up first."

"I ain't drunk," she said rolling off the side of the sofa before her feet were under her. She hit the floor. Lawrence just looked at her. "Can't you just answer me? Can't you just tell me why you're doing this to me?"

"Doing what Lizzy?"

"Why taking care of me ... sorta taking care of me."

"Lizzy, I was going to drop you off at DeGraff."

"Where am I now? I mean besides your home?"

Lawrence told her where they were, in the heart of the City of Niagara Falls only a couple blocks from the gorge.

"Christ I'm glad you didn't drop me at DeGraff. I been there so many times that the next one they was gonna commit me. You got some drink?"

"Yes, but I want you clean and sober before I give you any."

"Suppose I just up and walk out?"

"First of all, I won't let you. Second, you'll wind up falling on your face out in the street and probably get run over by a snow plow."

"God damn it's snowing again?"

"I'm exaggerating. Just a little. No plows yet."

Lizzy was trying to shake off the dizziness from last night. It was not working. She needed more sleep. She also needed to eat. Most definitely she needed to take a shower or bath.

She was getting teary-eyed. Coming from such a violent and aggressive person this surprised Lawrence.

"Mr. Lawrence, please tell me what's this all about?"

"I will Lizzy but I want you to understand something. I need to know about your son. You've got to get yourself together so we can talk without Jack Daniels getting in your way."

"I fucking wish," she smiled. "I ain't tasted something that good for years. I'm used to rot gut. Say that the Bills on the TV? Who's winnin'?"

"Bills by three. Norwood actually made a field goal."

"Lizzy, I'm going to make up some soup for you. I think that would be all you could handle for now. Trust me, you need to take a shower ... No, I think it best be a bath, don't you?"

"Yeah, I'd fall out of the tub taking a shower. I just don't know if I can make it to your bathroom and into the bath tub by myself."

Lawrence smiled, realizing that unlike Lizzy's previous discussions with Lawrence, she was not posing sexual innuendos now. With the odiferous bedspread from the trailer wrapped around her, Lizzy tried to stand but could not. Lawrence put his arm around her thread-like waist and escorted her into his bathroom. Lizzy sat on the toilet while Lawrence ran the bath water.

"Some of the grogginess is wearing off, Mr. Lawrence. I bet I puked a few times back home?"

"Few? How do you think I found the trailer? I just sniffed the air."

Lizzy grinned unsure if Lawrence was joking or just being sarcastic. She accepted joking. As the water neared the top, Lizzy got nervous, not knowing if she was sober enough to stand and actually get into the bath tub.

"I'll help you, Lizzy. I don't judge people by how they look, naked or not. Here give me the bed cover."

She accepted Lawrence at his word and stripped off the bed cover, exposing her naked self to Lawrence. He did not stare nor did he avoid her alcohol ravaged body.

"It might be a good idea for you to …" he paused trying to word his suggestion without sounding gross or childlike.

"Take a piss?"

"I couldn't have said it better. That I will leave to your privacy but I must help you into the tub, okay?"

She nodded as Lawrence left the bathroom to allow her a degree of self-respect. The pain was still there and she held in the agony she felt so that Lawrence would not hear her cries of pain. Standing and turning to flush, Lizzy saw the blood.

"I'm fine now? Can you help me?"

Lawrence came back into the bathroom and Lizzy was standing alongside of the tub, "it might be a bit too hot."

He held her right elbow as she lifted her foot over the tub rim and slowly put it into the water. She drew it back quickly. Lawrence reached around her and turned on the cold spigot for a few seconds. She tried again and slipped her leg into the water. Turning to face Lawrence she felt embarrassed about her disgusting body with her breasts that hung like sacks of flour nearly to her waist. They drew no reaction from Lawrence as she lowered herself into the water. It felt good, more than good, excellent. The warmth surrounded her naked body coming up to the downside curve of her sacked breasts. She felt her nipples harden when Lawrence backed off from the tub.

"I'm sorry. I used to be ..."

"Lizzy, just enjoy your bath. Nobody is as they used to be. We're all ugly in our own minds. Forget it. Here's a wash cloth. Get nice and clean and you'll be fine. I have some shampoo in the medicine cabinet. You want it?"

Lizzy nodded and Lawrence brought out a plastic bottle of Prell for her to use.

"Lizzy, just take your time. I've been there. Not as bad as you, but I've been drunk out of my mind quite a few times. There's nothing you can do but let it wear off. Okay?"

Lizzy smiled and laid back in the tub. Lawrence wished he could see in Lizzy Hawkins's naked body the same wish he had seen earlier - - a woman once of great beauty and sexuality. It had never been there in the Lizzy he knew. Maybe her body, skinny with ribs poking out the sides, was once enticing but her face was hard and ugly. He had sympathy for her but not pity. Lizzy's aggressiveness when intoxicated meant she knew as well as anybody, including Lawrence, that she had never been an attractive and sexy woman. That had to have been a driving force making her an addict.

Enjoy yourself, Lizzy, thought Lawrence. I will not hurt you.

Lawrence left her alone. After a half an hour, fearing she might have drowned, he left the soup on warm at the electric range, and knocked on the bathroom door. There was no answer but at least the door was not locked from the inside. He knew she was still alive even before opening the door because he could hear her snoring. Her now soaked red hair was draped back over the edge off the bathtub and her arms rested on the edges of the tub. Lizzy was sound asleep. He felt the water which was now cool and covered with used soap suds.

Rubbing the knuckles of his hand gently along the side of her face, Lawrence gently called her name, "Lizzy, Lizzy wake up. Your soup's ready. Get up."

Lizzy Hawkins had probably not had a fresh and cleansing bath like this for years. She smiled with a glow in her tiny eyes. "Why did you wake me? It was so good."

"Getting cold Lizzy."

"Nah, water's not that ..."

"Soup, Lizzy. I made you some soup." Lawrence partially closed the bathroom door so he could get his bathrobe from the hook behind it. "Here, you can wear this."

Lizzy stood up and for the first time since he had seen her naked body, Lawrence saw a freshness in it but also the tell-tale needle marks of a drug abuser.

"No, don't get out of the tub yet. Let me turn the shower on so you can rinse off the soapy water, " said Lawrence as he led her to the other end of the tub, unplugged the drain, and adjusted the shower to a warm flow. He pulled the curtain closed and waited with a towel. She opened the curtain, took the towel, dried off, and put on the bathrobe.

Entering his kitchen, she spoke, "Mr. Lawrence ..."

"Just Lawrence, Lizzy."

"I'm sorry. Lawrence, that bath did me a world of good."

"Sit down. There's a bowl of soup for you."

Lizzy sat across from him and using a tablespoon took a sip of the soup. "Wow, this soup's got a great taste. What kind is it?"

"Mrs. Grass Noodle Soup. Got that golden nugget in it.

"Good flavor."

Lizzy was nearly sober now. Lawrence brought up the why of his confrontation with her. "I need to know some information about Henry. If it's going to be too difficult for you to talk with me ..."

Lizzy had tears in her eyes. It was easy for her to forget her son's death when she was drinking or shooting up. This time, the time with Lawrence, was real time, sober. Lawrence slowed down, let her regain her composure.

Except for me and her, Lawrence thought, only three people were visitors to Henry Hawkins. Two of those people were sitting in this kitchen right now and the third was dead. Tears formed at the edges of his pupils. He did not want Lizzy to see his emotions over Eileen O'Hara.

"I know about your girlfriend, Mr. Lawrence. Henry totally adored her. He was hoping he'd be invited to your wedding."

Lawrence gulped, eyes watery, heart starting to pump, "I guess I've underestimated you Lizzy. You know death as well as I do."

Lizzy was exaggerating his and Eileen's relationship since he knew Henry would have never said what Lizzy just did. Lawrence sat down.

"Henry never said that to you."

Lizzy was startled and felt her anger rise as it always did when she was confronted with her own lies. She stopped short, from attacking, her usual reaction to being caught lying. This man, this Lawrence, was not going to be brow-beaten. Lizzy made a decision that she should have made years ago - - to be honest. Do not launch tirades because you do not like what is happening. She did not have a chance to apologize before Lawrence continued.

"Lizzy, Henry did an essay for me as part of his English grade. He failed that essay. But I never graded that it. It bothers me. It bothers me because by sheer accident I got a copy of the essay and don't understand why he failed."

Lawrence felt like he was walking on glass shards to get through to Lizzy brain without letting her know that Henry probably did not commit suicide.

"Why didn't you grade it? Weren't you his English teacher?"

It was a good question but one he could not answer. "You obviously know about Mrs. Ledger, his counselor and I."

Lizzy saved him from creating a lie. "They fired you?"

Not yet, thought Lawrence. "No, they did not fire me."

"Well I guess it was just all that publicity?"

Lawrence kept his mouth shut and let a sad smile speak.

Lizzy continued, "well it don't really make much difference to Henry anymore, now does it?"

"No, but it does to me. I liked your son. He was a tough kid, had hard lessons in his life. He brought a lot on himself ..."

"Mr. Lawrence, I brought a lot of them hard lessons on him."

"Do you have anything from his stay at the halfway house? Any papers or notes?"

"No, there was just some clothes, that's all."

"How about his father? Did he ever visit Henry?"

"Uley? That asshole gave up on Henry the day I brought him home."

Lawrence knew Ulysses Hawkins slightly since Uley, as everybody called him, was a school district maintenance man and substitute school bus driver.

"Will it upset you if I talk with your husband about Henry?"

"My husband?" Lizzy got a smirk on her lips and laughed, "why do you think Uley is my husband?"

"You both have the same last names?"

"Uley is my brother, Mr. Lawrence."

Lizzy Hawkins had a baby by her brother and both of them lived a married life like nobody's business. That did the trick on

Lawrence. Lawrence's ego and self-righteousness were stunned. He had to control himself, the first step being to not make any judgment. Obviously, Lizzy, Uley, and Henry lived a life where incest had little or no meaning. Whether Lawrence should or could accept their way of life meant nothing. Lawrence leaned back in his chair trying to shake it off. Lizzy would have nothing of it.

"You judging me, you mother fucker?"

Lawrence was going to lose her and lose any chance of discovery concerning Henry's death. Heaven would drop a storm on his head if he called her what she in truth was.

"No Lizzy, I'm judging me. You already did that by calling me a mother fucker, and you were right."

Lizzy put her scrawny right arm up on the back of the kitchen chair and looked at Lawrence. Lawrence shrugged and smiled.

"Uley never wanted anything to do with Henry. Nobody but him and me and now you know Henry was his kid and his nephew. But I'll give him this. Uley helped me all he could. Henry never knew that Uncle Ulysses was his father. Now Henry's gone, makes no difference. Uley can't help you."

"So there were no papers or notebooks or any kind of printed material that Henry left in his cell?"

"No, Mr. Lawrence. They didn't even allow me to bring things to him. Inspected everything. They let me give him candy but that's about it. I tried to take him a cake and they stopped me cold. No cake. I had to toss it in the dumpster outside before I could see him. Wouldn't even let Henry have any photos or pictures."

That was Lawrence's worst fear. The singular clue Lawrence sought was the word "pix" in the book <u>Papillon</u> and Henry had no pix. It was over.

"I don't know. How can they treat a child like that," said Lawrence. "They put him into this isolation chamber to detoxify him. They take away everything in his life, on, purpose so as to carte blanche his previous life. Shit, they won't even let him see pictures of what's going on ..."

"No, Mr. Lawrence. I said they wouldn't let him have pictures. I could bring him pictures but he couldn't keep them."

"And you did that?"

Lizzy brought her right arm forward and intermeshed the fingers of both of her hands. Lawrence could see the demeanor change in her attitude toward him.

"Just once."

Lawrence sat back and laced his fingers together. "You're afraid of something, aren't you?"

"You know that chances are that if you hadn't found me this morning I'd be dead by now?"

"Why? You were just shit faced, that's all."

"No, Lawrence, that's not all. You saw where I live. That old trailer's nobody's home, been abandoned for years. Since it's back in the woods, everybody forgets it's there. Well it's all I have. I live on welfare, Mr. Lawrence."

Lizzy pulled her kitchen chair around so she was within inches of Lawrence's face, "I get enough to just get by, Mr. Lawrence. Except for one problem. They don't give me enough to get drunk. That's why I live there. You saw the dog Lawrence."

Bile rose in Lawrence's throat.

"Dogs, cats, even tried a rat once. Too chewy, though. You can't go to the food store when you spend you welfare check at the liquor store."

"You need help, Lizzy. You need to be hospitalized."

"Ain't gonna happen. Medicare cut me off. Agent came out and found me near like you found me. No more Medicare unless I commit myself. I run my mouth off to you, it gets back to the government and there goes my welfare check."

"Lizzy, that won't happen. Do I have to prove my honesty anymore than by your being here?"

That stunned Lizzy. Lawrence was right. Nobody had shown her compassion and consideration like he did this Sunday.

She paused, stared Lawrence in the eyes, and spoke, "fuck probably means nothing anyway. Can I have a drink."

Lawrence smiled, "not yet, Lizzy. Talk a little first."

Lizzy smiled, sipped a bit more soup, found it cold, and pushed it across the table. Lawrence went to his stove to dish her some more. Returning with a fresh bowl Lizzy spoke, "Henry said he needed some photos to do some school work. I was on a visit to him on an really warm day in early spring. We were walking outside as he had requested of the security people at the halfway house. I had to memorize in detail what pictures I was to bring him. The photos were in one of those envelopes that K Mart gives you. You know? There's a flap in front of the envelope where they put the … What are those plastic strips called?"

"Negatives."

"Yeah, negatives. Anyhow, I was to bring an envelope with Christmas pictures from last year… that'd be two years ago.

Except I was to get an envelope marked "bus ride" which he had in the top drawer of his dresser. I had to take the negatives out of the "bus ride" pouch and put them with the negatives from Christmas photos. I did it and brought them with me on my next visit. Can you believe those security fuckers actually went through each and every picture, checking it out, making fun of people?"

"Sounds up to par to me."

"Except they never looked at the negatives."

"Kind of hard to do that."

"Henry put on this show about looking at the family photos. Called one of the security guys over to show him me and him in front of the Christmas tree. Did a real tune on him. They even said they were sorry when Henry asked if he could keep one of the photographs. Bastards checked that I had every photo when I had to leave."

Lawrence had it!

"Lizzy, have you ever tried a black Russian?"

Lizzy looked at him, "niggers? No, I did a couple. Lousy fucks. All they care about is getting off."

"No, Lizzy, I mean a black Russian as a drink?"

"Got booze in it?"

"Vodka?"

"Did I say something wrong? I got one more thing to tell you. You see …"

"No, just wait a few minutes while I make us both a black Russian."

Lawrence got out his bottles of Smirnoff Vodka, Arrow Crème de Cacao, and two 6 ounce cocktail glasses. He filled each glass with ice then two thirds Vodka, poured Crème de Cacao to the top. He stirred the dark brown mixture, and handed one to Lizzy. Lawrence knew his black Russians would put most people to sleep and hoped it would have the same effect on Lizzy.

"Lizzy, raise your glass to your son."

She did and they both took a sip of their black Russian.

"You drink this shit? Damn it's like drinking candy. Now let me tell you …"

"No, you sweet lovely lady I'll tell you. When you got back home and opened the photograph envelope with the Christmas photographs, the "bus ride" negatives were missing?"

"How the fuck did you know that?"

Lawrence just smiled.

***

The Niagara Falls School District halfway home was situated on the Robert Moses Parkway but could only be accessed via Buffalo Avenue which paralleled most of the southern branch of the parkway. It was very early, the sun just edging up under the Grand Island bridges. Lawrence had called in sick for his Monday classes. Lawrence's strength existed in how he dealt with problems, go at them fast. It was also a bad trait. Sometimes by not putting off what he felt he needed to do when faced with a problem, the problem would be exacerbated the problem, making it more difficult to solve later. Henry Hawkins' smuggling of negatives into the rehab building was an open wound. Sooner or later—if Lawrence's hunch was correct—somebody would find a loose concrete block caulked with tooth paste to the adjoining cement block. If he goes snooping around too soon, the person or persons responsible for replacing the shower pipe might be alarmed and do a meticulous search, block by block of the building. It would be hard to camouflage toothpaste as cement especially if you got close enough to smell it.

Lawrence could not just stop by and ask to search the premises. More than likely the staff had been told to keep Lawrence out, especially after his earlier visit when he discovered the shower pipe. This meant he had to go there when the day staff had not yet come on duty. Unless he had changed jobs, the morning facility supervisor would be there about 7:30 AM and he would be alone since the building security officers were usually late, especially on a Monday. There were two security officers and the senior officer who rarely arrived before 8:00 AM. On many days Lawrence had tutored Henry early in the morning before his high school classes started. He knew the routine and also knew that the senior officer was trouble, an arrogant black man blaming 'whitey' for every wrong in the world. Since Lawrence had only been a tutor for Henry, Lawrence no longer had any logical reason to ring the entrance bell. He did anyway.

"Mr. Lawrence? What ya doin' here? You ain't got no kid to teach here."

The morning facility supervisor was a middle aged black man from Philadelphia and Lawrence had no idea what his real name was.

"Hey Duke. Look, you've got to let me in," said Lawrence standing at the still locked steel door. The supervisor viewed Lawrence through a small window that slid open to Lawrence's left. Lawrence was holding his bicycle.

"I was biking down Buffalo Avenue and my stomach turned on me. I got to go and go real bad. Come on Duke, you know me. It's early. Let me in. I'll be done in a few minutes. If you don't, I'm gonna shit myself."

Lawrence heard the buzzer that released the door locks that clicked as they sprang away from the door jamb.

"Don't be long. Gwana gets here 'fer you out, he'll kick my ass and yours too," said Duke as Lawrence set his bicycle inside and out of view. "We'll probably both get fired. Let me get you my key to the staff toilet."

"No, I can't wait," said Lawrence as he went past the front desk, hustled down the student hall and made a left turn toward the student toilets. When he was out of Duke's sight, he stopped and turned back to the first student cell, the one where Henry Hawkins had lived. To make sure the morning facility supervisor did not get suspicious, Lawrence moaned aloud those pleasures associated with exhausting your bowels.

Once inside Henry's cell which the school district called learning cubicles, Lawrence knew this whole gambit was a waste of time. The cell was built out of 15 X 7 ½ X 7½ inch concrete blocks. Even a few half blocks were too much for anybody to clandestinely chip away at the half inch cement filled gaps between the blocks. One block probably weighed ten or more pounds. Lawrence lifted the hinged drop down bed to see if there smaller blocks under the bed. There were none.

Lawrence had been driven by a world of fiction. The books he had read about prisons made it so simple. Scratch out the cement joints between the blocks, pull out the block, and you had a secret hiding place for what few valuables you squirreled away while in prison. Squeeze out some toothpaste, mix in the crumbs and dust you made when digging out the block. The toothpaste looks like cement except its now easy to open your secret vault. Put the block back into the wall, seal it up, and one, two, three nobody will catch you. Always works in books and movies.

Time was running short but Lawrence did not want to give up. He had little time left before Gwana showed up, but Gwana was not his problem now. Duke was since he was walking back to hurry Lawrence up. Hearing the footsteps, Lawrence hustled to the open inmates toilet room, dropped his pants and underwear, and sat down only seconds before Duke made the turn.

"Mr. Lawrence, you got to … Oops, sorry. Got it that bad?"

"Give me two minutes and I'm out of here. Bills beat your boys yesterday. Did you watch it?"

Duke and Lawrence shared their mutual admiration of the Philadelphia Eagles since both came from the that area.

Duke turned to give Lawrence some privacy and spoke, "yeah, but it ain't gonna do them no good. They'll fuck up the Super Bowl again. Got two minutes, then you gotta get outta here."

As soon as Duke turned toward the front desk and was out of sight, Lawrence stood up, pulling up his and buckling his pants. To carry on with his ruse, he turned back to the toilet to flush it. As Lawrence reached for the steel handle attached to the water pipe coming out of the cinder block wall, he found Henry's hiding place. In order to put a pipe through the wall and into the toilet room, cinder blocks had to be cut. This was not done using since the drill would splinter the concrete block. Instead, a wet saw was used to cut a narrow slit, going from the back to the front of the block, no more than 2 inches wide. After the sawed block was cut and cemented in the wall where the toilets would be, a water pipe was run through the slit and a small piece of cinder block was cemented in to fill the gap above the pipe.

Quickly Lawrence ran his finger over the joint that spliced the section above the water pipe. It was smooth, definitely not cement, and even though Lawrence knew the back wall in the boys' toilet room was covered with misaimed urine, he smelled the paste on his finger tip. It was toothpaste.

There were three toilets. Maybe he had time to dig out two. Quickly snapping open the jack knife he always carried, Lawrence started at the small section behind the first. He smiled as the small section of cinder block fell into his hands. There was no need to dig any further since Henry would not need to create more than one hiding cache. He felt an envelope inside the crevice. Slipping his two fingers inside the crack, he was able to slide it out. Quickly he stuffed the envelope into his front right pocket and closed the jack knife, returning it to the left pocket. The security guard would be here soon. He placed the small cut block section back into its niche and smoothed what was left of the toothpaste around the joints between the blocks. A close inspection would show that the block had been tampered with. There was nothing he could do about it.

Lawrence walked quickly back to the front desk.

"You better get you ass moving Lawrence. You okay now?"

"Almost. Thanks, Duke."

Lawrence wheeled his bicycle out the front door and as it was closed and bolted behind him, he heard a car door in front of the building slam shut. Lawrence turned around and circled the building in reverse of how a visitor would normally enter or leave the building. Once out of view he stopped and heard Gwana telling Duke to open the fucking door. Lawrence waited for a few more seconds to ensure that Duke did not tell Gwana about his visit. Since nobody came out of the building looking for him, he returned to his car, dropped his bike into the trunk, attached rubber cords he kept in the trunk to hold the lid down, and headed home.

***

Going after Henry Hawkins's hidden cache had been a chance, a very bad risk. Lawrence pulled in front of his house elated. He had not been caught and contrary to what his rational thinking processes had told him yesterday, Henry had indeed learned from his readings and discussions with Lawrence. Now free from any detection, Lawrence pulled out the envelope and opened it. As to be expected the contents were damp and mildewed, but since the contents were strips of polyethylene, the wetness did no harm. Lawrence now had a set of ten 35 mm photographic negatives. He pulled his handkerchief out of his right rear pocket and wiped off the mildew and moisture. There were the reverse colors of people and large vehicles, probably buses, and some of the negatives had buildings in them with people in front of the buildings.

"That's the school district's administrative building, " Lawrence whispered to himself.

After going through all ten strips of negatives, he put them back into the envelope, got his bicycle out of the trunk, locked up his car, and went inside his home.

Yesterday's kidnapping of Lizzy was not bad enough, this morning he had left for his encounter with the halfway house with Lizzy still asleep on his living room couch. Lawrence had taken a very dangerous risk with Lizzy Hawkins. She could be dead right now, or she could have raided his liquor bottles in the kitchen pantry and be drunk as a skunk waiting to attack him. She was neither, because she was still asleep, or so he hoped as he checked for and found a pulse.

"Damn, pulse is normal," he said to himself as he felt her forehead and found it cool. His touch was enough to wake her.

"Whoa! I'm still here?"

"You mean like are you dead and dropped down into hell?"

"No, asshole! I mean that I'm still your prisoner."

Evidently she was not as recovered from her weekend drunkenness as they both had thought, "I'm a bit dizzy!"

"You're okay Lizzy. Got a good pulse and your head is cool."

"I slept here? You slept here, too?"

"It's my house Lizzy. Why shouldn't I?"

"Well, like I could have woke up before you and stole something and took off. Shit I could've just hauled off and killed you. You're pretty stupid trusting me like that."

"Lizzy, I just got back. I trusted you enough to leave you alone. How's your stomach doing?"

"Fine. Got anything to eat? How about some eggs and cat meat?"

Lawrence laughed at her joke. Still ugly, her face was not one you loved but when she smiled, a warm feeling about Lizzy Hawkins came over you.

"Got sausage patties. They came from K Mart. Maybe they were made from cats or dogs or squirrels. Never know, do you?"

Not waiting for an answer, Lawrence went to the kitchen, put a large skillet on the back electric range burner, turned the dial to medium, took two sausage patties out of the freezer, and laid them into the skillet. As he waited for them to brown, he got two eggs out of the refrigerator and placed them carefully on the coils of another burner which was not turned on. The eggs would not roll away on the coils. Taking two plain bagels out of his bread drawer, he parted them and put both in the toaster.

"You like onion?"

"Go ahead. Onion will do me fine."

As the sausages browned on one side, he flipped them to brown on the other. "How come Henry attended Niagara Falls when you live out of the district?"

"Henry didn't live with me. Well, that's not totally true. He'd spend a lot of days, even a few weeks, bagging school and doing dope with me instead of staying with his father."

His father, Uley, didn't tolerate the drug use?"

"Uley? Uley and I are boozers. Uley drinks booze. He deals weed and smack and a few other goodies."

"Is that how Henry got started?" Lawrence flipped over the onion slices and browned sausages. The bagels popped out of the toaster. He cracked open two eggs and spread them on the skillet.

When the whites got a brown tinges to their edges, Lawrence turned over the eggs on top of the sausages,

"The drugs were a gift to his son. Henry usually stayed away from liquor. Oh, I could get him drunk on some gin once and a while, but it wasn't the buzz he wanted. Smack was his ... What should I call it?"

Lawrence turned off the burner and moved the skillet to another burner that was not turned on so the skillet would cool down. He laid a half section of American cheese on each egg.

"Drug of choice."

"Yeah, drug of choice. I heard it called that."

Lawrence opened the pastry cabinet and took out two paper plates. After putting one bagel bottom on each plate, he slid his spatula under the sausage, egg, onion, and cheese combo, and quickly slid the meal onto the bagel.

"Here you go. I like tomato juice. Want some?"

"Can I have a little vodka ..."

"No, Lizzy, we've got to do some talking before you hit the bottle again. And you need a shower. Trust me! You do need a shower."

"This sandwich ain't bad."

Lizzy went to take the shower. Lawrence had no idea what she would wear once the shower was over. He let it be and got out the negatives. For now Lizzy did not need to know he had the negatives that she had smuggled to her son. Maybe she could help Lawrence work through the photographs once he got prints made. He decided that he would leave her here, still wearing his robe while he went to get her some clothes. There was no possibility that he would go back to the trailer to find her something to wear. He knocked on the bathroom door.

"Hey! Come on in. You already seen me buck naked. Ain't gonna to do any harm seeing me through this etched up glass shower door."

Lawrence went into the bathroom. It was totally steamed up, not the mirror nor was the window clear. The room was suffocating with steam.

"Lizzy, I'm going to go out, get you some clothes. When you're finished, put on the robe I gave you last night. There's plenty of food in the pantries and fridge. Help yourself. I'm sure you'll find the booze. Do I have to take it with me?"

"When you come back can I have a drink?"

"Sure, if I don't smell any booze."

"Two?"

"You want me to take it with me?"

"No ..."

Despite the noise of the fully powered, near scalding water raging out of the shower head, Lawrence could hear Lizzy sob a bit, catching her breath as she spoke, "been a long time since anybody trusted me. My guess is it'll get to me. I probably be shit faced by the time you get back. Is that your answer?"

"The booze's in the closet behind the kitchen door when you open it," said Lawrence. "Enjoy yourself Lizzy."

The drug store in the Summit Park Mall just south of the Niagara Falls Airport had a two hour print service so Lawrence figured that he could drop off the negatives and find some clothes for Lizzy in that time. As he headed out Pine Avenue to Niagara Falls Boulevard, his thoughts drew him back to the negative showing what was obviously the Niagara Falls School District administrative offices. Why did Henry take a picture of the building? Damn, I know why. It was his inspiration for the story he wrote. Which could mean that the superintendant was one of the figures on the negative. The story linked the superintendant with the Niagara Falls chief of police. That could be the other person on the negative. These were two well know figures in the area. Lawrence had only vague ideas about the other negatives as his mind kept turning over details from Henry's story.

Lawrence could not risk having some local citizen pull prints off the negatives. If the photo finisher recognized somebody in one of the photographs, he would probably not keep it to himself.

Lawrence was stuck. How to get prints without anybody else seeing them? Lawrence went past the Williams Road turn off to the mall, stayed on Niagara Falls Boulevard until he reached Nash Road. Heading south on Nash he wound up in North Tonawanda. Driving back and forth, street by street, he hoped to find a photo developing shop that could help him. The chances in North Tonawanda were less risky than in the town limits of Niagara Falls. He drove by an old house that had been converted into a photographic studio called Hilburger Studios. Circling back, he parked his car and went into the studio.

A young girl wearing glasses was sitting at a desk. "Hello. Say do you guys do photographic printing?"

"Well, yes but that's really not our business. What do you need?"

"I got some important negatives that got all mixed up and I need some prints from then to sort out what they're all about."

"All you need to do is just go down to the Boulevard Mall. There's a processing shop that'll do that for you."

A middle aged man walked into the entry way from the back rooms. The man reminded Lawrence of the actor Bill Murray. He walked up to Lawrence and shook his hand.

"How you doing? I'm Dennis Hilburger owner of Hilburger Studios. She told you right. Easier for you just to go to the mall and get them ..."

"Mr. Hilburger, could we talk in private?"

"Sure. Dennis, just call me Dennis."

Lawrence was carefully avoiding giving his name. "Dennis, I didn't want to embarrass your young lady. You see I'm not sure about these negatives. I'd kind of like to get them done without anybody seeing them so I know what they're photos of?"

The photographer gave him a smile. "Okay! Something your wife might not like to see?"

Lawrence smiled in agreement.

"Listen, I can do you one even better. There's a place on Niagara Falls Boulevard just past the mall on the right. It's called Campos. It's a white windowless building just before you get to Sheridan Drive. Can't miss it. They'll let you do your own prints. They show you how in just a couple minutes. Here, give them my card. You have any problem just ... Oops, I forgot. I'm playing golf with this guy who works over on Grand Island. He's a client so I let him cheat all the time. Funny guy though. We've got a tee off time at Beaver Island and I got to get over there in an hour. Campos'll take care of you."

"Hey, thanks. Hope you play well," said Lawrence shaking the man's hand and leaving.

Hilburger had called as soon as Lawrence left his studio and Campos Photography was opened earlier than their normal hours. Lawrence made a mental note to send a thank you note to Hilburger with a dozen Titleist golf balls. The owner of Campos himself took Lawrence through the process from using the dark room, adjusting color levels, exposing photographic sheets, and running exposed paper through the processing machine. He emphasized that nobody would see what Lawrence printed as long as Lawrence was waiting at the exit tray to pick up his work. At this time in the morning that would not be a problem because only special customers like Hilburger were allowed access. Lawrence assured the man that none of the photos were obscene or potentially illegal.

The very first job was to expose a contact sheet with the negatives spread over it so that the processor could see each individual negative photograph. Contact sheets expose the photographs frame-by-frame at the same size as the image on the negative. The contact sheet reversed the negative, so that a miniature correct photograph was visible even though it was only 35 mm in width. Lawrence wound up with three sheets of negative strips, They gave Lawrence a magnifying glass to view each small exposure.

While the images were very small and difficult to accurately interpret, Lawrence knew he had what he needed and more. Lawrence had read the one negative correctly, the Niagara Falls Administrative building with Superintendent Nuevello clearly handing something to another man. The other man looked familiar, but the image was too small to identify. Lawrence went through each contact sheet and marked with a felt tipped pen the photos he wanted to enlarge. He also boxed in areas on some photographs that he wanted to enlarge, especially the ones with Nuevello in it. There were 60 photographs in all. Lawrence ran 8" X 10" prints of those and five of those same prints cropped and enlarged. Lawrence stacked them carefully together and put them into the Campos mailers that he had been given.

"That's a lot of pictures. How did they come out?"

Lawrence told the girl ringing up his very expensive invoice, "not very good with the color tones. But I can see clearly what I was after."

"Hey, nobody comes in here the first time and pulls photos worth squat. You'll get the hang of it. It's how we make money. Sorry."

"Don't be. And thanks. You guys did a great job taking me through it," he said as she handed Lawrence a VISA charge slip for him to sign.

***

"You mother fucking asshole!" Lizzy came right at Lawrence as he came through the door, "where the fuck you been? I've been sitting here watching these fucking games shows all morning …"

She came at him swinging at his face but Lawrence blocked her left hand with his forearm, caught her right armpit with his left hand, and grasping her upper right arm, lifted her completely off the floor. Lawrence was stunned. She felt as light as tissue paper and he easily held her short body more than three feet off of the living room floor. The front of his bath robe, which enveloped her before the onslaught, exposed her emaciated body. Although it had improved since the odor of feces and death was gone, her alcohol ravaged body and sack-like breasts still nauseated him. He held back the gag rising in his throat. She tried to kick him in the crotch but it did not bother him since she had the strength of a mouse.

"Need a drink, don't you Lizzy?"

"You fucker! You promised."

"That I did. I promised when I got back. I'm back."

"Yeah, ten hours late, asshole!"

"Stop screaming," Lawrence said staring her in the eyes, his face inches from hers. Neither flinched and if it was possible to see a person's soul close up looking through their pupils, Lawrence saw Lizzy's. Her mouth was a raging catacomb of hate and vulgarity, mixed with fear but her eyes were malevolence and brave.

"Did you leave my pantries alone?"

Still hanging from Lawrence's strong grip, Lizzy's body slackened and Lawrence lowered her to the floor, letting go.

"What do you think?"

"Good. You've done good," said Lawrence as he walked past her into the kitchen. He opened the kitchen cabinet above the refrigerator and pulled out a large, elaborately adorned bottle of brandy.

"Have a seat," he said putting the liter bottle on the kitchen table. Lawrence took two small glass goblets from another cabinet, opened the freezer and added a few ice cubes to each, setting them on the table.

He poured the brandy over the ice and spoke, "this is my favorite, St. Remy's brandy. I got a couple questions to ask you. I got some pictures I want you to look at and comment on. But first, I owe you and I want to help you."

Lizzy stared at the brownish yellow liquor in the glass in front of her. She could feel her salivary glands oozing in anticipation of the liquor.

"Yeah? Go ahead," said Lizzy having cooled off considerably. "Help me."

"I want you to take a small sip of the brandy."

She went for the glass too quickly and Lawrence gently put his hand over hers, feeling the sinewy tendons and narrow bones, almost like those of a chicken.

"Slow, Lizzy, drink it slow. Let it go over your tongue and warm the back of your throat, but wait a second before you swallow," Lawrence guided her, hoping she did not let it rush down her throat and cause her to gasp for breath on it. She did not and Lawrence smiled.

"How did it feel?"

The brandy made a marked change in her attitude. "Different, it felt different. It ran through my head even before I swallowed it. Funny but I got a high and it weren't even in my gut yet. Can still feel it. Kind of bites at you, digs into your throat. Pretty fuckin' good rush for only a small sip."

"Wait a second before another sip. Second one hits your brain faster and deeper. But it's no good unless you take it slowly. Get drunk fast on the St. Remy and it's a waste of expensive liquor. Take another one, not a big slug, but a little bit more than the first."

Lawrence watched her eyes as the brandy ran around inside of her mouth and etched its way into her throat muscles as she swallowed, her stomach warming to the liquid. Lizzy took in a deep breath, through her nostrils. He could see her facial muscles twitch as the brandy triggered smooth spasms in her cheeks.

"Lizzy, you're an alcoholic. Probably I am too. I used to go through stages, quit the booze for a couple weeks but get right back into it. Just get the high was all the further I went."

"That ain't being a drunk, boy. I know what a drunk is."

"No, I wouldn't say I was a drunk. Alcoholic fits the image. I need it."

"Need it? So you're a drunk just like me. Fuckin' a, got a alky teaching me to sober up."

"Stop. Hold off on you next sip a second. What I found would not stop me from getting high, only stopped me from getting so high I'd fall on my face. You know don't you, Lizzy? So drunk that nobody could stand to be around you?"

"Go on. Can I take another swig?"

"In a sec. Did you ever realize that once you've reached that level of drunkenness where you're just pouring it down your throat, that it does nothing for you?"

Lizzy stared at Lawrence. It was a connection between two alcoholics that both understood.

"Look for it and enjoy the wait like it's a special occasion. Say to yourself, I'm only drinking on weekends, no Mondays through Thursdays, just Friday, Saturday, and if you have to,

Sundays. Fight off those no booze days knowing a drinking day is coming. Then when it comes, tell yourself how many, how many shots or high balls or brandies. When you take it slow, you'll be able to do only four or five. Sometimes I'll just put it off until around eight o'clock and fall asleep after only one or two St. Remy's."

"So you want me to do this. It's gonna solve my boozing habit?"

"No, Lizzy. I'm not trying to get you back on the wagon. I just want you to help me ..."

Lawrence stopped. Lizzy was too unpredictable to trust, especially if she stayed drunk. Lawrence needed her to give him answers to questions that now faced him. He had seen Henry's photographs, but he needed her. He could not tell her this.

"It bothers me that your son failed my class."

Lizzy held up her glass to him.

"Go ahead, another small sip."

She took it slowly, closed her eyes like she was having an orgasm, put the glass down and spoke, "come on, Sweetie, you've had kids fail before."

Lawrence knew she was mellowing when she called him sweetie. "Not like this. I've never had a student taken from me and failed by another teacher. I think the district is setting me up to be fired."

Lizzy was keeping her drinking pace right where Lawrence wanted it.

"Why would they want to fire you? Henry said you were the best teacher he ever had."

"That's what I would like to know. Henry can't help me anymore, but you can."

"How?"

"First, I need you sober or at least just a bit over the edge. See what's in your glass?"

She swirled it, staring into the glass.

"That's it until later tonight. Can you handle it?"

Lizzy again swirled the ice cubes around in the glass. As they melted it made for more to drink even though the potency became diluted.

"Sounds difficult doesn't it?"

Lizzy smiled and lifted her eyebrows. "Stuff's good, but you're right. Us boozers know. Once you get on a toot, makes no difference what you throw down your throat. I might get by with a few of these, taking it slow."

"Two, Lizzy. This is one and another later tonight."

Her back went up and Lawrence prepped himself for a violent and obscene onslaught. She leaned back in the kitchen chair, swirled the cubes around again hoping to melt them faster and thus creating more drink in her glass.

"I stopped at K Mart and bought you some clothes. No offense but I don't think what you've got laying around your trailer is even worth putting into a washing machine. I stopped by and gave up, but I looked at the size tags. Here, take the bag the clothes are in. Time to take a shower. I'm guessing you didn't while I wasn't here."

Lizzy stared into Lawrence's eyes and nodded. She got up, downed the rest of her brandy, which was now mostly ice water, and turned toward the bathroom.

"Hold off just a minute. I want to see if you can tell me who this man is. I got some pictures that Henry mailed to Eileen Ledger."

Lawrence could not let Lizzy or anyone else know that he had found the negatives at the halfway house. He opened the top envelope and took out an 8" X 10", borderless photograph. Hopefully, Lizzy would not ask how he got so large a print. He laid it down on the kitchen table.

"Lizzy, it's a photo of some man in a vehicle repair shop opening a metal box. See if you know ..."

"It's Uley. He's at the school bus garage. Henry took the picture. He'd go over to the shop after school to wait on Uley while he finished work. Henry took a lot of pictures. He'd blow them up in the photography class he took at the high school. Probably the only class he like besides yours."

Lawrence picked up the photograph and stared at Uley Hawkins. He was a very tall, gangly man. His face had that beaten look with crevice lines crossing his forehead and thin jowls hanging down the side of his mouth, like an alcoholic. His facial features were jagged, like crags in a boulder, and his hair cut had that characteristic look of someone putting a bowl on his head and taking scissors to his hair. What stunned Lawrence most was the fact that Uley Hawkins had to be at least fifty years, probably older.

"How old were you when you had Henry?"

"That's a bit personal, Mr. Lawrence. I was twelve if you care to know."

Uley Hawkins was in his late forties when he knocked up his twelve-year old sister. Lizzy stopped at the bathroom door and turned back to the kitchen. She took the glass and drained out a few more drops of brandy before heading back to take her shower.

CHAPTER TWENTY ONE

Feast of the Beast

Lizzy was becoming a risk. Lawrence had to be very careful what he told her. He could sense that she had her doubts about Lawrence's questions concerning her son Henry. Lawrence knew he could control her through liquor but it meant unleashing her alcoholic rages. Lawrence had gone through 60 prints from Henry's negatives and weeded out the ones that were close to identical scenarios and others that had bearing to his quest. There was a definite method, rhyme, and reason for the set of shots Henry had taken. Like a good photographer, Henry had taken multiple shots at scenes where he was not sure the first shot would provide the image he was after. Henry took these pictures because they showed a world that Henry Hawkins knew. This was exactly what Lawrence had told him to do when framing out his final essay. Framing was the key since obviously Henry took a space of time in his life and captured it not in words but in visible pictures of his real world. Learning from writing what you know as Jack London did, Henry captured images of his life as he saw it. He wrote his story looking at his real world with its protagonists making his life visible in his mind through the photographs. They were transferred into words for the essay paper

Lawrence looked at Henry's rough draft that Eileen's parents had given him. His essay clearly iterated that Niagara Falls had a drug problem and the photos showing deals going down in bathrooms and kids at parties smoking and shooting confirmed this.

Henry's essay moved to another protagonist, Henry's father. Until yesterday Lawrence thought he was his stepfather. The photographs matched Henry's written description of Uley in the school bus garage. Henry's father had been photographed driving students on field trips as a ruse to hustle drugs. Henry must have had a long wait for the return of one trip from Toronto since he had photographs taken at the Rainbow Bridge showing the school bus driven by Uley getting only a cursory examination by the bridge agents.

Henry took many risky photographs which were very dark although decipherable. One series showed Uley and one of the other mechanics in the garage, crawling under a bus to remove a grease-covered box, the next shot of the box being opened on a work bench, and then with it opened. There were plastic bags full of white powder inside the box. How Henry got the photo without a flash attachment was a mystery. One of the photographs was a close up of the drugs. Lawrence guessed that Uley had left the drugs in the case on the bench unguarded which gave Henry a chance to take a close up and quickly get back to where ever he was hiding. Henry knew the contents of each bag. On Uley's return the bags were sorted and put in K Mart shopping bags. Henry followed Uley's garage mechanic on a delivery right to the same place Henry went to buy drugs, a row house whose rear side abutted the Niagara School District's school bus garages.

The only gap in Henry's story board pictures was here. He probably did not want to take a risk of photographing how the row house deals worked, especially since the Niagara police where in on the deals. In his essay he explained how the police were able to justify not being able to stop the drug deals since they could only make arrests on a search warrant for one particular row house at this drug alley, better known as Falls Street. As soon as the police arrived, the dealers who worked out of the third floor scooted up to the attic and out a hole into the attic of the adjacent row house. They could not be touched in the adjacent house since there was no warrant for that house.

The riskiest photographs were taken when Henry followed one of the dealers. He biked behind a dealer leaving the school bus garage and took photos as he followed the man's car. In his essay he wrote that the vehicle did not go very far and he never lost sight of the car. Henry must have ridden with no hands on the handle bars since he had shots of the moving car and the license plate. He got a blurred shot of the man entering the back of the school administration office. He was carrying the box of the bagged drugs from Uley's workshop.

Henry had not identified who the well dressed, short Italian man that exited the building with the police chief, although he did recognize the police chief. Lawrence knew the man that Henry had photographed. The man shaking hands with the police chief of Niagara Falls and holding the drugs was Superintendent Nuevello.

"Hey! What's with these short pants you bought me?" Lawrence spun around quickly. Lizzy had finished her shower, dried off, and was now dressed in the clothes Lawrence had bought her from K Mart. She had a towel drying her bright red hair.

"I don't like people to see my feet. They're fucking ugly."

"Lizzy, you look good. Damn, your eyes have almost lost those blood lines. Slacks look good. I stopped at your trailer and checked out some sizes from the clothes lying all over the bedroom floor. Couldn't figure shoe size so I got you sandals. How's it going?"

"Is it time for my next drink?" The more she rubbed her hair with the large bath towel, the more it turned into frizzy. Lawrence had thought her large mop of frizzy hair was the result of how she treated it. Obviously it was just how her hair grew.

"Come here. I need your help," said Lawrence. He had to trust her now nor at least be able to con her enough that she would not become a threat.

"Hey look, there's Junior Jig! See that nigger coming out from under that school bus?"

Lawrence just ignored her racism and spoke, "I've got some questions for you. First, the easy one. When I stopped to get your sizes for those clothes … and by the way, how's the underwear?"

"Loose, asshole."

"Blouse looks good. Brings out your bright face."

"Fuck off. When do I get my next drink?"

"When I finish going over these photos with you. But listen. In Henry's final essay he calls Uley his step father. You've told me that Uley's his actual father?"

"Why the fuck you want the world to know that my brother knocked me up? Henry probably guessed at it but that's how we went around it."

"Makes sense. Second question. These are the negatives that you took to Henry in the halfway house. You told me that Henry had you take the negatives out of their original envelope. What happened to the prints?"

"You saw my trailer Mr. Lawrence. Real mess, weren't it? I don't live like that. But right after Henry hung himself, Uley came into the trailer and took everything that I had of Henry's. I have no idea what he did with all of it."

… "Wait?"

"Problem?"

"You know that son of a bitch got Henry's stuff the same night the cops came to tell me Henry was dead. The cops had my name listed first as next of kin and asked me to verify Uley's address. Don't make sense."

It did to Lawrence.

"Lizzy, just one more thing then I'll share a brandy with you. Come over here and look at these pictures. See if there's anything strange about them."

Lizzy took her time which was surprised Lawrence. He figured she would rush through them to get her drink. Some she skipped, but a few she pulled to the side and went back to.

"Henry took these? Wow he sure had guts, my boy did. You know what's goin' on here don't you Lawrence?"

"Tell me Lizzy."

"Fucking obvious Lawrence. They're just some pix of Uley running his drug racket. That's all. Only surprise is that Uley let him take these pix. The short wop shaking hands with that grease ball in the parking lot is the chief of police. He and Uley do a lot of business together. My guess is he's buying up his weekly stash from that suit in the parking lot."

Lawrence was stunned. Lizzy's account of what she saw in the photographs matched to near perfect the essay that Henry wrote on these story board pictures laying on Lawrence's floor. Her brother was smuggling drugs on a school bus with children crossing the border. Her son an obvious a part of the action that went on and the police involved with the drug market right since it was happening right under their noses. Lizzy acted like it was a normal everyday occurrence.

"Lizzy the only thing that surprises you is the pictures?"

"Yeah, if Uley ever found out he'd beat the shit out of Henry …"

Lawrence had pushed it too far. She began to grasp more than the photographs or her brother getting irate. She saw the violence that Henry's essay might have caused. Lawrence could see the look of stark horror on her face.

"Let me get you that drink."

"No! No, I gotta run this through again."

Lawrence got her a glass of brandy anyway and one for himself. Contrary to her declining Lawrence's offer, she took the glass but only sipped a few drams of liquor, "Jesus Christ, Uley killed Henry!"

Lawrence was in trouble. Lizzy could get both of them killed. He had to get Lizzy and himself out of harm's way, "Lizzy, that's not possible."

Lawrence knew otherwise.

"How? Uley sees these photographs and he'd kill Henry without any qualms."

"But he did not see these photographs Lizzy. Think, where were the photographs? At your trailer after Henry died. Uley never saw them."

Lawrence was playing with fire because there was a strong possibility that Henry showed the photographs to Uley. Lizzy would not see that possibility.

She took a larger sip of the brandy. The alcoholic sting was tapping into her brain telling her more, try some more. "That's right. I had the prints and Henry had the negatives."

"That's not all. Hanging Henry at the halfway house would have been too great a risk for Uley to take."

"God Lawrence, I love this stuff. What's a bottle like that one cost?"

"About forty dollars."

"Fuck it. It ain't that good," said Lizzy and Lawrence could see she had forgotten her fear of Uley. But Lawrence had not eliminated Uley.

"Lizzy, a final question. How close were Uley and Henry? I mean like did they do things together? Go fishing or bowling or anything?"

"Uley is an ex-addict. Nearly died. He broke the drug habit but mastered the drug business. You want hits, he'll do them for you. Cost you a pretty penny, but he's good to go. Don't fuck with him. His kind of life gives him a lot of contact with some bad bastards. He'd kill you as soon as give you change for a ten spot. Don't cross him. He took Henry in only because Niagara Wheatfield wouldn't. Henry lived with me, had a record of substance abuse, and they wouldn't take him. Uley did it because I threatened to make him cough up support payments. He never liked Henry but accepted him as long as Henry kept out of his way. Beat the shit out of him for the smallest thing. That's Uley. Used Henry for drug drops but never let him handle any money. I don't know for a fact, but I think Uley paid Henry with drugs, not cash. He's a bad mother fucker, Mr. Lawrence. Better keep out of his way, like I said."

Lawrence had gotten from Lizzy Hawkins nearly all he needed.

***

Lawrence knew he was in trouble when the security guard greeted him at the entrance to Niagara High School.

"Mr. Lawrence, you need to go to Mr. Scarpetti's office not your room."

"What about my students …"

"They're covered. I'll take you over to Scarpetti's office. Just follow me."

In the hallway to the principal's office were stationed other security guards, more than Lawrence had ever seen before. Usually they hung around the cafeteria before first class started.

Scarpetti had replaced Principal Rolanda Mosse two months into the first semester. Mosse was hired as the obligatory female black administrator two years ago when the news put pressure on the school board about the lack of minorities in the school district's administrative positions. Mosse had an axe to grind and superintendent Nuevello knew how to let a tyrannical black woman march herself to the gallows by trying to upstage and micromanage her mostly white and male staff. That same staff, excepting Lawrence, knew how to defeat a bad administrator. They filed grievance upon grievance forcing the elite school board to spend late night hours hearing them. It did not take the school board long to accept Dr. Nuevello's recommendation that Mrs. Mosse take an administrative position as co-coordinator of standardized testing.

Nuevello instantly put Bruno Scarpetti into the position. Bruno Scarpetti was obviously a good old Italian boy and also the husband of one of Nuevello's nieces. He was a rubber stamp and sycophant for Nuevello.

"Ah, Mr. Lawrence, we've missed you. Feeling better now?" said Scarpetti's secretary her tone conveying that she knew whatever Scarpetti knew, only she knew it before Scarpetti since her sister, Italian like her, was Nuevello's secretary.

"Mr. Scarpetti has been anxiously waiting for you to get here. Go on in."

Lawrence opened the glass door which once had Mosse's name written across the glass. The faint letters had been scratched off but were still casting an outline shadow on the door that awaited a Bruno Scarpetti's name.

"Here Lawrence. Here in front. Have a seat."

Lawrence wondered if Scarpetti could put together a sentence of more than five words. He had only talked with Scarpetti once since he took over and that was a cordial greeting and introduction in the hallway when Lawrence had lunch duty guarding the cafeteria doors.

"Got a letter here," said Scarpetti handing it to Lawrence along with a small sheet of paper from what must have been a receipt book used in purchasing. "Sign this first."

Lawrence read the sheet. Lawrence's signature would mean that Lawrence had read and understood the contents of the letter. Lawrence did not sign the receipt but opened the letter which was on the superintendent's stationery. Lawrence was in trouble, big trouble. He was being suspended with pay until a hearing was held to terminate his employment with the Niagara City School District. Not only would a judgment be made to fire Lawrence, but the evidence produced from the hearing would be given over to the City of Niagara police department for possible arrest charges against Lawrence.

Lawrence had pushed too far. He had gone too far with what happened to Henry Hawkins and now he had fallen. Lawrence eased back into the wooden chair. He heard Scarpetti again ask him to sign the receipt of the superintendent's letter but waved him off. How many times had he done this to himself? How many times had he fallen on his face, having to get up and rue his arrogance? Waiting, his mind almost flipped out.

"You got big trouble," said Scarpetti.

Lawrence signed the receipt and tossed it across the desk, "you know all about this?"

"Have to, I'm the principal."

"Wow Bruno, five words. Now if you would have said I am instead I'm, you'd have made a six word sentence. That'd be a record for you."

"I never liked you, Lawrence."

"We finished here, Bruno?" Lawrence did not wait. When he left Scarpetti's office there were three security guards waiting for him. They escorted Lawrence all the way to his car without a word. Lawrence sat on the hood of his car and read the suspension letter for the third time. One of the security guards told Lawrence he had to get off school property. Lawrence ignored him and the guards left. In less than five minutes a police car pulled into the parking lot. Before an officer could open the cruiser door, Lawrence got into his car and drove off.

The patrol car tailed him all the way to his house. It stayed parked across the street for the rest of the morning. At lunch time it left but returned around one o'clock. Lawrence was under surveillance and the suspension letter gave him the reason – Ulysses Hawkins.

***

The Niagara City School District bus garages reminded Lawrence of the times his Uncle Ralph took him to the engine houses for the Pennsylvania Railroad. They were almost cathedral in shape but dark and murky in atmosphere. The one wild card in trying to solve what had happened to Henry Hawkins seemed to be Ulysses Hawkins, the kid's father and maybe uncle. Never in the whole time that Lawrence tutored Henry did Uley Hawkins get discussed. Only through Lizzy did Lawrence discover how Henry got his drugs. Uley was the source and not just for Henry. The photographs showed beyond any doubt that Uley was running a drug syndicate that involved the school bus drivers and garage workers. It was also linked to the chief of police and the superintendent of schools. Were the photographs enough to convict these men? Probably but Lawrence wanted to push it a little more. The fucking edge, again!

… and he tripped and fell and didn't win.

Lawrence walked into the garage where Uley Hawkins worked. It was the day after he took Lizzy Hawkins back home. Lizzy had convinced Lawrence that Uley was indeed a drug dealer and had been one ever since she knew him. Uley himself had started on drugs but soon made the decision that dealing was better. Making money off of drugs was a better high than doing the drugs. Uley was an anthropomorphic misogynist whose goal in life was making other people uglier than he was. The photographs did not do justice to how ugly and evil Uley truly was. Lawrence felt a chill at the nape of his neck when he spotted Uley filing a brake shoe in an anvil at the end of a large, dirt covered work bench. Uley was tall, taller than Lawrence by at least three inches, but thin, and Lawrence guessed he outweighed Uley by sixty or seventy pounds. It was difficult to estimate Uley's age even though Lizzy made it clear that he was in his sixties. Lawrence had expected Uley to be muscular but he was not. His arms were boney and sinewy with purple splotches covering the front parts and blood lines stringing underneath a faint but visible pulse.

It was Uley's face that made him a match for a fight with Lucifer. Uley could probably win out of sheer fear from Satan's vision of him. Uley's face was like carved stone, broken in places to give Uley broad eyebrows, terraced cheeks, and a nose that stood out from his face like a giant crag in a lava mountain. Uley had an odor that took a second for Lawrence to identify. It was tobacco which Uley constantly chewed and spit out whereever Uley pleased.

"You Uley Hawkins?"

Uley did not stop filing the brake shoe. Turning his head toward Lawrence he spit a cud of wet tobacco at Lawrence's feet, "name's Mister Hawkins."

"Your son was Henry Hawkins, boy that died over at the Halfway House?"

"Fuckin' ugly bitch. I gotta see her more often and smack her around some more. That boy was not my son. That piece of shit was my nephew. What you want?"

Lawrence could not hold the man's stare. Uley's eyes scared Lawrence, made him feel like Uley could read into his head through Lawrence's eyes.

"Henry said if I needed a source you'd be one."

"A source for what boy?"

Lawrence was getting nervous now. There was no control that he had over the man and certainly Uley had no fear of Lawrence.

"I need to get some skag."

"Skag, huh? You know what skag is asshole?"

"Yeah, of course. It's H, heroin. I need a source."

Uley came within six inches of Lawrence's face. The smell of tobacco was now over ridden by the smell of dead flesh which Lawrence had knew from hunting. Uley did not blink. His eyes scanned every centimeter of Lawrence's face. They were hard eyes. When he spoke, spittle tarnished with pieces of chewed tobacco sprayed Lawrence's face. Lawrence could not back down. Uley had a two foot long metal file clasped tightly in his right hand. If he raised his hand, Lawrence would have to hit him. A bit of courage seeped into Lawrence's blood as he finally realized that he could take down this old man.

Uley did not move. "Jimmy Jig? What the fuck is skag?"

At the back of the garage a large brown man wearing an auto mechanic denim suit waddled slowing towards Lawrence and Uley. Lawrence caught sight of the man first, then noticed that at least five other workers had stopped to see this confrontation going on in their workplace.

"Skag Boss? Shit skag's an ugly woman that eats dead babies, especially rotten ones."

Lawrence knew he was in trouble when he saw out of the corner of his eyes that the doorway into the garage was sealed off by two workers, one carrying a sledge hammer and the other what looked like an old saw blade from a band saw.

"Alright, I guess I just made a mistake," said Lawrence. He turned but, Jimmy Jig blocked him.

Uley was not finished with Lawrence. "You come in my shop and accuse me of being a drug dealer. You out of your fucking mind, little boy? I'll bet you so scared now, you gonna shit your pants. Jimmy Jig, you a drug dealer?"

"No, boss!"

"You boys work for me? Any you want sell this little pussy some skag?"

They did not answer but laughed loudly. It was obvious they were expecting Lawrence to get beaten, beaten very badly. Lawrence had to go through Jimmy Jig since there was no way around his large body. Had he not thrown the first punch, Lawrence might have walked out of the garage only being humiliated not beaten.

"You gonna to move?"

Jimmy Jig just smiled and Lawrence caught him with a solid on this right cheek. The man's face was so fat, it felt like Lawrence had punched a pillow.. Jimmy Jig's hands went out from his sides as Lawrence caught the man's jaw on the left with a solid right jab with no effect. Jimmy Jig went at Lawrence's body, tackling him with both of bodies slamming into a school bus. Lawrence felt a rib snap in his back as the man lifted Lawrence straight up in the air and tossed him onto the work table where Uley had been filing. The whole garage was laughing as his back slammed down on the metal surface. Lawrence's head began to spin and the broken rib brought pain. He could hear the workers cheering the man on, yelling for a kill which would probably have happened except Lawrence always carried a jackknife with him. Jimmy Jig was getting hand slaps and knuckle bumps from his coworkers as he turned back to Lawrence. Lawrence's jackknife was the same one he used fighting Ledger. It was heavy, nine inches in length with a finely honed, four-inch steel blade. Lawrence pulled it from his pocket, eased the blade loose from the heft, and snapping it backwards with his wrist, opened the blade.

Had his timing been a split second slower, he would probably have been dead. Jimmy Jig had meshed his fingers together and came at Lawrence ready to bring down the clinched fists on

Lawrence's face. The sheer power of the man would have broken Lawrence's nose and driven bone matter into Lawrence's brain. Instead, Lawrence's left hand had the point of the jackknife at Jimmy Jigs jugular vein. He grabbed the man's left ear as a handle to keep the blade ready for the kill.

"One move and I'll put this blade through your neck."

Uley came over to the two men. Lawrence was on his back atop the table and the fat man's chin was raised above Lawrence's body, his face now red, fearing that the steel blade would kill him instantly.

"What ya goin' do now, Mister teacher man? You gonna kill Jimmy Jig? Jimmy Jig? You think he'll do it?"

Unlike Uley who was not in any grave danger, the man responded shivering, "Boss, Boss, don't push him. I see in his eyes. He do it. Back off Boss."

Uley came face-to-face with Lawrence, "I guess we gots us a standoff here boy. Gots us a bunch a witnesses too. Riley, go over to my office and call the city police. Tell them there's been an attempted murder done happened here."

Lawrence had fallen but he knew he had to rise, "Riley? Can you hear me Riley? Tell them to send an ambulance. Tell them one of your crew has had his throat slit."

Riley stopped. Uley got back in Lawrence's face, "you do it, it's murder."

Lawrence smiled, "back off you old fuck. I'm walking your buddy here out of that door and into the snow."

Uley did not move. Riley did not move. No one moved for nearly a minute. Lawrence pulled tightly on the man's ear, enough for him to feel the pain, and moved him backwards. He rolled himself off the work bench never letting the knife blade lose its life assuring contact with the man's neck.

It was still a precarious situation and Lawrence had to get out of it. Lawrence could not go to his car since no one knew he had a car parked outside and he was not about to let them know it. All he had to do was get through the garage doors and he was safe. Lawrence eased the man to the garage doors.

"You're some man, Ulysses Hawkins. Fuck your own baby sister, get her pregnant, and abandon her."

Lawrence kicked Jimmy Jig's legs out from underneath the man and when the man fell Lawrence cut his Achilles tendon and ran into the blinding snow. He could hear Uley yelling to Riley to call the police.

***

Lawrence took a slow sip of the Chevis Regal knowing that intoxication at this point would make his knowledge of the Remington Winchester 30.30 rifle lying under insulation between the rafters in the attic crawl space the final coup de grace. He maintained enough sober intelligence to embarrassingly pour the Chevis Regal into a Flintstones jelly glass. He had read Superintendent Nuevello's letter four times and Lawrence knew that he was in way too deep.

Lawrence pulled a wooden kitchen chair out to the sliding glass door in his dining area. He watched the snow and rued that he could not vent his anger and fear physically. Bicycling was out of the question. Not only had the weather locked him into self-ego molestation for his gigantic blunder, but the rib injury, only a severe bruise, prevented him from going to the gym to work out. He could surely use a good twenty minutes on the heavy punching bag.

The letter, the letter, the letter ran through his mind despite the numbing of the scotch. Nuevello had him out at all four bases. First, he was being charged with an attempted purchase of narcotics on school property, second he admitted using heroin to a school district teacher, third he committed abusive and threatening conduct on school property, and fourth and the clincher, assault with a deadly weapon on a school district employee.

Lawrence noticed on the second reading that a copy of the suspension and notification of a hearing to determine termination had been sent to the school district teachers' association representative. Lawrence imagined that he would get a call from them tomorrow since the letter was sent registered to the union representative the same day Lawrence received his notification. He knew that that rep would tell him there was nothing they could do until after the hearing since the letter did not specifically identify the entire incident and the people involved. There would be a response by the teachers' association once the hearing was over and the decision made. Discharge most certainly would be the decision.

Fired, he would be fired. That did not bother him as much as Nuevello notifying the police of the legal violations occurring during Lawrence's odyssey into the school district bus garages.

"From ghoulies and ghosties and long legged beasties and things that go bump in the night, Good Lord, deliver us!" Who wrote those appropriate words, Alfred Lord Tennyson or Robert

Burns? These were the words that raged through his mind when he faced Uley Hawkins and his demon henchmen. There was no doubt they would have killed him. Now they were going to bury him by putting him in jail. He would use the wounded yet innocent Jimmy Jig as a fallen employee, fallen at the blade Lawrence ripped unmercifully through his Achilles' tendon. Witnesses? Five, six maybe? First Nuevello would ceremoniously and degradingly terminate Lawrence in front of the school board. Once convicted as an immoral employee and exposed to the poor children of Niagara Falls City, Nuevello would hand Lawrence's head over to the city's chief of police for a maximum charge of attempted murder. Fired and disgraced, Lawrence would go to jail.

"How, how could I have been so stupid?" thought Lawrence running himself into the mire, erupting his emotions into self-pity, it was the edge he dared go over. If he could push Uley to sell him drugs, then he had Uley, Nuevello, and the chief of police bundled into a crime syndicate. Slay the dragon, cut off his heads, hold up your sword. When would the police come to take his sword away?

Wait a minute, Lawrence stopped as he emptied the jelly jar glass of scotch. That makes no sense. In fact, the whole scenario was badly constructed. Lawrence picked up the suspension letter for the fifth time and reread it. Now he would be charged with "assault with a deadly weapon on a school district employee." So why has he not been arrested? Obviously Jimmy Jig had received medical attention which meant he went to the hospital. A severed Achilles' tendon is extremely dangerous and the hospital, by law, and would have to notify the police that they had an obvious knifing victim in their emergency room. Did they? Even Dr. Nuevello could not stop that legal action. So why had someone not interrogated Lawrence?

Lawrence looked at the bottom of the letter and saw the names of the school board members. Nuevello had to be getting calls from all of them about this incident, demanding that Lawrence be arrested. So why had no one arrested him? Lawrence picked up the phone and dialed the teachers' association, asking for the union representative. Even though it was late in the day, the rep should have gotten his copy by now and hopefully would have called Lawrence. He had not.

"Why hello, Mr. Lawrence," said the union representative over the phone. "I don't think I've ever had the pleasure of meeting you. What can I do for you?"

This made no sense. The man should have gotten a copy of the letter by now. Lawrence had to be careful.

"Yeah, we got this new principal, Bruno Scarpetti. I had a little run in with him about my eating my lunch while I have hall duty. Basically he said I can't and I told him to go fuck himself. Well he wrote me up for disobedience and sent you a copy. I want to file a grievance against him. Did you read his letter of reprimand?"

"No, I haven't got it yet. When did you put it in the pony?"

"This morning."

"Well, I've got my mail from all the schools and central administration and I've got nothing from you. Want me to set up a meeting?"

"No, let's just wait until you read the reprimand."

"Mr. Lawrence?"

"Yes?"

"You were exaggerating when you said you told him to ..."

"Go fuck himself?"

"If you did say those worlds and all he did was write you up, I'd leave it be. I know he's a real jerk. You're not the first to contact us about him. I just don't think using that kind of rebuttal is going to do you any good."

"Yeah, I see your logic. I guess I got a little off the handle," said Lawrence with his mind thinking heft, not handle. "Look just forget about it okay? And thanks."

Lawrence hung up. There was now a new perspective to the conflict. He guessed that nobody listed on the bottom of the letter was contacted. Then why the letter? Unfortunately, at this point he not only had no firm knowledge of what was going on but, due to his lack of comprehension of the actions going on around him, Lawrence had no idea how to prepare himself for the battle. Nuevello was setting Lawrence up for the next attack. It was obviously not going to be the hearing with the school board. Lawrence went to the Bruce Springsteen Calendar hanging behind the kitchen door to check out when the next school board meeting was scheduled. The second Tuesday of this month was gone and three weeks stood in front of the next one. That was quite a gap and Lawrence knew how to hunt his prey. The hunt is experience, experience of seeing what the prey did in certain conditions. Spoor was a good detractor. Many a deer would urinate along a trail, then back track and take another path. The hunter would follow the laid down path by the smell winding up miles upwind from the prey.

Nuevello was setting Lawrence on a path where Lawrence could only be taken or be killed.

Lawrence rinsed out the Flintstones jelly glass, added some ice, and filled the glass with tap water. Rolling the ice around inside the glass, he drank down the nice cold water while staring out the sliding glass doors, the snow now three or four inches deep on his neighbor's porch roof. Snow is good to the hunter. Therefore, if you're being snowed, it is best to become the hunter. He sat back in the wooden chair letting his mind take over. The battle at the garage had been a loss but not a defeat. There was reason. Uley and his demons had Lawrence within their grasp, ready to make a meal of him. Did they back off only because Lawrence snared Jimmy Jig into a standoff? It seemed that way when he was fighting for what he thought was his life. Realistically would they have killed him? No, it would not only be too out in the open, but an execution of Lawrence covered by self-defense might expose Uley's and Nuevello's drug syndicate.

Chastising himself, Lawrence gently bit his lower lip, shaking his head.

There was no doubt that Nuevello or Uley had not set up Lawrence to be trapped at the school district bus garage. It was also obvious that neither of them cared much for a defensive position at the garage. As Lawrence learned from Henry Hawkins' essay and the photographs, the garage was only a transition place for removing smuggled drugs from their source and quickly farming them out to where they were vended. Just as quickly the profits cycled to Nuevello. Uley reacted more to Lawrence's accusations about Henry then to Lawrence's quest to buy drugs. The anger in Uley's face, especially the eyes, showed no fear. Looking back, Lawrence saw little protection of the drug operation in the attack on Lawrence but much violence in Uley's acceptance that Henry, his son, had ratted him out.

"Yep, Uley, deny it all you want," said Lawrence to nobody but himself. "Henry's got your eyes and your facial crags. He's your son and your nephew and you probably helped kill him."

Lawrence had escaped being the feast of the monsters. To stand up to the hunter makes you the predator.

CHAPTER TWENTY TWO

Who Are the Beasts?

Lawrence recognized his voice on the phone at once.

"How you doing Judi? This is Evelyn's son, Peter," said Lawrence talking to his mother's boy friend.

"Not bad, Petey. Your Mama has been on my case cause you don't call her anymore. You guys till fighting?"

"No, we're over this one."

"Listen Petey, I got a ask you something might get you upset. Can you give me some concern here and not bite off me head?"

"You're going to ask my mother to marry you, right?"

"How ... I guess it was becoming obvious. You have been talking to her? That's good. What do you think, Petey?"

Lawrence hated being called Petey but for some strange reason Judi's use of the name had stopped bothering him, "she's gonna to say no, Judi. I know she likes you very much, maybe even loves you, but she's kind of gotten use to being by herself."

"Ain't true, Petey. She wants me to move in with her. I been sort of avoiding doing that. I'm not a young man like you. Getting up there, getting close to biting the big one. I move in with her without us being married, it's a sin against God. Don't need that, Petey."

"I'll bet a priest told you that Judi?"

There was no response for a few seconds which meant Lawrence had hit the nail on the head, "so what can I do you, Petey?"

Lawrence smiled knowing Judi was going to avoid a response about the Catholic church, "you got any goombas up here in the Buffalo area that I might run across?"

"That's a strange one, Petey. Lotta Italians up there and quite a few Micks. Problem is they want a run their own game. Don't work that way down here. If they weren't so far, we'd a probably gone up there and bashed a couple skulls to straighten them out. Ain't worth it though. Not enough action cause the economy' s never good up there. Fucking Indians own the games, you know gambling."

"How about drugs?"

"Petey, I love you like a son. Don't want to see you get hurt." Lawrence listened while unconsciously rubbing his jaw where Judi had cracked him one. "They's some bad dagos up there. Don't talk about drugs with nobody. You wind up floatin' in Lake Erie."

"Judi, I gotcha. Here's why I called but I can't spell it out unless you tell me just yes or no. Understand? I can't do any explaining. I just need you to do two things for me. No questions about what I want to do unless they are questions to help me get done what I need. You got that Judi?"

"Been there and will be there with most people I know. What you need?"

"First, I want to set up a banking account that's one hundred percent out of reach by anybody but me. No cops, no FBI, and no IRS. And I've got to be able to make transactions directly over the phone and I might use this new internet computer gimmick."

"I'll have it set up for you by tomorrow. What else?"

"I need to use you as a conduit ..."

"Whoa! I ain't never been in jail."

"Sorry, Judi. Not a convict. I mean conduit like an electric plug. I need you to handle some transactions for me. Like if I call you, you can use my password and see what's happening with my foreign money account. I need you to hold some papers for me that ..."

Until now Lawrence had not breached anything involving potential jeopardy for Judi, "... look what I'm going to say could be risky, Understand?"

"Can't say yes or no unless you tell me Petey."

"I'm not sure how I'm going to work this out but I'm going to send you very confidential letters and photographs and maybe official documents. Like I said, I'm working on it. But I need you to sit on what I send and do exactly what I tell you to do with the materials."

"Materials? You going to be sending bombs or something?"

Lawrence laughed matching the laughter coming from Judi over the telephone line, "no, no real bombs. Can you do it?"

"Sounds pretty simple to me. I get the idea that you're setting somebody up? I'm not directly involved?"

"Yes, exactly. There will be no way anybody could tie you in with what's going on except me. I rat on you and I know you'll off me."

"Fix me with your mother and I wouldn't do that," said Judi with a small degree of begging attached to his voice.

"How soon Judi?"

"Tomorrow be soon enough for the money account? The other you got to work out so I know exactly what to do."

"No need to rush. I'm sort of waiting for the bait to be dropped."

"You doin' the fishing on some jamoke?"

"No, the jamokes are. Listen Judi. Can you go over to my mom's house tonight?"

"Yeah, was gonna to anyhow."

"Ask her to marry you tonight."

***

"Tim? Tim McVeigh?"

"Yes sir. Who is calling?"

"I don't know whether you remember me but I was Danny Costini's English teacher. That ring a bell?"

"Yes sir. Danny and his father were just at a gun show in Canada when I happened to be there. What can I do you for?"

Lawrence hated the current trend to butcher the English language with erroneous sentences and crimped words. "I'm interested in buying a pistol. Can you sell me one in New York?"

"Mr. Lawrence, it is very good to hear a person say pistol instead of gun. New York is a tough state in which to purchase any weapon, especially hand guns. I haven't a license yet but I could show you some weapons and recommend dealers in other states, sir."

Lawrence detected edginess in McVeigh's speech as if he was being careful as to what he would say to Lawrence, "that'd work. Can we get together ..."

"Mr. Lawrence, are you working for the police?"

Lawrence nearly choked, "I thought you were being a little standoffish with me, Tim. Here's my number."

After reading off his phone number, Lawrence angrily continued. "Call up Niagara City police and tell them I tried to buy a handgun from you. I'm betting they climb all over you for information and I'm betting they arrest me within the hour. Give it another hour for booking, then come down to the police station and put up bail money for me."

Lawrence hung up the phone and sat on his sofa waiting for McVeigh to call him back. No more than three breathes went by when the phone rang.

"Sorry, I didn't mean to accuse you of helping the police. I just have to be careful. How well do you know the escarpment area above Sanborn?"

A reflex went through Lawrence's chest causing a slight pull in his pulse. It was the area where he and Eileen began their tryst, "pretty well."

"The best place for me to show you some weapons would be my Grandpa's place off of Ridge Road just passed North Ridge Road. It's cold out there with this snow. You want to wait for another day?"

"No, I'm good. What's the address?"

Lawrence found Grandpa McVeigh's farm easily. As he pulled into the pebbled driveway, Timothy McVeigh came out the front door. He was carrying a rifle which Lawrence guessed was an AK47.

"AK47?"

"Yes sir. You know your weapons."

"Lucky guess," responded Lawrence which was a lie since Lawrence knew rifles very well. "Why the artillery?"

"Police are trying to shut me down. If you were the police or if they tailed you, I'd been in cuffs by now."

"That's a pretty dangerous chance you took."

"No sir," said McVeigh opening the chamber, showing Lawrence there was no firing pin, then rotating the rifle to show the barrel had been sealed. "It's only a model we use to attract people to our table at gun shows."

McVeigh led Lawrence into a small, barn shaped building and locked the two doors behind them. He turned on a hanging florescent light over a work bench which held several pistols lying on a blanket.

"Sorry to be so suspicious, sir. But every time I set up at a gun show, there are police trying to shut me down. What do you need the pistol for?"

"I've got some enemies. Don't want them catching me unprepared."

"What kind of enemies?"

"Enemies that would take me down without any qualms if I gave them a reason and an opportunity."

"Are you seeing demons in the shadows, Mr. Lawrence?"

It was the first time Lawrence had seen McVeigh smile. At first he did not understand why, but then he remembered their first time conversation at Lawrence's house when he accused McVeigh of seeing government demons in the shadows.

Lawrence looked over the pistols. He did not want a cylinder fed revolver even though they were least likely to misfire compared to an automatic. There were three automatics on the table. He hefted them, chambered each, aimed at the rear of the barn, and tossed them back and forth between his right and left hand.

"What's this one?"

"It's a Colt M1911A1. Want to try it?"

"Where?"

"Out back of the barn. You might have noticed my Grandpa's farm abuts the escarpment. Got a big cliff going up thirty or so feet at the rear. Not a neighbor close enough to hear a howitzer go off."

McVeigh led Lawrence out of the barn, turned and locked it, and motioned for Lawrence to follow him. It was getting near dusk but they were still able to see the pistol target stands McVeigh had built behind the barn.

"Ah ha! Jim Hawkins might be a cop hiding in these apple barrels to nab us firing illegal weapons," joked Lawrence and actually got McVeigh to smile. Immediately Lawrence stopped, realizing that Henry Hawkins had the same last name as the character from Robert Lewis Stevenson's <u>Treasure Island</u>.

"Is there a problem Mr. Lawrence?"

"Lawrence, just call me Lawrence. My head's starting to swarm a bit. I've got a lot of shit happening and maybe I am getting too jumpy, think I'm seeing cops coming after me and shoot outs like in some fucking movie."

Lawrence had let his mouth speak before his brain said talk.

McVeigh spoke, "You should be prepared. Remember the <u>Turner Diaries</u>? Maybe you shouldn't ridicule Macdonald's paranoia so much. Look at this country right now. We're an overtaxed police state. Hell, the ATF has a no-knock search warrant to go through everything we bring to the gun shows or have at home. They and the FBI blow away women and children so they can keep the power to rule the people."

Lawrence could see McVeigh's face turning red even in the sparse evening light. It was not the cold chapping his face but the anger that Lawrence had seen before in McVeigh. Lawrence needed to know McVeigh better. He was going to buy a weapon or maybe two from McVeigh. If McVeigh reported him, Lawrence would be arrested instantly, the coup de grace for Niagara City's police chief and Dr. Nuevello.

"Talk about paranoia Tim. Killing women and children?"

McVeigh's face was almost entirely red now, "you fucking blind? Don't you read the papers or watch the news?"

"Whoa, cool down. I'm overtaxed and living in a police state like you."

"Haven't you heard about Ruby Ridge? This past summer when the ATF and FBI attacked a family living in North Idaho?"

"Go on."

"The Weavers? Pete and Vicki and their three kids?"

"I know about it. They had illegal firearms or something like that and resisted arrest."

"Fuck you! You're just like the rest of the slaves letting the authorities walk over you."

McVeigh was livid and Lawrence had to bring him back to today, away from what happened last summer.

"I'm listening. Don't jump down my throat. You know as well as I do the media presents the government agents as the good guys. What do you expect me to know? Tell me. Don't attack me."

The redness began to fade from McVeigh's face. Lawrence had never seen a grown man get so upset, so violent over what happened to others. McVeigh had carried the Colt out to the shooting range. Laying the gun carefully on the gun stand about twenty-five feet from the targets, he opened a box of 7.45 ACP caliber rounds, inserted them one at a time into the pistol's magazine, clicked and locked the magazine into the pistol's grip, and fired off five rounds. All were within the center circle of the bull's-eye. It calmed him and he popped out the magazine, handing it and the Colt to Lawrence. Seeing Lawrence's unfamiliarity with an automatic pistol, McVeigh took the gun from him and ran Lawrence through a quick lesson in pistol shooting.

"Thanks, I'm a rifle person and probably would have shot somebody walking on top of the hill.

McVeigh smiled, "I'm sorry I got so riled. Just listen to me, okay?"

Lawrence nodded.

"The Weavers worked the gun show circuit. Randy, Pete as some people called him, pushed the edge too much. He got caught … Actually he got videotaped selling a sawed-off shotgun to a federal agent a couple years ago. Virtually ended his chances for legitimately selling firearms. Still he kept at it. Trained all his kids in firearms. Wife loved shooting and was damn good at it. Anyhow, they moved to Idaho out in the boondocks so the Feds would leave them alone. Fact was he ran off from a trial that put the Feds on him. ATF caught up with him and his family out in a cabin near the Canadian border, sort of had him trapped there."

"Listen, news didn't tell it like it happened. FBI and ATF didn't have the guts to go up after him. Can you imagine? Christ a man and a woman and a couple kids. They brought in snipers. You heard about the snipers, didn't you?"

"Not on my news channel, I didn't."

"Leon Horiuchi was the man they set up to gun them down. I knew Leon from my Army days. Cocky son of a bitch who was good but not as good as most of us."

"I remember you telling me about it. It got to you, if I remember correctly?"

"Oh, yeah. Even shooting the Iraq desert people who were suppose to be our enemies, it was disgusting, watching the poor son of a bitch caught by surprise, half his head blown away. I quit it but there were others like Horiuchi who thrived on it. Doin' that nigger high five shit when they mangled some person's face with a shot out of nowhere."

"Before he took any shots at the Weavers, he had trained so well that he could put a bullet in a quarter-inch target at two hundred yards every single time. Two hundred yards was the distance to take somebody out up on the hill. How good was he? All that practice and he missed the first time. He moved to where he thought he had a better shot, aimed the .308 Remington 700 at Kevin Harris who was hunkered down with the Weavers, and hit Vicki Weaver instead. Great shot? Right."

"Blood was all over the place, splattered over Vicki's ten year old daughter. Sara could remember the bullet whizzing by her head. He had shot a woman carrying a baby and the dead woman laid on the floor still cradling that baby. The bullet went through her head and left a coin sized hole in the arm of Kevin. His body was pockmarked with fragments from the bullet and Vicki's face bones."

"Jesus, they never tell you about this stuff do they?"

"I'll tell you what needs to happen in this country. You need some warrior to rise up and fight back, overturn the empire we live in. Like some kind of Jedi warrior. I know that sounds stupid but people don't care anymore, don't give a shit. Maybe <u>Turner's Diary</u> goes too far, but we need a terrorist to kill off some of these assholes like Horiuchi. You know he went out drinking with a bunch of his Fed buddies to celebrate his great sniper shot? The man is proud to blow apart a woman's face, and do it in front of her children? A woman who herself has committed no crime? And he did not even hit the person he was trying to snipe!"

Lawrence was dumbfounded. Like the other three hundred million Americans, he let it happen and he let it go by. It brought to Lawrence's mind what he had recently read in Howard Zinn's, A People's History of the United States. The human animal lives in a group called civilization like a whale lives in a pod or an eagle in a flock. Time has witnessed all civilizations and survived through each, since called by any name, they all represent the same society. Every human community from tribe to country or from empires to democracy winds up in three parts: the rulers, the soldiers, and the slaves. Go by other names, they still are the same.

Lawrence fired off shots with the Colt. He liked its heaviness, even though that could be a disadvantage when maneuvering during a fight. The weight made for stability, in exchange for holstering speed.

"How much and how do I get two of them as soon as possible?"

Lawrence was armed within two days.

***

Looking out his front window to the west, the snow blotted the Niagara Gorge. Not a good night to drive his car to the Niagara City Schools Administrative Offices. He should call for a cab or call Nuevello's office to see if their meeting was still scheduled. He did neither. Having his car in the administrative office parking lot was necessary for his plan. It protected him from being caught with illegal fire arms. Since it was over two miles in the snow, Lawrence finished his after dinner coffee, pulled on his hooded parka, bundled his hands into gloves, and grabbed the snow shovel next to the front door. Outside was not as bad as the view portended. The snow was light snow.

Shoveling and clearing off his car was a good warm up for what Lawrence would be facing. He had been called by Dr. Nuevello's secretary this morning before the snow came in from Ontario, to set up a meeting with Dr. Nuevello for this evening. While talking with the secretary, Nuevello came on the phone.

"Lawrence, how you doing Lawrence?" Before he could answer, Nuevello prattled on, "Listen my boy. I think we can resolve your problem tonight. This meeting is just between you and me. No teacher's union rep. Just man to man, boss to employee. I need you here tonight, Got to get this fracas ended … Gotten move on … You with me?"

Lawrence replied with a yes but before he could say anything else, Nuevello was off the line and the secretary was back on. He had no idea what Nuevello was planning. But it did create the first step in Lawrence's own confrontation plan - - get a private meeting with Dr. Nuevello. How to get that private meeting had been solved for him, a good move for going face-to-face with Nuevello, but a problematic enigma for knowing what Lawrence's prey was plotting. Lawrence went over in his mind what he had sketched out since meeting with McVeigh and talking again with Judi. The plan had been flawless until now. Nuevello had wristed a small degree of control by initiating their rendezvous. After scraping the snow from the driver's side window, Lawrence started up the engine. He threw the window deicer on full blast and sat waiting for the ice to loosen enough to run the windshield wipers.

Leaving the car running with the heater going full blast, Lawrence returned to the house, took off the heavy parka and got out one of the Colt M1911A1's and the trouser belt holster. He clipped the holster on the right side of his pant's belt toward the rear, put the Colt into it, and latched the safety strap. The ammo clip had been fully loaded ever since he left McVeigh's shooting range. He needed to have some maneuverability so Lawrence opted for a Buffalo Bill's extra-large hooded sweat shirt which hung well below his waist, not exposing his weapon. The looseness of the sweat shirt worker well and he had practiced quick draws from the belt clip holster until he had reached a good rate of speed.

Would Lawrence need the weapon? Had the confrontation between Lawrence and Nuevello been generated through Lawrence's maneuvering, there would have been little chance for violence. Lawrence's grandfather George had taught him to plan out every hunt, be it a deer or a bear, to accomplish the worst case scenario possible. Plan for the worse and enjoy anything less. Would Lawrence kill Nuevello? Before his meeting with McVeigh he would have thought it extremely unlikely but now he did not know. The horror of Ruby Ridge had meshed with the fate of Henry Hawkins. Power in many hands was out and out evil. Those people placed their power into soldier's hands and regaled in seeing a woman's face blown away while holding her baby. The rulers, the soldiers obeying, and the slaves slaughtered. The worse was the satanic pleasure taken by the killers like Nuevello and Uley, king and soldier. Would the system ever stop them? Lawrence knew better. Men like Nuevello were the system. What chance would he have against the system? Could his plans take Nuevello down for the count? Lawrence did not need a knock down tonight. Winning by his hits and his opponent's misses would be enough to start the battle. He knew that eventually he would have to make the kill but not until he controlled the battle. Then he could feast off the beast.

Lawrence had plenty of time despite the snow. Considering Western New York's history of snowfalls, this one was still puny, with slow winds, a few glimpses of the clear sky, followed by dark clouds and medium sized snowflakes which mostly melted since the temperature, though falling, was still just above freezing. Route 104, Lewiston Road became Main Street Niagara Falls just past College Avenue, and Lawrence made a left onto Walnut Avenue to get into the school administration's nearly empty parking lot. The snow had accumulated to about four inches and there were drifts in the parking lot. Lawrence, as was his habit, backed into a parking space, or at least a place he guessed was a parking place. He was at the back of the building and since he was twenty minutes early, he sat, letting the car run to keep him warm. He scrutinized the building. It was mostly dark now with only a few rooms in the building lit. The one room that was important in his plan was lit - - the custodian's office and work room in the basement.

With ten minutes to go before his appointment with Nuevello, Lawrence got out of his car, intentionally leaving his black leather attaché case on the back seat. In it was the ammunition to take Nuevello down. The entrance to the building was on Pine Street and had a flight of steps that took the visitor to the second of four floors. As expected, there was a security guard at the front door with a metal detector wand. Lawrence had taken a chance that there might not be a metal detection device when he holstered his Colt on to his belt, but he had also plotted how to not get caught with the weapon in the building if there was indeed a security guard waiting for him. Just as the guard pulled back the ten foot high left side door to allow Lawrence entrance, Lawrence spoke.

"Damn! I forgot my brief case. I'll be right back."

Back tracking he circled to the rear of the building, opened his car, unhooked the belt holster with the weapon in it, and slid them both under the front seat. He returned with his bag to the front door, was wanded and had his brief case searched for weapons. He was then directed to the Superintendent's office on the fourth floor. Shown where the elevator was, Lawrence said he would rather use the stairs. Lawrence noted that where he entered on the second floor, it was empty of all personnel except the guard. What he was specifically hoping to find, he did, on the third floor.

"Hey how you doing?" Lawrence said to the night janitor who was straightening chairs and emptying trash cans in the second room to Lawrence passed.

"Fine sir. How you doin'?"

"You all by yourself here?"

"Sure is, it being a Monday and all. Snow might keep the night guard out of here. Who knows? Have a good one, sir." The janitor headed to the next room.

Lawrence backtracked to the elevator, pushed the down button, and waited. When it reached the third floor and the doors slid open, Lawrence got in and pushed the basement button. Once in the basement he headed to the custodian's room and got lucky. The door was not locked. After entering, he quickly flipped the lock switch. He went to the exit door that led to the parking lot, slowly swung open the door, and propped it open with a cleaning solvent five gallon drum. Just as quickly he got to his car, opened it, removed the weapon, and was back in the custodian's office in seconds. He brushed off the snow, shook his head to get rid of some of the wetness, and after leaving the custodian's room, found a men's restroom. Once inside, Lawrence grabbed some paper towels to dry off the Colt, its holster, the brief case and his clothing. He was now armed.

He took the elevator to the fourth floor, got off and making a left turn, faced the superintendent's office, a set of large glass doors with three secretarial desks spread evenly around the entrance foyer. There was only one secretary working at this hour and she either recognized Lawrence, which was doubtful, or more likely had been waiting only for him to arrive.

"Ah! Mr. Lawrence. Is the snow getting worse out there?"

"Better be going home soon. It's getting there."

"Don't worry about me. Soon as I show you in, I'm out of here. Come on."

Lawrence followed her through the oak doors and into Nuevello's office. Nuevello's oversized mahogany desk faced the entrance doors and Nuevello rose immediately from behind it to greet Lawrence. Lawrence noticed that there was another man present.

"Lawrence, Lawrence, Lawrence! I don't know what to do with you. I should either adopt you or shoot you," said Nuevello as he shook Lawrence's hand. "This is Sean Fannon, our chief of police."

The hairs on the back of Lawrence's neck rose and his face turned ashen. There would be violence. Fannon was here to arrest him. Lawrence had already prepared himself for that outcome. His mind rushed through what he believed was the scenario Nuevello and Fannon had set up to keep the incident away from the public's attention. They would confront him with the charges here and then they would arrest him, which was highly unlikely since it would be bad for the school district's image or they would confront him with the facts, threaten him with the arrest, and then accept his resignation so that nobody tainted Niagara City Schools reputation.

While not truly expecting an arrest, the Colt ensured they would not take him down. This decision was made quickly. Lawrence would gun them both down. The problem was what he would do if all they asked was a resignation? Lawrence had prepared for this encounter but the challenge was greater than he expected. He was prepared to beat them at their own game, use their crimes to give him an advantage. Was his plan just another pushing the game to the edge? He had the control at his back and in his brief case.

He was on edge as he shook Fannon's hands. The man's grip was strong despite his pudgy fingers, two of which Lawrence deduced had been broken at some point. His face was also pudgy with a stubble he could not shave close enough to be considered clean shaven. While shorter than Lawrence he was still taller than Nuevello, as were most people. Lawrence's instincts kicked in. Wait, watch, be able to predict what the prey or as in this case the predator might do. If they asked for a resignation and he was cleared of all charges, should he accept? Thirty minutes ago, it was not a question to answer. He was ready to take them down, kill them if necessary. Stupid, it all seemed so stupid now.

"Chief Fannon's here because the problem ... Well let's lay it out on the table. Your problem involves some legal charges. You're basically in deep shit, Lawrence. You know I called up a few of the references you gave us when you were hired, even the schools you went to? Nobody could believe that you had a drug habit."

Lawrence did not even contemplate responding to Nuevello's query. Nuevello's concern was my drug habit?

"You're a good teacher, Lawrence. I don't want to lose you. But a teacher doing drugs is in total violation of school board policy."

Lawrence knew Nuevello was leading toward a resignation or was he?

"Policy or not, I want to help you. But first let's clear up the confrontation you had with James Gingham."

"Who?"

"The man you cut in the school bus garage."

Jimmy Jig was James Gingham, thought Lawrence.

"Chief, what do you think? You gonna to arrest him for assault with a deadly weapon?"

"I should. Hard to believe a teacher carries around a jack knife like that. You bring that weapon to school with you?"

Lawrence knew to keep his mouth shut and just shook his head no. He fought back a smile, knowing what was carried in the pit of his back bone.

"Good fucking thing cause then I'd have no choice but cuff you and take you in. As it is, it seems Mr. Gingham has a problem with pressing charges against you. Makes no difference though about you toting a deadly weapon on school property."

Nuevello broke in, "so Peter, all we've got is your drug problem. Gingham's being taken care of. We've given him a year off with pay to recuperate and we're paying for all his medical expenses. They were covered by insurance anyway. Back to your habit. Here's what I've come up with. I'll put you on personal leave with pay if you agree in writing to get medical help for your addiction. Soon as your doctor and I've got a few I'd recommend, soon as he signs off that you're clean, you're back on board. Except with an exception."

"What's the exception?"

"You'll teach at the middle school, not the high school. At least for a while. Maybe after a couple terms I'll move you back up. I'm trying to be as fair as I can, Peter. You got to help yourself before I can help you. Think about it. You're still on leave for another month. Use it. Go over what you've learned here …"

Lawrence did not hear anymore words from Nuevello. The man was as crafty as Satan. Before he knew it Nuevello would be telling him that he made Lawrence an offer he couldn't refuse. Basically, Lawrence would be let off free and clear. No loss of salary, no loss of job, no police charges and thus no legal proceedings. It was much better than resignation and it was his to accept. Tableau rasa, a new beginning, just forget Henry and the drug syndicate. Nuevello and Fannon rule. Here is a ruler, one of the best, Dr. Nuevello. His soldiers were Fannon, Uley, and all the good boys and girls driving school buses, fixing the school district physical plant. What Nuevello offered was absurd but Nuevello was ignorant of what Lawrence actually knew. Nuevello believed that Lawrence's assault at the bus garage was because Lawrence was an addict. Nuevello had no idea that Lawrence knew about the drug business running through the school system or the connection to Henry Hawkins's death. Yet Lawrence could right now walk away scot free. Forget what he had prepared for and destroy what he had in his brief case.

Lawrence had evaluated Chief Fannon well when they met and shook hands. Fannon was carrying a revolver under his left arm pit in a shoulder holster. Fannon kept the front of his jacket buttoned with one button giving him a bit of interference for a quick draw. Lawrence's sweat shirt was too bulky when he bought it and just bulky enough now to prevent Fannon from seeing the Colt bulge at Lawrence's spine. Besides, the security guard thoroughly wanded Lawrence with a metal detector and Fannon would feel safe. Nuevello sat looking eye to eye at Lawrence, his elbows on the desk top and fingers interlaced. Lawrence doubted that Nuevello was carrying a weapon but he had the make sure Nuevello had no emergency buttons under the desk.

"So I spend some time in rehab, get full pay, and walk back into a teaching job?" Lawrence rose slowly from his chair in front of Nuevello's desk. From the corner of his left eye he could see Chief Fannon's right hand slide off his thigh and inside his suit coat. He had to make a decision, one he could live with until he died even if dying was to be now. Accepting their concessions was not a choice he could live with since he would never forget who they were and what they did. Nuevello's eyes darted to Fannon as Lawrence walked to the massive windows behind Nuevello. Fannon nodded, showing he had control and Nuevello dropped his right hand to his lap. As Lawrence passed Nuevello's desk he could see the buzzer button attached to the inside surface of the huge desk.

Lawrence could kill both of them before Fannon could draw his revolver. That was no problem. Shots would be fired, Nuevello would set off the button alarm, police would come, and Lawrence would spend the rest of his life in prison. The rest of his life? Could he accept that for destroying two men who have killed and supplied lethal drugs to children? McVeigh's story of Ruby Ridge shot through his head. America was becoming a supply ground for people like Nuevello and soldiers like the man who shot a woman's face off. He knew he could not go down because of them.

"Snow's getting icy out there. Must be warming a bit, melting as it falls. Got a great view here Dr. Nuevello. I can see the lights from the Falls shimmering as sleet and snow drift and fly through their glare. You know something, Nuevello? I've never done drugs in my entire life. I've no reason to do therapy in drug rehab."

Nuevello nodded a "no" to Fannon and turned in his seat to look at Lawrence who had turned back from the windows.

"I got a better deal. How about if I just resign?"

"Resign?" Nuevello was turned with his back to the desk. He could see the snow speeding across the window panes behind Lawrence. "You want to just resign? No compensation?"

"Chief Fannon, do me a favor, grab my brief case and open it. You'll find two manila envelopes in there. Take out the bigger one, please. My resignation is it."

Nuevello was at a loss, completely stymied. He knew Fannon was armed and that a quick turn and a hit on the button under his desk would bring the security guard and send a signal to the police department. Lawrence was a loose wheel but not any danger to them.

Lawrence spoke, "compensation, you'd pay me some compensation for what I did? That sounds pretty good. How much?"

"You really brought your resignation with you, Lawrence? I'm surprised. I thought you'd put up more of a fight than that. Got it in that bag? Once you give it to me, you're done? You're let go. No charges, right Chief Fannon?"

"Yes, sir."

Lawrence spoke, "don't open the envelope yet. Compensation, huh? Okay how does two hundred thousand dollars sound?"

Fannon's head came up and his eyes opened wide but he kept the large envelop in his hands. Nuevello laughed, "Lawrence you slay me. My boy you want us to give you almost a quarter of a million dollars to get rid of you? You got some balls, Lawrence."

Nuevello started to turn to Fannon and was laughing until he saw Fannon's face go red and heard Lawrence's voice. "Keep your fingers, both hands, on that envelope or I'll put a bullet between your eyes."

Lawrence had reached behind his back, unlatched the holster strap, and drew the Colt. Nuevello turned and saw the pistol leveled at him.

"Fannon, listen to me and listen carefully," said Lawrence. He saw Nuevello starting for his desk. "You move again Nuevello, and I'll blast apart your left knee cap. Put your hands on top of your head, now. Fannon, hold the envelope with your right hand and reach inside your jacket. Using two fingers, pull out the revolver and gently lay it on the floor. Understand?"

Fannon did not move. Lawrence walked over to the police chief and slammed the Colt's steel barrel against Fannon's left cheek. "Now!"

The gun was laid gently on the floor.

"You're fucking crazy Lawrence! Even if you kill us, you'll never get away with it."

"Kill you? Why should I kill you? I've got an offer you'll never refuse. Go over and sit in the chair where I was seated."

Lawrence kept the Colt aimed at Fannon but it wasn't necessary. The man was in pain and blood was slowly seeping from the left side of his mouth where a mangled tooth pierced through his lips.

"I know when people are lying to me. Don't ask me how, I just can. If you lie to me, I will slam you like I did Fannon the first time. The second time I will blow away your knee cap. Do you want to know what happens next?"

He did not need an answer.

Lawrence sat down at Nuevello's desk and spoke. "You really thought I was after drugs at the bus garage?"

"Of course I did. What else?"

"You and Fannon and the good old boys down at the garage run a drug syndicate. That's why I was there. I wanted to see for myself."

"You're crazy, Lawrence. What gave you the idea we're running a drug syndicate?"

"Fannon, go over to Nuevello's bathroom. Keep the door open and clean yourself up. You're not that hurt."

The police chief did as Lawrence ordered. Both Lawrence and Nuevello watched as the man spit out the bent tooth, vomited up some blood, took one of Nuevello's expensive wash towels and wiped his face clean. Lawrence saw that Fannon's face was swelling when he returned to his seat.

"Now open the envelope, Fannon."

Fannon pulled out a stack of 8 X 10 photos and laid them across the coffee table in front of him.

"Remember Henry Hawkins Nuevello? Belafont said you read has essay. Said you told him to grade it a failure. Take a look at the photos he took. They're kind of a story board set that portrays Henry's essay. See them?"

Nuevello was speechless. He remembered almost word for word the Hawkins kid's story.

"These don't mean a ..."

Nuevello was too smart to continue his denial. "So you caught us, Lawrence. You're right, Lawrence. That's what I have going. Just one of many ventures I have my fingers in. Turning me in gets you zero, Lawrence. Probably I won't even be convicted. My guess is that all this would not stand up in court. You think I'm the highest step in this business? Ha! I'm small potatoes. I'm just one of many operations."

"Dana, Dana, Dana," said Lawrence. "You didn't say anything about the photographs of the Halfway House's shower room?"

Nuevello hated the name Dana and had fired a few employees that had used it in his presence. Lawrence was right. Nuevello had side-stepped the shower photographs.

"Chief Fannon, how we doing'?" asked Lawrence. "Reach down inside the other envelope and you'll find a piece of pipe."

Fannon pulled out a rusted shower head pipe and, despite his still swelling face, gave Nuevello a look of abject fear.

"I also busted that off when I took the photographs. It wasn't any trouble, just a slight pull down and back up, and bam I had a piece of rusted pipe in my hand."

Lawrence watched their faces. They were evolving from outrageousness to complacency to fear. "I also got this copy of a receipt from the school's plumbing vendor. It's for a shower pipe and just happens to be dated the day Henry Hawkins hung himself in that same shower. Look in the envelope, Fannon. There's a copy of the receipt. You guys need to find a new vendor. Damn little piece of pipe cost a hundred and ten dollars and thirty nine cents. At least you had a tax exemption. One I bought at Grand Island Hardware only went for fifteen bucks but I had to pay tax!"

Lawrence was getting irate. He was contemplating outright murder but he had already beat them at one level and was smart enough not to push it.

"What do you think the good people of Niagara Falls would do if they found out their superintendent of schools had committed murder to protect his syndicate for drugs?"

Fannon dropped the pipe back into the envelope and spoke. "Get to the point."

"The point? Where is the point? I think we're at an impasse here, Chief," responded Nuevello. "What do they call this in those western movies? A Mexican stand off? Well Lawrence, you're a smart man. Let's just break it down here and now," said Nuevello as he got up out of his chair and walked behind it. "I like to line up my objectives, Lawrence. You know, prioritize the problems. We have some basic problems here. First, you could just shoot us. But where does that put you? Regardless of what you have on us, you'll go to jail. Next we could tell you to fuck off and you leave with our promise to leave you be. Think that'd do it, Lawrence?"

Lawrence smiled.

Nah, didn't think so. How's about we go back to our original offer? Except we eliminate you having to do rehab. How about it?"

Lawrence continued to smile.

"Of course not. You know we'd get you. I'm just one small jamoke in a system across the whole East Coast. You know that, don't you Lawrence?"

Lawrence smiled, since having learned of Nuevello's connections from Judi's responses.

"Two hundred grand? I think I can come up with that," said Nuevello snapping his fingers.

Lawrence shrugged still smiling.

"What, no faith in me? We'll have to see. Except there's a major problem with paying you off. We're on the string. We're on that string that every time you run low on funds, you yank the 'I'll expose you' string and expect us to pay off. My guess is you've found a way around that? What say, Lawrence?"

Lawrence knew the time had to come and there was no avoidance. He no longer smiled. He dared not cry.

"Chief, there's another manila envelope in the big one. Get it out."

Fannon pulled out a small, brown envelope and at Lawrence's direction opened and read it aloud. It took all of Lawrence's strength to not call it quits and shoot them right now.

"Jesus Christ Lawrence! You killed Eileen Ledger? What the hell for?"

Lawrence was in pain. To survive this confrontation, to take down these malevolent villains, Lawrence would have to desecrate the woman he loved most in his life. Lawrence had written a confession admitting that he had killed Eileen Ledger. The confession claimed that she had gone back with her husband and abandoned Lawrence. She and Zig Fitzgerald had gone camping and Lawrence had trailed them and slain both of them. The confession went right through Lawrence's heart.

"She went back to him?"

"The guilt got to her. After you prodded Belafont to embarrass Zig, Zig pleaded and begged with her. He admitted that he had not shown her that they still had that love both brought to their marriage. His pain and crying got to her and she agreed to a trial to see if it could be saved, their marriage could be saved. To do so, the bitch told me I would have to wait and see."

Lawrence hurt like never before in his life saying these words. "She convinced Zig that an outing, an outing that she and I had done, might be a first step. Can you believe that she invited him to do with her the same camping trip we had done? I couldn't accept it. I found out from her parents where they were going and followed them. I knew right where the fucking bitch would take him, except I had a canoe and he had a speed boat."

Lawrence knew his words and his gestures had to convince them. "Chief Fannon, if I sign that confession in front of you since you're an officer of the law, will it hold up in court?"

"Of course it will."

Lawrence walked over to the suffering police chief, took the paper and signed it.

"Here's the deal Nuevello. If I rat you out or try to hit you up for more money, you've got me for murder in the first degree. It would be first degree murder, right Fannon?"

"Should be."

Nuevello's eyes were going back and forth, his mind playing over the situation. Lawrence was right. The confession had him by the short hairs. What was even better was that Nuevello could pay Lawrence off then send a hit man to nail him.

Lawrence was one step ahead of both men. "We do it now or I kill you both."

"Whoa! Hold on there! How the hell do expect me to come up with two hundred thousand in cash right now?"

Lawrence had to bury his shame for using Eileen this way and get back to nailing Nuevello.

"Good, I see you have a speaker phone. Here, you're going to make a call." Lawrence pushed the phone across the desk top to Nuevello who hit the speaker phone button and got a dial tone.

"Okay, what's the number?"

"Fannon, read out the phone number on the outside of the envelope," said Lawrence.

Chief Fannon read the number to Nuevello and they waited for someone to pick up on the other end. Someone did.

Judi spoke over the speaker phone, "yeah, this is Bruno. What ja want?"

Lawrence smiled hearing Judi's raspy voice. "Bruno, it's Peter Lawrence. You hear me all right up there?"

"I'm good. What you got, Petey?"

Lawrence grimaced but knew neither Nuevello nor Fannon could trace Judi's line, "you got the envelope I left with you?"

"Yeah, right here."

"Good. It's sealed, right?"

"Sure is, Petey."

"What's it say on the outside?"

"This envelope is to be delivered by hand with a receipt to the District Federal Bureau of Investigation upon the death of Peter Lawrence or upon his requesting it to be given to the Federal Bureau of Investigation."

"Good, Bruno. You got your second phone line working?"

"Yeah. All ready to go. Got the number you gave me right here and the information I need. What now?"

"I'm going to turn off the speaker phone up here and put you on hold. Before I do, what happens if you don't hear from me within a few minutes?"

"I start looking at the obits to see if somebody offed you."

"Thanks, Bruno. It'll only take a couple minutes."

After turning off the speaker phone and putting the line on hold, Lawrence continued, "here's where we stand, Nuevello. Bruno's got the same photographs you've got and copies of the pipe receipts like you have but he also has a letter from me detailing all that I know about the drug dealing up here, your involvement and the school's, and Henry Hawkins murder. He will not open that envelope but mark my word he will personally deliver it to the FBI if I don't call him back if he ever finds out that I have been killed."

"That's very clever, Lawrence. Damn, you got the standoff beaten. Except ..."

"Don't fuck with me, Nuevello. I know the business manager of this school district, Anthony Nuevello. Name sure is familiar. Call him on another line. Tell him you need a phone transfer of two hundred thousand dollars made to this account number at this phone number. So you don't get any ideas, it's an off-shore bank that even Uncle Sam can't touch."

Lawrence thought this would be the most difficult part, squeezing money out of the syndicate. Lawrence probably underestimated the revenues produced by this criminal mob. The drugs were not even their most productive ventures.

Nuevello picked up the phone and called his nephew Anthony, "Tony, I need you to transfer some funds for me. You okay with it?"

"Two thousand g's, Anthony. Anthony, shut up and do it. Here's the phone number and the account number. Just do it, you asshole! Do it now and call me when ..."

Lawrence waved Nuevello off his response and Nuevello muffled the receiver with his palm, "what? What's the matter? What do you want, more money?"

"No. Bruno has a direct line to the bank and they will tell him the funds have been transferred. Tell your nephew you'll call him back if there's any problem. Do it."

"Anthony, we'll know if you got them through, understand? If they don't go through, you'll be a cashier at the Indian Reservation Casino tomorrow. Understand? Good."

Nuevello put the receiver down and Lawrence picked it up, "Bruno, you connected to the bank? Good. I'll keep the receiver open so when it goes through just yell into the phone so I can hear you."

"You're fucking unreal Lawrence. I must say ..."

"Shut up. The line's open. Bruno does not need to know anything but what I already instructed him about and when the bank acknowledges the deposit."

The silence lasted forever and Lawrence noticed that Chief Fannon had passed out, his face still swelling from the blow with the gun. Too bad, thought Lawrence. Nuevello sat with his fingers meshed together, obviously contemplating how to get Lawrence. After what seemed an eternity which in reality was only fifteen minutes, Judi came on the line.

"Petey, it's Bruno. Money's in, full two hundred thou. I got the envelopes and they'll go in a security box where only I know they are. Anything else? Good."

Without waiting for an answer, Judi hung up.

Lawrence spoke. "We're on a funny kind of seesaw here, Nuevello."

"Seesaw? How's that, Lawrence?"

"You shoot me at the one end and you go down. I shoot you at your end and I go down."

"That's a fucking good analogy, Lawrence. You think you're hot shit pulling this off don't you? Two hundred g's? Small stuff, Lawrence. Think I'll come after you?"

"No, if Bruno's security deposit box doesn't keep you straight, small stuff isn't worth it. Is it?"

"No, but vanity is, Lawrence."

~~~***~~~

www.ingramcontent.com/pod-product-compliance
Lightning Source LLC
Chambersburg PA
CBHW071644260626
47170CB00001B/222